The Golden Princess

The Golden Princess

A NOVEL OF THE CHANGE

S. M. STIRLING

A ROC BOOK

ROC
Published by the Penguin Group
Penguin Group (USA) LLC, 375 Hudson Street,
New York, New York 10014, USA

USA I Canada I UK I Ireland I Australia I New Zealand I India I South Africa I China
penguin.com
A Penguin Random House Company

First published by Roc, an imprint of New American Library,
a division of Penguin Group (USA) LLC

First Printing, September 2014

 REGISTERED TRADEMARK—MARCA REGISTRADA

LIBRARY OF CONGRESS CATALOGING-IN-PUBLICATION DATA:

Stirling, S. M.
The golden princess: a novel of the change / S. M. Stirling.
p. cm.—(Change series)
ISBN 978-0-451-41733-6 (hardback)
1. Imaginary wars and battles—Fiction. I. Title.
PS3569.T543G85 2014
813'.54—dc 23   2014012527

Printed in the United States of America
10 9 8 7 6 5 4 3 2 1

Set in Weiss Medium

PUBLISHER'S NOTE

This is a work of fiction. Names, characters, places, and incidents either are the product of the author's imagination or are used fictitiously, and any resemblance to actual persons, living or dead, business establishments,
events, or locales is entirely coincidental.

To Jan, forever

ACKNOWLEDGMENTS

Thanks to my friends who are also first readers:

Thanks to Kier Salmon, unindicted co-conspirator, who has been my advisor and helper on the books of the Change since the first.

To Steve Brady, for assistance with dialects and British background, and also natural history of all sorts. Also for showing us around Stonehenge and Avebury!

Pete Sartucci, knowledgeable in many aspects of Western geography and ecology.

To Diana L. Paxson, for help and advice, and for writing the beautiful Westria books, among many others. If you liked the Change novels, you'll probably enjoy the hell out of the Westria books—I certainly did, and they were one of the inspirations for this series; and her *Essential Asatru* and recommendation of *Our Troth* were extremely helpful . . . and fascinating reading. The appearance of the name Westria in the book is no coincidence whatsoever.

To Dale Price, help with Catholic organization, theology and praxis.

To John Birmingham, for local expertise and permission.

To Walter Jon Williams, John Miller, Vic Milan, Jan Stirling, Matt Reiten, Lauren Teffeau, and Ian Tregellis of Critical Mass, for constant help and advice as the book was under construction.

Thanks to John Miller, good friend, writer and scholar, for many useful discussions, for loaning me some great books, and for some really, really cool old movies.

Special thanks to Heather Alexander, bard and balladeer, for permission to use the lyrics from her beautiful songs, which can be—and should be!—enjoyed by all. Run, do not walk, to do so at www.theheatherlands.com or via her heir, Alexander James Adams, at http://faerietaleminstrel.com/inside.

Thanks again to William Pint and Felicia Dale, for permission to use their music, which can be found at www.pintndale.com and should be, for anyone with an ear and salt-water in their veins.

And to Three Weird Sisters—Gwen Knighton, Mary Crowell, Brenda Sutton and Teresa Powell—whose alternately funny and beautiful music can be found at www.threeweirdsisters.com.

And to Heather Dale for permission to quote the lyrics of her songs, whose beautiful (and strangely appropriate!) music can be found at www.heatherdale.com, and is highly recommended. The lyrics are wonderful and the tunes make it even better.

To S. J. Tucker for permission to use the lyrics of her beautiful songs, which can be found at www.skinnywhitechick.com, and should be.

And to Lael Whitehead of Jaiya, www.jaiya.ca, for permission to quote the lyrics of her beautiful songs.

Thanks as well to Stephen Stills, for permission to quote from "Southern Cross," written by Stephen Stills (Gold Hills Music).

To Chris Hinkle and Jennifer Dowling, for help with Japanese idiom.

Thanks to Michael Moorcock, one of my foundational inspirations, for permission to quote "The Song of Veerkad" from his and Jim Cawthorn's brilliant Elric story, "Kings in Darkness."

Thanks to Dave Crosby (yes, *the* Dave Crosby) for permission to quote his lyrics from "Guinnevere."

Thanks again to Russell Galen, my agent, who has been an invaluable help and friend for a decade now, and never more than in these difficult times.

All mistakes, infelicities and errors are of course my own.

The Golden Princess

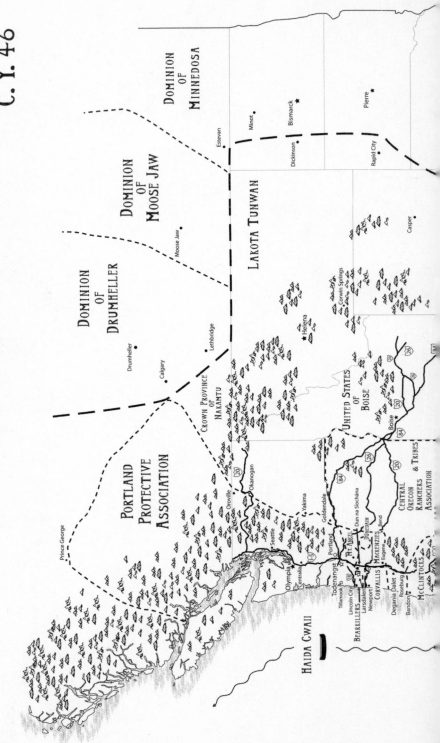

HIGH KINGDOM OF MONTIVAL
C.Y. 46

DOMINION OF MINNEDOSA

Pierre ★

Minot .

Bismarck ★

Estevan .

Dickinson .

Rapid City .

DOMINION OF MOOSE JAW

Moose Jaw .

LAKOTA TUNWAN

Casper .

Corwin Springs .

DOMINION OF DRUMHELLER

Drumheller .

Calgary .

Lethbridge .

Helena ★

CROWN PROVINCE OF NAKAMTU

PORTLAND PROTECTIVE ASSOCIATION

Prince George .

UNITED STATES OF BOISE

Okanogan
Oroville
Yakima
Goldendale
Seattle
Olympia
Centralia

Boise ★

Portland
Ft. Nisqually
Dun na Siochána
Dúnedain
MACKENZIES
Bend

CENTRAL OREGON RANCHERS & TRIBES

Tillamook ?o
Lincoln City
Larsdalen
Newport
CORVALLIS
Eugene
Degania Dalet
Roseburg
Bandon

BEARKILLERS

McCLINTOCKS

HAIDA CWAII

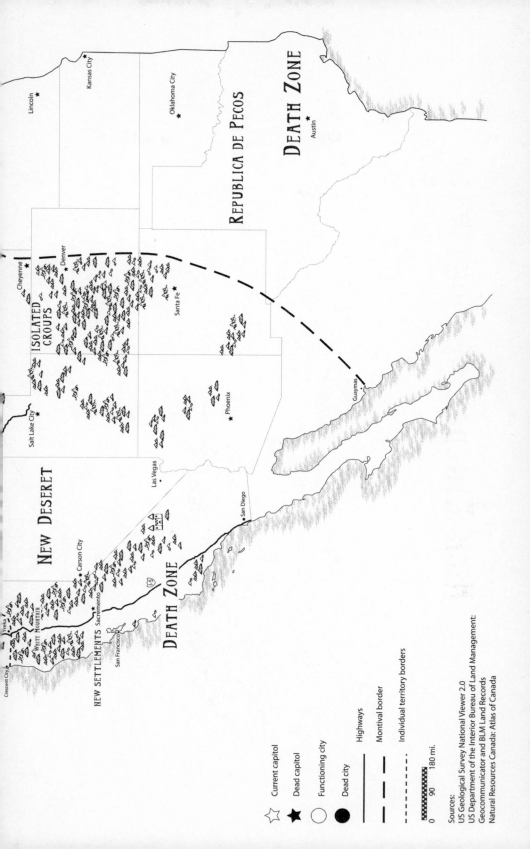

DEATH ZONE

REPUBLICA DE PECOS

Austin

Oklahoma City

Kansas City

Lincoln

ISOLATED GROUPS

Cheyenne

Denver

Santa Fe

Phoenix

Guaymas

NEW DESERET

Salt Lake City

Las Vegas

San Diego

Carson City

NEW SETTLEMENTS

Sacremento

San Francisco

DEATH ZONE

Yreka

WHITE MOUNTAIN

Crescent City

Current capitol

Dead capitol

Functioning city

Dead city

Highways

Montival border

Individual territory borders

0   90   180 mi.

Sources:
US Geological Survey National Viewer 2.0
US Department of the Interior Bureau of Land Management:
Geocommunicator and BLM Land Records
Natural Resources Canada: Atlas of Canada

CHAPTER ONE

NEAR THE *NEMED* OF DUN BARSTOW
COUNTY OF NAPA, CROWN PROVINCE OF WESTRIA
(FORMERLY NAPA COUNTY, CALIFORNIA)
HIGH KINGDOM OF MONTIVAL
(FORMERLY WESTERN NORTH AMERICA)
APRIL 30TH, CHANGE YEAR 46/2044 AD

Órlaith Arminger Mackenzie bore the first unlit torch forward to her father's pyre as the sun touched the low mountains to the west.

All I want is to crawl alone into somewhere dark and greep like a little lass, she thought. *Or run to my mother that we may weep together. But I've more than twenty summers now, Mother is far away in the north building* Dún na Síochána, *I'm his heir. I must do this for him.*

His big long-fingered hands were crossed on the hilt of the Sword of the Lady as he lay on the bier, shapely though scarred and battered. He was dressed plainly in the simple kilt and shirt and plaid, ankle-boots and knee-hose of the people who'd borne him. There was an inhuman peace now to the face that had been so lively with the play of thought and feeling, and the golden torque around his neck hid the wound that had killed him. Rudi Mackenzie—High King Artos—had been a tall man, still broad-shouldered and narrow-hipped in his forty-seventh year; his red-gold hair held no trace of gray, or his short-cropped beard, though there were deep lines beside his eyes. It was as if he were withdrawing before her eyes, from the living man who had sired her to the sculptured image of the King who'd forged a realm that stretched over half a continent.

From the light of common day into the time of legends.

At least she was among Mackenzie clansfolk, mostly, so they wouldn't expect her not to weep. Following the steps of ritual helped, she found. The tears trickled down her face, but her voice was steady as she laid the torch at her feet and raised her arms in her faith's gesture of prayer:

"He was High King and father to all the land, but to me he was my da," she said. "This memory I give, and it is my first of him: my mother lets me go and I run stumping towards him and he sweeps me up, high, so high, and he laughing up at me with the wind and sun in his hair, his hands as strong as the bones of Earth and gentle as the Lady's love. We will miss you, I and Mother and the sibs. Wait for us in the Summerlands beyond the Western Gate, Da, where no sorrow or evil comes and all hurts are healed."

She *knew* that would be so; as he lay dying they had grasped the Sword of the Lady together, and they had met and spoken in the world beyond the world. The eeriness of it was still with her a day later, but it was colder comfort than she would have thought. He'd said grief was for the living, and it was so. He still was . . . but he was *gone*.

The symbol of the High Kingdom lay naked on his breast now, by his own longstanding command for the day of his death-pyre. In its form it was a knight's weapon, what they called a hand-and-a-half sword; thirty-six straight inches of tapering double-edged blade, a shallow crescent of guard, a long double-lobed hilt of silver-inlaid black staghorn ending in a pommel of moonstone gripped in antlers. Merely a sword of superlative quality, until you looked closely. Then there were patterns in the metal and crystal—not quite seen—that led the mind inward and inward . . .

She'd heard her father say that the blade he had brought back from the Quest might not be a thing of matter at all as humankind understood the word. Instead somehow an embodied *concept*, a thought in the mind of the Goddess, one that could be touched in the light of common day. Though that was a perilous thing, very dangerous indeed to anyone not of the Royal kin.

The pyre was a large one, set in a deep pit so that the top was breast-high to the ground about, with a narrow trench to provide draught.

Mackenzies gave their dead to the fire and the ashes to Earth for the most part, and the High King had long made clear that he wished that rite. Dun Barstow was a new settlement that had spent hard labor clearing land here in the renascent wilderness that had once been California, and it was the eve of Beltane, a festival always celebrated with bonfires; there was any amount of dry timber on hand, even with the other funeral pyres that had been needed.

Edain Aylward Mackenzie came up next, to stand at the northern end of the pyre. He was commander of the High King's Archers, a stocky broad-shouldered man of about her father's age with a square weathered face, oak-brown curls and gray eyes. His voice held the Mackenzie lilt, stronger than hers:

"He was my Chief, and my friend from my earliest years, the brother of my heart, the one I chose, the one I followed on the Quest to Nantucket. My father Samkin Aylward taught us both the bow. This memory I give: when I first carried the Silver Arrow at the Lughnasadh Games, my da gave me a nod and a hand on the shoulder I prized more than the Arrow itself. Then Da turned and cuffed *him* upside the head and said he was a natural, he'd been slacking on his practice or he'd have done better than third place. He grinned, that smile that could bring the birds from the trees, and said: *Edain has the blessing of Llew of the Steady Hand as much as I, Sam, and he works harder at it; he earned it, it's his.* Ochone, my Chief, would that I could have died for you! But I'll look to the lass and Prince John and Vuissance and Faolán so long as a man may, I promise you that. We'll have a mug together and talk it over, in the Land of Summer."

The headman of Dun Barstow was Oak Barstow Mackenzie, a tall rangy graying man, one of the few here who'd been born before the Change—though he'd been a child of nine and couldn't remember it beyond fragments. He'd been First Armsman of the Clan Mackenzie for many years. When he laid it down he'd led a party of pioneers south to found Dun Barstow, including many of his own children and grandchildren.

He stepped forward and nodded somberly.

"I was an orphan of the Change, reared in Dun Juniper, and I knew Rudi

Mackenzie first as a brat running about underfoot, then a wild youngster always in a scrape. When he returned from the Quest with the Sword of the Lady and was hailed the *Ard Rí*, the High King, it was as a story from the old tales to me, and I cheered it mainly because I saw how it gave our folk heart in those dark times and united the alliance. This memory I give: when I led the full levy north from our dùthchas in the Prophet's War, I told him: *This is all we have, Ard Rí. If we lose it, the Clan dies.* And he nodded, and told me what he'd planned. As he spoke the memory of him tumbling with the puppies before the hearth dropped away, and my heart said within me:

"*This man is a King you may follow to the death. You may leave your bones on foreign soil, but he will save our folk.*

"The great battles lay ahead, and the march to Corwin, but I never doubted again."

Heuradys d'Ath came to the eastern side. Alone of them she wasn't a Mackenzie, though she was of the Old Faith: she was a noble of the Portland Protective Association from the north-realm, Órlaith's liege-sworn knight and her best friend. And of her own generation, only two years older, like her one of those who'd grown up wholly in the world the Change had made, children of those who had laid its foundations.

"This memory I share," she said. "When I came to be a page at Court, only Órlaith was my friend at first, and the High King seemed godlike to me, to be honored from far away. The other Associate pages were all boys and all Catholics, and . . . Then the High King came to the *salle d'armes*, and I'd just lost a practice bout. I was sitting there rubbing my elbow—and telling myself I would *not* cry where anyone could see me—and he just stood at the back, arms crossed, making this little gesture to the teacher to keep going, and watching. I got back up and picked up my practice blade and stepped into another circle and lost *again*. He watched me keep losing and keep going back time after time. I was the youngest there, and the smallest, and the others didn't dare bully me too badly in the open but they thought they could make me so miserable I'd leave anyway.

"I got back up . . . and he walked over and said to me: *And so you wish to be a knight, do you? My knight?* And I said: *No, Your Majesty. I'll be Princess Orrey's knight and fight by her side and be the shield on her shoulder!*

"And he smiled, and rested his hand on the Sword and looked . . . looked *through* the wall for a moment. And then he looked back at me and said, so that everyone could hear:

"And so you will be, girl, and glad of it I am, for I want only the best backing my Princess in the hour of her deadly need."

Heuradys lifted her gaze and smiled, though her eyes were wet. "And after that, First Armsman Oak, I also never doubted that I would win the victory, hard as it might be."

She turned to the bier and lifted her hands. "Go in peace to the Shades, my King, and rest content in the flower-meads of *Elýsion pedíon* before you drink of Lethe and return. I will fulfill my oath."

There was a moment of echoing silence, with the sound of the birds greeting the sunset the loudest noise, that and the wind in the treetops. Then a set of bagpipes began to play, a slow mournful pibroch of lament. The piper paced slowly ahead of the High Priestess of the Dun's coven, Oak's daughter Rowan, a lanky brown-haired woman in her thirties. She wore a black cloak over her white robe and a black scowl on her fair face as she raised a staff topped with the Triple Moon, waxing and full and waning. Behind her two muscular women carried a large wooden yoke, holding a cauldron loaded with coals, and another pair and another pair came behind, each with a cauldron packed with oak burned down to a savage white heat. A dry smell of scorched bronze and silver and iron filled the air, under the sap of the cut wood in the pyre.

A song began as the piper paced in a circle around the High King's resting place, walking *deosil*, sunwise, as the spirit traveled to the Western Gate.

"We all come from the Goddess
And to Her we shall return
Like a drop of rain
Flowing to the ocean—"

Órlaith met the angry hazel eyes calmly, more calmly than she felt. They'd had words; Rowan had thought the day wrong. This was Beltane Eve—which was the festival of love and life, as Samhain was of death and endings and the Otherworld. Few gainsaid a High Priestess of the triple cords in her own dun, and this one had all the bull-headed stubbornness Oak had shown on the battlefields of the Prophet's War, and all the strength of will of her grandmother Judy who'd been the Clan's first healer and Maiden of the Singing Moon coven before the Change. The cross-talk had rent the afternoon as the women washed the High King's body while the men had laid out clothing and gear to wear on his final journey. Finally Oak had stepped in, his gnarled hand gentle on his daughter's shoulder.

"*A leanbh na páirte;* hush now. Beltane is the rite of life and love, yes. But the High King has fallen on this eve, leaving us the young Queen to pick up the reins. So does her life as Queen begin; and his death is the sacrifice that renews the life of the land, his blood freely spilled upon it bringing the growth of spring, as the Lord of the Corn dies and is reborn. From death comes life. She is the Spring Queen indeed, her strength and youth that of the kingdom. So it is fitting that he should be sent on his way on the holy day, and by her hand."

They'd been silenced, and Rowan had bowed her head and agreed to the pyre this very night. But ill feeling lingered. And Órlaith was too shaken to be diplomatic.

Rowan came to Edain's side, the priestesses with the black cauldron following her. The white and the brass cauldrons were brought equidistant along the pyre, closer to Órlaith. Rowan looked across to the Princess and her face changed as she thrust back the cowl and shook free her hair. Each Priestess copied her, and after a second, Órlaith, Heraudys, Edain and Oak did likewise. Rowan cut a long lock of her hair and held it in her left hand. The small crowd beyond milled and seethed. Órlaith glanced back to see them holding up their hands, holding locks cut free. She swallowed, her throat tight again. That was the rite for close kin or *anamchara*—oath-sword brothers or sisters of the soul, for it sent part of your very self to the otherworld with the dead. Her father had been respected by all, feared by enemies of the peace he'd brought . . . but he'd also been loved by many. Her own grief was a wave on a great sea of sorrow that would wash over the kingdom. That didn't make it less, but it did make her feel a little less alone.

Rowan opened her mouth and took a breath . . . and let it out, again, and shook her head, tears suddenly running down her face; Órlaith heard them clogging her throat as she tried to speak through them. Edain turned and tugged out a handkerchief from his sporran and handed it over. Rowan gave a half-hysterical laugh that hiccuped and skidded sideways.

"I wanted to be so solemn, so perfect for the High King!"

"The honest voice of your heart is a greater tribute," her father said gently.

Órlaith felt her own anger fade. There had been times in her childhood when she was jealous of the way her parents seemed to belong to everyone—the King was Father to the land, and the Queen stood for the Mother. Right now seeing the echo of her grief brought a sense of fellowship.

The High Priestess turned to those watching—the folk of Dun Barstow, the archers and men-at-arms and varlets of the Royal party, and the others from half-built Castle Rutherford who'd answered the courier's call to arrive horror-struck to find the High King dead, killed by a prisoner's treachery after the short victorious fight. The Nihonjin who'd been rescued stood at a farther remove, and kneeled as they sat back on their heels, heads bowed in respect. Not that they hadn't borne their share of the fight, and more, and their own Emperor had fallen in it.

Rowan's voice rose, soaring sure now, as if something or Someone else joined its strength to hers:

"As it was said in the ancient days and now again—*The King is dead! Long live the Queen!*"

The crowd took up the cry, and Órlaith bowed her head a little at the crushing weight of it. In strict law according to the Great Charter she wouldn't be assuming the throne until she was twenty-six, still a few years from now. Her mother the High Queen Mathilda had always been her father's right hand and closest councilor as well as his handfasted wife, and Órlaith knew she would be doing the bulk of the work for years to come, she and Chancellor Ignatius and Edain and High Marshal d'Ath and the others.

Rowan was speaking as the Lady's priestess, at a level beyond human law and politics; or above or behind or beneath it. She went on, her voice ringing:

"And I say, *Mourn! Mourn!* You have seen the death of greatness; the swift daring strength of his youth and the steady hand of his ripe manhood we have had, but the wisdom of his deep age is taken from us and that we will never have, spilled with the blood he shed for us! Mourn, then, *mourn!* For he is lost and gone and we will send him to the sky and the earth and the sea. For his soul has gone on, gone on and left us here, bereft, but not unconsoled. Princess! Light the balefire!"

Órlaith shook herself and took up the torch. Edain, Oak and Heuradys copied her. Two steps took her to the brass cauldron and she thrust the soaked head into the glowing coals and pulled it swiftly out as it took flame with a sudden flare and dragon-hiss. Oak, Heuradys and Edain followed suit and she spun it around her head as a wordless cry of pain burst from her chest. She thrust it deep into the pile of wood, to the prepared pot of tallow, oil and spirits. A scream like a Harfang, a roar of the bison, the howl of a wolf echoed on the trailing edges of her voice as the others called on their totems. The fire roared up from the four quarters, huge and hungry and the Priestesses grabbed the yokes and tipped the coals in a stream along the edges, moving widdershins as the chant rose:

> "We all come from the Maiden—
> And to Her we shall return.
> Like a budding flower, blooming in the springtime.
> We all come from the Mother—
> And to Her we shall return.
> Like a stalk of wheat falling to the reaper's blade.
> We all come from the Wise One—
> And to Her we shall return.
> Like the waning moon, shining on the winter's snow."

Órlaith raised her voice into the dying fall at the end of the verse:
"God of Light, You of the Long Hand, Swift Striker, Lover, Warrior,

wise Father, Knower of Roads and Ways, in Your form he came among us, ever walking in Your power. Take him to Yourself now!"

She threw her handful of yellow hair at the fire and it flared, caught the air currents and danced even as it glowed, crisped and charred. With a shout, the crowd moved forward to do the same. The keening rose with the flames, the wail for the beloved dead. The flames caught swiftly . . .

She felt a prickle of awe break through the intense self-focus of grief as she flung up a hand to warn the others and stepped backward, and then again. The rest retreated behind her.

Yes, the wood was tinder-dry and cunningly placed furnace-style and there were tons of it, around the well-stacked kindling. But surely this torrent of red and gold reaching for the purple sky of sunset was something else again. Sparks flew upward, turning in a widening gyre like a dance of hot stars. There was no scent save the intense dry smell of the fire, and the tears dried on her face. She had to look aside, as the blaze grew to a white heat where steel itself might burn, a roaring amid a wind that torrented towards it from every side and cuffed plaids and hair and robes. That wind seemed to blow through her as well, a storm of fire and power and light, filling her and shining as if she were turned to glass that contained the very Sun.

Rowan looked at her, and her eyes widened as if she saw something as well. She turned her gaze away from the King's daughter, and then her breath caught again as she raised her staff in a gesture half of reverence and half of warding. More heads turned to follow. A raven was flying out of the setting sun, down the slanting rays that came from the piled clouds above the mountains.

"Morrigú," someone murmured, and then Órlaith realized it was herself. "Badb-Macha-Nemain. Moro-rīganī-s, Shadow Queen."

The pyre burned down swiftly, consumed in minutes and dying as if the flames were falling back into the earth. That left the drifting circle of sparks. Gasps rose from the crowd as the raven banked about them, midnight against gold, its wings a yard across and its beak a slightly curved blade like the spike on the back of a war-hammer. And in the center of the hot glow—

She hadn't expected the Sword of the Lady to be harmed. Her father had been certain it could *not* be, not by any flame kindled by men, not by the fires at the heart of Earth or the core of the Sun itself. But now it hung suspended, point-down in the middle of the golden coil. And it blazed, the crystal pommel a star brought down from the heavens. She advanced towards it step by step, each feeling as if miles passed, or distances of time and space beyond conception. Edain started to cry out in alarm as she reached for the hilt, but the staghorn and silver were cool and solid beneath her palm, and the blade swung upward like a living thing in her grip.

Chambers opened within her mind, currents of thought too vast and strange to even be given names, then surged away leaving a sense of *potential*, as if her soul was stretched like an iridescent bubble vanishing-thin, hollow and waiting to be filled. She would have staggered, would have cried out, but it was too swift and too large. Eons passed in an instant. When she came to herself again the raven hung before her, its wings beating about her head once and twice and thrice. The flint-sharp beak stabbed forward, landing between her brows with a quick pain that grounded her again, like her very self pouring back into her body. The little trickle of blood was cool fire, and the darkening wilderness glowed with meaning, a thousandfold millionfold dance with herself at the center.

She fell to her knees, panting, as the raven circled above her and turned back into the West.

"Are you all right, Orrey?" Heuradys asked.

Edain was at her other side, looking for once as if he could not decide what to do. Rowan grounded her staff and bowed her head, and the crowd had fallen silent.

"Are you all *right*?" Heuradys asked again, sharply.

"I'm—" Órlaith began hoarsely.

She rose. Earth *spoke* in her as she did, one sharp syllable that left an echo that faded but never quite died. The land of Montival, all of it from the deeps of the Ocean of Peace to the hot heart of the Valley of Death, all of it *her*.

"I'm . . . I'm what I need to be, Herry," she said.

A moment, then to the people: "Go, and feast in my father's memory. We keen the dead, and then we make merry at the wake. Sorrow, but also take what joy you may on this day. For there will be much to do before what begins here is finished."

When her father had finally found the time and labor to begin building a capital for the High Kingdom, he'd called it *Dún na Síochána*, the Citadel of Peace. Peace was good—in fact, it was divine, a face of the Mother, She who loved all Her children without distinction.

But Justice is also a Goddess.

And from the images they made of Her, even the ancients knew—

—*that Justice . . . Justice carries a sword.*

CHAPTER TWO

Near Dun Barstow
County of Napa, Crown Province of Westria
(Formerly California)
High Kingdom of Montival
(Formerly western North America)
April/Uzuki 30th, Change Year 46/2044 AD/Shōhei 1

The newly-made Empress of Japan took council with her advisors as the night wound down into silence.

Reiko looked at the urn with her father's ashes and swallowed at the sight of the plain, subtle gray curve and the three thin sticks of incense burning before it. As his only blood-relative here it had fallen to her to use the special chopsticks and pick the charred fragments of bone up out of the remains of the pyre with due reverence, for transfer to the ceramic container. It hadn't been as hard as she feared; concentrating on doing it properly had helped, as ritual was meant to do. When every motion was prescribed, you need not think. Nor was the memory gruesome. It had been a means of saying good-bye, a final act of love. But . . .

For an instant she closed her eyes, took a deep breath, and cleared her mind by feeling the mild air on her skin, the slip and slide of linen *haori* on silk kimono belted with the warm wool *hakama*; and the smells of warm canvas turning cool with night, and the alien greenery beyond, a scent drier and spicier and more dusty beneath the dew than her homeland.

When she opened them the men kneeling around the table in the center of the open-sided tent were waiting for her to speak, eyes politely lowered. The lantern hanging from the center-pole cast slight, flickering shadows. Everything was changed, now that she was *jotei*.

"We await your orders, Majesty," her Grand Steward said.

He was a thin weathered man in his late fifties named Koyama Akira, the only one of the senior men who'd been born before the Change. Few such had survived the terrible years since.

It was a little disconcerting to have them waiting on her word, since the half-dozen of them were all at least a decade more than her twenty years—commanders and advisors she'd seen working with her father all her life. They'd always treated her very politely, of course, and with increasing deference since it became clear that Prince Yoshihito was lost and there would never be another heir except her or her younger sisters.

Reigning Empresses were very unusual but not completely unknown. Her grandmother had been one, for all her short life, until she died bearing the son who had been Reiko's father. She had been the sole survivor of the Imperial line, brought from Change-stricken Tokyo through chaos and terror and death on an unimaginable scale, on a journey that had been an epic of sacrificial heroism by men determined that the seed of Amaterasu-Ōmikami be preserved at any cost.

"The *Renso-no-Gi* and the *Ryosho-no-Gi* are out of the question," she said quietly; those were the funeral rites. "Investiture with the Regalia . . . well, you all know why we are here. For the present we will simply take this meeting as *Sokui-go-Choken-no-Gi*, the First Audience of my reign. I hereby authorize it."

Koyama bowed and slid a sheet of creamy mulberry paper towards her, and then a leather-covered box. She opened it, hearing an intake of breath as the square gold shapes within were exposed to view; not everyone on this voyage knew that the State and Privy Seals were with them.

Reiko paused for a moment to clear her mind, then in one fluid movement held back the sleeve of her kimono, touched her brush to the wet surface of the inkstone and quickly signed the characters of her name on the paper. Then she pressed the seals home—they were heavy, being of pure gold and three and a half inches on a side, but her hands were strong and steady. The special cinnabar ink stood out below the plain black brushstrokes.

"Are there any objections?" she asked quietly, as she folded the box closed again. "No? Then we will proceed."

There had been whispers that the Emperor treated her too much like a son after her brother Yoshihito's ship was lost, as if grief had driven him to distraction. These were his most loyal followers, but they would be weighing her every word and action.

She knew that there had been many times in the long, long history of her people when the Emperor had been a revered but powerless figure-head, a puppet-prisoner in the hands of iron-fisted generals or simply presiding at the rituals of State while politicians ruled. This was not such a time, and her father had been clear that she must *command* as well as preside. Reaching a consensus was important, it provided the framework that made action possible just as the bones did for a man's body, but without a central focus it degenerated into paralysis all too easily.

"There is simply no time for ceremony," she said, after waiting a mo-ment, putting a decisive snap into her tone. "Nor do we have the other requirements for it. The Montivallans can conduct their rituals for their High King because they are on their own ground. We will give—"

She felt another wave of pain as she stopped herself from referring to her father by his name, or by any title he'd borne in life. That would be inauspi-cious, but it was like another step away. She controlled her breathing—if you ruled the body, you ruled the mind—and went on by using his posthu-mous name, called after his era, the Rebirth.

"—*Saisei Tennō* the proper obsequies when we can. In the meantime we will do him honor by carrying out his plan. Is that understood?"

"*Hai, Heika! Wakarimashita!*" the others replied, ducking their heads in formal agreement.

Nobody was happy about it, she judged, but necessity had no respect for law. Even custom must bow to it at times. They were probably grate-ful to have her say it for them, though. Most of these men had loved her father too, in their different ways.

"We will also take this as the first year of *Shōhei*," she said.

That was the era-name she had chosen: Victorious Peace. There was a very slight rustle at the boldness of her claim, though eras were named as an aspiration, not in retrospect. Only time would tell whether it was correct . . . or a bitter irony.

"I require a complete and frank analysis of our situation. Egawa, you will begin," she went on briskly.

Remembering to use his name alone this first time, as a marker of their relative positions. Another man might have been offended, though most wouldn't show it, but Egawa Noboru's eyes flicked very slightly in approval before he lowered his head in acknowledgement.

"How are we placed?" she said.

The Imperial Guard commander bowed.

"*Heika*," he said.

That was *Majesty*, as informal as was really possible, acceding to her unspoken command that they keep strictly to practicalities. Until she saw her mother and sisters again—and even then only in private—it was unlikely anyone would actually use her name to her face. The living being vanished inside the outline of the Heavenly Sovereign One.

Egawa's face was an iron mask, his voice flatly objective, though she knew his grief was if anything worse than hers—and tinged with shame that his lord had fallen in battle while he lived. The bandage on his left hand marked where he'd intercepted the throwing knife aimed at *her* by desperately and instantly putting his own flesh in the way, only moments later. She hoped that soothed his honor; if so it certainly made her glad. He would be the sword-hand of her reign, as he had been for her sire.

"The Montivallans have furnished all the supplies we could ask," he began.

She nodded. They'd had nothing left, and the food and water had been running short for weeks before they made land. For the last ten days of shattering labor at pumps and sails and catapults there had been only a handful of rice each, and barely enough water to cook it and give one strictly rationed cup to drink. Nobody had gone *quite* mad enough to drink the seawater around them, but some had probably been close.

And Father smiled as he refused the men who pleaded with him to take their ration, she thought.

Her people prided themselves on the warrior spirit that could overcome mere material things, but there were limits and thirst and starvation and scurvy were among them in the end. The beaching and desperate flight and savage battle that followed had taken the last reserves of everyone's strength.

Nobody showed it openly, of course, but just being able to drink their fill of clean water and feel it soothe the savage pain between the ears was inexpressible bliss. And it had required all the iron control samurai learned not to gobble and stuff themselves with fresh food like peasants at a festival; they had been very hungry, and for just long enough that it became a grinding, nagging ache without the numbing that followed in real famine conditions. The food here was not what they were accustomed to, apart from the fish, but there was plenty of it and they could prepare the raw ingredients in the fashion they preferred.

In a way she almost missed the physical misery, because it preoccupied you and the spiritual effort of suppressing it smothered the pains of soul and heart.

Father—

"And they have provided excellent care for our wounded, treatment much like ours," Egawa continued.

"That is most fortunate," she said, proud that her voice was steady.

And she'd noticed the same thing when she visited their injured. It was a comfort that those who'd suffered wounds in the Throne's service were being given the best possible care, though it was a pity that it was among strangers with whom they shared not a word. Still, the skill and sympathy of the healers and their assistants had been unmistakable. To a man in pain, no matter how brave, a smile and a gentle hand meant much.

"Not one man can be spared if recovery is possible," she said, with iron in her tones. "And we have no true healers left."

One of their doctors had intercepted a *jinnikukaburi* roundshot with her head in the Aleutians, and the other had been slashed to death in the brutal scrimmage around the ship trying to drag a wounded man back from the front line. Everyone learned field medicine, but that didn't make you a real doctor.

"We have thirty-two men of the Imperial Guard fit for duty, including some lightly wounded, and adequate gear for all though we are short of arrows," Egawa continued. "Two more have died, and six are seriously injured. I regret to inform you, Majesty, that Watanabe Atsuko-*gozen* never recovered consciousness."

Reiko closed her eyes again for an instant. Lady Atsuko had been the last of her female attendants; there had been three originally, all well-born young women a little older than her and selected for their varied skills. She could see Atsuko driving the point of her *naginata* into the face of the Korean swordsman who'd been about to strike Reiko . . . and to do it, ignoring the scar-faced savage who brought a stone-headed club down two-handed to shatter the plates of her helmet. Reiko could remember her frowning over the *go* board, too, or gently, patiently mopping the face of her friend Haru by the flickering light of a single swaying lantern when she was prostrate with seasickness in the endless storms.

"Duty, heavier than mountains," she said quietly.

They hadn't been friends, not exactly—there were barriers—but they had all become close, in the confined quarters and constant shared peril and hardship.

"Death, lighter than a feather," another voice murmured, completing the formula. Then: "But now you will have no woman to attend you, Majesty."

"We will do as we must. Continue, General-san," she said levelly, switching to the more courteous distant form of address with his title.

"Our ship *Red Dragon* is a wreck and most of the crew perished in the rearguard action there."

Young Ishikawa Goru, who had been *Kaigun Daisa*—captain—of the *Red Dragon*—leaned forward slightly at his gesture and supplied the precise information. Her father had directly ordered him to join the retreat because they absolutely must have an experienced navigator, and there had been tears in his eyes as he obeyed.

"The upperworks burned and there is structural damage to the scantlings, Your Majesty, from the fire, from the grounding, and from the storms—we were leaking like a ladle dipping noodles out of the pot for days before we sighted land."

"I remember the pumping," she said; her hands had hard calluses from weapons practice, but that had worn them sore.

He ducked his head. "Majesty. And the repairs we could make to strikes by roundshot and catapult bolts at sea were makeshift. So sorry, we would need a shipyard, timber and cordage and sailcloth, many skilled workers and even with all these things at least a month or so to make her seaworthy. Effectively, complete rebuilding. As it is, here in this wilderness the ship must be regarded as a total loss. To return to the homeland we will require a new ship, and at least some of the crew for it."

"The Montivallans have ships capable of the voyage. They trade regularly with Hawaii and even more distant lands," Reiko said.

"Mainly by the southern routes, Majesty," Koyama confirmed. "To avoid the savages who helped the *bakachon* against us."

"This is why the Montivallans took our side, Lord Steward?" someone asked. "They couldn't know what was going on. We were all warriors from nowhere, we and the *bakachon* and those savages they picked up."

Here Reiko could answer: "The savages fighting with our enemy, the ones whose ship kept us off the coast so long after we reached Alaska . . . they are called *Haida*. And evidently they are enemies of Montival—pirates, I think."

Ishikawa nodded thoughtfully. "*Ah so desu ka*. That would explain why the seas were so completely empty as we came across the Pacific from Hokkaido, though that is the best sailing route from Asia to this continent, Majesty," he said. "It is not that there is no sea traffic at all, as we feared, but that it avoids that route despite the favorable winds."

Reiko gestured agreement with her fan. "That came out when they made sure of where *we* came from. We are not stranded."

Nobody moved, but she could feel their relief.

"Continue, General Egawa."

He went on: "The ship is lost, but a good deal of the baggage and gear in the hold was salvaged by the Montivallans after they put out the fire, and promptly turned over to us, unopened. There is much goodwill on their part, I think, but communications are a problem; those of us who have some English have to use written messages. Thankfully they are all literate in the Latin alphabet and a number of us can use it, but it is still awkward."

Koyama said thoughtfully: "Their High King spoke perfect Japanese . . . Sado-ga-shima dialect, even . . . and apparently Korean as well. And now his daughter does. I still do not understand that. Certainly none of the others have any, Majesty."

"Yes, I recall, and I was astonished at his fluency even then," she said. "The difficulty in speaking with them is very awkward; we cannot expect a ruler to act as our interpreter whenever it would be convenient. We must master their language as rapidly as possible, and that applies to you all, and to your subordinates."

Her mouth twisted a little wryly. Her tutors had been convinced that she could already speak fluent English. She had studied dutifully, even though it had seemed a useless accomplishment to her.

They were very wrong, and so was I!

It would have been extremely useful to speak English now, but though she could handle the written language easily enough, several embarrassing attempts at the spoken tongue had proved incomprehensible to the locals. Nor could she follow more than a word or two per sentence when *they* spoke. The sounds that English-speakers actually used were excruciatingly difficult—many of them were identical to her ear but were distinct and crucial to meaning—and the spelling in the supposedly phonetic Latin alphabet was bizarrely useless as a guide. Why did *night* have a *g* and an *h* and no *e* on the end?

And while she was not sure, she suspected that at least two very different *dialects* of English were involved here.

The Kami know it's hard enough to understand someone from Hachijo, the way they mumble everything as if their mouths were full and call a field a mountain or say garbage for firewood. It might be something like that. And I don't even know which dialect is more important! But the important thing here is—

"It is the sword he carried, and that his daughter now bears, that did these things," Reiko said flatly. "It is . . . *shintai*."

She turned slightly and bowed to the urn. Everyone followed suit; it wasn't necessary to speak. *Shintai* was a word with many implications: literally it meant something that served as the dwelling of a *kami*.

Most commonly it was at the center of a shrine, and it could be a rock, a tree, a waterfall . . . or an object like a sword. Some considered the relationship merely symbolic, but the ancient tales could make the power embodied in a *shintai* sound quite bluntly literal. Her father's quest involved taking the stories very seriously indeed, and they now had direct proof in the light of day that he had been absolutely right.

Koyama went on slowly: "These people . . . they are not at all as I would have imagined Americans, from the records and stories. Even two generations after the Change. Though they recognized *us* immediately, what we were and where we came from. Even using our own terms; I heard their ruler's daughter say *Nihon* as soon as she saw us closely. Curious."

"As far as custom and appearance go, I suspect that we too might be surprising to someone who had no knowledge of Japan since Heisei 10," she said; that spring was when the machines had stopped. "Since we have returned to many of the older ways."

She reminded herself to think of the Western calendar as well, though it wasn't much used in everyday speech anymore: Heisei 10 was 1998 AD.

"And just as surprising to someone brought forward in time from before Meiji, Majesty," Koyama said, surprising *her* a little. "Though they might take a little longer to realize it. History cannot be completely undone, even by the Change, nor can the past be truly brought back even if you wear its clothes."

True enough, she thought. *I am not about to shave my eyebrows off or blacken my teeth or apologize for existing every time I speak to a man.*

"My father once said he felt as if he had awoken in a Kurosawa epic and could not escape," Koyama added.

They all ignored the mysterious last sentence; the Grand Steward was given to gnomic references nobody else could understand.

Egawa's second-in-command Nakamura Ichiro spoke; his left arm was bandaged and in a sling.

"These *gaijin* look so *strange*, though. More so than the pictures prepared me for. Hardly like human beings at all. More like characters in an ancient *manga!*"

Reiko tapped her fan on her chin; that had struck her too. Nobody born in Japan since the Change had seen a living *gaijin*, of course. When nine hundred and ninety-nine in every thousand perished, it wasn't to be expected that any of a tiny group of foreigners centered in the cities where devastation was worst would survive. For her generation, their parents hadn't seen one either, though there were surviving photographs.

A representation was one thing, the living reality another. The fantastic hair and eye colors were like something from a dream, and the odd angular features, even the way they differed so strongly one from another in things like the tint of their skin—she had seen everything from the commonest odd-looking pink shade through normal tan to a very dark brown almost the color of an aubergine. It all made it a little difficult to see most of them as individuals, though she supposed she'd grow accustomed to it.

And frankly, most of them are repulsively ugly. So hairy! Almost like oni. *Though this Princess Órlaith is striking, in a deeply strange way—hard to realize that the yellow hair and blue eyes are real. And her face is like a blade.*

"They seem civilized enough in some respects," she said thoughtfully. "Not too smelly, at least."

Everyone nodded. The communal bathhouse in the little village looked as if it had been among the very first things built there when the settlement was established a few years ago, and it had been almost exactly like the *sentō*, the equivalents back in the homeland. Almost as if it had been modeled on them, with provision for scrubbing down first and then soaking in a large tub of hot water. Hers were a fastidious people, when they could be, and it had been a deep relief to be properly clean again after so long. Though it had been a little strange and sad to be rattling around in it by herself.

"General Egawa, your military evaluation of our . . . hosts," Reiko said.

She wanted everyone to have the facts, and she was also interested to see if his judgment would match hers.

And the battle was so . . . chaotic. Despair, and then it was arrows and lances in the enemy's back. I could easily have missed something crucial. I am the descendant of the Sun Goddess, not Herself. And even the Great Kami are not omniscient.

"Majesty."

He passed his bandaged hand over the shaven strip on his head, back towards the topknot, and frowned for a moment as he organized his thoughts.

"Their High King's personal troops dealt with the *jinnikukaburi* who were about to wipe us out very well. From what I observed their individual weapons-handling with sword and lance was reasonable, allowing for different weapons and styles. The archers were truly excellent, as good as our *shashu*, and the heavy cavalry charge was fearsome, I've never seen anything quite like it. Or those horses!"

"Huge but graceful," Reiko agreed.

"Feeding them might be a problem, though—I've seen that they eat grain, General-sama," his second-in-command said thoughtfully.

Egawa nodded; it was a valid point. In Japan, animals ate only what humans couldn't, apart from the odd handful of barley to keep chickens tame enough to be easy to catch. The Imperial Guard commander went on:

"Coordination between arms was nearly perfect. Beautiful timing, which requires not only a commander with good judgment but a force with maneuver discipline. And the way they deployed indicates to me that they scouted carefully with those lightly armed horse-archers without either we or the enemy noticing them before they struck. The *jinnikukaburi* were taken entirely by surprise."

"Their High King assumed that any friend of the Haida was an enemy of his, and any enemy of an enemy was a friend," Reiko said. "Logical, but it is not easy to be completely logical in a situation like that, with so much unknown and so much at stake."

Egawa nodded. "*Hai*, Majesty, that was sound thinking, when he had so little time to consider and no precise information. Swift! Decisive! He saw the situation and struck precisely with all his force, and without a moment of the hesitation that might have let the enemy recover their balance. A great pity he was killed."

Silence fell for a moment as they thought of their own loss, until Grand Steward Koyama nodded.

"Very fortunate thinking for us," he said dryly. Then: "And perhaps not so much of a pity that their High King was killed."

"Explain," Reiko said sharply.

"Majesty, even without understanding the language well, it is obvious that the Montivallans are stricken with sorrow. And beneath their sorrow, a deep anger, hot but lasting; both as great as ours at the loss of our Emperor. The *jinnikukaburi* have killed a man, but they may well have awoken an entire nation. And filled it with a terrible resolve."

"That is a point," Reiko said thoughtfully. "Yes . . . yes, considering what I have seen, you may well be correct. Continue, General. You spoke of the household troops of the Montivallan ruler, who are presumably their best men. What about the rest?"

Egawa went on: "The militia from the village are good archers, and well equipped for light troops. I cannot say more without seeing them in action, but my impression is favorable. They resemble our *kosakunin-ashigaru*, our farmer-infantry."

More nods. Every household in the homeland kept weapons ready to hand, trained to arms in what spare time they had, and every fit man and every woman not pregnant or recovering from childbirth was ready to turn out with bow and *naginata* when the alarm-drum boomed out. Full-time samurai were a handful, their numbers set by what the land and the peasants and craftsmen who worked it could produce, but the raiders from across the Sea of Japan did not find an easy meal anywhere.

Her commander went on: "The reinforcements they've received since then look generally similar to the regular troops we saw fight, well equipped, well-fed and strong, with good march and camp discipline as well. They hold themselves with pride, care for their gear without being driven, obey orders promptly, work hard, and set alert watches."

Everyone nodded; those were good rule-of-thumb indicators of quality if you couldn't actually see men fight. Egawa continued in a slightly lighter tone.

"Some of the older troops have seen much action, judging from their smooth skins and beautiful looks."

There were a few smiles as he touched one of the scars that seamed his square pug face before he went on:

"Apparently they also have heliographs, gliders and observation balloons. And catapults. Probably fortifications, castles, too. The crossbows some of the reinforcements carry have a very ingenious rapid cocking mechanism, and I noticed a number of other good tricks that might be worth copying. Unless there were implausible stockpiles before the Change, most of what they use is of modern make, done to a very high standard."

"So your appraisal is on the whole positive?"

Egawa nodded. "*Hai*, Majesty, very much so. They would make formidable allies, if we can persuade them. If I could combine our own total forces with an equal number of troops of the quality I have seen here, and the necessary ships, I would pledge to lay all Korea at your Majesty's feet in two campaigning seasons."

At the thought his expression changed slightly. To something you might glimpse on the face of the very last tiger you ever saw.

Ishikawa Goru was only ten years older than her, which made him the second-youngest present, and the sailor was also inclined to headlong brashness.

"But their country seems to be very thinly populated, General-sama," he said. "How many of them can there be?"

They all looked at him, and he flushed and mumbled: "So sorry."

Reiko made a tapping gesture towards the naval captain with her closed *tessen* war-fan in mild reproof, making allowances for the way he'd kept them afloat through weeks of storms in the frozen wastes of water north of Hokkaido as they ran before the gales and the relentless pursuit of the *jinnikukaburi* squadron. And for the fact that the *Red Dragon* under his command had sunk several of the enemy ships in brilliant slash-and-run engagements without taking crippling damage or heavy casualties. If those extra *jinnikukaburi* crews and marines had been on their tails when they came ashore here not one of the Japanese would have lived long enough to be rescued.

"This is probably only a fringe territory, like our new settlements on the main islands," she said gently. "The equipment, weapons and tools we have seen . . . there must be plenty of large workshops *somewhere*, with highly skilled specialists, *their* tools, and a labor force. Which means many farming villages like this one we have seen to support them. Hundreds, at the very least. Probably thousands."

Koyama nodded. "Yes, Majesty. I have definitely learned from maps they have shown me and what conversation we have been able to manage that this is the southernmost of their inhabited territories and far from the center."

There was an old map of western North America on the table, and he used a finger that had been broken long ago and healed slightly crooked to point:

"From what I was able to learn, the heart of their realm lies here in the valley of this river to the north, the Columbia, and the other rivers flowing into it, from the coast far into the interior. This was where the largest number survived the Change. Rather as Sado-ga-shima or Hachijōjima or Goto and Oki-shoto and the other islands of refuge are to us, but I suspect they have more people than we do. Possibly *many* more; that river and those seaports were the path by which huge quantities of grain were exported before the Change, and much would have been available in ships, storage elevators and trains. There were a few large cities which doubtless perished, but also very broad farmlands with few inhabitants. Very few, by our standards."

"Ah, yes," Egawa said clinically. "With organization, that could have made quite a difference to the logistics."

His was not the only nod of agreement. Famine had been the greatest killer everywhere in the year after the Change, closely followed by the chaos and plague that inevitably came in famine's wake and brought everything down in wreck. There had been a hundred and twenty million people in Japan in 1998; thirty-five million in Greater Tokyo alone. She had learned those numbers from her tutors, but it was difficult to think of them as anything real. Sado-ga-shima had been a rural backwater, and not many of the few surviving adults from the cities willingly spoke of that time. Or of the battles on the island's shores to keep out starving refugees, fought by men weeping as they killed.

All her people together were perhaps a third of a million now, and that was much more than it had been at the lowest point. When a city of thirty-five millions found itself with only a week's food, and no light or clean water or sewage disposal or transport or ability to communicate faster than a man on foot . . . Tokyo and Osaka had burned for months. The skies had been dark that year, the elderly said when they spoke of it at all, and stank of smoke, and the cold rain left stains like liquid soot. Her father's generation had been more haunted by it than hers, but it would be centuries before the memory of horror lifted entirely.

The Grand Steward concluded: "Montival *claims* the whole western half of this continent. I have not yet determined how real that is."

Reiko nodded; her government *claimed* all of the old Empire, but most of that was howling wilderness and haunted ruins. Her people were the children and grandchildren of remnants preserved on offshore islands with enough food—just. And not too impossibly many mouths as the Change flashed around the globe like a flicker of malignant lightning and the great world-machine stopped in its tracks. On some of those islands the aged and infirm had refused food or opened their veins or walked into the ocean lest they starve the children, or overburden those strong enough to work and fight and breed.

"Not entirely unlike us in the breadth of their claims, then," she said dryly. "However little substance there is to either."

"Every reality that we can make begins with a dream, Majesty," the Grand Steward said. "The Seventy Loyal Men who brought your grandmother to Sado dreamed, and made the dream truth in the face of the wrath of the *Kami*."

"*Hai, honto desu ne,*" she conceded to the unspoken reproof. "Unquestionably true. Or I would not be here."

Some of those men had paid with their sanity, most with their lives, many with both, and none were still among the living; but every child in Nippon learned their names now, and made offerings to their memories in summer at the Obon festival. Their *giri* had been fulfilled, but an unbreakable burden of obligation remained with the living.

This too passes to me with Father's death. All the generations past and those to come look to us now, their fate balancing on the blade of the sword we hold. Duty heavier than mountains, neh? But we may not escape it through death; we must triumph and live and hand down our heritage. The first duty we owe our ancestors is that they have descendants.

Her shoulders moved as she set herself to it, but her face showed nothing. Koyama acknowledged the point with a gesture and continued:

"But certainly they are pushing new settlements into the wilderness here in what the maps call California. Here the Change struck as badly as it did in Japan. Our hosts recognize the name California, by the way, but do not use it. I also have . . . mmm . . . an impression that this High Kingdom is a federation of very different units. No details yet, so sorry, Majesty."

Reiko made a small hissing sound of frustration, and there were nods of agreement.

We know so little! And we cannot make sensible decisions until we do know more.

The *jinnikukaburi* raids had kept Japan's survivors isolated from any real contact with the outside world all her lifetime. There was an occasional ship from the mainland looking for salvage or trade or just fleeing chaos, but the coasts of China were mostly a wreck as bad as the main islands of Japan. And from what they had heard the interior was a bloody murk of warlords fighting each other and Tibetan and Mongol invaders, seasoned with flood and disaster as the dams and dykes and canals of the old world broke down and spilled the great rivers across their floodplains.

The rest of the world was barely even rumors. And all her people had *wanted* to do was begin the long slow process of resettlement of their homeland, until the enemies of humanity forced them onto another path.

"There is another matter," Reiko said; after her first reminder, it was time to drive the lesson home. "You all watched the cremation of their High King."

Another series of bows. This time they masked deep unease. They had been politely distant, but close enough to know that something entirely strange had taken place.

"You saw what happened then. I know many of you thought *Saisei Tennō* was . . . possibly unwise . . . to seek *Kusanagi-no-Tsurugi*. You thought it was a piece of mysticism, perhaps even madness, to follow visions seen in dreams. I suggest that you reconsider. The Grass-Cutting Sword is exactly what he said: our only hope."

CHAPTER THREE

The varlets would have the tent down in minutes when she was finished, but some things should be done with due form when you could.

Heuradys d'Ath stood before the folding table and poured *khernips*, lustral water, into two identical glasses, crystal flutes salvaged from one of the dead cities long ago. They were part of the traveling altar given to her by her adoptive mother Tiphaine d'Ath when Heuradys became an Initiate and they realized that they had the same patron deity. The gift was a bronze votive case, a foot on each side and four inches deep, with padded velvet recesses in the lower half for the glasses and flask, a small golden tripod and a libation cup like a shallow bowl, fine pottery with sprays of olive-boughs and owls painted on it in black.

When it was opened, as now, the low-relief silver image of the Owl on its inner lid made it a miniature shrine. The dim light of dawn glistened softly in a diffuse blur through the gauze windows of the tent she shared with Órlaith, carrying the smell of woodsmoke and frying bacon, the scorched iron and horse odors of a camp.

"Tegea," she said softly, touching one glass, and then for the other: "Tritonis."

She poured a little from the first over the dark-auburn braids coiled on her head, feeling the cold drip down her bare back, and murmured:

"I cleanse myself by the waters of the sacred Tegea, Waters of Refuge."

Then she poured some from the other onto her hands and touched her face with them, concentrating on an image of sunlight sparkling in clean cold water bubbling from the mountain spring that had supplied the *khernips*, and of the incense and burning twig that had sanctified it.

"I purify myself to receive the Goddess, by the sacred waters of the Tritonis, Spring of Abundance. Make me clean, I pray, of any offenses I may have committed against You knowing or unknowing."

She wiped the glasses both reverently and replaced them, set up the little golden tripod and lit a small sprig of olive wood and leaves in its cup—fortunately common here in the south, she'd had to use Russian Olive before. It was the symbol that counted, but the best symbol for something was the thing itself, and the pleasant slightly musky scent curled up with the smoke as she poured in a drop of olive oil and wine from the libation cup. Then she took out a long black and white feather from a Harfang, the great northern Owl, passed it through the smoke, planted it upright before the image and stood back with her arms raised and outstretched and palms up in the gesture of prayer.

"Athene, Bright-Eyed Lady, unwearied One, Shield of the City, Former of Plans, Granter of Victories, You I honor and to You I pray. I, Heuradys d'Ath, have worshipped you above all others in the past, with libation and placing such offerings as are acceptable to You on Your altar. I give thanks that You locked shields with me in the vanguard as I fought for my liege-lady. Grant to me sharp insight and an undeceived mind and well-taught hands that I may fulfill my oaths and guard her whom I am sworn to uphold, and through her the Kingdom. In league with You will I set my own hand and mind to work with all my strength, as is ever pleasing to You, Who loved Odysseos of Ithaka for his many skills and undaunted cunning. Accept now my offering of wine and Your sacred olive, I pray. Be You always by my side, Shining Lady."

She touched the feather to her eyelids and lips and tucked it into its holder, wiped the tripod and libation-cup clean and replaced them, fastened the straps and then closed and locked the case. It went into another, slightly larger and of plain hard olive wood; that went into the saddlebag hanging from the tent-pole. The brief ceremony always made her feel better, more focused and determined and *sharp* somehow.

Today it also helped with the odd dislocation of grief, that flux between moments of normalcy and the sudden realization *he's gone* hitting you over and over, fresh each time.

Though of course her patroness understood if circumstances forbade; there were advantages to being a follower of a *rational* deity. Some of the other Olympians . . . Ares, for example . . . she shuddered.

It still got her odd looks up north in the Protectorate, the Association territories, though things were much better there than they'd been in the old days when the first Lord Protector had his tame antipope running an Inquisition, complete with Auto-da-fé.

Her mother Lady Delia had had to be a Church pagan—pretending to be a Catholic—all of her childhood and much of her young adult years. The Great Charter didn't actually say all the realms of Montival had to practice religious toleration, though it *did* say anyone who wanted to could move, but the High King had certainly encouraged it even when he didn't have the power to command. By his own example not least.

Damn, there it goes again, she thought, as a stab struck her. *He's gone. But you built well, my King.*

She dressed quickly in traveling garb, knit cotton drawers and sports bra, snug doeskin breeks and turned-down thigh boots with gilt spurs, and a loose persimmon-colored linen shirt fastened by ties at throat and wrists. Her armor was on a stand beside her cot, as Órlaith's was beside her camp-bed. That was standard procedure in any camp; getting into it in an emergency was hard enough without having to rummage through a trunk, and it was the reason why surprise attack was the great weakness of men-at-arms. She certainly wasn't going to wear the full suit of plate today, with no danger within miles that anyone could tell; nobody did that unless they had to, for training or combat or on occasions of ceremony. Just for starters, you needed skilled assistance to put it on *and* to get it off. She considered wearing half-armor instead, just the vambraces and back-and-breast, but . . .

But we're all reacting irrationally. The horse has already left the stable, alas. Anyway, the High King was wearing full armor, everything except his bevoir and helm, when that prisoner got him with the throwing knife . . . and the bastard was aiming at Orrey, at that. Her father threw her back, I've never seen anyone move another full-grown person in plate so fast, I swear he started moving before we saw the knife. And I got my shield in front of her and then he jerked his shield-arm up and wasn't quite quick enough to protect himself. That old shoulder wound . . .

She forced herself not to play the scene over again in her mind imagining a better outcome; the past was done and had to be accepted, and her immediate responsibility had been to her liege-lady.

Instead she shrugged into a supple, sleeveless thigh-length black jerkin of kidskin that had a layer of light meshmail between the leather and its silk lining, held together by patterns of flat rivets made of gilded brass. It being a warmish spring day she decided against a houppelande coat and instead pulled on a short-sleeved divided T-tunic of fine thin cinnamon-colored merino wool that came nearly to her knees, embroidered with silver thread at throat, deep V-neck and cuffs and with her arms—Sable, a delta Or on a V Argent, with a crescent of cadency—in a heraldic shield over her heart.

A habitual quick glance at the mirror showed the effect was quite striking, given her height and build, and went well with her mahogany hair and amber eyes. The look was not in the least masculine, despite the fact that it was decidedly male dress by the standards of the northern nobility.

Elegant, but ever so slightly threatening, she thought. Dashing, *that's the word I was looking for.*

She had a reputation as a bit of a fop about dress whether she was in hose or skirts, and it wasn't undeserved. Right now she was still feeling too shocked at the High King's murder to take her usual full innocent pleasure in a good turn-out, but it never hurt to seem as you wished to be and vice-versa. Or to keep up standards.

Heuradys cinched the belt that held sword, dagger and pouch around her hips, tucked a pair of long leather riding gloves through it, and picked up her chaperon hat—a round thing with a rolled brim and long dangling liripipe and a livery badge that quartered her own arms with the Crowned Mountain and Sword of the High King's house. A chaperon was almost as much a marker for gentlefolk as the spurs.

"Droyn!" she said briskly.

Droyn Jones de Molalla was the senior Household squire, a grandson of the first Count of Molalla and a younger son of the current one; Molalla was a smallish but very rich County southeast of Portland, one of the first established by the PPA after the Change, during the Foundation Wars. The young man was three fingers taller than her five-ten-and-a-half, with a cap of curled black hair and skin somewhere between dark olive and very light brown.

He *was* in armor with his visor up as he ducked into the tent, and his kite-shaped shield was slung over his back, but then he was on duty. There was a clash of steel on steel as he brought his clenched right fist to his breast in salute.

His face might have been carved from seasoned oak, but she thought he'd probably been weeping himself, when he was alone. There was enough sorrow to go around, a kingdom's worth, a continent's. Millions would be mourning, soon enough.

Then they'll want blood. Hades in the Underworld, I want blood. Armies will march and cities will burn because of this, she realized with a slight chill.

"My lady?" he said, and inclined his head with formal deference.

Quite properly; she was a knight, even if she hadn't been in his chain of command until now, and he wasn't one yet, though he was about Órlaith's age. Heuradys was two years older but still young to wear the golden spurs in peacetime, though she'd passed all the tests and done very well in tournaments and won a couple of duels to first blood. Including one where she was pretty sure the man who'd challenged her had been planning to kill her and claim it was an accident. There hadn't been any wars to speak of since she came of a squire's years, though.

Until now. I'm young for the accolade in what was *peacetime,* she thought grimly. *That's about to change too. And obviously, I'm going to be close to the Throne, and Droyn realizes that.*

They were about equal as far as birth went, though that counted less in the Household. Her father Rigobert de Stafford was a Count too, of Campscapell just north of the Eastermark in the Palouse, and had estates in the Willamette as well—he'd been Baron of Forest Grove since the Lord Protector's time, not long after the Change.

There was the added complication that her adoptive mother Baroness Tiphaine d'Ath was a noble in her own right, seigneur of Ath and Harfang and a tenant-in-chief, but Heuradys wasn't in line to succeed to those either. Her elder brother Diomede d'Ath would be Baron under the Association law of primogeniture, as their eldest sibling Lioncel de Stafford would inherit the Barony of Forest Grove and the County of Campscapell.

She'd take livery of seisin of three good manors on Barony Harfang eventually, held in free and common socage, which would make her a vavassor—a minor but well-to-do landed noble holding directly from the Crown, rather than from a baron or count or duke. That was as much as she really wanted, that and being Orrey's household knight. She'd absorbed the knowledge that being a baron involved a lot of hard dull work through her skin as a child. At least if you wanted to do it right.

The complex balance of status went through both young Associate nobles' minds in a subliminal instant; that sort of calculation was as natural as instinct.

"Droyn, Her Highness isn't to be troubled with matters of precedence and Household organization yet. Grief aside, there are high matters of State that demand her full attention."

He frowned. "Yes, my lady. Everything's all ahoo, but . . . yes. We can improvise and work around. We'll leave the High King's tent and trappings with the baggage we're having sent on, and leave most of the staff with them. The . . . the High King wasn't traveling with much state anyway."

Heuradys nodded; Rudi Mackenzie had been a knight but not an Associate despite being married to one, and he'd always retained the infor-

mality of the Clan's chieftains when he could. The north-realm's ideas of
how to show the consequence due to rank weren't popular in the greater
part of Montival outside the Protectorate, anyway. They were a legacy
of the Association's precursor, the Society for Creative Anachronism, a
pre-Change brotherhood. Who'd practiced them, and the other arts of
chivalry . . . as far as she could tell from what her adoptive mother had
let fall in private moments, simply as a pastime. They were deadly serious
matters to their descendants, most of whom didn't think of the centuries
between modern times and the days of Charlemagne and Arthur and the
Black Prince as important . . . or even very real.

A tradition had to start somewhere, and enough belief made it as real
as a rock.

"So we can . . . ease things in," Droyn said.

"Good idea," she said.

She was relieved that he was thinking along the same lines. Being the
son of a Count didn't guarantee you weren't a natural-born damned fool.
On the other hand, it didn't mean you necessarily were, either. She'd
dealt with her share of well-and-high-born idiots, though they were rarer
than in the general population. Foolish or timid people just hadn't survived the Darwinian process that had produced the Associate nobility's
survivors in the first generation, and there hadn't been enough time for
much regression to the mean.

"Select a minimum number of varlets to handle this tent and Her
Highness' baggage. Young and strong ones and good riders, because we
want to make all speed we can north. It wouldn't hurt if they at least knew
which end of the sword goes where, just in case."

"Guard relays?"

"Sir Aleaume will handle that as usual, under Captain Edain's direction; they'll set the rosters. I've consulted with both. Just remember that
we do *not* want to start formally treating the Crown Princess as if she
were her father, or as if she'd been crowned High Queen Regnant. High
Queen Mathilda wouldn't get *very* upset, but a lot of other people *would*.
Starting with Her Highness, which we do not want!"

"St. Michael and the Virgin, no!" Droyn said, crossing himself.

"Glad you understand that. We'll be taking most of the horses to use as remounts at least as far as White Mountain; the carts can wait here for more to arrive. So no gear that won't fit on a pack-saddle. I'll coordinate with Sir Aleaume, but I think I can rely on you to be inconspicuous and still get things done? The Household has to keep as much off of Her Highness' shoulders as we can, right now."

His clenched fist in its armored gauntlet clashed on his articulated breastplate again. "My lady!"

"And one final matter."

She turned to a steel box about two feet on a side, turned the key in the lock and opened it. Within rested a vase twenty inches high, a tulip-shape of sleek silver-colored glass with a design of reeds and flowers that made you think of warm early-summer days beneath the shade of a riverside willow-tree. It had been intended as a gift from Dun Barstow to the High King because of its beauty, an ancient thing found in the ruins of a mansion in Napa. Now it held his ashes.

And there wasn't anything left but *ashes,* she thought with a slight shiver. Usually even a hot pyre left bone fragments. This time . . .

Ashes. Fine as dust, almost. Impossible to tell where the wood-ash left off and the body began. Even the buckles and the gold of the torc were gone.

The box was sturdy, and the thick glass of the vase was packed carefully with dense soft lamb's-wool.

"The most vigilant care must be taken with the High King's remains," she said.

"My lady!" He crossed himself. "My men and I will guard it with our lives, and bring it to the High Queen."

"Good man," she said. "I'll leave you to it. The Crown Princess and I have full confidence in you."

His face looked more alive after that, though still very solemn. She'd found that with men of his sort giving them an important task to focus on was the best way to get ten-tenths of capacity working. She settled her hat, draped the liripipe over her shoulder and came out of the tent, making her stride brisk and nodding to the squad of the High King's Archers outside as they brought up their longbows in salute.

High King's *Archers?* she thought grimly. *That's going to change.*

Her own status was going to change; everything would. The ground was shifting under her feet, and Droyn's attitude had been a foretaste.

What was that ancient saying? I expected this, but not so soon?

As she walked away there was a concerted rush of varlets behind her; the baggage was coming out and the canvas coming down before she'd gone a dozen paces.

The camp in one of Dun Barstow's fields was larger now that the reinforcements from Castle Rutherford had joined the party that had first accompanied the High King and his heir on their tour of the new Westrian settlements. The broad flat expanse had been in wheat last year and was thick with green burrclover and medic now, knee-deep where it hadn't been trampled and sweet-smelling where it had, starred with yellow and purple flowers and murmurous with bees and hummingbirds.

The breakfast table stood beneath a great live oak, one that must have been growing here when Napa was a sea of vines. Possibly before the old Americans or even their Hispano predecessors had come, in a distant pre-dawn past when only the tribes of the First Folk dwelt here. The Mackenzie settlers establishing Dun Barstow had left it in their turn when they ripped out the thickets of dead and living vines and brush to make their crofts, for looks and shade for livestock in the fierce southern summer.

And as an act of piety to the Goddess in Her form as Lady Flidais and to the Horned Lord, Cernunnos of the Forest, Master of Beasts. It was a recognition that humanity was not over and above the other kindreds, and held what they did on sufferance. Órlaith was just lowering her arms from her own morning devotion to the rising Sun, and her expression froze for an instant as she turned. As if *everything* in the world reminded her of her loss and her dead.

"I know, Orrey," Heuradys said softly, and rested her hand on her liege-lady's shoulder.

Órlaith laid her own hand on the knight's and squeezed briefly. Heuradys saw the Gods thanked for her for a moment, which was comforting; it meant she was making a difference. She loved all three of her own parents and would grieve when they died in the way of nature, but Ór-laith had been much closer to her father than Heuradys was to the Count of Campscapell, who was more like a wonderful uncle in many ways. And the brutal surprise of the assassination made it far worse, like a raw wound on the soul.

Plus Orrey is probably feeling guilty that he took a knife meant for her. Illogical, but the heart has its own reasons that the mind does not know.

The camp looked different without the High King's pavilion, sparser somehow despite the greater numbers, and all the banners flying at half-mast. Even the bustle of packing up and getting ready for departure was somehow subdued. It was odd to think that in most of Montival things would still be completely normal, the High King merely gone on a prog-ress with his heir to inspect the remote southern frontier.

The news of his death would be spreading northward already, of course. As fast as relays of couriers on horseback could take it to the edge of the heliograph network, and then by coded flashes of light from hilltop to hilltop, city to city, castle to castle, mirrors reflecting the sun's rays in the day and burning lime in darkness. They would know in Portland in a few days, and eastward to the Lakota country and north to the Peace River in a fortnight. It might be months before it filtered out to the most remote villages and ranches, or even years in the vast wilderness border-lands. Large chunks of those weren't inhabited at all, or had a few wild-men who weren't even aware that they *were* part of the kingdom.

But there will be a great stirring, a sharpening of blades and a stringing of bows. Whoever those strangers were, they made a very bad mistake when they shed our King's blood on our own land.

"I've asked the Nihonjin ruler . . . *jotei*, Tennō, Empress . . . over for breakfast," Órlaith said. "Her and two followers, and you and me and Edain."

"Are you ready for that, Orrey?" Heuradys asked bluntly. "If you're so stressed your judgment's off it would be better to wait. You took a heavy hit, we're all here to handle things for you, and our guests aren't going anywhere soon."

"No, I can push it," Órlaith said calmly, after glancing aside for an

instant. "It's not a council, just a talk. I think this could be really important and we need to set things off on the right foot. There will be plenty
of time for detail on the way north."

Heuradys looked at the Sword of the Lady hanging in its black tooled-
leather scabbard at Órlaith's left hip. The High King had always worn it
on his right, and it looked a little odd there.

*And I could swear it's a bit smaller. A weapon sized for her father would over-blade
Orrey, but that looks as perfect for her as it did for him. Brrr!*

"Talk?" she said. "You can understand them?"

Órlaith nodded as she turned and walked towards the meeting-place.
She was wearing a loose saffron shirt and Mackenzie garb, a pleated
knee-length kilt in the Clan's brown-green-orange tartan. A plaid of the
same fabric was wrapped around her chest and under the right arm,
pulled firm to the body, pinned at the left shoulder by a sapphire and gold
knotwork brooch that left the trailing end with its fringe hanging down
behind to her knee-hose. Her hair hung loose past her shoulders under
the flat blue Scots bonnet with its spray of Golden Eagle feathers in its
silver clasp, and the morning sun brought out the hint of copper in that
thick yellow mane. She put her left hand to the pommel of the Sword.

"Yes, it's working for me the way it did for . . . for Da."

She swallowed, and visibly forced herself back to calm. "It feels . . .
odd. For a moment there was . . . was this balloon swelling in my head,
then it popped and I knew the language. As if I'd always known it, somehow. No, as if I'd grown up speaking it. I could tell that some of the
people with her speak different dialects, and I just . . . knew what the
honorifics and so forth meant, not just literally but all the implications. I
can switch over to thinking in it like turning a tap and when I do the
whole world looks a wee bit different."

"Useful!" Heuradys said. "But better thee than me, my liege."

"*Arra*, tell me. Being warned isn't like feeling it. There's all sorts of stuff
that comes *with* it, too. I think 'food' and . . . what comes into your mind
when you're after thinking the word food, Herry? Comes first, at least."

"Bread," she said instantly.

A loaf was what you thought of immediately. A nice long crusty loaf right out of the oven and off the baker's wooden paddle, butter melting into the steaming surface when you broke it . . . damn, but she was ready for breakfast. Feeling sorrow didn't stop your digestive system, outside the more romantical chansons, she found.

"Me too. But I switch over to *Nihongo* and suddenly for a moment I'm thinking of a bowl of rice . . . or noodles . . . with little separate dishes of things on the side, and I look at an ordinary plate and go *euuu* at the way everything's mixed up. Fair disgusting . . . for an instant."

"How many times have you eaten rice? Really, I mean," Heuradys asked curiously.

It wasn't grown in Montival, not yet, and anything imported was a hideously expensive luxury. Though it still grew wild, seeded from old plantings in the Sacramento Delta not far from here. Perhaps someday folk would settle there to raise it.

"A few times. Rice puddings at Yule, mostly, and sushi on occasion in Portland. But when I start thinking in *Nihongo* my mouth wants it steamed and sort of sticky . . ."

"The Sword of the Lady is a cookbook, too?" Heuradys said, chuckling.

Having been around it so long at court, from her childhood as page and then squire and now household knight, she didn't have *quite* the awe of the Sword that most people did.

Not quite, *and that still leaves a fair degree of awe. And not that I'd touch it willingly.*

"Not recipes exactly, but sort of . . . an ideal of what food *is*. Or I think 'hello' and I know how to say hello to people of different ranks and in different circumstances and a whole bunch of stuff like that. I think 'clothes' and it's various robes that come to mind, not a kilt or hose. Kimono just means *the thing you wear*. I get the language, and how to *use* it. It doesn't . . . I mean, I still want bacon and eggs. But I can sort of . . . switch."

"I don't know what we'd do without the Sword this time. Though there's the other stuff."

"No need to mention that just yet, I think."

They both nodded slightly. The bearer of the Sword of the Lady could detect falsehood—or as Rudi Mackenzie had put it, the speaker's belief that what he was saying was false, the *intent* to deceive. Everyone in Montival knew that and virtually all of them had believed it by now; it had been a long time since anyone but foreigners and the densely stupid tried to lie to the High King. There was no need to explain that to their new . . .

Guests, Heuradys decided. *Possibly allies, but not until we know a lot more.*

"Is there anyone in Montival . . . besides you . . . who speaks Japanese?" she asked.

"Not that I know of, though there are almost certainly a few tucked away somewhere. Ones who learned from their grandparents."

A weary smile; Órlaith hadn't slept much. "Reiko . . . that's her name, it means something like *Child of Courtesy* . . . or possibly *Courteous Lady* . . . actually speaks English quite well."

"It didn't sound like it!" Heuradys said.

She'd *thought* the woman was trying to say *Thank you very much* to the people who'd saved her outnumbered party from being overrun and slaughtered where they'd been brought to bay, but she hadn't been at all certain, and she was well-traveled and versed in the weird and wonderful ways the English language had evolved in Montival since the Change. It was amazing what could happen to a language if a few hundred people were cut off from most outside contact for a half-century, and that was just accidental stuff and not counting deliberate alterations, which were also common.

"All right, *knows* English. She learned from people who'd learned from people who'd learned English as a second language. For someone who grows up hearing nothing but *nihongo* the sounds are difficult. She's got the grammar and vocabulary quite well; it's just a matter of learning to pronounce them."

Edain came up and saluted briskly.

"Sir Aleaume has matters in hand; we'll be ready to march as soon as breakfast is over, Princess," he said. "And once we've talked to the foreigners."

He scowled a little at that. Órlaith laid a hand on his arm below the short mail sleeve, where it was corded with muscle and scars.

"It's not their fault, my old wolf," she said. "And they suffered a like misfortune. We have a common enemy, at the very least."

He drew a deep breath. "Yes. Yes. I saw the one who did it—"

And you put three clothyard arrows through him in less than three breaths, Heuradys thought.

The commander of the guard regiment was known as Aylward *the* Archer for good reason.

I'd heard about you doing things like that in the chansons *about the old wars, but I'd thought they were exaggerated. And the dead man didn't stop moving. I'd hoped that those stories were exaggerated too, but apparently not.*

"—and he was like a magus of the Church Universal and Triumphant; I haven't seen the like since Corwin fell in the Prophet's War, nor missed it, but it's not something you forget. It was fated that your da would not live to see his beard go gray. It's not just Fiorbhinn's songs. The Chief told me so, long ago on the Quest. And not a month past, just before we came south . . . he told me he'd dreamed of wading across a river, and seeing blood flowing by his feet from the clothes an old woman beat on the rocks."

Heuradys shuddered very slightly, and she and Órlaith made the sign of the Horns with their left hands. The scarred archer did so too; they all knew what it meant to see the Washer at the Ford in your dreams. The knight shared a look with her liege-lady, and saw she also knew why the High King had spoken no word of it to anyone else but his trusted life-long comrade: he'd wanted Órlaith to have the joy of their last time together on this journey, not to blight it with pain come before its season. The Princess' eyes closed again, then opened as her face set.

Edain gave a crooked smile. "So don't worry, lass . . . Princess . . . I'll keep an open mind with these strangers." Thoughtfully: "They're bonny fighters, and that's a fact. So let's go break bread with them this spring morn. And speak of the fine red revenge the both of us will be having, to brew bale-wind for the chieftains we've both lost."

A dozen of the Archers were drawn up a tactful twelve paces behind the folding camp table, in brigantine and short mail sleeves and kilts, with their longbows cradled in their arms; equally tactfully, they were wearing their flat Scots bonnets rather than their helms, with the raven-feathers of the High King's sept-totem in the badges. A man-at-arms in a full suit of armory-issue plate held the banner of Montival. You couldn't tell much when the visor of the sallet helm was down and he wasn't wearing a tabard with his own arms, but Heuradys knew it was Sir Aleaume de Grimmond, commander of the mounted guards on this expedition and son of the Grand Constable of the Association, Baron Maugis de Grimmond. He'd probably taken the duty so he could keep a close eye on the Crown Princess without openly violating orders to be inconspicuous and tactful. To be fair, the foreigners wouldn't know him from Prometheus.

A similar number of the Japanese followed their Empress; the equipment wasn't quite what Heuradys recalled from pictures of ancient samurai in the *gusoku* armor of the sixteenth century, but closely similar—lamellae and plates mostly laced together, and flared helmets much like northern sallets but larger. The surfaces shone with exotic combinations of colored lacquer in liquid brilliance, and the man in charge of the detachment had a flag on a short pole in a holder on his back with writing in spiky script and a visor shaped like a grimacing face complete with mustache.

The overall effect wasn't frivolous at all, despite its vividness and touches of fancy like crests set on the brow of the helmets.

More like a collection of giant killer wasps, she thought, remembering the brief battle.

When the Montivallans showed up and pitched into the enemy's rear these folk had risen from the ruins where they sheltered and charged instantly with a uniform scream of *Tennōheika banzai!*

When they hit, it had been like a many-legged mincing machine flinging sprays of blood and body-parts in every direction. She swallowed a little at the memory; she'd trained for war since her childhood and to live and die by the sword was her inheritance, but that had been her first real combat. There hadn't been time to be queasy about it then, but the memory was a bit . . . unpleasant . . . even now. At the same time she couldn't help but wonder how they'd fare against Associate knights or Bearkiller cataphracts or Boisean legionnaires. . . .

The armored men halted and bowed; the Archers responded by tapping their bows to their brows and the standard-bearer thumped his gauntlet to his breastplate and ducked his head. The three walking forward were in civil garb, the men on either side in plain dark short kimonos with round embroidered *kamon* symbols on either side of the chest that her education said corresponded to heraldic blazons, and *hakama*—broad loose trousers of striped fabric with pleats, almost like a divided skirt. Heuradys carefully hid a grin; in the north-realm, in the territories of the Portland Protective Association, something very similar was the usual dress for ladies when traveling on horseback.

The ones who don't scandalize the respectable by wearing breeks or hose, like me, she thought.

It was known as a riding habit, but the original inspiration had been precisely the sort of clothing she was seeing now, and Delia de Stafford had made it *the thing.* Her birth mother had always been a leader of fashion and had a huge library on the history of textiles and costume worldwide. There weren't many people in Montival who had several walk-in closets full of classic kimonos simply because they were interesting, but Lady Delia was one.

The young woman called Reiko—evidently Japanese royalty didn't have a surname, though apparently you didn't call them by name either—was wearing a longer kimono of very dark blue silk, dyed with tiny dots in black and paler blue that made patterns that might be either clouds or dragons, and with golden *kamon* badges in the form of a stylized chrysanthemum. She was within a few years of Heuradys or her liege, give or take, though shorter, and under a studied formality of movement walked with the cat-grace of someone who could wield a mean *naginata*, which the knight knew was true from personal observation.

When she took off the shallow bowl-like straw hat she was wearing the face beneath was marked by grief and probably lack of sleep, but strikingly regular from high cheekbones down to rosebud mouth, small straight nose and narrow cleft chin. Not quite delicate, the bones were too pronounced, but verging on it; her long black hair was parted in the middle over the forehead and then gathered at the nape into a woven

knot, with two long gold-headed ebony pins. There was an indefinable
air of taut, controlled thought to her as well. Altogether it was an attractive face, and strong.

Exotic, too, the knight thought. *Striking.*

Heuradys didn't have the slightest erotic interest in women—which
had been disappointing to at least one of her mothers and which her father Count Rigobert liked to say with a chuckle she'd gotten from him—
but she could appreciate the ensemble aesthetically.

All three of the strangers had broad sashes around their waists, tied at
the back and with long katana and short *wakizashi* thrust through it on the
left, the blades nearly parallel to the ground. Their left hands rested on
the sheaths in a way that must be utterly unconscious, thumbs lightly
pressed against the guards in a gesture that made it possible to flick the
blade forward in an instant, an aid to the draw-and-strike technique that
could give you a crucial extra fraction of a second.

These are serious people, she thought soberly.

That term too was a legacy of the Foundation Wars in the early days
of the Association. Besides his fellow-members of the Society for Creative Anachronism, the first Lord Protector had recruited what were eu-
phemistically referred to in the heavily mythologized chronicles of
family history kept by noble houses as *freelance men-at-arms,* to help him
hold and extend the power he'd seized in the chaos.

In areas of Montival outside the north-realm she'd heard the same men
referred to as *gangsters* and *thugs.* They'd mostly taken up Society ways with
the enthusiasm of converts, but the traffic hadn't all been one way.

Órlaith and Reiko bowed—at moderate angles, simultaneously, with
their hands before their thighs and to exactly the same degree; the two
male Japanese bowed with their hands to their sides, and rather more
deeply towards the Montivallan leader. Heuradys exchanged a glance
with Edain, and then they both made the gestures of respect they were
accustomed to—Edain bowing slightly with the back of his right hand to
his forehead, Heuradys sweeping off her chaperon with a flourish and
making a leg. That was safer than trying to fathom the depths of a system
of etiquette they didn't know well.

The Japanese hesitated at the sight of the chairs; she got the impression they knew about them but didn't use them much at home. Heuradys drew out Órlaith's and held it for her, a motion which one of Reiko's attendants copied; they were utilitarian collapsible canvas-and-aluminum models. The three Nihonjin removed their sheathed swords and laid them on the table before they sat—on their right sides, and with the curved cutting-edges in.

Ah, Heuradys thought. *That would make them* hard *to draw quickly. Probably a gesture of courtesy or trust.*

The three Montivallans unbuckled their sword-belts and hung them across the backs of their chairs before they sat. That was polite too. And wearing a sword sitting down was plain uncomfortable; they were always catching in things, especially the long knight's weapon.

Heuradys studied the three across the table carefully. Even the friendliest negotiation was a battle of wits, a matter of controlling the exchange of information. She suspected that her side had one advantage here, at least at first. People of that East Asian physique weren't common in Montival, especially unmixed, but they weren't vanishingly rare either. Sir Aleaume's mother was one-quarter Japanese by descent for instance, a legacy of her grandparents back before the Change. From what she'd seen and heard, the newcomers had never before met anyone who wasn't of their own physical type before they landed on these shores. Probably that made it more difficult for them to read the more subtle expressions, piled on top of differences in custom and body-language.

One of the male Japanese looked as if he were a few years either way of sixty, with a lean impassive face and a slightly hooked nose; she guessed that the bare strip up his pate to the topknot at the rear was mostly natural by now.

A fighting-man in his day, she guessed. *But more of an advisor now, or senior administrator, probably both.*

The other man was about Edain's age and stocky-strong, with a formidable collection of scars and a weathered complexion, the sort you got from being outside all the time regardless of weather—warriors and peasants both looked like that, and she didn't think this man had spent his life growing rice. He and Edain were appraising each other, and after a second gave a very slight nod of mutual recognition.

This one's a man of the sword—a commander, I'd judge, and tough enough to chew iron and crap caltrops, as the saying goes.

Sharing a meal was a gesture of welcome almost everywhere. Varlets came forward with plates and a basket of maslin penny loaves, the rough one-pound ration issue made from mixed flour of barley and wheat. The strangers looked very slightly apprehensive, then showed equally well-hidden pleased surprise when they were presented with bowls of noodles in broth and plates with a grilled trout each.

Relieved that they don't have to pretend to enjoy revolting barbarian swill, Heuradys thought, amused behind an impassive face. *Nice touch, Orrey.*

Not too difficult either. Fish swarmed in the Napa river and its tributaries, and with a civil settlement at hand finding pasta wasn't difficult. For that matter, it was where the risen bread was coming from; in the field you mostly made do with tortillas unless there was a chuckwagon along. But the Crown Princess was being . . . tactful . . . again. The foreigners each brought out a little lacquered case and set their chopsticks on a rest built into it, the sharp-tapered points to the left.

Well, well, Orrey's really getting benefit from the Sword, she thought.

The Japanese pressed their hands together before their faces and murmured something, then sat impassively; Reiko drew a folding metal fan from her sash, probably a habitual gesture, but the edges glittered like razors. Órlaith and the Empress introduced their companions—Heuradys caught the words *bushi* and *samurai*, terms which had been part of her military education, and shaped the names *Koyama Akira* and *Egawa Noboru* to fix them in her memory.

Right, surname first, I remember that. And only family and very close friends use the personal name.

They all sat, and the Japanese laid pads and writing-sticks before them.

And this is going to be a bit of a strain, the knight realized. *Well, at least the breakfast looks good.*

"Harvest Lord who dies for the ripened grain—
Corn Mother who births the fertile field—
Blessed be those who share this bounty;
And blessed be the mortals who toiled with You
Their hands helping Earth to bring forth life."

Órlaith signed her plate with the Invoking pentagram as they murmured the Blessing, and she and Edain dropped a crumb of the bread. Heuradys flicked a drop of her hot herb tea aside as a libation. Órlaith would have offered the Nihonjin real tea if there had been any to be had, but it was an expensive luxury in her kingdom, imported or grown on a few experimental plantations, not the sort of thing you dragged along on a trip through wilderness.

"Is that a religious ceremony, Your Highness?" Koyama said slowly and carefully, pronouncing each word distinctly.

Órlaith nodded, her lips quirking in a slight smile. They *knew* she spoke Japanese like someone who'd been born among them, but it seemed hard for them to *grasp*.

"You may speak normally. I think you will find I speak your language reasonably well," she said.

His face was entirely expressionless as he looked at her chin. The habit of avoiding direct eye contact after a first glance was a little disconcerting, but she copied it. They were also avoiding watching the Montivallans wield knife and fork on their bacon, scrambled eggs and fried potatoes, which they seemed to find mildly revolting.

"You speak it perfectly, in fact," Koyama said. "Even with the same distinct regional accent as myself or the Majesty, and with post-Change Court diction. Which is remarkable. I understand it is due to that . . . sacred weapon?"

They were stealing occasional glances at the Sword of the Lady; slung across the back of the chair, the crystal antler-cradled pommel was just visible. She nodded and continued:

"The Sword of the Lady. And yes, this is a religious ceremony, a minor rite. We give thanks to the Earth Mother and the dying and reborn Lord, and an offering to the . . ."

She dropped into her own language for the term before she explained it in theirs:

". . . the *aes dana*. The spirits of place. *Kami*, I think you would say. My religion believes that each place and thing has a spirit, parts of the greater Gods but also distinct, as They themselves are aspects of the Lord and Lady, who in turn make up a greater Oneness that is all that is, or was, or might be."

The Japanese looked at each other. Reiko cleared her throat.

"We . . . ah, were under the impression that most Americans were Christians."

Órlaith smiled. In a way it was like meeting time-travelers. They would have no idea what had happened on this side of the Pacific, nothing but surviving stories and books that ended with the death of the old world.

"Well, things have *changed* rather drastically here since the Change. We usually refer to the Americans as *the ancients*," she said.

Leaving aside some of the old diehards in the United States of Boise who insist that the Change was just a broken carriage wheel on the upward road of progress, but let's keep it simple at first, for all love, she thought to herself. *That's sort of . . . sad, anyway.*

Aloud she went on: "And yes, there are plenty of Christians in Montival, more than half the total, probably. Catholics especially. My mother the High Queen and two of my siblings are Catholics, for example. As it happens my guard commander here and my *hatamoto* Heuradys are of what we call the Old Faith."

She could tell that Heuradys stirred a little at that because it was an oversimplification. The knight was a pagan but not a witch like Órlaith or her own mother, strictly speaking. Still, it was close enough for government work.

And since I am the government . . .

"And there are also Mormons, Buddhists, Jews, I think there are some

Muslims about somewhere, and then the First People—Indians—have their own rites and beliefs, differing between their tribes. It varies regionally, too."

She held up a hand and glanced over her shoulder. "Arbogast? Did you find it?"

A senior varlet slid forward and handed her a slim book, with *The High Kingdom of Montival: a Regional Study* stamped on the leather of the spine.

"Yes, Your Highness. Young Ghyslain is taking a correspondence course."

"Ah, good. Thank you, Arbogast, that was quick. See that he draws funds to replace it." To the Nihonjin:

"This is published in Corvallis for students . . . that's a great center of learning. One of our cities with a university."

It's actually more of a case of a university having a city-state, but let's keep things simple for now.

Aloud she continued: "It'll furnish some background information. I thought it might be useful, since for now you all find written English a little easier than the spoken language."

Which was a polite way of saying *can read it but might as well be deaf and dumb.*

Koyama looked at the textbook with a trace of eagerness, Reiko with interest, and Egawa with resignation.

The conversation became more general. Órlaith listened carefully. Reiko was trying to reply in English occasionally, and managing the sounds a little better, working at it doggedly.

"Yes, we have seen something like that . . . thing . . . that killed our fathers before. Have you?" the Japanese woman said.

The Crown Princess nodded. "Yes. There was a war here, we call it the Prophet's War, against a . . . religion . . . of sorts, one that saw most people as . . . worthless, tools. Their leaders were like that at times. As if something else looked out through their eyes, and at deep need they could do things that ordinary men could not—keep moving for a little while after they should have been dead. Even their blood could be perilous. This ended the year I was born, you understand, when Corwin . . .

their capital . . . fell, and my father killed their Prophet on the steps of their Temple. The last of them was hunted down before I rode my first pony, and I have only heard of it, not seen it . . . until . . . the day before yesterday."

She swallowed pain and fury, that the enemy defeated so long ago had come *back*, and slain her father in the end.

Who then has the victory? she thought. Then: *He bought us a generation when common folk could reap what they sowed with no one to put them in fear. He and Mother built the Kingdom on strong foundations. That is his victory, and nothing can take it away so long as we keep faith with him. To every generation their own task.*

But the sheer fact that she had something important to do, something that required her full concentration, kept the misery at bay. Her father had been fond of the saying that work was the best cure for sorrow, and it was true. The three leaders across the table looked at each other. Pure envy seemed to be involved in the subtle play of feeling on their faces.

"The *jinnikukaburi* leaders are like that," Egawa said. "Their ruling dynasty, and some of the lesser ones."

"*Jinnikukaburi?*" Órlaith asked.

That wasn't an ordinary Nihongo word; it was a compound that meant roughly *human flesh cockroach* or perhaps *cockroach in human flesh* and to her it . . . tasted . . . as if it were a new coinage. There was a freight of loathing and unacknowledged fear to it.

"What we call the *bakachon* these days," Egawa went on. "Cannibal bastards."

One of Órlaith's brows went up. *Baka* was the word for fool or imbecile. *Chon* translated in her mind as *Korean* and at the same time as something like—

Her consciousness stumbled, as the new language tried to flow into concepts not present in her mind, superimposing on what she'd grown up speaking in a way strange to her. Terms she knew only vaguely floated by at the back of whatever part of her paid attention to the way the Sword amplified her knowledge of words: *dink* and *gook* among them, with *Canuk* a more familiar but very distant and qualified third.

Here in Montival people insulted each other all the time over things like religion, tribe or clan, old feuds, occupation, social class and neigh-borhood, and they did it in ways ranging from rough half-friendly teas-ing to an active will to harm. But not in quite *that* way.

Finally she got a sense that the closest rough equivalent in her native dialect of English would be something like *Korean* crossed with the con-tent of the phrase *stinking retarded monkey;* the whole process took less than a second, though it seemed longer.

Right, "Chon" is not *a compliment. I don't think they love each other, so.*

Reiko made a slight sound, the equivalent of an English-speaker's *tsk-tsk,* and touched her folded fan to the man's wrist for an instant.

"That is not quite fair, General Egawa," she said gently.

To Órlaith: "We are not sure of the details, but from prisoners we know that there was a terrible war in Korea, not long after the Change. The enemy believe that the man who was their ruler then, who had es-caped Pyongyang and hidden with his closest followers in a mountain fortress, received a divine revelation that enabled him to reunite Ko-rea . . . what was left of Korea. He emerged when the chaos had de-stroyed all that went before and imposed his rule, claiming that the spirits had made him a *kangshinmu,* seer and sorcerer and priest, and that those who pledged allegiance to him alone were pure, and were entitled to make cattle of all others. Those who resisted were . . . disposed of, though it took years of fighting. We only really became aware of this afterwards, from interrogating prisoners we took when their raids began, and so we know only the story as the victors told it."

"Ah. That would be where the *human flesh* and *cannibal bastards* comes in?" Órlaith said with distaste.

We were lucky here. I've heard oldsters laugh when we say that, but it's true none-theless. Luck is always something you say when thinking of someone with less of it, or more.

"Yes. So they survived the terrible times, until there were crops again. That is why there are so many of them, for the stronger ate the weaker. That happened in many places, but not so . . . so organized, so disci-plined, so deliberate. We Nihonjin and the folk of Chosen have never been what you would call friends—too many old wars and grudges—but they are not evil in their natures or corrupt in their blood, any more than we. They have been forced and twisted to become the enemies of the human race. Fate, neh?"

Egawa looked obedient, but not altogether convinced: Órlaith thought he must not be a man much given to that sort of fine distinction. To him an enemy of his nation and ruler was just an enemy, and scum were just scum.

And it says something about Reiko, that she does make that sort of distinction. Even now. Da always said a ruler couldn't afford hot hatreds, and she seems to know that too. Be careful not to underestimate this one!

Edain leaned close and murmured to her after she translated: "Sounds as if they had a Prophet's War of their own, these Chosen folk. But the wrong side won."

Órlaith nodded. "My grandmother Juniper said visions had shown her the same conflict in many lands," she said softly. "Why suppose the outcome would always be the same? It was a close-run thing here."

"We apparently have a common enemy," she said across the table, in Japanese once more. "And for that at the very least we owe you transport back to your homeland, and possibly much more . . . and more would be my inclination, as of this moment."

Then she held up a hand. "But I am not High Queen Regnant yet. Not until I come of age, which is twenty-six for heirs to the Throne. Five years from now. Until then my mother is ruler, though she will listen very carefully to my advice. My . . . my father has been killed, but we need to know much more before we send the kin of many to die. Much more of what is gathering on the other side of the Mother Ocean."

CHAPTER FOUR

"Huzzah! Huzzah for King Birmo!"

"Good on you, JB!"

Prince Thomas frowned at the informality: "Cheeky fucking peasants."

The King of Capricornia snorted at his son as the carriage rumbled slowly through the crowd over pavement that had started out as tarmac and been patched with whatever came to hand over the generations since. He turned a wave to the crowd into a mime of a clout over the ear.

"You were born a peasant, or a bloody commoner at any rate, and don't forget it, you little prick. The whole fucking realm is only as strong as the lowliest peasant. They carry us all, in the end, the poor bastards. Remember that, and respect the truth of it."

The King was eighty-two, unbelievably ancient in this new world. There were a couple of hundred thousand people in Capricornia, counting everyone from his family to the ones living on grubs, roos and other assorted bush tucker in the outermost outback down towards Uluru. Out of all of them there probably weren't more than a dozen older than he was, and most of those had been on remote cattle stations when the Change came and spent the first year comfortably eating the beef they couldn't sell anymore. *He'd* been in bloody Brisbane, ninety-nine percent of whose population hadn't survived those twelve months.

New world?

He snorted again, but quietly and to himself this time. This was a *new* world that looked like it'd been stitched together from a madwoman's patchwork quilt of the old, the not-so-old, and the *really* old. What he liked to refer to as *Ye Fuckin' Olde* when he had a few quiet drinks under his belt. But never aloud, and never in public. King John knew that the new world took itself very seriously indeed. As deadly serious as edged metal and liquid fire.

He turned inwards, away from the happy, caterwauling crush of his subjects.

My subjects? *Sweet baby cheeses isn't that a sour fuckin' fate for a bloke who'd once been a member in good standing of the Australian Republican Movement? But not as sour as starvin' to death or being eaten by Zed or chopped up with a shovel or stabbed with a pair of garden shears on a stick, which was what happened to most of the people I knew in the way back when. Along with typhus and cholera. But sour enough.*

He sketched an expression somewhere between grimace and grin at the idea of the old British monarchy carrying on up there in the cold, gray isles, turning into a fierce squint at the tropical sun before Thomas asked him what was wrong. That nearly led to a giggle: he'd gotten a letter from the King-Emperor of Greater Britain in Winchester last year, addressed to *His Majesty John I* and hoping for a continuation of their *brotherly* relations and a discreet hint that they had a surplus Windsor princess or two they needed to place usefully if any of his grandsons were interested. He wondered what poor old Lizzy II would have thought of it, since he'd been born *her* not-so-humble subject.

And after all, what could be wrong? He was only the most powerful wrinkly in the world, lord and master of a fairy-tale kingdom he couldn't have dreamed up in the wildest drug-addled days of his youth.

His youth.

The King stifled a sigh, hid it away behind a wave and thumbs-up gesture for an especially rowdy concentration of well-wishers, the front row of the Backwater Rugby Club if their banner didn't lie. They cheered him past.

"Hats off for JB!"

"Pants down for JB!"

Raucous laughter and another frown from Thomas.

"Go you good king!"

Ah, his youth. Nineteen sixty-four, he'd been born, under the old calendar. The Age of Mystery to most of his subjects. A long lost Golden Time, to him.

God I miss television. And espresso. And rock music.

He found himself recalling the distant past more and more often these days. Sometimes it was a comfort, but often it just made him grumpy for what was lost.

Being grumpy was acceptable when you were older than God, or at least thirty-four years older than the Change, but he tried to avoid it. Had to work his benevolent dictator mojo, after all. He waved back to the crowd and shouted:

"Have a cold one on JB. And if you're goin' to the bar grab your mates one!"

He felt the high sun on the parchment-thin skin of his hand when it crept out from beneath sheltering shade of the parasol.

Another stifled sigh.

Yeah, that's right, a fucking parasol. What of it?

His rapidly advancing years made riding in the open carriage with a parasol top totally bloody acceptable. His subjects were a hard people, as unforgiving of weakness in themselves as they were upon finding it in any of their many foes. But beneath the armor of that sometimes callous stoicism he knew them to be a good and even kind-hearted mob. They indulged him in his twilight years and increasingly quaint fancies, after all.

He pulled a bottle of Saltie Bites Lager out of the cooler; the label had a lively print of the giant seagoing crocodile in question biting a fishing boat in two, something which did happen now and then. They were a lot less cautious around people now that guns were gone and catapults rare.

He tossed the treat to one of his enthusiastic subjects in the dense crowd, who snatched it out of the air with a broad grin.

"Thanks, JB!"

The grin was all the more conspicuous because the face under the shock of white-blond hair was very black; he pulled out the cork with his teeth, spat it aside, then poured the icy beer down with a blissful expression and an evident determination to transfer the frosty beverage from bottle to stomach without touching the sides of his gullet. It wasn't an especially hot day for the tail-end of the Big Wet, which meant it was a hundred degrees and steamy, literally so as the puddles on the pavement smoked vapor upwards. King John decided what was good enough for the freeman was good for his Lord and fished out another longneck for himself, his Adam's apple bobbing up and down under a snowy beard as he drank. He lowered the bottle and belched.

"He necked it in one," cried out a voice from the crowd.

"Huzzah! Huzzah for JB! Long live the King!"

"Long live the People of the North!" he crowed back, summoning up a hint of the residual power in the voice that had more than once called the whole city to arms.

"The People!" roared Prince Thomas, already on his feet.

"The King, the blood, the People and the Land," they roared back.

Who'd-a-thunk an undergrad degree in politics and bullshit psychology would lead to this? he thought.

The King belched softly again, his head a spinning a little from the cold, heavy lager. Brewed from the finest barley malt and Tasmanian hops. None of your Sorghum Specials here.

Thomas resumed his seat and leaned forward to speak to his father under the roar of the crowd. "Come on, Dad, do you really have to whip up the Bogan Horde like this? It's been a long time since you had to call them to weapons. The bad times are done with. Passed. You don't reckon you could throttle back the politics a bit?"

The King had been a heavy-boned muscular man for most of his life; he was stringy now and nearly hairless except for the beard, but still spry enough, especially for a man with his collection of scars. Those were mostly visible, dusty white against his tanned skin, because he was wearing the national costume; khaki shorts, sandals on knobby bare feet, a sleeveless vest, and a low-crowned, broad-brimmed hat with corks dangling on strings around the edge to encourage the ubiquitous flies to move along.

Part of him still thought the hat a ridiculous piece of costumery, but one that had become necessary about five minutes after the last aerosol can of insect repellent had run out. He still remembered fashioning his first one a year after the Change, when feeling like an idiot was less important than keeping the flies out of the sores that had opened up on his face after the scurvy caught up with them on the road.

His son and heir sat across from him dressed much the same, save for the kerchief tied around his graying blond hair and knotted at the rear.

"Bad times are like the Big Wet and the Dry, son, they always come around. And at least I don't have tickets on myself like you," King John said affectionately. "Wanker."

"Your time has passed, old man," Prince Thomas smiled, a long-running family joke. "At least make yourself useful and fetch me a Saltie."

King John leaned forward and flipped up the top of the cooler, pulling another bottle from the slurry of lightly salted water and ice. Very, very expensive ice. He waved an informal salute to the Captain of the Royal Escort; six mounted troopers of Capricornia's First Light Horse, in old-fashioned bush hats, one side of the brim pinned up with a long ostrich feather; their bowl helmets hung at their saddlebows. They were armed with Golok knives—heavy single-edged chopping swords—at their belts, lances in scabbards at the rear of their saddles, and cased bows at their knees. Each man carried a heavy slingshot on his right hip, and a leather pouch full of heavy warshot on the left. The Captain of the Guard also sported a long boomerang in a scabbard on his back. The sun glinted on the razor sharp steel embedded in the shorter, killing arm of the throwing stick. A highly polished ceremonial weapon, to be sure, but no less deadly for it; it stood up from the fancy off-the-shoulder tigerskin cloak the officer wore, product of some demented idiot's decision to let his beloved big kitties go feral when he couldn't feed them.

THE GOLDEN PRINCESS 59

The King hoped they'd eaten him first of all; their descendants were all over the Top End, meeting the lions spreading up from the south and tucking in to livestock and the odd farmer and bothering the roos. There were even giraffes around now, ripping the tops off the gum-trees. He could remember when the worst intrusive exotic animals had been rabbits and cane toads and Englishmen. . . .

"Poor fellah my country indeed," he muttered.

Three of the troopers rode before the carriage and three behind, with pennants in the black-white-ochre colors of Capricornia snapping below the honed steel of the lanceheads, and its symbol of a stylized Desert Rose on their lacquered buffalo-hide breastplates and the round shields slung over their backs, seven white petals around a seven-pointed black center. Occasionally their sergeant would shout:

"Out of the fucking way, you bludgers!" with a strong nasal Vietnamese accent peeking out from under his impressive command of the local dialect.

The replies of the crowd were even less polite, when anyone bothered to reply at all. Many just waved the sergeant off with a middle-fingered salute. They were *not* a deferential peasantry, and King John regarded that as one of his greatest achievements. A bubble of space let the Royal carriage proceed, but at nothing better than a brisk walk. The crowds were thick, as always towards sunset when the heat eased up a little and people came out to finish the day's business or make a serious start on the piss: Darwin had fifty thousand people now within the city wall, not counting transients. Which made it either the largest city on the continent or the second behind Cairns, whatever those apple-eating retards from Hobart said about the fading glories of their chilly village.

Workshops lined the street, their fronts open and samples of the merchants' goods spilling out under awnings—knives and edged tools, bolts of cotton and wool and silk cloth in colors ranging from utilitarian khaki to glittering embroidered splendor, pottery, glasswork, leather, piles of spices in gaudy colors on wicker platters, books . . . and anything else anyone on this continent or half the one to the north thought would sell. Craftsmen and vendors bellowed or shrilled the high quality and low prices of their wares; here and there an iron-barred shopfront and staff with cutlasses at their belts, crossed arms over muscled chests and stony faces behind their wraparound shades marked a jeweler or goldsmith or small banker.

Carts drawn by oxen, water buffalo, horses and mules fought their way past pedestrians, rickshaws and handcarts. It sounded to his old ears as though curses in a dozen different languages rode the thick, tropic air. But that was probably a few curses short of the truth. A string of snorting, spitting, stinking camels caused a bubble of chaos as it passed; there was even an elephant about the town somewhere, which some clown had trapped as a calf from one of the feral herds and tamed for heavy work. For a while the King had thought on an expedition to trap more of the giant beasts, perhaps to add a squadron to the city's defenses, but in the end there were too many other calls on the Royal Treasury and he had always believed in meeting the enemy as far forward as possible. That meant aggressively patrolling the island chain to the north.

Not constructing a fucking heffalump zoo here in Darwin, he harrumphed to himself.

There were certain strategic truths that even the Change had not changed. Any threat to the city or to the continent beyond had to come from or through the old Indonesian archipelago. Java and the other densely populated bits were wastelands with nothing left except ruins and Zed, but the still inhabited portions of the islands had shattered into a kaleidoscope even more patchy than Australia. Threats would always come from there, just as so much of the city's trade and people did.

The vehicles choking the streets of the busy town were piled high with everything from sacks of Papuan coffee to salt fish from Timor, Balinese furniture, kegs of Sumatran palm oil, musky-pungent hides from as far away as Borneo and Kalimantan. The royal procession halted for a moment at an intersection blocked by a cart loaded impossibly high with reed baskets, heavy with rice from Ceram and the much prized millet of the Eyre Peninsula. The Captain of his guard detailed two of the troopers forward to encourage the merchant to get a move on. The King sipped at the dregs of his Saltie and enjoyed the thick aromas of Darwin's famous food carts, a heady blend of deep-frying meat, grilling fish, garlic and chilies, piles of dripping peeled mangos under gauze and bunches of bananas and a color wheel of tropical fruits, many of which remained an utter mystery to him, even after all these years.

Truth is, a lot of those stupid hippie fruits give me the runs.

"What are you smiling at?" asked Thomas.

"Hippies," said the King. "Memories."

A nearby street vendor whipped two skewers of barramundi, onions and peppers off a grill, wrapped them in flat gray sorghum pancakes and ran over to offer them up to her sovereign. King John waved off the Light Horse captain who had moved his horse to block the woman's progress. The officer backed his mount off a few paces with an expert's ease and grace. His hand did drift down towards the worn hilt of his Golok knife, though. It was his job to be paranoid, even about a young woman with a sandwich in either hand and not enough clothing between her conical straw hat and her sandals to conceal a nail-file, much less a hidden cross-bow. He was lucky the man didn't insist on taking a bite from the sandwiches first.

Prince Thomas took the offered gift with a nod and a wink, and King John flipped a small silver coin back at her. About ten times the value of the meal, and having King and Prince tucking in to her stock-in-trade in public wouldn't do her business any harm at all.

"Cheers, luv," he called out over the din of the crowd. "I do like me a fish finger sandwich."

The flaky white flesh had been marinated with onion juice, tamari, lemon and black pepper before it went over the coals, and he savored every bite, wishing he hadn't necked that whole beer in one go. It would have gone down a treat with this. They said that knowing hunger, real hunger, changed the way you tasted food forever, the way you thought about it. It made even the plainest meal something to be savored and thankful for. Every bite, ever after, a joyful thing. He'd heard some survivor of a Japanese POW camp in Burma say that on the television when he was a kid.

God knew he'd done some starving of his own in the year after the

Change—he and his young family had made it out of Brisbane early, which was why they hadn't quite died by the roadside like millions of the slow, the stupid and the unlucky.

Then again, he thought, *I always loved a feed, even in the old days.*

A memory shook free and dropped on him, wholly formed and heavy with significance; a dinner date with his late wife, his one true love, at a restaurant by the ocean in the golden days. They had ridden an elevator—an elevator!—to the top floor of an old, whitewashed building on the bay at Bondi Beach. It was the first time he had ever had real French champagne. He . . .

"Dad? Earth to Dad. You've gone to your happy place again, haven't you?"

King John shook his head, the memory gone, only sadness left. For his wife. For a whole world. It had been so real.

"Come on," said Thomas. "Focus. At least give them a wave."

His hand came up automatically, a thumbs-up gesture for the crowd that brought forth another cheer as the traffic snarl at the intersection cleared. The mounted troopers clip-clopped back into formation and the carriage lurched forward again. King John shaded his eyes, which were no good for close reading work anymore, but not bad over longer distances.

Northeast from here you could just see the thick forest of masts at the docks, pennants hanging limp in the hot moist air, dirty canvas sails visible above the roofline of the waterfront. The port grew busier every month, though he could still remember the first outside trader in the fifth year after the Change—a schooner from New Caledonia with a hold full of yams, taro and coconuts looking for metal tools and cloth. Today the warehouses were stuffed with goods from as far away as Puerto Mont and Hinduraj, Zanzibar and Astoria and Newport; there was even a ship or so from Europe per year. A goodly number of those ships down the harbor were built and crewed right here in Capricornia, merchantmen and Navy frigates, fishing boats and the half-piratical salvager craft working the dead cities, crewed by mad fuckers who risked becoming dinner for Zed, all to bring back cargoes of metal and lenses, gearwork and sometimes even art treasures or precious metals that could make such a crew rich for life. He'd seen long ago that Darwin could be the meeting-place and entrepôt of continents, and by God it was coming true.

The odd tall building still reared skywards, but most of them had been disassembled for materials as the township rebuilt. Two or three stories of brick or timber was typical now, with lots of verandahs, tall slatted windows and overhanging roofs, and for the better-off, courtyards with shady plantings within. Colorful signage was everywhere, with paper lanterns waiting to be lit.

Anyway, he thought, *old Darwin was a low rise joint.*

Now the highest points were usually church spires; there were a dozen different varieties, along with gaudy Buddhist temples, even gaudier Hindu shrines covered in writhing sculptures and flower offerings, the odd mosque and a couple of synagogues. Another of life's insulting ironies. He had once been quite the fiery atheist. Now he was Protector of the Faiths. All fifty-seven flavors of them.

Well, most of them.

He beckoned Prince Thomas forward again, waving a suntanned, liver-spotted hand around.

"You're gonna be right with all this, aren't you, mate? You're gonna do the right thing? Look after 'em all?"

Thomas frowned.

"Well yeah, but where do you think you're pissing off to, you lazy bugger? You've still got years of work ahead of you."

King John leaned back and grinned with pride at the crowds; Stationbosses in from the remote countryside with their outriders, cockies with carts of vegetables from the small farms around the city, a Papuan merchant in grass skirt and mother-of-pearl nose pendant, a party of chattering Surabayans in sarongs with kris-knives thrust through the waistbands, a band of Koori Warriors from Arnheim-land leaning on their spears and watching the pageant. Altogether livelier than any other town in Australia, and a lot more interesting in his opinion.

"I'm almost done, I reckon, son," he said. "On the back nine, as Greg Norman used to say."

"Norman who? That mad black knight prick in America? Shit, he's long dead."

"Not that wanker, no. Classical reference, forget it. But don't forget what I've taught you and your sister."

Prince Thomas seemed to catch himself before he could sigh. Instead he sat up and rather than reciting the lessons, as he had a thousand times before, he spoke them as if revealing a truth for the first time.

"The kingdom is the people. The people are the land. Without them we are nothing."

"Good lad. Say it like a prayer, every night. God knows you're gonna have the fucking bunyip aristocracy in your ear before my scrawny carcass is even cold, and the merchant prince wannabees are even worse because they're smarter. They're gonna want to tighten their grip on things, on people. But it's plenty tight enough already and could even do with some more loosening up in my opinion. Might be we should offer up a little more power to the Council and the Guilds."

Thomas look alarmed.

"Bloody hell! Really?"

King John smiled, a wicked mischievous smile.

"Oh, yeah, make it an offer they can't refuse but with a rider they wouldn't otherwise go for. True universal suffrage. One man or woman, one vote, and none of this bullshit about property requirements. You come of age. You serve your time in the militias or the army, you get a say. A small one at first. You don't want to freak the station-bosses too badly. But from little things . . ."

"Big things grow," Thomas finished for him. He stared at his old man, searching his eyes for something as the noise of the crowds seem to fall away. "You know things can never go back to the way they were, don't you? Before . . ."

"Before the Change, yes, I know," said King John testily. "I understand that. There will always be a King in Darwin. Just like there's a Premier of Hobart and a Mayor of Launceston, a Colonel in Townsville and a fucking idiot in Cairns."

Thomas grinned for a moment. "The Lord High Moron Joh III? You think that dynasty's going downhill?"

"Nah. They started in a pit under the Seventh Circle of Hell. They'll be right." He went on seriously: "We've done well here, son. But we can do better. For them and by them."

He waved his hand at the crush of townsfolk on the sidewalks. He knew visitors from the south referred to Capricornia's capital as Wogland and Slopetown or the City of a Thousand And One Frights; the polite ones with an air of disbelief, but many with open distaste.

About what you'd expect from a bunch of inbred bogans.

Down south the Change had all but erased a century of migration by killing off the big coastal cities while sparing the Outback and, of course, gallant little Tasmania. He'd noticed that a fair number of their youngsters drifted up here, looking for something more exciting than a life spent growing spuds or staring up the arseholes of sheep.

Tasmanians. Those self-important pricks, he thought, even as anxiety at the latest reports from his spies in Mindanao stabbed at him: *Christ, there's a whole* kingdom *of Zed up in the islands? We might just* need *those self-important pricks.*

"And we'll need *them,*" said King John jerking a thumb at the throngs of peasants and commoners. "More than they need us."

The driver took his bare foot off the brake lever and sat up as they came up to the wrought-iron gate and the four mules pulling the carriage slowed. The guards rapped the butts of their pikes on the brick roadway, or presented their crossbows.

A banner over the arch read: *Darwin Welcomes The Regional Security Conference Delegates.*

"Because I've got a bad fucking feeling about this. It's going to be bad. For us and everyone else."

CHAPTER FIVE

Dúnedain Ranger outpost Amon Tam
(Formerly Mt. Tamalpais)
Ithilien/Moon County, Crown Province of Westria
(Formerly Marin and Sonoma Counties, California)
High Kingdom of Montival
(Formerly western North America)
May 10th (Lothron 9th), Change Year (Fifth Age) 46/2044 AD

"Three kings in darkness lie
Gutheran of Org, and I
Under a bleak and sunless sky—
The third beneath the hill . . ."

Faramir Kovalevsky snorted. "Oh, shut the fuck up, Malfind," he said. "That one sounds better in the Common Speech, anyway."

It was the late morning of a fine day, more than half-way through their eight-hour shift, with high white clouds in the blue sky. May was late spring, by the standards of their home here in Ithilien, and from the walls of this lookout station on the mountaintop you could see across a huge stretch of green-gold meadow, olive-green chaparral, leaf-green oak grove and ravines where conifers stretched tall. In the distance they faded to a dreaming blue-purple.

The Bay and the lost cities lay blurred with miles to the south, and westward long steep slopes led down to the white line of surf that marked the Mother Ocean three thousand feet below. Beyond were the black specks of the rocky islands called the *Haeron Thavnath*, the Far Pillars, just this side of the horizon. Gulls were thick along the shore below, white specks floating against the blue water, and sometimes the wind carried the echo of their massed quarrelsome squabbling. Closer a red-tailed hawk soared just below them, flight-feathers extended and moving with a subtle grace like a harper's fingers on the strings as it danced with the currents of air.

Morfind Vogeler stood silent lookout while her twin, Malfind, blew a raspberry at Faramir, and then lifted his flute, which *was* shutting up, technically.

Behind them eastward were the valleys where human-kind lived again, however thinly spread the new settlements were. Where the wheat would turn gold for the harvest in a few weeks, the folk whose fields and children and sleep the Rangers guarded, and beyond it all the faintest blue-white hint of the Sierra peaks. The air was cool enough to be comfortable wearing Dúnedain field gear with their cloaks around their shoulders. It smelled faintly of sea and more strongly of mountain herbs and the pink-and-white blossoms of the wild roses that grew shaggy over the chest-high walls, making them look like any other set of tumbled boulders and broken concrete in the ruins hereabouts.

Faramir was in charge of the lookout patrol at this outpost as part of his training and he knew his cousin would do whatever he was told, just as Faramir would when the positions were reversed. For example, if he told him to put the flute away, he would. Though he'd probably suggest Faramir putting it somewhere extremely uncomfortable while he tucked it into his haversack. The Dúnedain Rangers were highly disciplined and they all understood that you couldn't get into the habit of sitting around arguing about what to do in the field.

They were also a family business and the three of them had grown up together, and they were all just eighteen years old. He wasn't going to get the sort of deference an Associate nobleman expected up in the north-realm, even if it had been a much happier day than this. Dúnedain had ranks, but they didn't have an aristocracy. Or to be more precise, they all thought of themselves as nobles whatever work they did. That meant he wasn't going to get the sort of military punctilio you could expect from Boisean legionnaires or Bearkillers either.

Still, he took a breath to speak. This sort of thing was *why* you practiced being in command. Watching other people do it or talk about it was one thing, and helped you see the right thing to do and when it needed to be done. Doing it *felt* different, and less agreeable.

Morfind snorted from where she stood at the heavy tripod-mounted binoculars they were using to keep the western approaches to the Golden Gate under observation. At the same time she tossed a pebble at her brother over her shoulder . . . accurately and fairly hard.

"Ouch!" Malfind said, as it smacked into his forehead and then bounced away; it didn't draw blood, not quite.

"Stuff the flute up the back way, dear brother," she said. "This isn't a Ring Day dance."

"It's makework," Malfind grumbled, rubbing the red spot. "It's staring at nothing!"

"So what? It's still a scout, so play the flute when we get back. And if you ever miss the first sharp on 'Sing Ho to the Greenwood' again I'm going to hang your severed head in a tree and say the *yrch* did it."

Faramir turned his head so that he could smile for an instant. Malfind would take that from his sister and remember it better, since it didn't involve butting horns with another young ram. He was bored; so was Faramir. He'd much rather be hunting, or fishing, or even singing along with Malfind's truly terrible version of "Sing Ho to the Greenwood," which the poor fool actually thought would help him with girls. Or working on a woodcarving project he had going to make illustrated printing blocks for the press. Or even just weapons drill or barnyard chores.

Malfind chuckled. "All right, I'd better practice where you're not listening, beloved sister from Udûn."

A lot of what Rangers did was pretty boring. Much of the rest was . . .

What was the old-world word? Stressful, that's it. Stressful.

"You used the old loan-word, too," Morfind said disapprovingly to Faramir, also without turning around. "You should use the pure Noble

Speech when you're telling someone to shut the fuck up in Sindarin. Particularly when they *really need* to shut the fuck up."

"Oh, shut the fuck up, Morfind," Faramir said, but this time he used the true term as she did, and smiled.

It was more authentic, but somehow . . . and it was the word the Sword of the Lady had given the High King when he returned from the Quest, before any of them had been born. There was a reason they were all feeling prickly today; it was an alternative to being depressed, and you couldn't spend time on watch weeping and mourning.

The High King was dead, murdered by a prisoner right over in Napa.

And I sort of feel . . . numb about it, he thought. *Like when you've just broken a bone and you're looking at it and thinking, uh-oh, damn but that's going to hurt in a second.*

That had happened to him a few times. Falls as a child, since Rangers learned to climb like squirrels, and fractures in two ribs once in a fight in the ruins, from an Eater's flung stone when they'd snuck around to attack the apprentices serving as horse-holders for the Ranger *ohtar* and *roquen*. There he hadn't had time to feel anything but terror at how helpless he was with the maneaters near until a shower of arrows drove the savages off and friendly hands pulled him out of the hole where he'd been pinned, trying to hold a knife ready despite every breath feeling like blades in his body.

And after that it hurt a lot, *but I almost* didn't *mind even when they threw me across a saddle. Not at first.*

He knew the pain from this loss was going to be even worse; it wasn't just the death of a lord, however much respected and revered for his great deeds and firm hand and fair justice, but of an elder kinsman who he'd always liked. Though Stath Ingolf was a long way from the center of things, his parents had gone on visits to wherever the Court was, or to Stardell Hall in Mithrilwood in the Willamette where the founding lords of the Dúnedain dwelt, and the High King's kin were always welcome at Dun Juniper too. They'd seen one or the other every second year or so, and the High King and his family had visited here about as often. Sometimes just to see his half-sisters and his other old comrades from the Quest and their families rather than any reason of State.

I think part of that was getting away from the crowds and the pomp, here where there's room to breathe and he could let the man out of the King, with people who knew him when he was a kid.

So High King Artos was also Uncle Rudi, his mother's elder half-brother. A man he could remember telling stories that kept them all silently enthralled while the youngsters crowded around his feet at the hearth in *Tham en-Araf*—Wolf Hall in the Common Tongue—over in the Valley of the Moon. Or throwing ten-year-old Faramir Kovalevsky into the hill-pool reservoir there on a hot summer's afternoon, and jumping from the Leaping Rock himself and sputtering and roaring with laughter and mock-growls as his nieces and nephews swarmed on and gleefully tried to drown him in the cold spring water.

Or once giving Faramir a quick wordless slap on the back after he'd done something needful and risky and just at the margins of his fifteen-year-old strength on a boar hunt, when a massive projectile of bone and gristle and goring tusks nobody had noticed had exploded foaming and squealing murder-rage out of a thicket.

And *that* man had died by treachery not a day's travel from Stath Ingolf and none of the Rangers had realized it until a frigidly-polite messenger in the tartan of the Clan Mackenzie had delivered the tidings from Dun Barstow. He'd found everyone still getting ready for the Royal visit. That made it a matter of honor, too. Under the Great Charter the Dúnedain were direct vassals of the High King wherever they lived, holding from his hand and charged with the burden and proud duty of keeping the High King's peace and borders.

His own father Ian and the twins' sire *Hîr* Ingolf Vogeler had taken a keg of brandy into the woods when the news came and gotten monumentally drunk together, drunker than the legendary guards of King Thranduil, off on their own where they could . . .

I don't know. Sob, I suppose, or howl. Or maybe just tell stories of their friend Rudi and not have to be formal in what they said about High King Artos.

He suspected they welcomed the pain of the hangovers as distraction and punishment. Mary and his mother Ritva had occupied themselves with drawing up new patrol and guard schedules, however far the horse was from the locked stable door. Which was why this mountaintop post was now crewed full-time. That was done on rotation out of the Ranger station in the *Eryn Muir*—named for a friend of trees. Back in those days forests had had few friends, and needed them badly. A number of Dúnedain families lived there full-time and others including his parents usually did during the summer. Which made the new arrangement easier, though not easy.

"We didn't even make it for the cremation," Malfind said morosely. "Not us, not one Ranger from Stath Ingolf. Our mothers are . . . were . . . the High King's half-sisters and they and our fathers were on the Quest with him."

Well, pretty much, Faramir thought.

His own father had joined the Questers as they came back through the Dominion of Drumheller, which was a northern realm friendly to Montival but not part of the High Kingdom. He'd won Ritva Havel's hand, though, and fought through the Prophet's War and joined the Rangers and helped found Stath Ingolf.

Ingolf Vogeler—widely known as Ingolf the Wanderer—had gone all the way to Nantucket on his own from his birth-home in the Free Republic of Richland in the Midwest, carried the message of the Sword to Dun Juniper, gone all the way back there with the Quest and returned, a feat nobody else since the Change had equaled. It would have been notable nowadays, when it was a lot easier to travel, at least between Montival and the Mississippi. Uncle Ingolf had done it when the Prophet's bully-boys were running rampant over half a continent with orders to kill him on sight.

"And . . . you're right, not one of us at the side of the pyre," Faramir said. "I suppose there will be a delegation from Mithrilwood at the formal funeral in Dun Juniper, *Hiril* Eilir will be there of course, and *Hîr* Hordle, but . . ."

"We didn't spot *four ships* sailing through the Glorannon either," Morfind said, pointing to the Golden Gate. "Three ships chasing a fourth ship and shooting at it all the way to the mouth of the Napa. I'm not surprised the Princess is angry and didn't want to see any of us."

"Órlaith's likely not angry," her brother said. "She just wasn't thinking about us at all, I'd guess. Just wanted to get it over with fast and take his ashes back to the High Queen Mathilda. The Mackenzies over east at Dun Barstow were pretty angry, though."

Malfind's a bit goofy, but he's not stupid, Faramir thought.

They all brooded for a while; Malfind and he shared a glance and knew what it meant, and Morfind was probably thinking of the same thing. That was confirmed when she murmured:

"The Doom of Men."

The death had been a shock for any number of reasons, but one was that their own parents were of the High King's generation, pretty much. Ingolf the Wanderer was nearly ten years older than Rudi Mackenzie had been, and only just what the older generation called a Changeling, one born after the Change or too young then to remember the old world first-hand. Nowadays the term was less used, and less needed as the last who'd been grown then passed their three-score and ten and faded from the scene.

His own father, Ian Kovalevsky, was a few years younger than the High King. You didn't like thinking of your parents as mortal, but they all were even if they were heroes of song and tale as well. As a child your parents were eternal and unchangeable as the stars, or the trunk of a redwood.

But even redwoods don't live forever.

When you made the transition to being an adult yourself the thought came unbidden now and then. It would have been worse if Rudi Macken-zie had met his death from a heart-attack rather than an enemy's knife, which after all was something that could happen to anyone at any time, but they didn't expect their mothers and fathers to start staying safe at home just yet either.

"We weren't *supposed* to keep a constant lookout for ships," Malfind said defensively. "There have never been Haida raiders this far south before, not striking on land, there was nothing for them to steal except the lice in Eaters' hair until we started resetting Westria. Haida don't do salvage expeditions themselves, they just loot what other people find or make."

Faramir blinked; Malfind *was* smart enough, but he tended to make assumptions and sometimes to take things *everybody knew* at face value. That was supposed to be a fault of guys their age, but Faramir Kovalevsky had never been prone to it. Possibly he was less happy than his cousin because of that, but all in all he preferred it. It couldn't be in the blood, because neither Uncle Ingolf nor Morfind was that way. Mary Vogeler *certainly* wasn't, since she was his mother's identical twin and he strongly suspected that Ritva Kovalevsky was the smartest person he'd ever met.

"They don't do salvage expeditions *that we know about*," he said. "There isn't anything *to* salvage up where they live. Not much but fish and fog and trees at all, and the Navy doesn't let them into Vancouver, but we wouldn't *know* if they'd been going to LA, say. Not unless they left a note with the Topangans there."

Morfind nodded; Wolf Hall got the Crown's intelligence reports, and she liked reading them.

"They make *ships*," she pointed out. "By Ulmo, Lord of Waters do they ever! Those *orcas* of theirs have plenty of range. They could have been sailing across the Mother Ocean to Asia, and we wouldn't have a clue."

"The only ships that call *here* are merchants and salvagers, and not many of those," Malfind went on doggedly. "And nobody ever *heard* of any of those sets of weird foreigners with them—"

"Japanese and Koreans," Morfind said. "Koreans chasing Japanese with Haida helping the Koreans."

"That's not going to make the Dun Barstow folk any less angry," Faramir pointed out with what he knew was infuriating reasonableness. "It saves them being angry with themselves—they were a lot closer and didn't do any better than we did. I bet they're scared of what Lady Juniper is going to say."

"Lady Maude's the Mackenzie Herself now," Morfind said thoughtfully.

The first Chief—and founder—of the Mackenzies was in her seventies and had stepped down in favor of her middle daughter a decade after the Prophet's War, when the three of them were still toddlers. The Clan's *Óenach Mór* had hailed Maude with no dissent. Beyond the inevitable joke candidacy of someone in a Green Man mask calling himself *Robin Goodfellow Mackenzie*, who'd run on a platform of universal drunkenness and fornication during the summer and sleeping the whole winter away, and gotten precisely one vote from each Dun in the dùthchas before he danced off into the woods waving his wapping-stick with two bladders on the end.

"And she's the High King's half-sister, like our mothers, only shield-side," Faramir reminded her.

"I know that! And Lady Juniper's like everyone's favorite grandmother, anyway," Morfind said. "I can't imagine her cursing anyone who didn't really deserve it."

She meant *curse* in a very technical sense, not just using bad language. They all nodded; they certainly liked her more than their actual maternal—shield-side—grandmother, Signe Havel.

Who is a grim old bitch, frankly, Faramir thought.

Their fathers' families were impossibly far away for real contact, though they got a letter every couple of years. Their aunt Lady Maude was all right too, though rather serious and with a tendency to ignore youngsters beyond an occasional pat on the head.

"It's just . . . mothers are different, you know?" Morfind said. "I mean, our mothers are pretty even-handed, but imagine how *they'd* react in her place."

"Lady Fiorbhinn . . ." Malfind said, naming the youngest of Juniper Mackenzie's four children. "She's First Bard of their Clan. They say she can raise a blister on your face with a satire and after hearing her I sort of believe it. I bet she could make a Mackenzie just drop dead, or run off into the Wild and throw themselves into a pit, and she's a lot more impulsive than Lady Maude *or* Lady Juniper. Or *Hiril* Eilir, of course. Not cruel, but sort of . . . wild."

"Lady Juniper isn't chief of the Clan anymore but she's still Goddess-on-Earth to the witchfolk, and her son got killed on *their* land over at Dun

Barstow," Faramir said. "Napa isn't even in Stath Ingolf's area of responsibility, after all. Our Charter stops at the ridge of the Mayacamas."

Probably Lady Juniper will just mourn but they can't be certain, so they take it out on us. And the Mackenzies really didn't *do any better than we did despite being right on the spot.*

That last bit was comforting, in a guilty sort of way. Usually the Rangers got along fine with Mackenzies. After all *Hiril* Eilir, the other original founder of the re-formed Dúnedain, was the eldest daughter of Juniper Mackenzie, born before the Change. Most Dúnedain were of the Old Faith like them, though not witches strictly speaking. There was a certain rivalry as well, though. Not least, many Mackenzies thought the Rangers put on airs, and that the Clan's folk were better archers and just as good in the woods. He thought *some* of them were, but most weren't though they certainly had high standards . . . for outsiders. None of that had anything to do with the death of the High King, but it was certainly going to be part of how everyone felt.

"It's not going to make *us* feel much better to know that they shouldn't be blaming us, either," he concluded with depressing realism. "Even if the Princess isn't, we're all going to feel like she *should* blame us."

Órlaith was older than they were. But he liked her, beyond and above a wholehearted teenage-male appreciation of her looks; she wasn't snotty with people just a little younger than she—

Well, over three years younger, he admitted to himself.

—the way most people the other side of twenty were. She hadn't tried to act as if there was some sort of unbridgeable gap of experience between them. The three of them liked to tell themselves they were adults. He knew deep down that what they really were was just trembling on the brink of *junior probationary* adulthood, eager to prove themselves and secretly anxious that they weren't ready. They all sat and brooded a little more, keeping watch with ingrained care in turn and trying not to think of Uncle Rudi.

When the time came they silently opened their lunch bag and spread the contents out on a flat-topped rock as the sun passed its zenith and turned the surface of the ocean westward to an eye-hurting brightness like hammered silver. The leather sack held two long loaves of brown bread fresh out of the oven that morning. Besides that there were three hard-boiled eggs, a flask of olive oil and a bowl to pour it in, some salty, sharp-tasting black pickled olives, filaree and chickweed, yellow-topped hedgehog mushrooms and other wild greens they'd picked on their way up, a lump of pungent sheep's-milk cheese the size of a small fist wrapped in leaves, dried figs strung on straw twine and a few slices of the inevitable smoked roast venison from last night's dinner for relish.

An old joke defined venison as *Dúnedain potatoes.*

There was a small clay jug of wine, too, to be heavily diluted with the water in their canteens; here in the south-country most drank wine with every midday and evening meal, it being a staple rather than a treat. Everything came from the Stath Ingolf house-lands except the bread; they got the flour from the settlers down in the Sonoma lowlands or the newer ones in Napa as part of their fees.

The three Dúnedain stood together facing the west for a moment before they ate, their right hands over their hearts.

To Númenor that was, and beyond to Elvenhome that is, and to That which is beyond Elvenhome and will ever be, he thought, knowing the others did likewise.

The ritual was calming, reminding them of things beyond their own troubles. Then they sat to share the meal, in positions that gave them good views down from the lookout and half-rising occasionally to make sure no pirates were using the interval to sneak in. Faramir ripped a piece off a loaf, dipped his chunk into the oil, cut some cheese with the smaller knife he wore tucked into the top of his soft calf-high elf-boot, smeared it on top of the bread and took a moody bite. Morfind tore her bread into small neat bits before dipping it, and her brother cut his with his knife, which was slightly eccentric though not actually bad manners. After a minute he passed around some sea-salt in a twist of rag to use on the greens.

"The stranger ships came in very early, in thick fog," Faramir said thoughtfully.

His eyes narrowed as he swallowed a few mouthfuls of bread and oil and cheese and crunched up a nutty, slightly bitter mushroom. Then he tossed a few olives into his mouth, working off the flesh with tongue and teeth and spitting the pits over the wall. Something was teasing at his mind, a thought struggling to be born.

"Oh, let it rest, *hethren*," Morfind said to him, spitting an olive pit over the wall herself and disturbing a blue-winged scrub jay that flew off with a peevish cry. "We Rangers of Stath Ingolf are going to be remembered as the ones who didn't save the High King, and that's all there is to it."

Hethren meant cousin, and most Dúnedain of the same generation called each other that casually in day-to-day speech, just as they referred to each other's parents as uncle or aunt whether there was a blood relationship or not. The equivalent was common in small close-knit communities throughout Montival . . . which was to say, most communities.

But the three of them here actually *were* first cousins by blood. Tow-haired Malfind and black-haired Morfind were fraternal twins themselves, similar in their sharp-featured looks and blue eyes, and very slightly younger than Faramir. Morfind was about an inch under Faramir's five-nine, but Malfind was nearly up to his father's six-two. Although he was lanky so far, while *Hîr* Ingolf was built like a balding, battered-looking bear with a beard that was broadly streaked with gray in the brown. Mary and Ritva were tall blond women; the Havels and Larssons ran to that, and to twins. Malfind and Morfind were the oldest of three sets in *their* family; Faramir had two sisters and a younger brother, but his mother grumbled that she'd had to do a lot more work for fewer kids since they were all singletons.

Faramir's own father was fair-haired as well, which made his son's pale yellow-gold locks no surprise, but Ian Kovalevsky was of no more than average height and slender and Faramir took after him in that too.

I wonder who provided the freckles, snub nose and high cheekbones? he wondered; and his eyes were dark blue with gray rims, unlike either of his parents. *And Dad's beard has always been sort of sparse, so I shouldn't be surprised mine's nonexistent so far.*

Their mothers had been children of the High King's father Mike Havel . . . but by his handfasted wife and consort among the Bearkillers

Signe-born-Larsson, not Juniper Mackenzie. What it meant in essence was that through her father Crown Princess Órlaith was *also* their cousin.

Which now made the whole situation rather worse.

"No," Faramir said thoughtfully. "That's not what I meant, I'm not making an excuse for what happened. I'm just . . . I mean . . . I hope the old folks have thought of it too."

The Vogeler siblings looked at him; sometimes they did things in disconcerting unison.

He wiped his smaller knife carefully, checked the edge, then rubbed a bead of olive oil over the metal with a fingertip before he slid it back into the boot sheath. It was the one he used for general camp chores and eating, being more convenient than the slightly curved ten-inch fighting blade at his belt. A little film of grease wouldn't hurt it, quite the contrary, but you had to make sure there was no salt. Then he went on:

"I'm not just blowing smoke now to make us feel better. If we'd been *here* and watching we probably wouldn't have caught them, not with darkness and mist. What are we . . . Stath Ingolf, that is . . . going to do about watching for ships at night or in fog, now that we know enemies might approach by sea? We get night every night, and the Glorannon has fog as often as not for half the year. Whoever they are, we can't count on them making it easy for us by keeping running lights on their ships."

They went on with the lunch in a less gloomy mood now that they had a problem to think about, rather than chewing the crust of failure. Most Dúnedain settlements were well inland, but this one included a big chunk of coast and a landing-place where ships called. They were more conscious of matters maritime than Rangers elsewhere.

"I can see why they"—meaning their mothers, basically—"put us up here; it's better than nothing. We've got a good view in daylight and it's the only secure location with this view we have ready. But it's . . . I mean, it's not really *good*, you know?" he said. "Not to make sure ships aren't sneaking in when the visibility's bad."

"We'd have to put watchers on the *Glorannon Iant*, for that," Malfind said as they tossed the diminishing string of figs from one to the other, and jerked his thumb to what the old world had called the Golden Gate

Bridge, which meant exactly the same thing in the Common Tongue. "On the bridge deck . . . or maybe up one of the towers? Hard to get up but you'd be safe enough."

"No," his sister said. "The fog lies low a lot, you know how you see the bridge towers rising out of it first thing? So you'd be nearly as blind to something on the surface as you would up here. Blinder than you would be on the actual bridge deck, at least. From the deck you'd be able to *hear* a ship most times."

Good point, Faramir thought, and both the young men made gestures of agreement.

Wooden ships inescapably creaked and groaned a lot if they were moving at all, what sailors called *working.*

She went on: "Or maybe see the masts, unless the fog was really thick on a moonless night. And how would a ship run the bridge passage if it was totally fogged in or completely dark? The sailors say it's bad enough in broad daylight."

They all looked south for a moment. You could see the bridge from here, of course. The view all around was magnificent, which was the point of a lookout station, and it was a pleasure to see on a nice day like this and exciting in a storm, though they'd all been familiar with it from childhood. Even the bridge was beautiful, which was more than you could say for most of the giant works of the ancients; it would be a pity when it finally collapsed, in a generation or two or three.

Stath Ingolf had been established when they were about nine and they knew these hills and woods like the kitchens of their homes or the Stath's dancing ground over on the other side of the valley.

"Row it in?" Malfind said. "Sweeps from the deck, or a longboat tow-ing?"

"Even noisier," Morfind said.

"You could probably hear or spot a ship from an observation post on the bridge even at night or in bad weather," Faramir said.

Then he added: *"But."*

Both the others pursed their lips as they followed his thought. They were young, but they knew the family business from watching their parents run it. They'd been helping out with it as they could all their lives, more so as they grew, the way children everywhere did with whatever their elders' trade was. Just lately their help had been as *ohtar*, squire-warriors formally fit for anything but command.

"Yes, that's one of those things that would work . . . if only it worked," Morfind said. "Like, if the Eaters would only not do anything like the things Eaters really do."

Most of the Ranger business here had originally been leading the effort to clear out the Eater bands roaming the wilds, the descendants of those who'd survived the collapse of the old world by preying on—eating—other victims. There hadn't been many, for reasons made clear in the old tale of the Kilkenny cats. And they patrolled to keep more from filtering up from the ruins around the Bay. Some of the ones in the wild had been human enough by then to send back to civilization, just crude backwoods hunters whatever their parents or grandparents or great-grandparents had done to survive. Split up as individuals or small family groups they could fit in among the many places looking for more hands to work and not too picky about backgrounds, and make lives for themselves. Others had still been orc-like and bestial, with only the young children capable of forgetting and so spared.

The ones who still haunted the city ruins southward and their outskirts were mostly pretty bad. The rest were either very, *very* bad . . . or even worse than that. They were quite good hunters now, living in territory swarming with game and fish and fowl, and they lived the way they did because they wanted to rather than the necessity that had driven their ancestors. Being *killed* by them, or even killed and then eaten, was far from being the worst nightmare a Ranger of Ithilien faced. Which was why Rangers generally referred to their kind as *yrch*: Orcs.

Besides tending their own properties and ordinary peacekeeping, the rest of the Stath's work mostly involved salvage in the dead cities, or escorting outside salvagers for a fee and a cut of any unusual finds. Even with their experience and local knowledge that was still deadly dangerous, though also very lucrative and a great service to Montival.

It would take an army of thousands working for years to sweep the

Bay cities clean the way Eugene and Seattle had been in the north, which wasn't going to happen for a long time given the Crown's other priorities, but the Rangers did what they could. They'd cleared the roadway across the bridge and some of the main roads of the wrecks of cars and trucks so that escort parties could reach the ruins more easily. Some of the springs had still been useful, and much else went to blacksmiths and glassblowers. Waste offended the Valar.

But as I said, there's a big fat but involved . . .

"We can cross the bridge in daylight," Morfind said, eating the last fig in two bites and tossing the little dried stem over the wall too. "We can go into the ruins in a strong armed party, though that means fighting. Especially if you're there for more than a day."

The young men nodded solemnly. They'd all three of them served on several escort patrols of that kind, a mark of their promotion to *ohtar.* That had involved fighting, or skirmishing and night work, and they'd all seen blood and faced blades at least a little. The Eaters didn't challenge armored warriors marching in ranks during daylight, they'd learned better than that, but those steep tangled overgrown warrens were never safe. And they were riddled with hidden passages made by collapsing buildings and old tunnels and corridors. Despite attempts at mapping, many of them were unknown, or worse still improved by the *yrch* knocking holes through walls and installing ladders over the years so they could move unobserved.

After dark the ruins were the stuff of very bad dreams. Drums and obscene shrieking war-cries in the night and knife-work done amidst inky blackness . . .

"But they'll push back *hard* if it looks like we're trying to run our boundaries farther south, not just escort salvagers on an in-and-out. They know what happened to their kind up here north of the Gate. It would be like standing up in front of a target at the range to *stay* there on the bridge all the time. You're right about that, Faramir. It would have to be a fortified post. With at least a dozen in the garrison, or they'd all get eaten some dark foggy night."

"Better *two* dozen," her brother added, and mixed more of the water-

and-wine in their canteens. "And a couple of catapults. Or even better, flamethrowers."

Faramir drank. It was good wine, though being mixed three-to-one with water didn't help with the bouquet. He rubbed his obstinately smooth chin. Malfind had a point.

"Some of the *yrch* bands on the peninsula can muster fifty or so fighters, the ones farther south are bigger, and four or five might get together if we left them a really juicy tempting target like that," Faramir said.

"You think so?" Malfind said. "They hate each other like poison."

"They don't love *us* much," Faramir said with what he thought was elegant understatement.

"Can't imagine why," Malfind said, and laughed.

"More to the point, they're *afraid* of us. And they're not stupid just because they're crazy-bad," Faramir said, staying serious. "They know we're just the point of a spear aimed at them. The stupid ones all went into one stewpot or another long ago."

Though sometimes they ate their prey raw over many days, hung up alive on rope or hook to keep it fresh. Morfind nodded and ran one finger over her lower lip with her eyes rolled up in thought.

"But twenty or more for an outpost garrison . . . building it would be a one-off and doable, but that many blades tied up in one spot full-time would be a big problem just by itself," she said.

There were about three hundred Dúnedain within the bounds of Stath Ingolf's patrol territory of Ithilien—Moon County in the Common Tongue—but that included all their noncombatants as well, from the hundred-plus children below fighting age to those who just didn't have the inclination or talent or the physical abilities, and some were only fit to defend the home-places at the last gasp. There were a score or more *ohtar* from other Ranger communities here at any given time. Dúnedain youngsters often spent a few years going from Stath to Stath, usually from the less to the more active ones like this to get experience in varied environments, not to mention the social benefits. The Dúnedain had an exchange program with the Morrowlander Scout Pack of Yellowstone too, and Faramir had been trying to get into that.

But even including their visiting kin, there were only sixty or seventy or so warriors at any one time. Tying up every fourth member on the active list sitting in an improvised fort and watching the seagulls for month after month . . . and so far from quick help if they needed it . . .

"We'd have to get the *galor* militia to do it," she said. "It's not Ranger work. Too passive, and it would leave the rest of our ops too short-handed."

"And the farmers would say it *is* our job," Faramir replied. "And not theirs to march far from their homes and stay under arms full-time, even in rotation."

The word *galor* meant literally "grower" and it was Ranger slang for ordinary outsiders. At least among youngsters, who did not use it as a term of endearment, though it wasn't actually an insult. Not technically, since most people you met were in fact farmers at least part of the time; even Dúnedain, in the sense that they tended groves and gardens and ran livestock. Despite that their parents, Stath Ingolf's leaders, tended to get shirty if they heard anyone using it, and downright testy if anyone did in front of . . . *galor*. On the grounds that the farmers *knew* it wasn't an endearment, and it made it harder to get everyone reading from the same page. Not many outsiders knew the Noble Tongue, not least because it was Ranger policy to speak the Common Tongue to them, but a few always picked up a bit if there was a Dúnedain Stath around.

"The Mist Hills people might pitch in," Malfind said. "Baron Godrick Godulfson has always been a good friend to us."

"Yeah, but that wouldn't be enough either. We really need to get the Crown involved," his sister replied.

Malfind nodded, but Faramir snorted.

"After what happened to the High King?" he said. "I should *think* the Crown will get involved! Everything's changed now. We're not out of sight and out of mind anymore."

They packed away the remains of their meal and settled into position again, taking turns with the binoculars, mostly keeping silent. Two hours past noon a bird called from not far away, one among many. Faramir inclined his head. It was a series of five buzzy calls, with the second-to-last high and sharp. Either a small black-gray-white bird was following its mate with nesting material rather late in the season, or . . .

He held up a hand for everyone's attention and for silence, and gave the same call in return. It was answered with a repetition. All three of them had picked up their bows, gracefully shaped four-foot recurves of laminated horn and yew and sinew with risers of olive wood, set a shaft through the cutout and nocked it to the string. They watched alertly with their cloak-hoods drawn over their heads and their eyes just over the sides of the post, keeping a three-hundred-sixty-degree lookout. Three more figures came cautiously into view, standing for an instant and throwing back their hoods to be recognized.

The Stath was still small enough that everyone knew each other by sight, even if their families lived at different ends of Ithilien. These were the Mangjŏls, Damrod the eldest at twenty-five, then Mablung and their sister Tathardes, who were younger by two-year intervals. Their grandfather had been a retainer of the Larssons somehow back before the Change when all that sort of thing had been different in ways he'd never bothered to study. Their parents had joined the Rangers very early, when they were barely pubescent and the reborn Dúnedain were very new, really just a band of teenagers playing in the woods up north under *Hiril* Astrid and *Hiril* Eilir. Albeit even then the games were deadly serious at times. All three had a strong family resemblance, narrow slanted eyes of brownish hazel with flecks of green, olive skin and hair as black as Morfind's, except that Tathardes' developed faint reddish highlights if it had been in the sun very long. Everyone relaxed and stood.

"*Mae govannen, 'wanur nîn. Prestad?*" Damrod Mangjŏl asked as he and his siblings walked towards the post.

"Well-met to you as well, my kinsmen, and no, no trouble. Birds, deer and a bear was around last night from the scat," Faramir said. "Grizzly, I think; cinnamon-colored hair, at least."

"Speaking of scat, no problem with monkeys throwing their crap in your hair, you two?" Mablung said to the twin brother and sister, grinning and taking a couple of ostentatious sniffs.

Faramir grinned himself and then suppressed it; that had been most of a decade ago, but he remembered his cousins' discomfiture when he'd tricked them into climbing a certain tree during a children's game they'd cheated at. That band of scat-slinging macaques no longer lived in the big live-oak near *Hîr* Ingolf's hall, but the memory of the day lingered yet in local legend. The beasts were common enough all over the area that everyone knew their feces-slinging habits.

Malfind and Morfind didn't think it was nearly as funny as other people did, for some reason; as he recalled, he'd danced after them chanting *cheaters* and *poopy-heads.*

"And some whales out to sea," Faramir went on diplomatically. "Apart from that, nothing."

Tathardes smiled now, though she'd remained tactfully poker-faced at her brother's joke despite a sparkle in her eyes. He thought it made her look very pretty and extremely kissable when she smiled, except that it also made her look as if she thought *he* was a child to be teased and chaffed. Which was precisely what she did think. Maybe three years shouldn't make that much difference, it didn't seem to be any great matter with people in their thirties, but somehow when you were eighteen . . . just . . . and she was twenty-one . . .

"You cousins can go back home"—she meant the station at Eryn Muir, where the Mangjŏls lived full-time—"and sit around moping *there*," she said. "Why not, since everyone else is? Except me!"

When her brothers scowled at her: "Look, the High King, may Lord Mandos receive him with honor in his hall and give him Beren Erchamion's old chair, was a great man. I loved him as our sworn lord and I would have fought and died for him, we all would. But he fell in battle . . . well, after a victory . . . and well, he was never going to end his life in bed surrounded by grieving great-grandkids! Everyone's who's listened to the 'Song of Bear and Raven' knows that it was fated he not grow old. Vairë weaves all threads."

"And the malice of the Shadow never sleeps," Faramir agreed. "But look at all that he did with forty-six years!"

The older Dúnedain woman went on: "So . . . there's no point in beating ourselves up. Grief, yes: guilt, no."

Morfind laughed. "Well, at last *someone's* being sensible."

"*Gellon ned i galar i chent gîn ned i gladhog,*" Tathardes said to her, bowing with her hand over her heart and a wink.

"*Ai!* How come you don't love the way *my* eyes shine when I laugh?" Malfind asked, half-seriously.

"Because you're too young," she replied.

"She's my twin! I'm the same age minus fifteen minutes!"

"That's in boy-years; they're different, like with dogs. You're a spotty kid, she's just the right age for heedless play amid the spring flowers."

"And then harsh waking to the real world ends your happy dream, willow-girl," Morfind said dryly in the Common Tongue, punning bilingually on the meaning of Tathardes, and everyone chuckled.

The Mangjöls climbed into the outpost and they all exchanged the hand-to-shoulder greeting Rangers used and helped with packing and unpacking respectively. The newcomers had more supplies and some basic cooking equipment with them because they were taking the two-to-ten shift and would be making their evening meal here. They also each had a ring-tailed pheasant hanging from their belts, gutted and headless and drained but not yet plucked of their iridescent blue and green feathers. There was very good hunting on the mountain, if you were alert and walked quietly.

Some liked to use pheasant wingfeathers for fletching their arrows, though Faramir thought it was showy and preferred goose, or seagull when it was available.

The center of the outpost's floor held a deep pit where, with care, a cooking-fire would be invisible after dark, and Faramir noted Damrod's eyes flick to make sure the stack of dry firewood had been replenished, along with the damp rotten branches needed to turn a blaze into a daytime fire-signal in an emergency. That was a day-shift duty.

The newcomers wore the same gear as the three cousins; loose tough pants and shirt-tunics of hard-woven linsey-woolsey twill, with leather patches on knees and elbows, mail-lined elk-hide jerkins cinched by broad equipment belts of the same, soft-sided leather boots that came to just below the knee and were fastened by horn buckles on the outside, and cloaks that had loops sewn to their outer surfaces and loose broad hoods. All had bows and quivers, climbing ropes, round shields and light helms slung over their backs, and tomahawk-hatchets through a loop at the back of their belts; tomahawks were something of a specialty of this southernmost Stath. Two-foot brush-swords hung at their left hips or over their shoulders, straight and thick in the back with a curved, waisted leaf-shape to the blade on the other side.

Everything was colored in muted, mottled shades, mainly olive and green, steel carefully grayed, copper and bronze fastenings let tarnish. Close-up you could just see the blazon on the jerkins and shields—a tree and seven stars surmounted by a crown—but the whole faded into a blurred gray-green at more than a pace. Malfind picked up his spear in addition as they vaulted easily over the low wall to leave.

"*Novaer, mellyn,*" Damrod called after them softly.

"Good luck to you, too, comrades," Faramir replied over his shoulder.

The downward path they took was very steep in parts. As a matter of course they were taking a different route back from the one they'd come on, or that their reliefs had used. The Dúnedain of Stath Ingolf had a network of trackways over the whole of their territory, and memorizing them was part of their education. On the more level parts the packed dirt still had crumbled remains of old asphalt, for there had been a road here once. Now it was much narrower and more direct, and only reinforced here and there with log or rock to keep it from washing out in the rains of winter. Nobody brought wheeled vehicles up here anymore; backs served, or the odd packhorse.

A small group of twenty or so tawny-coated tule elk grazed on a ridge of open land covered in tall grass just turning from green to yellow. They threw up their heads and moved slowly away as they caught the humans' scent. The herd were mostly spike bulls, young males without the antlers and heavy dark throat-ruff of grown herd-lords. The females would be dropping their calves about now. They liked privacy for that, though normally they were very social.

The three Rangers bent low to avoid being silhouetted against the sky as they went over the ridge and took a knee when they were below the crest to look down the slope. It had been a bit wetter than average this last winter, and the waist-high grass was still heavily starred with silène, the tall stalks bearing flowers white and purple and pink, and with crimson poppy and yellow mariposa-lily. There was a strong minty aroma as they knelt, from the crushed leaves of a patch of low-growing herbs that the ancients had called Yerba Buena and Rangers knew as *athelas*.

Malfind leaned his spear against his shoulder and spoke with his hands to avoid spooking the elk further: all Dúnedain learned Sign in their earliest childhood along with the Common and Noble Tongues. *Hiril Eilir*, their co-founder, had been deaf since birth, but it was extremely useful for everyone.

Take one? Malfind asked, flicking his eyes towards the herd.

Faramir thought for a moment. The fresh-grilled liver and kidney were the hunter's right, and always tempting because they tasted so marvelous right out of the beast with nothing but a little salt, but . . .

No. We don't know if they need that much fresh meat at the Wood and it's the wrong season for salting down.

Ranger law was strict that you ate what you killed, and frowned on wasting horn, hide, bone or anything else useful about the animal unless you really had no choice, that Oromë the Lord of the Trees not be angered. Their supple, durable belts and jerkins and most of their boots were brain-tanned, for instance, and their bows needed sinew and horn and glue. Anything left over could always go for compost and then onto a kitchen-garden.

Morfind nodded. *Anyway, one of those bulls will dress out at fifty pounds for each of us, not counting the hide. Do you want to pack that for hours, brother, and without carrying frames? It'll be dark before we get back, especially if we have to take time for a stalk, and then draining and gralloching and skinning it.*

That's a fact, her brother admitted. *It would take time since they know we're here already.*

Let's go, Faramir concluded. *Malfind, you're point.*

They were within the Stath's regularly patrolled territory, but rather far south; Eryn Muir was only about an easy day's stroll from the ancient bridge, much less if you really pushed it. It wasn't absolutely impossible that a lone Eater might sneak across to try for a Ranger; eating the heart and bringing the head home would be strong magic and enormous status. They trotted across the savanna at a swinging pace. It was scattered with small round-topped oaks, and cinnamon bush with its pungent bay-scented leaves.

Then they took a path that cut through thick madrone chapparal. The twisted limbs were joined by coyote bush, with young golden-fleece standing like green plumes. They took care to avoid the poison oak, and the orange flowers of the sticky Monkeybush. You needed good eyes or a guide to realize it *was* a path, more an amending of naturally weak spots in the barrier of hard-leafed spindly scrub than a roadway, with an occasional inconspicuous mark in the Tengwar runes.

Then into a steep ravine, through tanbark oak with its serrated leaves, sweet-scented blueblossom and chamise with bunches of stiff white blooms, then dense Douglas fir and hemlock standing tall and thick and meeting in a canopy of scented green above. The air grew cooler and damper and smelled of wet earth, and the undergrowth was thick with moss and fern. Water trickled and tinkled.

They'd walked in silence among the chuck and birr and buzz of insects and birds, in a row each three yards from the next; Faramir was bringing up the rear, halting occasionally to glance behind them. Even their footfalls made little sound. The soles of their boots were complex constructions, tough but supple leather with a bottom layer of the increasingly hard-to-find tire-tread. That was much more expensive than conventional hobnails . . . but they also gave better traction and were much quieter. Stath Ingolf had finder's claims on several large warehouses where their explorers had found vast numbers that had been stored away from sun and weather since the old world fell, still on their shipping pallets in buildings that were shapeless mounds of honeysuckle from the outside.

Farther down the ravine were young redwoods, or at least young by comparison to the millennia-old giants of Eryn Muir that was their destination, trees that had been ancient in human terms when the first Hispano explorers arrived in this land. This canyon here had probably been

logged a century or more before the Change, which you could see because the trees stood in rough circles where saplings had sprouted from
around the long-vanished stumps. Young redwoods, the ones less than a
hundred years old, put on better than a yard of height per year on a favorable site. These didn't have the overwhelming mass of their elders, not
yet, much less of their cousins in the Sierras, but while only a few were
two hundred feet high many were respectably close to it. The ground
beneath was open, thickly coated with their brown dropped needles and
too shady for much other growth.

A stream ran down the ravine, still fresh with the spring and running
quickly over brown stones, making a low chuckling music. They slid
down beside it, sometimes jumping from rock to rock, and once down a
sort of steep ladder carved beside the foaming jumps of a cataract-
waterfall. The flow of the white water wasn't very large, since the stream
was only a few feet across, but it was refreshing in the still air of the
canyon and comely enough that you half-expected to see a water-sprite
tumbling in it. At the bottom Malfind leapt down and trotted half a dozen
paces on to shed momentum along the shore of a small pond, prodding
with the butt of his spear at muddy dirt and watching where he placed
his feet.

Then he stopped, stiffened and thrust the weapon up. Faramir felt a cold
prickle in his gut as he saw it. That was Battle Sign; it meant *hostile tracks*.

"Overwatch," he said quietly to Morfind, who'd stiffened as well; then
he joined her brother.

The black-haired Ranger went down on one knee and put a little draw
on her bow, ready to snap-shoot as her eyes scanned the undergrowth.
They'd been walking for about an hour, and the shade was dense here—
the sun was far enough past noon to be partially blocked by the ridgeline
to the west, but they'd have been back to base before the full night came
and the stars came out in the east. The prickle between Faramir's shoulder blades grew worse as he squatted where the butt of Malfind's weapon
pointed. Nobody hostile should be around here, not this close to the
Ranger station in the Wood where his folk dwelt.

Malfind was an indifferent-good archer by Dúnedain standards, but a fine spearman. Wordlessly he took the scabbard off the head of his spear and tucked it into his belt; it was normally worn on to keep the edges from glinting if they caught sunlight. Then he slid the round shield off his back and took it in his left hand by the central grip beneath the boss, before he faced in the opposite direction from his sister, weapon poised for the quick underarm gutting thrust.

The sharp edges did glint, a very little, though the rest of the steel was a bonderized gray. It was about nine inches long, starting out as broad as a man's palm and tapering to a vicious point; the spearshaft was seven feet of seasoned brown-gray ashwood, thick as a quarterstaff, with a foot of stainless-steel wire wound around below the head and a similar length of butt-cap at the other end. A strong man with long arms could reach twelve paces with a single darting lunge.

Faramir opened his eyes and his mind and looked at the tracks; then he closed his eyes, thought, opened them again and repeated the process for several seconds. They called the technique *Kim's game* in his folk's schools, and he'd always been rather good at it besides liking the book it came from. That way he could call back and move the images like cutouts in his head, like multiple drawings, without needing to keep staring down at them. A good deal of Dúnedain training had come from Lady Astrid's consort Lord Alleyne, and Lady Eilir's, Lord Hordle. As youths they'd both joined an esoteric warrior brotherhood over the eastern sea just before the Change, known for some reason as the SAS.

The tracks were of bare feet. They were broad across the ball, and you could draw a straight line from the tip of the big toe of one particularly good print through the middle of the heel at the rear. There were distinct gaps between all the toes, with even the little toe turned noticeably outward. As if the foot were a hand, with the fingers splayed. Those were the marks of someone who had never worn shoes for any length of time; if you'd gone shod from childhood your foot was narrower and the toes all pointed ahead, or even inwards if the shoes were bad.

"*Yrch,*" he said softly, rising. "Eaters. At least a dozen just here."

Individual bare feet were as distinctive as palm-prints, and as easy to tell apart. That there were so many meant . . .

"Moving fast and taking chances to do it."

The others didn't look around, but he could feel a subliminal crackle. That sort of enemy raid hadn't happened since the very early years of Stath Ingolf. There *weren't* any Eater bands left north of the Bay and hadn't been since before they reached their teens. That meant a war-party from south of the Glorannon, and that was very bad . . . and hadn't happened in many years either.

He blinked again and the images were summoned back; the mark of the right foot was twisted in a bit from that of the left, pigeon-toed but only with one foot. An old injury that had healed not-quite-right, sufficient to affect the man's stride just a little. Not many who ran with the Eater bands down around the Bay lived through an injury that needed time and help to heal. Not in the grisly game of stalking and hunting and dreadful feasting that made up their lives. One who did would be very tough and very cunning, and probably a leader whose followers feared losing his wits and ferocity more than they did the effort of keeping him alive until he was strong again.

"I make it less than an hour since they passed," he said very softly.

The edges of the footprints had just begun to blur a little, soft soil flowing, water seeping into the bottoms.

His voice was gently soft but not a whisper—the sibilants of a whisper carried, if not the meaning of the words. A quiet tone died closer to the source.

"Cousin?" he asked.

"About the same," Malfind replied, concurring.

He didn't turn his head towards Faramir, or stop its slow tracking across a hundred and eighty degrees of forest. When the track was made said absolutely nothing about where the *yrch* had gone. They could have left it deliberately as a trap and be hiding half a bowshot from here ready to ambush anyone following them.

"Farther down, Morfind," he said. "Sweep for signs. I think there may be other bunches."

Moving through brush in hostile country you split a party of more than ten or a dozen up into a number of small columns moving in parallel whenever you could. That put them close enough to support each other but far enough apart that your group's progress didn't turn into an inch-worm crawl and become utterly obvious to anyone looking or listening. At least Dúnedain did, and he was willing to bet whoever had made these tracks did as well. A dozen Eaters was either too many to try and cross Ranger-patrolled country, or too few. Any others would have to cross the little stream too, and the soft ground was where they'd leave evidence.

"Malfind, take my back. Morfind, across."

She took two strides, leapt, and landed on the other side of the pond near where the rapid fell into it. Faramir walked quickly along his side as she paralleled him, and Malfind walked behind him a little farther with his attention on their surroundings. Morfind was walking a little bent over; Faramir looked up occasionally to scan behind her, and kept his bow ready.

"Here," she said, in the same soft tones they'd all been using.

They didn't want to face each other for Sign, not when the brush might spew howling cannibals at them any instant. He knew this ground intimately, but suddenly it *felt* strange and alien, like a dream of Mirk-wood.

"Not *yrch*, but not ours," Morfind amplified.

"Overwatch," he said again, and she turned to face the woods.

Faramir trotted to the spot opposite her, went down on a knee and looked at the ground again. There were no tracks in the soft dirt, but someone had scratched and furrowed the ground with a branch and then used it to drag leaves and litter over the spot. He gently brushed some of the dead vegetation aside with a finger, and the pattern of water in the scratches became more obvious.

"Covered their tracks," he said.

He might have missed it altogether if his cousin hadn't made him examine this spot with extra care, and the stroke with the brush had de-stroyed detail anyway.

"Malfind, follow."

He jumped the stream himself; it would only be knee-deep, but there was no point getting your boots and socks wet if you didn't have to.

Where Morfind had been looking were scuff-marks a little farther from the bank—tracks, but nothing specific, where the ground was dry and covered in dead needles. Conifer forest made for bad tracking ground. That and the shelter of the canyon walls from viewers at a distance were probably why the *yrch* had taken this route.

A little bit closer to the water was a fern just in the right position to sway aside when a shin brushed it and then sway back quickly to hide the resulting footprint. He used the tip of his bow to move it, and beneath was the mark of a boot or shoe. Not any form of footwear he was familiar with, not even the shapeless home-made ones local farmer-settlers often used. It was canoe-shaped, but broader at the front as if the toe of the shoe were upturned. And deep, either a heavy man or one carrying a full load. Armor, perhaps.

"Two parties, traveling southeast about a hundred yards apart, say thirty all told, maybe as many as fifty," he said. "One Eaters, one some sort of foreigner *and* Eaters. No Haida moccasins that I can see, but there might be some of them as well, they're supposed to be good woodsmen."

"Foreigners? And the Eaters didn't *eat* them?" Morfind said.

"Good point," her brother said. "That means something odd. Something bad."

Faramir's hand went to the signal horn hung at his belt, a bull bison's horn carven with the story of the Three Hunters In Rohan and with a mouthpiece and reed, the raw material imported from the far-off high plains beyond the mountains. Unfortunately they were still far too distant from the nearest point they could be sure Dúnedain were listening.

"The report said there was only one shipload of Japanese to start with," he said. "So the only foreigners who could possibly be around here I can think of are the ones who killed the High King."

He was surprised for a moment at the way his lips curled back from his teeth and flood of hot lust behind it. They said revenge was a dish best served cold, but right now it didn't feel that way. Hot and steaming seemed more attractive.

"Especially if they're keeping company with Eaters."

"But they all died or were . . . oh," Malfind said.

Faramir nodded. "They were all killed or captured *that we knew of.* I'm point."

He was the best tracker.

"Malfind, you behind me."

He wanted that spear nearby if he suddenly ran into anything hostile within arm's reach.

"Morfind on rear."

She was the best archer of the three of them, particularly at quick instinctive shots.

"Helms on."

They all reached over their shoulders and put on the light open-faced sallets Dúnedain wore for scouting work when there was a real risk of a fight, simple ridged pots with enough of a flare that they protected the neck but blocked neither sight nor hearing, covered in the same mottled cloth as their cloaks. He worked his with a hand to set it properly and buckled the strap under the chin; the feel of the internal felt pads clamping around the crown, brow, sides and back of his head made him swallow a bit.

"*Gwaem,*" he said. "Go!" and led off at a swinging lope.

Now that he knew he *was* following a band, it was much easier, easier than following a running deer though not nearly as obvious as a sounder of boar. He didn't try to look for specific sign every moment, just for an impression of dislocation, a wrongness in the overall *feeling* of the woods, and every score or so of paces something stood out from the background. A twig broken, a branch bent, ground-cover crushed down, a human hair caught in bark.

With only three Rangers it was a hideous risk to pursue such a large *yrch* band—not to mention the foreigners, the reports had said they were much better armed and organized than either Eaters or even Haida. Leaving an ambush party behind you was one of the standard tactics of a pursuit, and the only way to completely avoid it was to travel so slowly that you couldn't keep up with the people you were chasing.

They simply didn't have any choice, though. From the angle that the tracks had cut the path he didn't think they were headed directly for the

Eryn Muir. They were probably trying to reach the water of the inner Bay where they'd hidden boats. Aluminum canoes lasted like the hills and some Eaters were skilled watermen with them.

Why they were doing this was a complete mystery right now. But that path might well take the *yrch* across hunters or foraging parties . . . which might be a few children gathering herbs and mushrooms with only the sort of guard needed to make sure no bear or tiger got ideas, or a school party being taught plants and terrain and wildlife. He had absolutely no doubt what the *yrch* would do then, whatever their other motives were. And evidently the enemy from over the sea were a hard and cruel tribe as well. There might be Haida pirates with them both, and the northern raiders were slave-takers though not maneaters.

They had to follow the enemy, and they had to get within signal range of the Eryn Muir, whichever came first. He knew what his cousins knew; when they did, he was going to sound that horn.

Whether it brought the *yrch* down on them or not.

CHAPTER SIX

Dùthchas of the Clan McClintock
(Formerly northern California and southern Oregon)
High Kingdom of Montival
(Formerly western North America)
May 16th, Change Year 46/2044 AD

"It's always sort of awkward meeting a former lover," Órlaith murmured quietly, inhaling the scents of pine and cold spring water trickling over moss-grown stone. "Especially when you haven't told him it's *former* yet."

The track still had fragments of old asphalt in it. That showed as gray-white flecks when dapples of light penetrated the swaying branches high overhead. It had been shored up in perilous spots with smooth rocks and logs but mostly it was a forest track now, kept open by hoof and paw as much as shoes or wheels. Up ahead Edain winded a horn, a long low sonorous huuu-huuuu-hurrr sound repeated once and twice and again, which was manners hereabouts—if you didn't signal and come in by plain sight when you approached a home-place, by McClintock law you could be treated as hostile.

There were still outlaws around here, and until well within living memory there had been the odd Eater band filtering up from the death-zones of old California. The Royal party were expected and so it was a formality, but her father had always been punctilious about respecting local custom. The infinite varieties of which he'd also said was a large part of what made life interesting.

"Former lover?" Heuradys said, raising a brow.

Diarmuid Tennart McClintock had his holding near here, and he had been her first man. Five years ago, almost exactly, at a Beltane festival in Dun Juniper, far north of here in the Mackenzie dùthchas. They'd met every once and a while since, and enjoyed each other's company, in and out of bed.

The Royal party came out into a hillside meadow with only scattered oaks, dropping away towards the river northward. Órlaith blinked in the flood of light after the deep green gloom of the forest of Douglas fir and Jeffrey pine and ponderosas; to east and west mountains lined the horizon, and some of the peaks of the Cascades on her right were still snow-clad. The bright green grass of the mountain spring was thick and starred with blooms: the last blue camas, the flower called farewell-to-spring with its four pink petals, a scattering of orange paintbrush and the purple blossom-balls of ookow nodding on their tall thin stems. It was cropped by a mob of three-score shaggy but bare-legged Icelandic sheep under the guard of a kilted shepherdess with a bow and two collies who ran silently to bunch the flock before they faced the strangers suspiciously, crouched belly-down.

Their mistress waved, but stayed near the ewes and the lambs that stopped their play to huddle close to their dams, pointing upward in explanation.

"Former lover, now, yes. Sure, and something tells me. Not in the mood anyway, of course."

Órlaith glanced upward herself. A pair of Golden Eagles were turning in the updrafts overhead, their great wings stroking the air like caressing hands. She thought they were the most beautiful of birds, and they were her totem, the spirit she'd found in her dreaming quest. There was no denying they loved lamb, though. Of course, she did herself. Her stomach rumbled slightly at the thought of roast spring lamb with mint, and she suppressed a—totally senseless—stab of guilt at the way the body's needs went right on even when fathers died.

Da would have laughed at her, and said *Leave the guilt to the Christians, poor spalpeens . . .*

"He'll understand that," Heuradys said. "And if he didn't, his leman would explain what his dense male sensibilities couldn't grasp. Caitlin's a girl with her wits about her. He should get off his backside and marry her."

Órlaith smiled a little; it helped to think about someone else. "Speaking of backsides, I'll be just as glad to get mine out of the saddle for a day or so."

They'd been winding through densely forested mountains for days, and not taking any more time than they must, gobbling trail-rations and falling into instant sleep every night. Her own retainers and escorts had borne up well, though the knights and men-at-arms had left their tall coursers behind to be brought on in easy stages when they passed the courier station at the north end of the Central Valley near White Mountain. Everyone was on hardy sure-footed rounceys now, and the gear and supplies on pack-mules. Except the High King's Archers, who'd left their mounts and just trotted afoot up hill and down dale at a pace that could have killed the horses and even the mules if Edain hadn't taken pity and ordered a rest now and then.

"You look more tired than I'd have expected," Heuradys said. "You're sleeping well enough . . . something else?"

Órlaith suppressed a stab of irritation. Heuradys was concerned as a friend, and moreover it was her *job*, as Órlaith's liege-knight.

As much as possible they'd followed the King's Way—what the ancient world had called the I-5. Those works were proof of the awesome powers of the old Americans, who'd carved the bones of earth as if it were a Tillamook cheese. But half a century of wind and water, snow and frost and earthquake and the slow inexorable grip of growing roots had shown that the Mother was stronger still. A lot of the journey had been on rough trails. The light cavalry scouts were nervous; most of them were from the dry open ranching country of the interior beyond the mountains and found all this forest oppressive. Usually Órlaith loved being in the woods, but . . .

"Bad dreams," she said quietly. "Not . . . not about Da. In fact, when I dream about him it's happy. I keep getting this . . . I'm not sure. I don't remember much of it, but there's something to do with a desert. Not one I remember from the waking world, but it's desperately important in the dream. And then there's this castle . . . odd-looking castle, distorted . . . and eight heads . . ."

Heuradys frowned. "Well, you remember *something*."

"A little more each time, actually." Órlaith grimaced. "Probably it's not important."

Heuradys' shrug was non-committal. They both knew that dreams *could* mean something, particularly the dreams of a monarch. Which didn't mean they necessarily would; she'd dreamt of her first dog for years after the poor beast took his final illness, and all it had meant was that she missed him and had had to put him out of pain herself.

She shifted her attention to their guests. The Nihonjin were keeping up; they were reasonable riders if not expert by her standards, and they were as hardy and uncomplaining as any Scout or Dúnedain Ranger.

"Though I get the impression that they're not used to trips this long," Heuradys said when she mentioned it. "They looked a bit stunned when I told them how many weeks we'd been on the road, and how long it will take to get back to civilization. Then wrote notes to check they hadn't misunderstood. Twice."

"Which makes sense, to be sure," Órlaith replied.

"Why?"

"All the islands of Japan together are barely the size of Westria Province, and they only live on the smaller ones the now. Just starting on re-settling the rest, from what they've let drop. At that, there are more folk alive there than anyone I know who considered the matter thought they'd have. At the Change they had four times the numbers of old California packed into the same space, and the flat land fit for tillage a smaller proportion—and look what California was like."

Heuradys shivered. "It's a miracle anyone's left in Japan but Eaters."

"The geography helped. Islands are easy to defend, so, and there's a mort of tiny and not-so-tiny ones about the place there, with nobbut a few fishers and farmers on them when the Change came. Britain was the same, with Wight and Mona and the rest, from what I hear. Still, I've no doubt it took luck and hard fighting and careful organization. They're not used to living any place else, though. Little islands like pimples on the sea's broad backside."

"Ah," Heuradys said, then with a chuckle: "A day's travel at most and then you hit salt water and have to take a boat. Hard to imagine. Sort of like being locked in Little Ease in Todenangst, actually."

Órlaith winced slightly even as she made a gesture of agreement at the metaphor; Heuradys *was* an Associate noble, and even now they tended to be a little . . .

. . . *hard-edged*, she decided.

Little Ease was a dungeon cell under the Onyx Tower at Castle Todenangst up in the Protectorate, carefully designed to make it impossible to stand, sit or lie comfortably in the chill damp blackness. Designed by her maternal grandfather Norman Arminger, the first Lord Protector, in fact, in imitation of one his hero William the Bastard had built into the Tower of London. Though he'd outdone the Conqueror in many respects, as warlord and builder both. There were times she'd wished she could have met him, but mostly she was glad he'd died in battle more than a decade before her birth.

She'd known and admired and loved her mother's mother, Sandra Arminger, who'd died of natural causes when Órlaith was in her early teens. But under a smoothly amiable, cultured exterior *she'd* had a cold ruthlessness that could make you blink in astonishment, or horror, when it did peek out.

Like a razor in a ripe fig, she thought.

Órlaith had just started realizing it before her Nonni's final illness. Common story had it that the ancients had been rather soft, but that certainly didn't apply to the ones who'd survived the Change Year. Doubly so to the ones who'd come to power then, for the most part.

And according to all the stories, Grandfather Norman made Nonni Sandra at her worst look like a loving auntie with a tray of cookies always in her hands. Da called him a bold bad man and said it was fortunate for his reputation he died when he did, when he talked about him at all. Mom rarely does mention him aloud; I think she loved him, but then she was only ten when he died and it wasn't until long afterwards anyone talked truthfully to her about his deeds.

Her mother was Lady Protector now—it was a separate title from the High Kingship, specific to the Association territories, and she'd been that rare thing, an only child, and hence sole heir. She didn't use Little Ease nearly as much as Nonni Sandra had, or the prerogative Court called Star Chamber that met in secret to send people there. . . .

Perhaps when John becomes Lord Protector he can abolish it. It's convenient, sometimes . . . but that's just the point, it's too convenient. What's that old saying Grandmother Juniper likes? "Boys throw stones at frogs in jest, but the frogs die in earnest." It's so easy to break things . . . break people . . . if you're a monarch.

"I notice you haven't been pushing our guests much for information," Heuradys said thoughtfully, looking over her shoulder. They'd clumped together where the road came out of the forest, looking down over the vast tumbled stretch of hill country ahead that vanished into blue distance. "Not even about how they ended up here on the other side of the Pacific."

Órlaith nodded. "Yes, and that's no accident. They've been honest"— she touched the hilt of the Sword—"but a little close-mouthed about some things. Sure, and in their position, alone among strangers, even friendly strangers, I would be too until I had my feet beneath me. And until I knew what and who were where and what."

"No hurry, I suppose," Heuradys said. "But eventually . . ."

"Yes, we need to know the details. But they're here and they won't be leaving any time soon, so."

Heuradys raised her brows. "Not interested in getting a ship from Portland straight back home?"

Órlaith smiled through her weariness; there wasn't a real question there, despite the way it had been phrased. She *had* been raised at Court, and so had her friend.

"I think some of them would like nothing better. But not Reiko; she has something she wants to *do* here, wants very badly. Let their trust in us ripen. And let them see something of our land. It's very strange to them, the size being not the least of it but by no means all, either."

Montival was big—well over a million square miles, counting the wild lands—and many of the inhabited portions were widely scattered clumps separated by stretches empty of human-kind even now. It might well be the largest single realm on earth, though with well under five million people not nearly the most populous. That was almost surely distant Hinduraj, which might have ten times that number, and its storied, fabled capital of Sambalpur was the greatest of all cities now. People and the work of their hands were the wealth and strength of any kingdom, but she sincerely hoped Montival never had *that* many.

Both the young women had traveled with the peripatetic Royal court for many years, by horse and carriage and railway and ship, traversing thousands of miles, from the edges of glaciers to the fringes of the lowland deserts. Órlaith's parents had made a point of spending some time anywhere there was a significant clump of people, to let them see the High King and Queen in person; monarchy *was* a personal thing, the living breathing persons of the Royal kin, not some bloodless bureaucratic abstraction of laws and regulations. Traveling about gave the rulers perspective too, and it also meant you met plenty of dwellers who did *not* travel much. Most common folk never went more than a few days' travel from where they were born unless war called or disaster struck.

The valley below was cradled in heights rising blue-green all about, in a sky where the distant snowpeaks seemed to float disembodied on the horizon under the noonday sun. Wildfowl rose like a twisting spiral of air and smoke from the water, and the first faint trace of the scents of damp turned earth and burning fir-wood hinted at men's dwellings. It was a new note in the intense green freshness of the springtime forests, a benediction of that purity rather than a violation.

Reiko brought her horse up by theirs and paused to look east and west along the stretch of river. The far faint rumble of fast water over rock reached their ears from the willows and ash that grew in dense thickets along the shore. Below, field and pasture and orchard made a subtle patchwork of shades of green and textures of growth. It was an island amid the wilderness. A gust of wind scattered a last swath of white blossom from pear trees like distant white mist, and trailed smoke from a scattering of chimneys set in roofs of flower-bright turf.

"*Yūgen*," she said.

"Beautiful," Órlaith said softly in her own tongue.

Koyama and Egawa nodded agreement behind their *jotei*. Then Reiko went on: "*Yūgen*, that is beautiful, yes, but also it means . . ."

Órlaith was a little surprised when it was the scar-faced soldier Egawa who recited:

> "*To watch the sun sink behind a flower-clad hill.*
> *To wander on in a huge forest without thought of return.*
> *To stand ashore and gaze after a boat that disappears behind distant islands.*
> *To contemplate the flight of wild geese seen and lost among the clouds.*"

Her father had been fond of saying that even a horse or a dog might always surprise you, and that the true inwardness of any among humankind was like a forest at night, mysterious and full of the unexpected, with much hidden even from the self that dwelt there and walked beneath those trees. And prone to poking you in the eye if you moved heedlessly.

She blinked; the beauty of the view merged with the pain of missing him.

I will never share this with him, or anything like this, ever again.

She looked over at Reiko for an instant; their eyes met, shared a moment of communion across all boundaries of people and custom, then looked aside.

"*Yūgen*," Órlaith agreed.

They crossed the sloping pasture and headed into the valley of the Rógaire River on a track that switchbacked down a rocky slope overrun with purple-flowered deerbrush. The name of the stream was post-Change, bestowed during the years of chaos and violence when the Clan McClintock had taken form in these comely but rugged lands south of the Willamette Valley. Their first Chief, the McClintock Himself, had been a man of odd skills, esoteric knowledge and strong will who ended up founding his own small nation. One that modeled itself on him and his first core of helpers, as a saturated solution crystallizes around a seed; that part of physics hadn't changed with the Change, and her instructors had demonstrated it in her chemistry lessons. It was much like what Órlaith's grandmother Juniper had done in founding the Clan Mackenzie.

Only in a manner rather less sane, she thought.

One of the first McClintock's many obsessions had been slapping names from the tongue of his ancestors on any piece of local geography that didn't actively fight back, and by now many of the older terms had dropped out of living memory. Though he hadn't quite been able to get his new clan to *speak* that language, if only because it would have taken too much time and effort when both were at a premium.

But they do mine it . . . or pull plums out of the pudding.

Diarmuid's grandfather had been one of the first McClintock's right-hand men, what they called a *feartaic* or tacksman, and Diarmuid had succeeded to this land when his father had demonstrated the risks of tackling a grizzly with a boar-spear several years ago.

Reiko came up again as the way broadened out from the narrow track into open oak-savannah, accompanied by her two closest advisors. She untied the chin-cords of that curious straw hat shaped like a flat-bottomed bowl and fanned herself with it for a moment; it was noticeably warmer in this sheltered hollow than up the mountainside.

"This man Di-ar-mu-id is . . . your . . . vassal?" she asked, in her own tongue and then in much-improved English that had even acquired a very slight Mackenzie lilt.

Órlaith nodded a little reluctantly; the knowledge she'd gained through the Sword warned her that *vassal* and *fudai* weren't exactly the same thing. It wasn't anything explicit, more a matter of a slight mental stumble, as if on an uneven pavement.

"More or less," she said. "Through the McClintock himself, himself, Colin, the *ceann-cinnidh.* Clan chief," she added, again frustratingly conscious that *shi* and *clan* weren't exactly the same thing either, nor was *ichizoku.*

Knowing a language was much better than not, but it didn't mean perfect communication. Not even with Da's magic sword. Her mother had said that once while she was teething her parents had come in to a room and found her gnawing on the pommel. There were times she still felt like doing that.

You have to work at getting across what you mean. And Reiko works, by Ogma of the Honey Tongue! She can follow most speech now.

"The McClintocks were early allies of my father's birth-Clan, the Mackenzies," she added, to clarify. "From their beginnings, soon after the Change. When my father returned from the Quest with the Sword of the Lady—"

She touched it with her palm on the crystal, the same gesture her father had used.

"—they were among the first to hail him High King; and they fought for him in the great battles of the Prophet's War, and he confirmed them in their lands and a good deal more when Montival was founded and the Great Charter proclaimed. They . . . hmmm . . . resemble Mackenzies somewhat in their customs."

Edain had trotted back, saluting and leaning on his bow to listen for a moment as she spoke. She'd been repeating each sentence in English and Japanese and he grinned at the last part.

"Resemble us? That they do. Somewhat as a donkey resembles a horse, so," he said.

"That was not tactful, old wolf," Órlaith said affectionately. To Reiko: "Some . . . ah . . . consider the McClintocks a little . . . I think you would say *soya*. Rustic."

Edain snorted. "And some consider them a bunch of drunken savages from the arse-end of nowhere," he said cheerfully; almost the first time since her father fell she'd seen him so.

Egawa spoke; Reiko started to translate and then made a graceful gesture of apology.

The Imperial Guard commander looked at his sovereign, tucked his head when she waved him on, and asked:

"How do they fight, your Highness?"

"Understand, General Egawa, I haven't seen them in combat myself."

In fact, that fight when we rescued you and Da fell was my first real battle. But not the last, by the Dagda's club and the wings of the Morrigú! Not while those who killed Da walk the ridge of the Earth.

"My father's appraisal was that they were fine skirmishers and raiders in broken country, especially in wooded land like this."

She inclined her head to indicate the mountains and foothills they'd been traveling through.

"Good at scouting, good at ambushes—both ways. And very fierce in a massed charge, especially if their enemy isn't expecting them. They're weak against cavalry on open ground, or against disciplined foot-soldiers, if they don't win by a quick rush. And they have no artillery—no field catapults—or engineers. They can't take fortified places, except small ones by scaling ladder. Da would say . . . that they have all the courage in the world, but not so much staying power."

Egawa nodded. "I knew your Royal father only by watching him command one small battle," he said thoughtfully; it was a manner she recognized, a craftsman speaking of his trade. "But that was enough to show him to be a man whose judgments in war were to be taken very seriously."

The words were praise, but they were sincerely meant. Órlaith swallowed and took a deep breath; it was getting a little easier to think of him without actual physical pain, especially when she had something to focus on.

"How many of them are there?" he asked. Casually, but there was a slight edge of tension in his voice.

"Nobody knows exactly," she said. "They don't take censuses, they had some . . . unfortunate experiences with that soon after the Change. The Lord Chancellor's office thinks somewhere between one and two hundred thousand. They sent more than ten thousand warriors to the great battle in the Horse Heaven Hills the year I was born, and there are certainly more of them now, they've been spreading. They don't like being crowded, which means to them being able to see a neighbor's smoke."

The Japanese were as difficult to read as any people she'd met, not least because they were also apparently free of the impulse to fill a silence with talk just for the sake of it. Reiko blinked quickly, and Egawa squinted thoughtfully. Koyama gave no reaction at all, simply noting what she said. She still thought they found that a large number.

"There's a many of them at the tacksman's steading now, Princess," Edain said. "Gathered for Beltane, and stayed for a handfasting; the party was just splitting up and the wreath still on the bride's head."

She nodded; the May feast was a lucky time for joinings, as for beginnings in general, and weddings were common in this month among followers of the Old Faith.

"Whose handfasting?" she asked.

"The tacksman himself, to be precise. The bride's name is Caitlin Banaszak McClintock, who I think—"

He raised his eyes tactfully, and did *not* grin.

"—I think you know."

Órlaith exhaled slightly; that would simplify things. She had no intention of taking a consort until she came of age for the Throne.

Heuradys murmured: "Oh, good," and the three of them shared a glance. "Cry hail to Aphrodite, and to Eros, You Goddess gentle and strong, You powerful God," the knight added piously, but with a grin. "And may Hera of the Hearth bless them. She's probably pregnant, too."

I've never thought Diarmuid was ambitious that way, Órlaith thought. *But being the High Queen Regnant's consort might be tempting to any able man, if he thought he could gain it.*

They came out into the pocket of flattish land on the south bank of the broad swift Rógaire, noisy with the spring melt and still rising as the mountains warmed and shed their white winter coats.

The river ran westward several hundred miles from the High Cascades to the Pacific at *Tràigh òr,* mostly through mountains and often in deep narrow canyons. Land that wasn't too rocky or steep to farm came in patches along river and tributaries, some quite extensive and others small like this; canoes and rafts afloat and pack-beasts through the forests and folk on their own feet were the links that held the McClintock dùthchas together, as far as anything did. The mountain winters with their storms and huge snows hadn't been kind to the ancient world's roads and bridges, and the dwellers here lived widely scattered, each family or little kin-group to itself.

Hooves and feet thudded and drummed on the rutted trail that led them on, flanked by planted walnut trees. Diarmuid's steading showed him to be a great man, by local standards, though in some places—Corvallis or Boise, for example—it would have been about what a well-to-do yeoman farmer might have.

Unless you count the warriors he could call out at need.

Sixty or so acres along the river were planted to wheat and barley and oats, hay and fodder and potatoes, orchards of cherry and apple and pears and other fruits, truck gardens and a small patch of gnarled goblet-trained grape vines. A shift of the wind brought a waft of smoky, pungent odor from long huts by the river that told of brine-cured salmon being smoked; the big fish swarmed thickly here in spring and even more so in the fall. A flume led from a creek to an overshot waterwheel, standing next to a small stone-built mill that would grind grain, saw timber, break flax and lift some of the labor of fulling woolen cloth for all the neighborhood. The forests themselves would yield as much or more than the fields, game for meat and hides, bones and fat and horn; wood and fuel; dyestuffs, honey and wax; nuts and other wild provender and pasturage for cattle and swine and sheep.

Eight crofts shared the land, little log-and-fieldstone cabins standing back from the bank and possible flooding amid their own gardens that included flowers as well as vegetables, and the intense blue of patches of blossoming fall-sown flax wove bands of color near the houses. There would be more homes tucked away in suitable pockets for many score miles around, and upstream and down. Families who followed the Tennart sub-chieftains to war when the Red Arrow went around, and met here for worship at the great feasts of the Wheel of the Year or in assembly to vote on disputes or for something like cobbler's work when traveling artisans came through on their rounds.

Diarmuid's house was larger, though quite modest compared to a north-realm manor or a rich merchant's mansion in Corvallis. A two-story block of deep-notched logs rested on a foundation of mortared fieldstone; lower wings in a U shape stood around a cobbled court. High-pitched roofs reared above, shake and birch-bark covered in dense flower-starred green turf, and the rafter-ends snarled in the shape of dragons. The log walls were carved in sinuous running patterns based on a three-armed spiral where they weren't covered with trellised roses just coming into full crimson bloom.

The house was on a rise of ground. Not far away, but beyond the scatter of tree-shaded barns and sheds, corrals and stables and workshops, was a low hill with a rough circle of tall trees. It was surrounded by a screen of the sacred Rowan, planted many years ago when the Old Faith swept this area. That was the *nemed*, the Sacred Wood. You couldn't see the altar from here, but two carven trunks of old-growth incense cedar had been set in stones where the path wound up to it, each a thick baulk thirty feet high.

One was wrought at its top with the image of stag-headed Cernunnos, two torcs of twisted gold in His hands. The other was Flidais, with Her sacred white deer crouched at Her feet, the Goddess standing naked and bold, cattle-horns raised in Her grip. The colors of the figures glittered fresh under a coat of varnish.

The carving was cruder than it would have been in the Mackenzie dùthchas; for that matter, most of the northern Clan's duns would have used Lug of the Many Skills leaning on His spear and Brigit the Bright holding the wheatsheaf of abundance and the flame of inspiration for the images, as they did outside the gates of Dun Juniper. But Mackenzies were village-dwelling farmers and craftsfolk who also hunted and fished; the McClintocks were hunters and fishermen who also farmed and practiced crafts. Here in the vast steep tangle of forest and mountain, glacial lake and swift tumbling river, their first worship went to the wild Powers of the lands beyond the tamed tilled fields, the Ones who dwelt in the rustling green silences that shaped their souls. There was a raw strength in the images that made her hand move in the Invoking gesture.

Flowers and boughs were piled at the feet of the god-posts, and a chain of flowers linked them, marks of the festival just past.

Diarmuid's folk were gathered on a cobble-paved space before the outer doors of his house to greet the Royal party, about forty of them including some who must be guests. The shock-headed children might wear anything from nothing whatsoever save an anklet of luck-beads to a shift-like shirt. Adults were in the baggy wool *Feileadh Mòr*, the wrapped and pinned Great Kilt in the blue-brown-red tartan of their Clan. This folk preferred that one-piece garment to what Órlaith privately considered the more elegant phillabeg version that Mackenzies used, with its separate plaid. Though it was a matter of opinion; McClintocks had been known to refer to the Little Kilt as a *little pleated skirt*, something which had started brawls. Some here wore the Great Kilt alone, with its upper part thrown over a shoulder, and very little else down to their bare callused feet; except in the coldest parts of winter it would serve as cloak and blanket as well.

Diarmuid himself wore ankle-boots, knee-hose, a broad tooled-leather belt with a golden dragon buckle to hold his basket-hilted sword and dirk and sporran with its edging of badger fur, and a sleeveless shirt-tunic of fine saffron linen embroidered with green thread at the neck and hems. A slim torc of twisted gold circled his neck now—the mark of the handfasted in both Clans—and two chased gold bands were on his bare muscular upper arms. He was a young man of medium height, slim but broad-shouldered, with dark-blue eyes and seal-brown hair in a long queue, his chin shaven unlike most McClintock males but a mustache on his upper lip.

His new bride stood beside him in a fine embroidered linen *leine*, a long shift, under a newly woven arisaid in the Tennart colors. An arisaid was the most formal of woman's garb and not much worn by those below middle age on anything but the greatest occasions . . . such as a wedding, or a Royal visit. It was much like the everyday kilt that all usually wore, but with the lower portion far longer, down to the ankles, and only a dirk on the belt. She had high cheeks and narrow gray eyes above a snub nose. Hair the color of birchwood flowed down in many long plaits confined by a flower garland of creamy white meadowsweet, often called Bridesblossom when put to this use.

One of the Japanese muttered: "Tattoos!"

Well, yes, Órlaith thought, suddenly conscious of them through a stranger's eyes. *And the way he says it . . . it feels like tattoos are something . . . dangerous and risqué.*

It was what you'd first notice if you weren't used to McClintocks, which not many apart from their immediate neighbors were. Diarmuid himself had elongated blue curves on his arms and legs, body and face; his lady Caitlin had the wings of a monarch butterfly around her eyes, the colors tawny-orange and black. Many of the others were both more gaudy and more crude.

There were a few non-McClintocks present. Their leader seemed to be a stocky man of medium height with ruddy-brown skin and his graying black hair in braids, dressed in plain homespun trousers and deerskin hunting-shirt and moccasins, and a few others with a family resemblance.

Yurok, she thought, nodding in his direction and getting a sober inclination of the head back. *Have I met him?*

She'd have guessed his tribe even without the Sword and the new-found communion with the Land of Montival—that was curiously muffled and incomplete as yet, probably because she hadn't gone through the Kingmaking.

The Yurok folk still dwelt along the Klamath River south of here and more towards the coast, very far out of the way. Which accounted for their survival in their ancient homeland both in the days of the Americans and after the Change; her parents had made one visit there, when she was eleven, and it had been a hard trip. The Yurok had become autonomous again when the ancient world fell, absorbing most of the other dwellers in the region, and they'd made alliance with the first McClintock chieftain for mutual help against bandits and Eaters. Though they were part of the High Kingdom, such few dealings as they had with outsiders were mostly through his Clan.

And didn't Diarmuid once tell me a family story of the Tennarts . . . yes, there's some of that heritage on his father's side. When the ancients first came to these lands two centuries ago one of his ancestors married a Yurok woman and brought her north to the valley of the Rógaire. He wasn't the only one hereabouts. Not surprising. Even conquer-

ors as hard and stark as the old Americans rarely sweep a land absolutely clear; some of the blood of the vanquished endures, however scattered or unknown, as water moves unseen through sand. Da's father Mike Havel was a quarter Anishinabe, after all. Nonni Sandra had a Nez Perce great-grandmother married to a Quebecois trapper, and Grandmother Juniper had some Cherokee, very far back.

Órlaith reined in and raised her hand in greeting. The McClintocks cheered, a high ululating sound, pipers added the raw wail of the drones, and a drum boomed.

The adults—which with McClintocks meant anyone big enough—all brandished their weapons thrice in the air as they shouted, a gesture of greeting and fierce loyalty. That included a good many yew bows, spears, tomahawks, gruesome-looking Lochaber axes with their hooks and two-foot blades on six-foot poles, and swords that might be either basket-hilted claymores or the original *claidheamh mòr*, greatswords four feet long worn over the back in a rawhide sling. Nobody was wearing armor, beyond round nail-studded shields with a central spike, they'd come here for a festival-feast and a wedding after all—the nailheads were polished bright. But McClintocks didn't so much as go out to the privy without something in the way of a weapon. That was a habit that had been fading elsewhere lately, but it remained quite lively here.

The Japanese attracted looks and murmurs and some plain dropped jaws—most of these forest-dwellers would never have been outside their dùthchas in their lives, save for some of the older ones who'd marched off to the Prophet's War and come home to tell the tale. A few started to bristle dangerously at the strangers, and Órlaith cut in before scrambled backwoods rumor about who'd been responsible for what got out of hand. These were a fierce folk, readier with their steel than her father's people.

"These *Nihonjin* are our guests, and they share our feud," she called, her hand on the hilt of the Sword to remind them that she could not mistake the truth of the matter. "As our guests and allies, they are under the Crown's protection."

The scowls turned to smiles, or sheepish foot-shuffling when Diarmuid turned and glared at them for breaking the peace of his greeting.

She dismounted and handed off the reins of her horse before she went to one knee briefly and took a clod of earth in her hand to touch to her lips.

When she rose she spoke formally:

"I, Órlaith, daughter of Artos and Mathilda, of the House of Artos and the line of the High Kings of Montival, ask welcome on the lands of Clan McClintock and the sept of the Tennarts. I come as a guest claiming guest-right for me and mine, by the leave of the Clan and its Gods and its folk, and of the *aes dana* of rock and tree and river, bird and beast."

Diarmuid and Caitlin stepped forward and each exchanged the ritual kiss on both cheeks with her. Diarmuid's clean male scent of hard flesh and woodsmoke and wool was familiar and comforting even just as a friend, and Caitlin's garland of bridesblossom had an overpowering sweet lushness that had soaked into her hair.

"The House of the *Ard Rí* and our *Bana Ard Rí* to be are always welcome on this land and among our folk," he said gravely. "For our land is the land of Montival and we are of the High King's people."

His voice had the McClintock accent, a deep burr that rolled the "r" sounds and swallowed others: *our* became *ooorr* and *to* became *tae*. That was a legacy of the first McClintock too, as the soft Mackenzie lilt was of Grandmother Juniper. The early followers of both had adopted the habits of speech as a sign of belonging and it had spread as more joined them. To their children and grandchildren and now great-grandchildren it was simply the way they spoke, changing slowly as a living speech rooted in a settled place and people did. Few realized it had ever been otherwise, or that many had thought the original fashion excruciatingly artificial.

Especially Grandmother Juniper. Whereas the McClintock reveled in it. Ah, well.

"A hundred thousand welcomes, tae ye and all yours!" Caitlin added, with what seemed like perfectly genuine enthusiasm.

It is, Órlaith knew with a slight chill. *She means it . . . and sure, I can tell that she does. Useful, but I can see now why Da thought the Sword a burden and a danger to the bearer.*

"In the name of the Mother-of-All and the Horned God and all the kindreds o' land an' water and sky who dwell wi' us here," Caitlin went on.

One of Diarmuid's followers handed Caitlin a carved cedarwood plat-
ter piled high with little wedges of dark wholemeal bread beside a bowl
of salt. His eldest sister Seonag was about twelve, and stood with a frown
of grave concentration on her face and a great carved ox-horn in her
hands, brimming with red wine, its tip and rim bound in pale gold. Their
mother Gormall—who was also High Priestess here, in the usual way—
wore a white robe bound with the Triple Cords and carried a carved
rowan-wood staff tipped with the waxing and full and waning moons in
wrought silver. She signed the plate and horn with it before it was brought
forward.

Órlaith took a piece of the bread and dipped it into the salt in the
carved wooden bowl, ate the morsel and took the horn, raising it to the
four Quarters before pouring out a small libation, taking a sip of the full
strong liquor and passing it on; when it came back she drank the last
drops and ceremoniously turned it upside-down. Mackenzies would
probably have used mead instead, but the ritual was much the same as
that of her father's birth-folk.

So were Gormall's words, more or less: "Holy and peace-holy is the
guest beneath our roof and on our land," she said proudly; she was a gaunt
woman in her late forties, with graying dark hair. "Keep ye all the *geasa*
of *a'ocht*, of sacred guest-right, or suffer the anger of the Keeper of Laws
and the Wise One."

With the formalities out of the way, Diarmuid's face was intent as he
studied hers.

"So it's true, then, Orrey?" he said quietly.

She nodded, and he bit his lip and shook his head. "Och, he was a
man in ten thousand, a hundred thousand," he said. "We bewailed him
here when the courier came, but I'd hoped . . ."

His mother shook her head as well, in disagreement rather than nega-
tion. Her voice was somber:

"Naen wi' the Sight could hae doubted it. The Earth's very self wept
and keened him, when his blood lay upon it. It weeps yet, and rages, that
the sacred King was slain untimely by the weapons of foreign men, and
that his life was spilled on the holy eve of life's beginnings."

Órlaith swallowed and nodded. "I've no wish to darken your handfasting," she said. "Or to strain your stores, it being spring"—the hungry season, farthest from the last harvest and before the earth yielded much in the way of crops or garden stuff—"and you having had your own feast to find these past days."

Diarmuid smiled a little. "Nae, we're well-placed for food-stores this year. The first salmon run was very good, and the wildfowl abundant, thanks be tae Modron, and the wild herds are as thick as I've ever seen now that they're moving up tae the high country."

Edain nodded, and flicked the string of his bow with a thumb. "We took two elk and a young boar yesterday. Cernunnos was generous; fair ran into us, they did, and us so many and making enough noise to fright the fae. They're gralloched and slung over a pair of mules, but I'm thinking they'd do more good in your kitchen than over a campfire, if you don't mind being offered your own, *feartaic*."

That was both true and tactful. The prime cuts would go on the table tonight and however long the Royal party stayed, and the rest would go into the icehouse and help stretch the household's supplies for days to come.

"I don't mind in the least, master-bowman, ye've lang had leave tae hunt oor land," Diarmuid said. "Enter then, a', and welcome; the bathhouse is heating and the stoves are ready."

The bagpipes sounded, overpowering within the little hall as the pipers strutted around the inner side of the hollow square the tables made, their plaids swinging as they paced. Behind them solemn youths and maidens carried the platters—mostly grilled salmon brushed with oil infused with garlic, onions and ginger, baked on cedar planks that still smoked and sputtered aromatically. But they were accompanied by roast boar and elk and a smoked bear-ham, baskets of loaves, vegetables in the wicker containers used to steam them, and salads of wild spring greens and much else. Órlaith found herself sniffing at the scents with interest; they'd been many days with nothing but trail rations.

"*Ith gu leòir!*" Diarmuid called.

The pipers downed their drones, the helpers set their burdens within everyone's reach between the butter-crocks and wheels of cheese, and sat on the benches themselves; the thirty or so diners said their thanks in their various ways. Órlaith drew the Invoking pentagram over her plate and murmured the Blessing.

"Eat plenty!" Diarmuid added, translating the ritual cry into the common speech.

His new wife smiled up at him, and his mother fondly at both of them. The older woman had a wistful look to her, probably because she saw her man in her son, and her own youth in her daughter-in-law. Diarmuid himself beamed around with pride.

He'd seen the splendors of the north at court and on visits; Órlaith thought the better of him that his standards of judgment remained solidly grounded here in the land that had born and nourished him, in his own *heimat*.

Her father had picked up that word from one of his companions on the Quest to Nantucket, a Midwesterner called Ingolf the Wanderer by many. Though she'd mostly known him as Uncle Ingolf, since he was married to her father's half-sister Mary.

Heimat meant the little homeland of the heart, the *patria chica*, small and very dear, the place your kin dwelt in a landscape dense with their stories and deeds and where you expected to lay your ashes in turn and your children after you. This was Diarmuid's however he named it, the house his father and mother had built, the land they tilled to feed him, the river that had sung him to sleep in his cradle, the *nemed* where he worshipped with his clansfolk and the hills where he'd hunted and dreamed as a boy.

That didn't lessen his loyalty to the High Kingdom; if anything, it strengthened it with the strength he drew from deep-rooted heartstrings. Montival was a mosaic of little homelands within the greater, some very strange indeed, but all rightly and greatly beloved by their dwellers.

And I don't really have *a* heimat, she thought a little sadly.

She didn't grudge Diarmuid his contentment, even if her heart was still raw; if anything it was comforting. This . . .

Normal life, she thought. *Just . . . life, with its ordinary sorrows and its sweet common joys as one generation follows another.*

. . . was the reason for the Royal kindred's powers and its burdens. But she was inclined to see the melancholy side of everything just now, and supposed she would be for the natural term of grief.

Da was a Mackenzie at seventh and last; the dùthchas was his heart-place, Dun Juniper especially. And Mom is an Associate—for her it's the core of the Protectorate, the Crown's demesne land around Portland and Todenangst, castle and manor and village. But I've traveled all my life. I love those places but they're not mine *in quite the same way. Because everything is, so nothing is. Not in that special fashion.*

The core of Diarmuid's house was a rectangular hall with a second-story gallery around it. Many of the wedding guests had tactfully—though reluctantly—departed homeward to leave room for the newcomers. Most of the stripped-down numbers of the Royal party were being feasted in the outbuildings where they'd doss for the night. That left room for the ones seated at the trestle tables if they didn't mind touching elbows. Diarmuid's kin and retainers were there, and the core of the Royal party and Reiko and her closest advisors of the *Nihonjin* guests. The spring night in the mountains was cool enough that the low flickering of the log fire on the hearth was welcome.

That and the lanterns on the gallery rails cast uneasy light on pillars carved in the shapes of Gods and heroes, walls covered in pelts of wolf and bear and tiger, or with the horns and skulls of beasts preserved to honor their beauty or bravery, or weapons and shields and a few helms and mail-shirts. Equipment in the corners under the overhang—disassembled looms and spinning-wheels and more—showed that this room was used for crafts as well, though mostly during the short days and long nights of winter when snow and rain and mud bound field and forest. Up on the gallery were shelves with several hundred books, some of tales, more of instruction on everything from magic and ritual to how to compost manure, volumes which the *feartaic* kept but all the neighborhood could consult.

Órlaith sat at the head table nearest the hearth, in the seat of honor on Diarmuid's right. That put Reiko and her advisors within hearing distance despite the buzz of conversation, and the fact that it was in another language made it easier to pick things up from what they said. She heard the Imperial Guard commander mutter:

"Majesty, how do these people manage to avoid eternal constipation, with all the meat they eat?"

Her folk don't seem to be vegetarians, or most of them aren't, but I'm not surprised they look on red meat as an occasional treat, Órlaith thought.

Heuradys nodded too when she murmured it in English.

"Not much land to use for pasture," she said. "Not surprising that they like seafood, either, if they can't have big herds and they all live close to saltwater."

Órlaith looked at the four Japanese leaders and thought of the others in their party. "Notice they're none of them what you'd be calling big men?" she said. "They're very fit and they all seem strong, but not one of the men is as tall as you or I—most of them are shorter than Diarmuid, and he's middling to our eyes. Reiko is what, five-six? And she looks tall-ish in their company the way you or I do in Montival."

"That might be hereditary, like their looks. Height runs in families, sometimes."

"To be sure, though both my grandmothers were short women and I'm after being a bit of a tall poppy. But you know how feeding works."

They both did; even in generally prosperous Montival there were places where you could trace the history of the last half-century simply by looking at successive generations—the few tall elderly survivors who'd been near adult at the Change and who came of long lines of the well-fed, their shorter children born to grinding want, and then *their* children and grandchildren inching—literally—back up. It was largely a matter of how long it had taken each to adapt to the new world.

Heuradys looked at the Nihonjin. "They're a bit short but not scrawny. On the other hand, they're nobles or nobles' retainers where they come from, right? If they live on those little islands you mentioned, maybe even the gentry are used to eating sparely—enough but only just, and not of rich foods."

Reiko was deftly using her chopsticks to free a morsel of the salmon fillet before her while the two Montivallans spoke. She and her followers had all chosen the fish, except for one who'd taken a slice from the haunch of the boar and was eating it with relish.

"This salmon is excellent, General," she said to the older man who'd grumbled, and ate the morsel with delicate precision. "Different, but not in the least repulsive. And there is plenty of fiber in this bread."

She broke a piece from her loaf and nibbled cautiously. Órlaith noticed she was averting her eyes from most of the feasters. Even Mackenzies considered McClintocks a little rowdy at table, though nothing outright disgusting was going on—the Tennarts were tacksmen, after all; this wasn't a woodsrunner's single-room cabin twenty miles from the nearest neighbors. No doubt the woodsrunner would consider Diarmuid a trifle citified and sissy, or awesomely sophisticated, because he used a fork and napkin and didn't chuck gnawed bones directly to his dog.

"It's not entirely different from *anpan*," Reiko went on; thanks to the Sword Órlaith knew that meant a sort of bread-like dumpling. "No bean-paste filling, of course, and it's a little sour, but fine if you make an effort. They are providing us with the best they have; it would be ungracious to quibble."

Even Reiko was avoiding the cheese and butter, Órlaith noticed. All of the Nihonjin seemed to find dairy products viscerally repulsive. The dried fruit pastries that ended the meal were well-received. Heuradys leaned forward slightly and spoke to Reiko:

"One of your men seems a little uncomfortable, Your Majesty. Perhaps it's the chairs?"

"Which one?" Reiko said.

"The younger, handsome one."

Órlaith looked herself. One of the Japanese *was* shifting a little when he didn't focus on it, as if the wool-stuffed leather cushions were rasping something tender and he had to remind himself to sit still.

And yes, he's sort of handsome; sort of dashing in fact, all whipcord and that slightly tousled hair despite the odd haircut, and he's got a nice smile. Younger than the others, too, and a bit less dour. Altogether more pleasant to look at; I wonder why he's here with the leadership?

The rest of Reiko's close associates reminded Órlaith all too much of her father's advisors, only more so and all men; rather grim middle-aged men at that, of the sort who'd been irritating her for years by refusing to acknowledge that she wasn't twelve anymore . . . often without realizing they were doing it, which was *doubly* irritating. A few still expected her to be playing with dolls and chattering about her new pony or goshawk.

She hadn't gone through the butting-heads-with-father stage many teenagers did; that seemed to be more of a thing for boys anyway. She *had* had her quarrels with her mother, though that was years past, and there had been a while when she found both her parents excruciatingly embarrassing. Which was embarrassing and sad too now that she looked back on it.

But those old men made her sympathize with the boys' tantrums at times; and she admired the way Reiko seemed to have hers well in hand.

"Ah, Ishikawa Goru," Reiko said, giving him a look.

Suddenly she laughed a little, holding one hand over her mouth as she did; it was the first time Órlaith had seen her lose her solemnity, and it made her look much younger for an instant. Then she spoke in her much-improved but still somewhat shaky English:

"I will not tell him that you say. He also thinks he is handsome. But he is one sailor, ship captain is not used to be on horseback long time. Sore, neh? Not . . . not so dignified as he like to be."

The three young women shared a chuckle; Ishikawa had caught his name, looked up to see their eyes and smiles on him, started to preen and then winced again as straightening his back rubbed the sensitive portions of his thighs and buttocks the wrong way. Then he smiled ruefully himself.

Yes, quite a charming smile.

McClintocks had no greater proportion of drunks among them than most folk, despite what Edain might say, but they did drink deep at a wedding feast—or at a wake. After the wine that went with the food on this special occasion, decanters of brandy and fruit cordials and a smoky, potent whiskey were set out, with bowls of nuts and raisins as accompaniment. Órlaith took a glass of the barley spirit and sipped, welcoming the way it put a slight wall between her and the pain.

After the first toasts, the Yurok she'd noticed rose and stood before Diarmuid. In the ritual of the place he reached out and the head of the household touched his hand; the buzz of speech died down at the sign that someone was to address them all. From behind the chief table the firelight made his craggy brown face a thing of gullies and mysteries. He looked at Órlaith and raised his hand in a gesture of greeting.

"*Hoyeee,*" he said, which meant hello in the Yurok language—though in their own tongue they actually called themselves *Puliklah,* which meant *downstream people.*

She would have known that much without the Sword; the Yurok spoke English among themselves for the most part, but they kept the old language alive for ceremony and she'd heard it when her parents brought her there.

"*Hoyeee, Segep,*" she said. "Hello, Coyote."

She wasn't sure whether his name was her own memory of that visit a decade ago or supplied by the Lady's gift. It was actually a nickname. The Downstream People had an elaborate system of taboos on what name could be said where and when and by whom, formal names were often limited to use by close kin, and all of them *changed* names at least once during their lives. Using the right name was important, because the wrong one or the right one in the wrong context could be a mortal insult, extremely bad luck, or both—

And I suddenly understand how to use the names, she thought. *It's the Sword, sure and it is.*

"*Hoyeee, Sun Hair Tall,*" he replied, then dropped back into English: "I remember your visit."

"You showed me the sea-otters," she said.

And smiled slightly at the sudden image of that tumbling playfulness in the waves. That at least was her own and unaided, and she could suddenly recall how she'd run to her parents jumping with the wonder of it.

"And . . . *ayekwee,*" he said: the sorrowing farewell to the dead.

After a moment of silence he went on: "I came because my sister said it was a . . . wise thing that we meet. She is . . . *mahrávaan.*"

Órlaith felt a prickle of alarm as that woman came to stand beside her brother. Literally that term meant *One Who Hunts,* or *Tracker.* In English, it was most commonly rendered as *shaman*. Among the Yurok they were almost always female. She must have hunted true, to be here just when the Crown Princess and her folk passed through. There weren't any heliograph nets in the McClintock dùthchas, and doubly so in the Yurok land; they'd have had to start before the High King's party met their foes down in Napa to be here now.

Segep's sister was quite a bit younger and somewhat less stocky than he was, and had a hard face that Órlaith would normally have called *clever*. Right now she looked . . .

Alarmed, like me, Órlaith thought.

"I had a dream, Sun Hair Tall," the Yurok woman said, in the old tongue of her people. "I went into the mountains, up the Stair, and I danced, I took pain, I sang."

She came forward, but when she spoke it was to Reiko, and in English . . . mostly. "You from across the western sea," she said. "*Uema'ah* are after you, they track you, they seek you."

"Devils," Órlaith whispered to her, and her face changed; it wasn't a word the Yurok used lightly. "She says devils are after you."

The shaman continued: "They run through the night, they make black flame, they seek to shoot you with the obsidian arrows of death. You need a . . . a great thing to defeat them. Like the war-club of a hero, like *Puelekuekwar*, Downriver Peg. It rests here in this land, the thing you need, somewhere, somewhere south, through the lost City of Sky Spirits, towards the Valley of Death. It shouldn't be here; it should be yours in your own country. A good thing can become a bad thing in the wrong place, and my . . . helpers . . . can see it because they are altogether of this land, they know what fits and what doesn't. You have to go and get it and take it home to its proper place—but you will need the help of everything that does belong *here*."

Then something seemed to go out of her, and she licked her lips and spoke in a more normal voice.

"And *don't* ask me what that means, because I don't want to think about it again. Once was enough. And damn, but I need a drink."

Reiko had been straining to make sense of the unfamiliar language.

"I am . . . I am afraid I *do* know what it means," she said, when Órlaith had explained a few things she had missed.

The shaman and her brother returned to their places at table, where she did begin to punish the plum brandy, to nobody's surprise. Another buzz of conversation arose among the McClintocks. Órlaith pointedly did *not* listen to the *jotei*'s conversation with her countrymen, whose eyes were widening as she explained.

Diarmuid stood after a moment. "This is a serious matter, and aa' o' we should take the words of these oor Yurok kinsmen and friends seriously," he said, as complete silence fell. "Sae heed the wisewoman's foresecht."

His mother the High Priestess nodded vigorously, and her son went on.

"We're at feud for certain, blood feud, and soon at war, like enough. Don't chatter like magpies, or foemen may hear an' tak advantage."

"Aye, or things worse than foemen," his mother said bluntly. "I know you're aa', each and every one, clapperdins who love tae chew the claik better than meat, and spilling secrets better than suppin' whiskey, but you'll keep yer mouths shut aboot this."

Diarmuid glared to make sure everyone had taken his message and his mother's, then turned to two of the young men sitting down towards the end of the table on his left. They might well be relatives and were certainly retainers, probably living with him and helping with the family's work for a few years to get a little polish and see a bit of the world beyond their parents' crofts up in the hills.

"Dòmhnall na Cluaise"—this Donald was indeed missing an ear, from the looks via an encounter with something's, or possibly some*one*'s, teeth—"and Ìomhair a' Bhogha Mhaide"—Ivor who might well be a bowman, from his shoulders—"get tae it."

The household men sprang up and pulled a blanket from a shape in the middle of the room; it was a harp, the tall triangular *Clàrsach*, strung with metal and with its long sound box hewn from a single trunk of willow.

The smooth curves of polished wood glittered, wrought with knotwork patterns, and a sigh went through the room as the tension flowed away. Diarmuid's mother went to take the stool before it, and his sister stood beside. The brilliant notes of the harp rang out as the older woman's hands moved, and Órlaith recognized the slow tune.

Suddenly the whiskey was no protection at all, and she bent her head as the young girl's sweet pure voice rose in ancient unbearable lament:

> *"The Flowers of the Forest,*
> *that foucht aye the foremost,*
> *The prime o' our land*
> *are cauld in the clay . . ."*

CHAPTER SEVEN

I t was the smell that alerted Faramir Kovalevsky and made him suddenly fling up his clenched right fist, open the hand and swing it down. All three of them went to ground within a stride, and he chose the moss-grown trunk of a Douglas fir that had been as thick through as his body before it fell. His cloak spread out over him as he did a controlled fall, which it was designed and cut and weighted to do. The loose hood wasn't so different from the color of the dead tree that it would betray him as he raised his head just high enough for his eyes to clear it, and it broke the distinctive outline of a human head.

Nothing to see.

Nothing except the trees, a mixture of goldcup oak and fir and pine and eucalyptus, green and silent with long slanting rays of sunlight breaking through and painting spots in shivering gold. Bright yellow broom edged them where the light penetrated.

They'd been heading southeast along the tracks of the *yrch* bands, downslope and into thicker woods again. That had taken them almost to the *Estolad Rhudaur*, an ancient campground as the name—Eastwood Camp—implied. It was more a thinning of trees than an actual clearing now, but there were ancient water taps that had been repaired, with tables and firepits and an open-sided roofed structure to keep firewood dry and shelter travelers in the rainy season. Which gave him an idea, if they could reach the spot. The outer layer of that wood would still be damp.

Beyond this stretch the land flattened out into the valley-bottoms of southern Ithilien, much of which had been built up before the Change, though not with large structures for the most part; it was still an unbelievably perverse way to treat such good farmland. The wooden buildings had all burned to the ground in the summer of the first Change Year, and much of the forest immediately around them. Then they'd been overgrown with brush and scrub, but the woods were reclaiming them fast. Not least because the runoff from bits of old roadway and foundation pads concentrated enough water for large trees to grow quickly, and their roots in turn ground the stony parts of the ruins to rubble and then slowly to dust and shaded out competitors.

Those trees included species from all over the world, descendants of those in parks and lawns, but the undergrowth was still thick and spiny beneath the canopy in many spots, or wound into tangles by masses of feral grape and multiflora rose that only boar could penetrate. Right beyond that were vast swampy tidal longshore marshes scattered with small creeks and inlets and overgrown spots of firm land where it would be easy to hide small boats . . . or in spots, even large ones. They were also favored dwellings for boar and Tule elk and the tiger who fed on them, but that just meant you had to be careful.

While his mind reviewed the terrain his eyes were still busy, and his nose. The scent came to him again faintly on a sough of wind, hard and dry, a combination of never-washed bodies and badly-cured hides and an undertone of rot. The wind was from the east, giving him an advantage. And precisely because of times like this Stath Ingolf's Rangers always washed themselves and their clothes with soap that included essences taken from a dozen types of local vegetation. Except at point-blank range, they smelled like forest and grassland or even the mass of matted vegetation that covered much of the dead cities. Or just vaguely green.

More silence. Then, off to his right—southward of due west, three o'clock in the system his people used—a flock of birds broke out of some brush. More and more of them, spiraling upward like smoke amid a clamor of harsh screaming cries.

Bornaew, he thought.

They were medium-sized iridescent long-tailed green birds with fiery red heads and heavy hooked beaks, common all over this area except in deep closed-canopy forest, and they swarmed in the ruins. This flock was medium-sized, five hundred or so; he'd seen thousands together in late summer, and farmers and gardeners cursed the sight of them. And they were quite sensitive to certain types of disturbance by mankind. Dúnedain didn't eat them, but *yrch* did, along with anything else they could catch, something at which they were actually fairly good.

They didn't *need* to eat men anymore. It was more in the nature of a tradition, and possibly a sport.

He lowered his head, smoothly and neither too quickly or too slowly. His hands moved, and both Morfind and Malfind were close enough to see if he exaggerated the movements a little.

Did you notice the bornaew?

Nods, and he went on: *The yrch are circling to our flank, that's what spooked the birds, I think they know we're coming but aren't sure of our exact location or our numbers.*

Dúnedain didn't travel alone around here, but a pair would be common enough or the standard three for a patrol.

I'm good here, but, Malfind, shift so you're covered from that direction. Morfind, up and snipe on your judgment or when you hear me call. And for later . . . do you have an incendiary in your quiver?

She nodded. *Two.*

Both of you, rally point is Eastwood Camp if we get separated. Fire the woodpile if you can, they'll see that at home. Go!

Malfind found a section of concrete, broken long ago and sticking up from the earth like a tilted slab and overgrown with creeping fig like fur on a really shaggy dog. His sister slung her bow, leapt, caught the lowest branch of a live oak and swarmed upward at the same speed as a brisk walk on the ground; she didn't need to extend the climbing spurs built into Dúnedain elf-boots or slip her hands into the similarly-equipped gloves they all carried. In instants she disappeared behind the rustling leaves.

Malfind was almost as invisible burrowed into the glossy mass of the creeping fig, his mottled cloak nearly disappearing even to Faramir, who knew where he was and wasn't more than twenty paces off either. Usually that plant was an absolute tree-killing nuisance, but he blessed the Lord of Woods for letting it grow there now. The other Ranger put his spear down just to hand, but with the head concealed under more of the vine. Then he put his shield leaning beside him with the grip-side out and made his bow ready.

Everything depends on how many there are, Faramir thought, easing his own shield off likewise.

He took three arrows out of his quiver and put them in his left hand, held against the wood of his bow's riser by his index finger, an old speed-shooting trick.

They wouldn't have left too many behind . . . I hope. Not when they have to pick them up again when they hit the water and their boats. Assuming they are heading for the water and boats, but it doesn't make sense to try getting all the way around the Bay on foot.

His mouth was dry enough to make him think of his canteen with longing, and he was suddenly glad he'd stopped to water a tree not long ago.

Tulkas the Strong, You who laughed as You wrestled with Morgoth Bauglir, lend me from Your strength and courage, he thought.

Slowly he raised his head again, just enough to bring his eyes over the log, and brought out a pre-Change relic from a pouch at his belt. It was a treasure his mother had given him last Midwinter Feast, a little metal tube known as a *Vanguard monocular.* Through it the distant became close. Hiding was important, but if you didn't keep the approach to your hiding-place under observation the first hint that the enemy had found you would be a blade through the kidney.

That gave him a good view as the first Eater eeled past the screen of madrone about five-score paces away. The Ranger was slightly shocked he hadn't seen him before, since that was no more than easy bowshot.

The foliage barely moved more than the wind would have done and the man's bare feet touched down without so much as a twig crackling.

The Eater was short and wiry, his muscles not huge but knotted and moving taut under his skin as he stepped with the loose-tight care of a cat on a stalk; to Ranger eyes he looked to be thirty at least and was probably no more than two or three years older than Faramir. The monocular let the Ranger see his eyes flicker, bright blue and tracking back and forth.

Not all the scars were from battle or accident. Three parallel ones marked his nose like the rungs of a ladder, and there was a bone—almost certainly a human finger-bone—through the septum, and two more through his earlobes. His skull was crudely shaven except for a lock at the back, and he wore a twisted loincloth made of a wisp of ragged pre-Change cloth, a more intact-looking belt, and a whole deerskin worn as a cloak and tied around his neck by the forelimbs.

A Cut-Nose, Faramir thought.

Their usual territory was far south around the southwestern corner of the Bay and down into *Imrath Ivor,* the Valley of Crystal: they called themselves the Altos, from a pre-Change place-name. They were a biggish group by Eater standards, and they'd been pushing north lately against the many small Peninsula bands weakened by the long struggle with the Montivallans.

More worrisome was the rest of his gear. The Eater bands had taken to imitating Ranger bows lately, as best they could. They didn't have anything like the craftsmanship needed to make composite bows from scratch . . . but they had access to a *lot* of salvage. Some cannibal genius with a vocabulary of a few hundred words had decided that the top couple of feet of two skis could be cut off to make good limbs for a bow, proving his Uncle Ingolf right when he pointed out that you shouldn't confuse education with native wit. All the Eaters had to do was carve a piece of hard wood into a riser-grip like those of the Dúnedain weapons and carefully peg the curved fiberglass shapes to it.

That *was* within their skill-set and required no toolcraft more sophisticated than a knife, a hammer and an experienced eye. The result wasn't nearly as good as what Montivallan bowyers turned out and the draw-weights were modest, but it was also very much better than the nothing the Eaters had had before. Faramir's father had once told him that if you played chess with good players long enough, you got good. That axiom was from his far-northern homeland in the Peace River country where there wasn't much else to do over the long dark winters, but as a meta-phor it was proving to be dismally true here in sunny Ithilien too.

It was two generations since the Change. The stranded urbanites so helpless without their machines that they were unable to catch anything but other humans as ignorant as themselves had become fairly effective savages. And apparently the inhabitants of pre-Change San Francisco and environs had been mad for skiing, despite having to travel all the way to the Sierras to do it, judging by the abundance of raw material resting in ancient buildings.

This *orch* had a perfectly workable if odd-looking recurve made in that fashion, with bits of leaf and straw stuck to the limbs to disguise it, and a bark quiver full of shafts fletched with gull-feathers at his hip. He also had a long knife and a machete, modern rawhide grips on pre-Change steel, and a hatchet with a yard-long lemonwood handle much like the Dúnedain tomahawks if less graceful and well-balanced.

The Eater padded forward. Faramir didn't move; the monocular was well under the shadow of his hood, which would disguise the regularity of the outline as well as the distinctive curve of a human head. If he stayed immobile, at a hundred yards the *orch* would almost certainly miss seeing him despite being alert and good at the work. Miss him long enough to think the coast was clear at least.

There's going to be a fight, the Ranger knew. *At least it's not them ambushing us from close range.*

That would have been a very *short* fight.

The teeth of the Cut-Nose were yellow, except where broken ones had turned black. They all showed in snarling rictus of rage and fear. The Eater knew that he'd been sent forward as an animated target to draw fire, a provocation to a keyed-up hidden enemy to reveal themselves with a couple of well-placed broadheads. A watching eye and a prepared mind could trace the first arrow's flight back to the bow without even really thinking about it. It must have taken some powerful compulsion or persuasion to shove him into the open like that.

Minutes passed. The Cut-Nose relaxed fractionally and stood more erect. Faramir remained just as motionless; if anything, the man's peripheral vision was probably better now. His instructors had taught him that most people's sight closed in like a tunnel when they were in fear of sudden death. The effort required for relaxed stillness helped the Ranger keep his breathing and heartbeat under control too, which improved *his* ability to see and sense.

The *orch* scout made a chittering noise and four more Eaters came forward out of the undergrowth, all Cut-Noses. One didn't *have* a nose and there were other things wrong with her as well, though they didn't seem to affect movement or senses. The Eaters were notably careless about eating fish and seals and birds from the Bay.

The life there was swarmingly abundant now, probably more than it had been for hundreds if not thousands of years, but there were still some spots livid green and iridescent blue and blood-crimson from leaking poisons that concentrated worse and worse as they went up the food-chain, and others more dangerous still because they were invisible. Stath Ingolf kept continuously updated maps based on careful tests and mostly confined their fishing to migratory species like salmon anyway, but the savages just ate anything that didn't look or smell too wrong.

Two of the gang had bows like the first, and another carried an axe, an old woodchopper, which made it too heavy for a good battle tool even in a very strong man's hands. The third had a spear whose head was a butcher-knife ground to a point, and a shield made from an old trash-can lid, hammered out until it was a shallow bowl around the handle and then covered in wet hide that turned iron-hard when it dried.

And then one more . . .

No. Not all Eaters. That one must be Haida. Six in all, damn.

Not many Dúnedain had fought the northern raiders, since the PPA nobility didn't like having the Rangers set up Staths on Association lands. But some had, and pictures had circulated from the office of Marshal d'Ath. Most of the Cut-Noses were shorter than Morfind and none were taller than Faramir, but this man was between him and Malfind, nearly six feet.

He wore a close-fitting blackened steel helm shaped like the upper half of a raven's head with the bill projecting over his face and a spray of feathers across the crown. The countenance beneath the bill was square and strong-boned and heavy-jawed, sparsely bearded with brown hairs and somewhere between ruddy and olive in complexion, the eyes long and narrow and nestled in a seaman's net of squint-wrinkles. His clothes were a long leather tunic sewn with small iron rings like miniature bracelets, with trousers and boots of sealskin. A cape over his shoulders was fashioned of a mixture of wool and the soft inner pith of cedar-bark, woven with a subdued pattern Faramir couldn't make out, and a long fringe around the edges; around his throat was a necklace of bear and beaver teeth and his hands were densely tattooed.

All the gear looked worn with use and stained by the sea but well-kept, and of good materials and workmanship to begin with. There was a serviceable-looking sword of cutlass style in a scabbard of sinew-bound whalebone splints at his side and a sheathed dagger like a narrow triangle clipped to one of the rings on his jacket. His hand held a short carved staff shaped like an oddly elongated double-ended paddle with puffin beaks strung to it, rather than a weapon. The markings were colored and highly stylized, but Faramir thought the main shape was two orcas eating a seal, the bodies of the great sea-predators in turn carved with ravens and eagles and, oddly, frogs. Something similar was painted on the leather surface of a small round hand-drum hanging at his side over the scabbard of his sword, shaped rather like a Mackenzie bodhran.

He doesn't look nearly as mean as the yrch.

The Eaters looked like vicious, half-mad killers and barely human; which of course was precisely what they were. The Haida just looked like a man, albeit a hard, formidable, competent man about a decade or a bit more older than Faramir.

But they're afraid of him, the Ranger realized. *And it can't be because he's such a great fighter. That would just mean more of them would mob him.*

It sent an icy trickle even through his concentration. The Cut-Noses were openly cringing as they did to acknowledge a superior in their own band. That left a gap of yards between themselves and the Haida, and they were shooting him the odd worried glance even though they were on Ranger territory and suspected Dúnedain were hiding somewhere near. Eaters had a simple concept of social rank, what learned humorists of his people called a *Great Chain of Beating*. Though it also functioned as a *food* chain sometimes.

If the *yrch* feared this man so, it was with good reason. He must be a *skaga*, a shaman. There were stories . . . The raven-billed helm swept back and forth.

He can't see me. He really can't see me, or he'd be pointing and shouting. He's still looking, I think.

The thought would have been more reassuring if he'd been absolutely confident that the Haida was just looking in the conventional sense. The man took a few shuffling steps forward, stooping and lifting his feet in what was almost a dance, then went down on one knee. He slapped one end of his staff into the earth with a rattle as he did so and brought his left hand down sharply in the same motion to bang out a rhythm on the little drum.

The sounds skittered over Faramir's nerves like blows of a padded club inside his head, and then the man spoke. Or chanted, since it had the rhythmic feel of someone reciting, even though the language was so wholly unfamiliar that the syllables twisted away from him almost as soon as he'd heard them:

> *"Gíisgaay uu k'asdláang?*
> *Xáldaang!*
> *Dáakw st'i us?*
> *Xáldaang!*
> *K'adii bláa!"*

The Haida barked it out, in a high singsong almost like a wail. The call wasn't particularly loud, but it seemed to make the earth ripple beneath the watching Ranger in an entirely non-physical way. That was interesting, even fascinating—how could the fabric of the world flex without moving at all?—but not enough to make him pay much attention. His head was too heavy. Everything was heavy, soft, drifting, like the feeling you got the night of the Ring-bearer's Birthday Party festival when everything was winding down. So heavy and sleepy and contented. Though he also felt like he was about to throw up, and that once he started he'd keep going until his guts were hanging out his mouth raw and red. He would feel better if he just put his head down and—

A high shriek from above and behind him, the alarm call: *"Tiro! Tiro!"*

Faramir barely managed not to scream in panic as he jerked his head back up, tasting bile at the back of his throat burning like acid.

Thock!

The Haida had—impossibly—jerked his little wooden staff into the path of an arrow that had come slashing down from the big oak, and the shaft spun to one side. A paler spot marked where it had taken a chip out of the wood, and the shaman looked down at it with a frown of annoyance. Morfind must have shot somehow; perhaps whatever the *skaga* had done hadn't been pointed *up*. The Cut-Noses were bounding in a full-tilt zigzag across the ground towards the hidden Rangers, screeching every time a foot hit the ground:

"Meat! Meatmeatmeatmeat!"

It rose into the wordless insane trilling of the blood squeal, and the ones with bows were loosing on the run. That meant they would hit only by accident, but an accidental hit would kill you just as dead and they were putting plenty of arrows into the air, going past him with *whrrrt* sounds or slapping and chunking into dirt or wood. Even a mild wound meant death now if it slowed him. The *skaga* was walking along behind the Eaters, frowning and twirling his staff in one hand like a baton.

"Malfind!" Faramir shouted. *"Dago hon!* Kill him! *Dago i ngollor!* Kill the magician!"

Meanwhile the Eaters were coming straight at him, looking five times the number they were. Black-fletched arrows buzzed overhead and by his ears. Faramir rose to one knee and drew, the limbs of the recurve bending into a deep U-shape. He had only seconds until the Eaters were on him. Targets, just targets, let everything but the target zone blur out of sight . . .

The flat unmusical snap of his bowstring sounded. There was a *tick* as it struck the very edge of the Eater spearman's shield. Then at almost the same instant the wet *smack* of impact: *tick-smack*. The shaft went into and transfixed the shoulder of the Cut-Nose, not immediately fatal but slicing muscle and vein and hammering into bone, taking the man out of the fight.

Faramir was stripping the next shaft out of the three held under his finger almost before the first struck. It had been chancy with the shield covering most of the man's torso, but he wanted that spear out of the balance or they weren't going to survive past the next few seconds. The decision wasn't something he thought of; it just happened, far too fast for the waking mind.

His eyes had shifted away from the man the instant the arrow came off the string, but his peripheral vision saw him make a neat heel-to-face turn that started with the mailed-fist impact of the arrow. Then he ran, clutching the wound and making hoarse grunting sounds. The Eaters' habit of devouring their own wounded helped with their supply situation, but it had tactical drawbacks.

Whap-whap, and he shot twice, even less conscious of the hard physical effort of repeatedly lifting ninety pounds weight than he had been in interminable hours on the range and the hunt. More of Morfind's arrows went by overhead, from her invisible perch in the tree; none of the Eaters had even realized she was up there yet. Some distant part of him was mildly surprised that having cover and a steady shooting position when under direct attack was just as big an advantage as his teachers had said it would be.

Another of the *yrch* went down, an arrow through the thigh next to the groin, bright blood spouting from a femoral artery slashed across—unconsciousness in seconds and certain death afterwards, the axe flying from his hand. Faramir didn't know who'd shot that one, but he half-expected the survivors to flee. Instead the three of them came on, screeching, steel naked in their hands. Possibly more frightened of running away with their backs bare in a hundred-yard killing zone, or just crazy, or more terrified of the man behind them than they were of death itself.

Malfind was concentrating on the *skaga* as Faramir had commanded. And while he wasn't the best archer in Stath Ingolf he wasn't the worst either, and he was shooting at less than fifty yards, point blank range, zero deflection with a target coming at him at walking pace. The Haida shaman flicked out his staff again, knocked an arrow aside with a hard *tock* sound, turned his torso to let another go by an inch from his chest, ducked under a third as he tossed the staff into his left hand and drew his sword. There *should* have been at least two solid hits.

He wasn't moving blurring-fast, more at a pace that was brisk enough but *unhurried* somehow, despite the fact that the arrows he was dodging and deflecting were streaks through the air moving at two hundred feet per second. It was as if time itself was passing at a slightly different rate for the man from the far northern isles, and even in the midst of battle it was the most terrible thing Faramir had ever seen.

Maybe it's at least distracting him!

The last Eaters threw down their bows and made their final bounds. The one coming for Faramir had a knife in one hand and a hatchet in the other, spreading out in unison like the claws of a crab. The Ranger came up, drawing his knife as he did. But instead of trying to fall into a full fighting position he simply rammed himself forward, neck tensed, head tucked and chin on his chest as he head-butted the man in the middle of his screaming, contorted face with the front curve of his helmet.

Dúnedain called it *i vidh dath galen*, the Kiss of Greenhollow.

The Eater had strings of gummy froth flying from his lips; he almost certainly had too many of the juices of rage and fear in his blood to notice most ordinary wounds. Faramir was a young man of average height, a little slender though fairly broad-shouldered, but all of that was hard solid muscle and bone. He weighed a hundred and sixty pounds not counting his gear, and he was driven now by leg muscles that let him jump straight up to chest height from a standing start with a sword in one hand and a shield in the other. The head-butt effectively slammed a two-hundred-pound, metal-tipped club into the Eater's face at their combined speeds.

Faramir didn't feel the blow immediately. Instead white light flashed through his brain and the universe vanished. The impact threw him back on his heels, so dazed that he *almost* fell over and *almost* lost his grip on the knife. The *orch* was two inches shorter and skinny, plus being naked except for a deerskin loinclout and in mid-leap off the ground rather than solidly planted. Nose, jaw, cheekbones and several teeth shattered with a crackle like breaking ice as he flipped backward in the air. He didn't quite do a full circle around his center of mass, but he hit the ground face-first. That might well have broken his neck, but he was dead by that time anyway. The body fell so limp that there wasn't even any final twitch.

Faramir flogged himself back to function by sheer willpower; it was easier if you *expected* a hard blow to the head. And if you knew right down in your gut and groin that someone was going to kill you very soon if you weren't at ten-tenths. And if you were wearing a steel helmet with internal padding, of course. And if you knew you had to help your kinsman right away, regardless.

My neck's going to hurt like a bastard in a little while, he thought. *Unless I'm dead and on my way to Mandos, of course.*

When his eyes had cleared enough to see again less than two seconds had passed. He sheathed his knife, stooped to grab his bow and shove it into the case that was part of the quiver, and snatched up his shield by the central grip in mid-stride with his left hand as he stepped towards Malfind. At that instant the spear in his cousin's hand snapped out like the tongue of a frog licking for a fly. The left-most of the pair of Eaters dodged almost quickly enough, caught the sharp edge along the side of his neck just under the hinge of the jaw where the carotid ran, and sat down to die.

The other darted in with his machete raised; he was on Malfind's spear-side and inside the range that the point of the weapon could be used. The counter to that involved clouting the attacker with the spearshaft, or with the butt if you were strong enough to twirl the whole weapon like the blade of a winnowing-fan . . . though both were long-shots.

Faramir solved the problem for his cousin more directly, though it involved forcing himself to move fast when he just wanted to lie down and cry: he punched with his left hand still gripping the handle of his shield and the disk parallel to the ground. That rammed the metal-shod edge into the Eater's neck, and the man dropped away sprattling and yammering. It also let him swing the shield up between him and the *skaga* as he drew his bush-sword and put the two Rangers shoulder to shoulder.

It was only then that he noticed he was wheezing like a pump with a loose cylinder, and the point of the bush-sword was shaking a little. Mor-find had run out on a waist-thick branch of the spreading oak above them and had her bow drawn to the ear. He opened his mouth to shout . . . But Malfind was already making a stepping lunge. The Haida stopped and flicked his sword up in an arc. *Ting* and the flat of it deflected the spear, and hard enough that the spearman was thrown off balance. Morfind shot, less than twenty feet away and she *was* a first-rate archer, more than good enough to aim so close to her own. The arrow should have taken the *skaga* in the chest; instead it deflected off the steel rings on his shoulder.

They were close enough now that Faramir could hear the sharp ring-ing sound, and his enemy's slight grunt as the force of the blow staggered him a little. Swordsman's reflex told him to step in with a lunge to the throat before the shaman could recover.

There seemed to be plenty of time to know what to do, but much less to actually do it. Faramir shoved his shield-arm across Malfind's body and heaved him back in a half-stagger.

"*Noro lim!*" he shouted.

That meant *run fast;* it was the order for hair-on-fire flight.

"Now! Do it!"

The three turned and bolted into the forest.

Behind them the *skaga* looked after the fleeing Dúnedain, sighed, and looked around as he sheathed his sword. Then he knelt beside the dying

Eater and grasped him by the back of the head with a hand that felt like a hydraulic grab.

"Look . . . at . . . me . . ." he said, and his voice seemed to stretch the world, like a heavy boot on taut canvas. "*Háws . . . bl . . . díi.*"

Or like a very bright light, one that left everything washed-out and unreal. The flow of blood from the severed arteries slowed as muscles clamped involuntarily around them. The Eater obeyed, and then screamed like a rabbit caught in a wire snare as he met the *skaga*'s eyes.

"Just a moment, and you may die," the shaman said soothingly. "And death is only the beginning. There is another we must speak to. Aid me, Orca-might . . ."

The Eater's second scream was fainter only because there was less strength and breath behind it. The whimpers that followed continued for a little while after the man had died.

CHAPTER EIGHT

DÙTHCHAS OF THE CLAN MCCLINTOCK
(FORMERLY NORTHERN CALIFORNIA AND SOUTHERN OREGON)
HIGH KINGDOM OF MONTIVAL
(FORMERLY WESTERN NORTH AMERICA)
MAY/SATSUKI 17TH, CHANGE YEAR 46/2044 AD/SHŌHEI 1

"That looks like a training kata as much as a dance," Reiko said to her guard commander the morning after their arrival at Diarmuid Tennart McClintock's steading.

I must ground myself in practicalities for now, she thought. *That dream . . . I wish I could remember more.*

Heat and light, desolation, thirst, fear. Then the looming castle, and the knowledge that death or transfiguration awaited within.

Or do I wish to remember more? Father told me of his visions, but I also saw how they rode and drove him. Have I the strength to bear that burden without breaking? Because I must.

A drum thuttered and a flute played. Two of the McClintocks moved in perfect unison, the broad four-foot blades of their greatswords flashing in the early sun. Every dozen or so moves they would face each other, parrying with a hard clang of metal on metal as the flats met, then turning and slashing at arm-thick wooden posts with a great shout . . . and taking a section off with each blow. Reiko blinked at the hard *thock* sounds—when her people used live steel in practice like this, they struck at water-soaked mats of woven rice straw rolled up and tightly bound around a bamboo post.

"It *is* a kata, Majesty," Egawa said, frowning intently. "And those things aren't as clumsy as they look. Not as fast as a katana, of course, but then they are more than twice the weight—around five pounds, from the one I hefted. In a duel, I would be confident against either of those men, but in a melee . . . even in my armor, I would not like to be hit by one."

This was evidently a slack season for the local people, whose way of life didn't involve nearly as much steady grinding toil as that of the rice-growing peasants and sea fishermen she was familiar with. The fall-planted crops here wouldn't be ready for harvest until later, and the spring crops were in the soil and needed only weeding. At home they would be planting the first early rice; this month was named for that.

Out in the river was a curious device like a waterwheel on an anchored boat, which operated a helix-like rotating wicker scoop that lifted salmon into holding pens. It wasn't working now, though if you looked for a moment you could see the four-foot forms of the Chinook working their way upstream; a question had revealed there was a strict quota enforced by some religious taboo she couldn't quite grasp on how many of the great fish could be taken in any one spot or time, to preserve the breeding stock. The allowable numbers taken from the first run were in brine-tubs and smoking-racks or waiting in wicker-fenced ponds to be eaten fresh. They did some hunting here all the year around—winter was the main trapping season for furs—but late fall was both the main salmon run and the time to hunt fat beasts migrating downward from the mountain pastures, and preserve them for the cold season by smoking and salting and pickling, in jars and in underground pits lined with ice. She couldn't imagine wanting to live this way, but in the abstract it had its merits.

So this was a time for visiting and music and the arts, or dancing and sport of the sorts difficult in winter; sport mostly consisted of running, leaping, wrestling, shooting, tossing rocks and logs, and practicing with their arms.

"Individually some of them are not bad at all," Egawa said. "Their coordination is elementary at most, though."

A few of her Imperial Guards were shooting their *yumi* at the targets, weapons that looked very odd to the McClintocks because their grips were two-thirds down from the upper tip. So did the shooting style, which started with bow and arrow held high and then drawn as it was lowered. The results opened their eyes though, and produced some enthusiastic cheers.

"But there are many of them," Koyama said, startling her a little; he'd been very silent since the . . . alarming incident with the shamaness yesterday. "Majesty, I think that book the Princess gave us speaks the truth. The *jinnikukaburi* outnumber *us* by about three to one. The Montivallans outnumber *them* around four to one . . . which means there are . . .

"Twenty of them for each of us?" Egawa said, sounding slightly alarmed.

"Somewhere between twelve and twenty," Koyama said. "If we wish to involve them in our war—and yes, we do, we must—it would be well to keep in mind *all* the implications."

She nodded at that, including the parts which would be tactless to speak aloud; she didn't think anyone but Princess Órlaith spoke her language, but she wasn't absolutely sure. According to the records, Japan had been more or less a client state of the old Americans between the end of the Pacific War in Shōwa 19 and the Change in Heisei 10, though it had been a gentle overlordship if you didn't count the terrible destruction at the end of the struggle, the hand of power mostly kept hidden in the sleeve. Certainly Japan had achieved unimaginable heights in numbers and wealth during that period.

Nippon's need for help against the *jinnikukaburi* was urgent . . . but it would be unfortunate if the price in the long term was a renewal of tributary status. On the other hand . . .

Egawa grunted. "The Montivallans are six thousand miles across the Pacific from our homeland," he said. "While the *jinnikukaburi* are far too close across the Sea of Japan. It is good to think in the long term, Grand Steward Koyama-san, but first we must ensure that there *is* a long term for us, other than as *jinnikukaburi* night-soil fertilizing their paddies."

"*Hai, sore ba ichiri aru,*" Koyama said, acknowledging the point.

"And six thousand miles is much farther than it was before the Change," Reiko said. "For good and ill. And as General Egawa says, the Americans . . . Montivallans, rather . . . do not wish to *literally* devour us."

They looked over to the target range. The High King's Archers were unlimbering *their* weapons, ready to make a contest of it. Órlaith was with them. She strung her bow by stepping through between string and belly, bracing the lower end against her left boot and bearing down with a thigh as she pushed up on the other limb with a twisting flex. That made the long hard muscles of her leg and arm stand out for a moment like living metal.

Odd style, but it works, Reiko thought, fascinated.

At first glance the Mackenzie yew longbows looked unsophisticated next to the seven-foot *higoyumi*, with their complex laminations of bamboo and hard wood and rattan, their binding bands of silk cord and coats of lacquer. Órlaith put an arrow to the string; the nock point was marked by a lead ring crimped to the hemp cord, which Reiko thought was clever. The Montivallan flicked a glance at her target—a man-shape of wood about a hundred and fifty yards distant—then drew and shot in a single motion. The method also looked odd to Japanese eyes; it started with the bow held *down* and the arrow pointing at the ground and the torso leaning forward, and ended with the body slightly crouched and feet wide-braced. In between was a twisting, writhing motion that looked as if it threw the torso between string and bow.

A whirr of cloven air and a solid *thunk* an instant later. Two more shafts were in the air when the first struck, and they grouped tightly in the target's chest.

"Those yew bows are more than they appear at first glance," Egawa said thoughtfully. "I examined several. The handpiece is a solid block of hardwood, with a cut-out so that the arrow can shoot through the center. And the yew of the limbs is a natural lamination—heartwood for compression on the belly, sapwood on the back for tension. They shape each into a double curve, you cannot see it when they're strung. Quite effective. I prefer ours, I think they have less vibration and hand-shock, and we do not need a separate type for horseback use, but these are much quicker and cheaper to produce."

Koyama nodded; his position as Grand Steward made him a connoisseur of costs and benefits. Reiko made a gesture of agreement as well, without taking her eyes away.

Edain came up to the archers. He was wearing only his bracer, kilt and knee-hose and ankle-boots, and the thin gold torc of a handfasted man; there was more gray in the disturbingly abundant hair on his chest and belly than in his oak-colored curls, and you could see the way the scars— mostly—stopped where his body-armor would cover his blocky thick-muscled torso. He spoke to Órlaith, and they both planted a dozen arrows in the short dense green turf at their feet. When they began to shoot the master-bowman moved with the unhurried precision of a hydraulic machine.

"Fetch my bow," Reiko said over her shoulder.

One of the troopers hurried off; when he returned Reiko removed the *haori* she was wearing with her riding *hakama*. She tied on the black leather *muneate* plastron, slung a quiver with the golden chrysanthemum *mon* on its red lacquered surface, and donned the shooting gloves. Then she bound on a headband of white cloth with a single red dot in the middle of the forehead.

Egawa coughed discreetly. "Majesty, you are quite good with the sword and very good with the *naginata*, staff and spear. So sorry, but with the bow you are merely . . . good."

Reiko nodded. "*Hai*, sensei," she said.

Teacher was both irony and truth; he'd overseen her martial education and administered much of it personally. When he had you under his thumb in a dojo or on the practice ground, there was neither deference nor mercy in Egawa Noboru.

"But I am good enough not to disgrace us, and I need the practice," she said.

Egawa and Koyama watched as she adjusted her swords and walked off with bow in hand. After a moment Koyama spoke consideringly:

"The loss of Saisei Tennō was a terrible misfortune. But since then . . . we are lucky. So far," he added when Egawa stirred.

"Don't call anyone really lucky until their grandchildren are polishing their grave marker at Obon and lighting incense," the soldier said dryly. "But, yes, so far we are . . . less unlucky than we might have been."

"Now that's interestin'," Edain said with fascination in his voice, watching Reiko shoot. "Doesn't seem natural, with the grip at the arse-end of the bow like that . . . but it doesn't hurt either, eh? At seventh and last, it's what the *arrow* does that counts."

"Handy for horseback, too," Órlaith said, moving her right arm in a circle to make sure the tendons were loose.

With the bow she was a bit above average even by Mackenzie standards, but unlike her father not even close to Edain's level and she would probably have had trouble enlisting in the High King's Archers. Mainly because she didn't have the time to focus on it; Mackenzies were a people of the bow, and started around the age of six. The exercise today was welcome. She hadn't lost any edge, but it had been harder than it should have been. Physical skills like shooting the bow were things that had to be continuously maintained, not learned and set aside.

And today felt better than yesterday, more like a real day.

She didn't want to rest too long, though. When she stopped she could feel the loss catching up with her again. Part of her wanted to just stop and let it crush her. It was going to be like that, a climb with falls.

"You can't really use a longbow for mounted work," she went on.

"Aye, you can, that," Edain objected stoutly; the Clan also tended to be a bit defensive about their preferred weapon's limitations. "It's not easy, granted."

"Granted a dog can walk about on its hind legs; the which is neither pretty nor swift and the amazement of the thing is that it's done at all," Órlaith retorted. "But for all it's longer than a longbow, that she's using would be near as easy as a horse-archer's recurve, mounted. The height of it being all above the gripping hand and so not likely to hit horse or saddle."

"Heads up," Heuradys cut in to the technical discussion.

A drum was booming somewhere distant. The McClintocks all tensed for a moment, then relaxed at the pattern.

"Traveler coming, no' a McClintock, but nae danger either," Diarmuid said. "Tha *gocaman* are aa' at their work, forbye. Gocaman, watchers," he added, out of courtesy to the guests.

Reiko shot, lowered her bow, and frowned—Órlaith thought because she was trying to follow what the tacksman had said. That turned to a sober nod of approval as she parsed it out and realized he meant that the sentries at the approaches were alert.

They're a ceremonious lot, these Nihonjin, the Montivallan princess thought. *But there's a streak of hard common sense in most of what they do. Businesslike, you might say. And Reiko not least. They've all learned in a stringent school, with no holidays.*

Diarmuid went on, slightly louder, as his household began to chatter and point northward: "No need to cluck aboot like chickens, twa guests from outside in twa days is nae the sea rising to crush the land, nor yet the sky fallin'!"

Though it's certainly not usual, Órlaith thought. *From what he's told me over the years, four outsiders a year is normal here, counting tinkers and peddlers.*

A rider with a remuda of remounts came into sight on the north bank of the river, which was steeper than this side on the stretch of the Rógaire that held Diarmuid's holding. There was a ferry, a flat-bottomed scow linked to a cable rigged between two tall trees on either bank. The river wasn't so wide here that a bridge would have been expensive beyond bearing, but the ferry was something that could be taken up quickly in an emergency without losing a capital asset.

The tiny figure dismounted, shoved the little craft into the water, and convinced all three of the horses onto it, not without what looked like some sharp argument involving tentative hooves and vigorous head-tossing at the insecure footing. That loaded it to full capacity or a bit more, and the passenger cautiously worked the crank that carried it across the swift current. On the south bank the rider vaulted easily back into the saddle and cantered in their direction.

"Royal courier," Órlaith said after a moment.

She recognized the tack, the breed of the nondescript but enduring ponies, and the tight riding leathers that made it easier, or less hard, to take the brutal pounding of their duties.

"Aye," Diarmuid said. "Dòmhnall, he'll need stabling fra those thrae nags."

"We've nae room, nor much hay, nor oats," the young man with the ragged ear pointed out. "I cannae magic them oot o' the ground, ye ken, nair pull 'em frae ma backside."

"Well, find wha' ye can!" Diarmuid said.

He looked slightly harassed; the Tennarts kept only a few dual-purposes horses of their own, and were massively overloaded with the Royal party's beasts. The manure for their fields was only a partial compensation.

"We'll be on our way soon, Diarmuid, that we will," Órlaith said gently.

It was a perfectly legitimate anxiety, since there was simply no easy way to get more fodder or oats into the steading; no amount of gold could compensate for the simple fact that there was no wagon road. He'd already driven all his own livestock up to the shielings, the mountainside summer pastures, considerably earlier than was wise given the possibility of late freezes or snow on the heights. Bad weather now could cost his family assets it would take years to fully replace. She reminded herself to check on that later; gold *could* replace livestock, since an animal carried itself, and though Diarmuid wouldn't ask she'd see any losses made good.

The courier drew rein and raised a hand in salute. It was a woman; Órlaith recognized her, one of the small corps of endurance riders the Crown reserved for urgent work. Susan Mika—Clever Raccoon—was a slender dark wire-tough youngster in her late teens or early twenties, with her black braids done up high on the back of her head in a fashion out of the eastern marchlands of the Kingdom. Right now she looked a decade older with exhaustion and a liberal coating of mud and dust and mixtures of the two, and anyway she'd never specified her birth-year.

She'd shown up at court eighteen months ago with a recommendation from the High King's friend and blood-brother Rick Three Bears, who was prominent in the loose government of the Lakota *tunwan* . . . and her uncle. And accompanied by a private note that the bearer had good if unspecified reasons not to want to go back to the *makol*, the short-grass prairies where her people hunted the buffalo. Not anytime soon, if ever, and as a favor to his old comrade-in-arms could Rudi find her something to do anywhere *else* in Montival, please.

Even for a Lakota she rode well and had passed the tests for the couriers with flying colors, though this wasn't generally the sort of work women did among the folk of the Seven Council Fires. Which might have been involved in her wanting to leave home, though she had said not a word about it. She had all the quick hot pride of the lords of the high plains though, and had added a few Lakota touches to her standard gear: fringes down the outside of her pants, and beadwork on the sheath of her shete, the broad-bladed curved cutting sword common east of the Rockies, and on her bow-case.

"*Scephaŋši, lila tanyan wacin yanke,*" Órlaith said, in her tongue: "Good to see you, cousin-who-is-female."

It wouldn't have been polite to use personal names while she was speaking Lakota. Not in public among strangers; and anyway, she actually was a cousin by that people's rather elastic definition, since Órlaith's parents had been formally adopted by Rick's father's extended family while they were on the Quest before she had been born. She'd spent a long summer stay there in her teens that she remembered very fondly, and had acquired a Lakota name herself: *Wanbli win*, Golden Eagle Woman.

"*Han, mis eya, scephaŋši,*" the courier replied. "You too, cousin."

In English again, Clever Raccoon went on a little awkwardly: "I'm really sorry to have this duty, Your Highness. Your father . . . sorry if I'm putting my foot in it, but . . . he was always really good to me. He . . . he *understood* and . . ."

It was getting easier to accept condolences. She was starting to feel them as tributes to her father, rather than blows on her own heartstrings to make her soul quiver in pain. She'd yet to come across anyone who'd known him who hadn't been touched in a good way when their worldlines crossed.

Except for his enemies, and they're mostly dead, Órlaith thought dryly. *Though he always said the best way to destroy an enemy utterly was to win them over.*

The messages were rolled in sealed tubes of boiled varnished leather. She took a deep breath and accepted them.

The first had the Chancellery seal. It was from Father Ignatius, the priest-monk from the Order of the Shield of St. Benedict who'd been Lord Chancellor of the High Kingdom as long as there had *been* a High Kingdom. He'd also been one of the original nine who'd gone on the Quest to Nantucket with her father and mother after the Sword of the Lady, and was the only person who'd ever made her seriously consider being a Christian. If her father hadn't been . . . well, her father . . . it might have worked. She could see the calm tilted almost-black eyes and steady, almost compulsively reasonable voice in her mind as she broke the wax, twisted the cylinder open and read.

The first part was simply information, typewritten: *Your father's funeral will be held at Dun Juniper in late October, with your grandmother Lady Juniper presiding.*

She nodded: that was Samhain, the festival of the dead, though the Christian priest wasn't outright saying so. And who else to conduct it but his mother, she who had been Goddess-on-Earth for so long?

In the interim, Her Majesty your mother wishes you to return to her and the remainder of your family at Castle Todenangst, bringing your father's remains and traveling as quickly as is possible without giving offense, and recommends that you mainly use the West Valley Railway with as few diversions as possible. A special hippomotive—

—which was a treadmill arrangement with gearing to let horses propel a train much faster than they could on their own hooves—

—*will be waiting at the Eugene salvage station and relays of fresh horses at the appropriate rest points. The High Queen strongly recommends that your Japanese guests be invited to stay at an appropriate estate near Todenangst until the most urgent family matters are concluded. I concur.*

Beneath that was a note in his own neat script:

My child, your father was my King, who it was an honor to serve before all others, saving only God, the Virgin, and Holy Mother Church. But even before that he was my comrade-in-arms, and we fought together against the Adversary's minions. Presid-

*ing at his and your mother's wedding was the proudest purely human moment of my life
as a priest. Above all, and always, he was my friend. No man ever had a better. Beloved
child, I grieve with you as at the loss of a dear brother.*

Her mother's was shorter and simpler: *My golden girl, bring him home
to us.*

She shuddered and bent her head, holding the stiff rolls to her forehead until a stab of physical pain broke the moment. Then she took a
long breath and looked up. Heuradys was standing ready, not pushing
forward, just . . . there.

Thank her Gray-Eyed Lady, Herry always will be there for me, all our lives.

It made everything seem less . . . crushing. Not less painful, but less
hopeless.

"Herry, Mom wants me to join her at Todenangst. And . . ."

She handed over the messages. "Family only," Heuradys said, reading
them quickly and nodding. "I completely understand, Orrey. Look, why
don't I put up Her Highness and the rest of her *menie* at Ath?"

"Can you?" Órlaith asked, sighing a little with relief; that would be
very convenient, since Barony Ath was close to Todenangst—not to
mention being near a railway line and hooked into the heliograph net.
"They'll be there for a while, not just a day or two. They're probably going to feel isolated enough without trying to split them up. But Mom and
the Chancellor are right, it'll be better to keep them out of town or
Todenangst for now. Close but not right there."

"I think so . . ."

She paused to consider. "Right, my lord my father is out at Campscapell being Count—there's some vassal dispute that needs to be tamped
down before the swords come out, barons being barons—and Lioncel is
with him and so are Audiarda and the kids, by Hera of the Hearth it's
almost indecent how much my lord father loves being a granddad . . .
Diomede is out on Barony Harfang with Ysabeau and the rest of my dis-
gustingly numerous nieces and nephews."

"Who swarm like vermin upon the earth," Órlaith said with a faint
smile; that was an old joke between them—in fact, Heuradys delighted
in being an aunt and was an adored presence in their lives.

"Exactly. No rugrats in residence, so it's just Mom and Yolande the Little Sister from Hell and Auntie Tiph at the manor house. Between Castle Ath and Montinore Manor there's plenty of room and supplies for the whole Nihonjin party. We'll put Reiko in the Royal Suite."

"Tell your lady mother to bill the Crown."

"Oh, don't worry about that, she's never shy about sending in receipts. And Mom will love having exotic guests, an Empress will be just nuts and cream to her, and Auntie Tiph will want to know what's going on and take a look at their gear and methods, so it's no problem at all. I can shuttle back and forth to Todenangst as needed, then bring them up when it's time."

"Let's do it, then," Órlaith said. "I want to see Mother and John and Vuissance and Faolán . . . but I'm afraid of it, too. It's going to tear everything open again."

Heuradys put a hand on her shoulder, and then they hugged.

"It's like pulling out an arrowhead," she said. "You have to go through it to get to the other side."

"If there's time," she said. "Da . . . what happened to Da was just the beginning, I think. You know the saying: sometimes you just have to go on fighting with an arrow in you."

CHAPTER NINE

Faramir leapt over a rock and ducked under a madrone limb as he ran, bow pumping in his left hand and right a little up to protect his face. You could run full-tilt along a rough trail you knew well, even if it was through thicker brush than this, if you didn't care how much of a track you left. They'd all practiced that many times over the years, on paths all over Ithilien. You could even talk as you ducked and wove and leapt and sweat rolled down your face to sting in your eyes and in scratches and nicks.

Of which he now had plenty. You *couldn't* run this way and never get lashed across the face, not on this sort of narrow track. If he hadn't been wearing a helm there would have been raw scrapes in his scalp too from times he'd ducked to save his eyes.

"What . . . the . . . fuck . . . was . . . *that?*" Malfind gasped as he hurdled a log.

Even with the effort of the run his teeth seemed to be chattering. Faramir understood how he felt, but they couldn't stop to have hysterics now, strong as the impulse to gibber and beat his head on a rock was.

They were gambling that the Eaters and Haida and whatever wouldn't leave *two* ambush parties behind them. It also just felt good to be running away from what they'd seen, even if they were running straight towards more of the enemy.

"*Gollor*," Morfind said waspishly; that was the way she dealt with fear. "A magician, or didn't you *notice?*"

"*Skaga*," Faramir agreed. "Slow down to sustained pace, you two. We may need our wind pretty soon."

There was just no *time* to be terrified right now, though some things were much more exciting in the Histories than when they happened in real life. Or more heroic in print and less . . . obscurely disgusting than they were in reality, somehow. The more he thought about it, the more he profoundly didn't want what had just happened to have happened, or even be a possibility.

"Malfind, when we get there, you and I will distract them. Morfind, fire the woodpile when you hear the horn. Then we all run for the Eryn Muir or a good hide, whichever you reach first."

That gave them *some* chance of living through this. Though not much.

Morfind slid the arrow on the string of her bow back into her quiver and took out another to replace it, something that needed real agility to do without looking around, especially when you were moving along at a pace one step down from a dash. Then she took out a second just like it and held it between her index finger and the riser of her bow. Both were slightly longer than normal arrows, and they had heads that were pointed cylinders shaped like fat pencils as long as a man's middle finger. From the point of each extended a stubby pin with a flattened end; you twisted that until it clicked, then shot.

"Break left!" Faramir said to her.

The trail forked here. She turned and dashed down the left-hand branch. Faramir and her brother took the right-hand way; the trees were larger and fewer here.

Don't think about it, don't think about it, he thought. *Come on, Ranger, just keep breathing.*

They were in deep shade, the crowns of the trees meeting high overhead, but he could see the diffuse golden afternoon gleam of an opening ahead. Three hundred yards, then two hundred—ten-score paces was long bowshot for him but doable. Hopefully just *beyond* long bowshot for the Eaters and *not* doable.

How far . . . I've got to give Morfind a decent chance . . . closer . . .

The underbrush got thicker as they neared the beams of light spearing down from above. There was a glitter of metal ahead, which there shouldn't have been. Then he could see several dozen figures ahead and downslope, instants before they saw him. Eaters, more of the Cut-Noses, but also Mud Hairs and Sharp Teeth, squatting in separate clumps. No more Haida that he could catch at a glance—thank the Valar!—but at least four or five men in helmets and mail-coats.

He jerked to a halt and raised the mouthpiece of the horn to his mouth. He had to work his lips and spit because his mouth was so dry, and then he took a deep breath and blew, the fingers of his right hand moving across the three holes.

The sound that it gave was *brighter* than most trumpets made from the horns of beasts, higher and truer and with less of the deep braying note. Two long blasts, then three rising ones, and repeat. The echoes spread off through the forest, fading as they carried in every direction—mostly, he hoped, straight south to the Eryn Muir. The Eaters would most certainly know that call, though the Dúnedain changed the others now and then.

It was: *Enemy! Enemy! Enemy!*

Heads jerked around, yelps and snarls rose, metal blinked as blades and spearheads pointed towards him.

"*Lacho calad! Drego morn!*" he and his cousin shouted in unison, the ancient Dúnedain war-cry. "Flame Light! Flee Night!"

Some deep corner of his mind gave an actual giggle, and the temptation to shout *can't catch me you poopy-heads* was strong.

The men in mail turned and would have started running towards him if the Eaters hadn't thrown themselves in the way, yammering. That was notably altruistic of them, but it was probably simply reflex born of the long war: just chasing someone hell-for-leather was a good way to get ambushed. A squat but massive Cut-Nose led the effort, putting his hands against the mailed chests and pushing. Then he turned and snarled at the *yrch*, and instead dozens of bows were raised. All of them seemed to be aimed at Faramir . . . which was more or less true, if you included his cousin.

As the big *orch* moved to shove his archers into position there was the slightest hint of a limp to his movements. This was the one whose twisted track beside the creek had drawn his eye. His hand chopped towards the Rangers.

"Shoot!" Faramir shouted, and did; Malfind followed suit.

The shafts from the recurves arched out. Two hundred yards wasn't easy, but he could hit a man-sized target that far away about seven times in ten, if the air was still. Targets didn't dodge, though; these did, and he couldn't tell whether he'd hit anyone or not. It didn't really matter, since two bows weren't going to make much impression on that mob.

There have to be at least—he began to think.

Whrrt. Whrrrt. Whrrtt.

Arrows started going by.

—*at least fifty of them*, he completed.

Some of the shafts went *thock* into the tree he jumped behind, but not very hard. Others were falling short. The ski-limb bows weren't nearly as powerful as the weapons the Dúnedain crafters made, though even a minor wound now didn't bear thinking of.

He put a shaft to the string, dodged out again and shot, and there was a shriek of pain an instant later. The *yrch* were coming forward in short rushes, pausing to shoot betweentimes. They probably hadn't coordinated it, but the fact that there were three separate bands of them meant that they were covering each other . . . and once they got close, their bows would be quite deadly.

Then: *crack*.

A shaft transfixed an oak sapling not ten feet to his right, the end emerging in a shower of blond splinters through a trunk over three inches thick. It was long and made of bamboo, with a narrow pile-shaped point of tempered steel—designed to pierce armor—and fletchings of pheasant feathers, four of them rather than the three vanes common in Montival. The strangers from over-sea had gotten into the act, and there was nothing at all wrong with *their* bows.

A quick glance around the tree showed them starting forward with three men in the forefront holding up big strong-looking rectangular shields, with only their eyes and the peaked helmets showing behind them, crests of horsehair tossing from their tops. The second rank were the archers, though they also carried swords and wore the alien-looking armor of small plates held together with mail.

He grinned tautly, because he *also* saw wisps of smoke starting up from the great pile of split timber under the roof of the storage shed that stood on the other side of the clearing, near the firepits and the tables where feasts were held in summertime. The wisps turned to streamers in seconds, and yellow flame showed. Morfind had been at work, two arrows that nobody noticed and then away. It must have been tricky shooting to get them in under the eaves of the roof, unless she got very close.

When you turned the pin on a fire arrow, you aligned it with a groove inside the head. Then you shot, and the strike on impact drove the pin back and set a friction primer going, much like a match. That ignited the magnesium fuse, and *that* ignited the thermite packed inside the metal tube with a blaze of sputtering violence that was very hot indeed. At those temperatures steel would burn, much less the soft thin aluminum from salvaged beverage cans actually used. A bucket of water would just spread it faster. The Change hadn't changed *that* reaction at all.

Dúnedain used fire arrows for many purposes, though swailing was the most common, controlled wet-season burns to manage the vegetation in wild areas. Arrows could be precisely placed in spots hard to get to safely on foot. When you shot a couple into stacked dry timber, though, the result was dramatic.

"Noro lim, Malfind!" he called, and ran himself.

The danger was worse now, but he felt a curious sense of relief. Whatever happened, every Ranger in the area would see the pillar of smoke that was pulsing into the air. Gongs and horns would be sounding within seconds, bows would be strung and Rangers would assemble. And eventually the *yrch* and the foreigners and please the Valar, the terrifying *skaga* would all realize that their only hope was to get out of here as fast as they could.

More arrows went past him as he ran and dodged and hurdled obstacles; they hadn't gotten the message yet.

"Look behind you, you Shadow-sucking idiots!" Malfind screamed as he ran not far away, spear held ahead of him like a plow. "Smoke! Stop chasing us and run away!"

Maybe some of them were taking his advice, since the rain of arrows was less. One would do, of course, if it hit in the right place. A shaft banged painfully against the shield slung over Faramir's back, and he stumbled and cursed and recovered in a flailing scramble. He didn't see the shaft or pieces of it go pinwheeling past or hear it crack, so it had probably pierced the sheet metal and boiled leather and plywood. There was absolutely no way of telling whether six inches of it was pointing at his liver right now, ready to drive through his jerkin and its light mail lining if he fell the wrong way at speed. The only consolation was that they were almost certainly gaining on the pursuers, because they weren't in heavy armor and knew where they were going.

Correction. We're gaining on those foreigners who are in heavy armor.

He'd had only a brief long-distance glimpse, but it looked like little rectangular plates set into a knee-length mail coat; at least forty pounds, not counting shields and helmets and swords. That precisely matched the report of the equipment of the men who'd killed the High King.

The Eaters aren't wearing anything but loincloths or carrying anything but their weapons. On the other hand, at least we do know the path better than they do.

Another arrow hit the shield that covered his back from his neck to the base of his spine, and he swayed in mid-stride and recovered again. This one definitely penetrated; he could feel the outer, leather surface of his jerkin catching on the point a little with every long stride. The breath was burning in his lungs now and his pulse was loud in his own ears; he was young and strong, but he'd been walking and running and fighting all afternoon. The sun was low on his right hand when he could see it, but that wasn't often. The trees were higher now, and more and more were the king redwoods, ones that had been left to complete their natural cycle in a rare act of forbearance by the ancient world.

And that arrow had hit at the very bottom edge of his shield. Which gave him a chill even with sweat soaking his clothes and running in drops off his chin, because an inch lower would have gone right into his pelvis. But it also meant the foreigners with the powerful bows were farther behind. The yelping of the *yrch* was a little fainter too, though he didn't dare look over his shoulder.

After you with the ambush, foreign allies, he thought with flash of grim humor. *That's what they're saying. Or maybe it's a promise to eat their bodies afterwards.*

He wanted to get out of this as soon as he could, but he couldn't look back. He couldn't run at this pace all the way to Eryn Muir, either. And if he slowed down, the Eaters would send their best sprinters after him, forcing him back to all-out effort and breaking his wind, leaving him exhausted and helpless when the main band caught up. That was standard hunting technique.

He saw a streak to his left past some bushes, left and a bit ahead. For one throat-squeezing instant he thought it was a *yrch*, and then he recognized Morfind . . . or at least another Ranger, and there wasn't likely to be anyone else in this chase. And Morfind could run down deer; he'd seen her do it, and seen her outrun people with much longer legs over anything but a sprint course. About a hundred yards ahead she angled in to a two-hundred-foot giant with a body seven feet through at chest height.

It was good they were getting bigger; it meant they were closer to home. It also meant the view would open out, because ancient redwoods shaded out most undergrowth, and it would make it impossible to run fast, because they bombed the ground beneath them with a constant litter of branches and chunks of bark. Close to the Ranger station the falls were policed up because they had dozens of uses of which fuel was only one, and they needed the floor free of obstacles. Out here, they weren't.

Morfind looked over her shoulder as she did what looked like a dance-step with her hands at her waist at the base of the tree. She gave him a grin for an instant before she turned, leapt and ran *up* the trunk nearly as fast as she'd been dashing through the undergrowth, only the motion of her cloak visible at all. Before they passed her chosen redwood she was out of sight in the crown.

The dance had been unlatching and swinging out the climbing spurs on her elf-boots—you could do that with the toe of the opposite foot, with practice—and putting on her climbing gloves. You couldn't wear them all the time because the claws on the palms meant you couldn't carry anything else. Malfind gave a panting whoop of joy and relief as they passed the tree.

"Go, Sis!"

Faramir reached over his shoulder. Just beside the quiver was the haft of a short folding grapnel, and reeved through the loop at the end of the shaft was the end of a long rope of thin strong cord, knotted every yard. The blades of the grapnel were spring-loaded, rather like a fancy umbrella's ribs, though there were only three and they were short and stout.

He'd use the grapnel because redwood bark was up to a couple of feet thick, soft and dry and fibrous. That made it marvelous for everything from insulation to fishing floats, but it tore away far too easily for him to trust himself to a spur-and-claw climb like Morfind's, not at speed, not when he couldn't take the time to test each grip and foothold. She was lighter than he was; even so it had been odds-on a foot or hand would come loose fifty feet up, and big redwoods didn't have branches to grab until just below their tops. Trying to do the same would be insanely risky for him, and outright impossible for Malfind.

The tines of the grapnel came out with a sharp metallic *click*. Faramir began whirling the instrument on the end of its rope as he ran, paying out to increase the speed. Ahead a redwood had fallen in some storm well before he was born, possibly before the Change. The great trunk lay moldering, but the nutrients it had released and the water around it meant that it was thickly grown with moss and ferns and the shoots of larger vegetation clawing for the light the giant's fall had let penetrate. Beyond it was his goal, a living tree, but it had taken a scar from the same storm or perhaps a later fire. The opening in the bark had let fungus penetrate to the vulnerable sapwood, and a cavity grew. Eventually it might heal over, but right now there was a dark slit twenty feet up.

He leapt to the six-foot height of the log and cast with a looping overarm throw as soon as his feet planted solidly. The line paid out across the palm of his right hand, twisting behind the head of the grapnel like a coil of smoke. One of the tines of the instrument clunked against the lip of the scar and Faramir's throat clenched for the precious seconds already lost, but it spun into the hole and locked solidly in place when he slung his bow and gave it a two-handed tug.

"Clip and brace the line!" he called over his shoulder to Malfind as he ran towards the tree taking the rope in hand-over-hand to keep the tension on.

The other Ranger grabbed the end and snapped the fastener there to a loop on his belt. When Faramir reached the base Malfind was right behind him, and he knelt and braced the rope so that it didn't fall flat against the trunk of the tree either. Faramir leapt, caught the line by a knot twelve feet from the ground and went up it in a writhing scramble, arm-over-arm lift and driven by the quick inchworm thrust of his legs. It bit at his callused palms, but each knot provided a good lifting point to be clamped between his boots. Though the rope was strong he didn't want to test the set of the tines in wood against the combined weight of himself and his cousin and their gear. Having two men going up the rope would also make it sway enough that it would be slower than having each climb in succession.

He tumbled into the hollow and instantly turned, bracing a boot-sole against the grapnel to make sure it didn't tear free. Malfind weighed nearly thirty pounds more than he did to start with, and there was the spear besides.

"Go!" he said, tossing aside his cloak and shield and unlimbering his bow.

The little cavity had contained human bones when the Dúnedain came, apparently some luckless victim of the Change who'd climbed there and then died of injuries or sickness or thirst. The Rangers had buried them, though without much ceremony; even then after nearly four decades there had still been too many to do otherwise, especially the resistant skulls, and you found them in the most astonishing places. Then they'd smoothed the interior, and left a few essentials like sealed glass and metal containers of water and hardtack and raisins, a bucket and so forth, checked and renewed regularly. If he could just get Malfind up here, they'd be cramped but safe while the enemy ran for it. However long that took. Or until the gathering Dúnedain caught the Eaters.

He could hear the other Ranger wheezing as he climbed; the spear was over his back to free his hands, with the shaft thrust beneath the bandolier that held his quiver. Looking north Faramir could also see the thick column of black smoke rising from the woodshed at *Estolad Rhudaur*. It would be visible over half of Ithilien by now.

Just a moment more . . .

"Shit!"

A flicker of movement. He drew and shot, but half a dozen arrows came back; one thunked into the wood near the entrance to the hollow as he ducked back, the soot-darkened feathers brushing against his cheek. It would be like standing up against the bull's-eye in a little kid's target range. He stepped back into the opening, shot, ducked . . . he could see half a dozen Eaters and this time an arrow came right through the slit and chunked into the soft wood at the back of the little cave. He thought he'd hit one of the *yrch*, but that left far too many.

Aragorn son of Arathorn couldn't have *fought* his way out of this situation, not with an elf-lord thrown in.

Malfind gave a bitten-off cry and the tension came off the rope. Instants later there was a muffled thud below as he struck the ground.

"*Shit!*"

Faramir dropped his bow—he'd need his hands for this—stepped out of the crack, turned in the air and caught the line. That jerked him to a halt, and nearly jerked his arm out of its socket, but it stabilized him long enough to get the rope between his crossed ankles. He wasn't going to do his cousin any good with broken legs; he probably wasn't going to do much good anyway, but . . .

The knots bumped between his boots as he came down in a controlled fall, getting out of the way of arrows as fast as he could. One went into the redwood above his head with a muffled thump, but that was the closest. Malfind was down at the bottom of the rope with one right through his thigh. The point came out just above his knee, with the fletching pointing down on the other side. It was bleeding badly; he clutched it with his left hand and waved his knife with his right. It wobbled.

Faramir let go ten feet up and landed with a grunt at the impact that drove him into a crouch. As he steadied he'd already stripped the spear free of Malfind's harness; his cousin gave a hoarse cry of pain at the way it wrenched him around, but there wasn't time to be gentle. The *yrch* were charging, four of them with blades out. Behind them the big one, the Cut-Nose leader with the slight hitch in his stride, waved a double-bitted axe back the way he'd come and yelled in a thick gobbling dialect:

"Na! Ufukinrun, a' puzzis! Na, na, *ufukinrun!*"

The four rushing at the two Rangers ignored him, squealing in their eagerness. Something else curved through the air; it was Morfind, swinging down from somewhere near at the end of her own climbing line, cutting a long arc and doing what his folk called a *flâd 'lân.*

"Lacho calad! Drego morn!" rang out in a hawk-shriek from above.

One of the Eaters whipped his head back to look over his shoulder as she let go of the rope and landed in a crouch. That gave Faramir time to snatch up Malfind's shield and jerk the point of the spear up with the butt braced beneath the instep of his foot. One of the Eaters ran right on to it with a smack that vibrated all the way down the shaft and the Ranger's hand and boot. The broad point ripped his body from above the navel and came out his back, carving a palm-broad slice through several major organs and veins and arteries as it went. He looked down at the shaft, goggling, then shrieked and grabbed at it with both hands and collapsed backward.

Faramir was already whipping out his brush-sword as he let the spear go and bounced up. He blocked one blow with the shield, another with the sword, a flat cracking sound and an unmusical crash. Something else ripped along his ribs, hard enough to make him gasp, but the mail lining of the jerkin stopped the edge reaching for his guts. Morfind was dancing about another *orch* with a long knife in one hand and her tomahawk in the other. . . .

The Cut-Nose leader came bounding forward, screaming in rage—at his own followers, probably. He wasn't very tall but broad enough to look squat, with thick scarred arms and a network of white tissue on his face that lifted a corner of his mouth even when he wasn't shouting. Morfind spun and slashed at his leg; he hopped over it and cut with impossible speed for the heavy weapon he bore. She flew backward, a plume of blood lifting from her face like an arch of red feathers. The backswing came down and hit Faramir's borrowed shield so hard that it spun out of his hand with the frame cracked across and a section hanging loose. He tried to stab at the ridged belly of the *orch*, and this time something hit his helmet.

The ground hit him next. There was a sound like thunder through the earth. Blackness.

Are these the Halls? Faramir Kovalevsky thought.

That would be interesting.

I could talk with Hiril Astrid, *and maybe they'll let me do some sightseeing in Valinor before I move on to wherever it is Mortal Men go.*

Then he stifled a scream; mostly stifled it, and the rest came out as a dry croak. He *hurt* too much to be dead, unless his people were extremely wrong about the afterlife. Though it was very dark indeed.

His eyes fluttered open. There was a tube down his nose and throat; he coughed and choked as it was withdrawn.

Right. My eyes were closed. *That's why there wasn't any light.*

It wasn't dark, though it was after sunset and the soft yellow-blue glow of the lamp still pained his eyes. Faramir recognized where he was, as much by the cool, somehow bright scent as anything else. It was the infirmary at the Eryn Muir. Like most buildings and all dwellings in that station it was well up in one of the great trees, built in a circle round the trunk. His head hurt, with a throbbing that went in from his temples in time to his pulse. His neck hurt too, and his ribs.

There was nothing that *didn't* hurt; some parts just hurt *more*.

A hand reached gently under the back of his head and he whimpered. He hadn't been conscious of anyone else's presence until now, which showed how out of it he was. It was Ioreth, the senior Ranger medic here, a woman of about his mother's age with close-cut graying brown hair and a ready smile, though she was grave now.

"Here," she said, examining his pupils for an instant and then holding a cup to his lips. "You've been out for more than two days."

He drank a little, coughed—which hurt too—and then took some more. It was rainwater collected as it dripped through the boughs above and tasted faintly of them. Presumably water had been going down that tube, but his mouth and throat seemed to drink the water like dust in an ancient tomb.

It also seemed to start his mind up again. *Is there anything missing?* he thought, with rising panic. *Am I crippled? Is that why it hurts so bad?*

"You're all right, Man of the West," Ioreth said. "You had a concussion, and your neck was sprained, and there are contusions and cuts and bruises. You're very lucky there wasn't neurological damage."

Something in her expression suggested an unspoken codicil: *as far as I can tell. So far.*

"The others got there just in time, a mounted party. Most of the *yrch* got away, though."

He turned his head, very slowly and carefully. The bed to his left was empty, blankets tight and brown linen sheet neatly folded above. The one to his right was occupied. Most of Morfind's face was covered in bandages, but he recognized her anyway. Her mother Mary sat on the other side of the bed, holding her hand and talking softly. She and his mother Ritva had been identical twins, until Mary lost her left eye fighting a magus of the CUT on the Quest; the black eyepatch on its silk cord had been familiar all his life.

The single bright blue eye looked at him for an instant. He rolled his head back and looked up at the whitewashed beams and planks of the ceiling.

"Malfind?" he said; his throat felt a little more like working.

Ioreth shook her head. Faramir winced again when he heard a stool clatter on the planks beside his bed. A hand gripped his, long and hard and careful in its strength.

"Faramir."

He looked up into the beautiful, damaged face of his mother's sister. Wisps of sun-faded blond hair haloed it, too fair for the first gray threads to show.

"So sorry—" he began.

"Faramir, I know everything that happened. There was absolutely nothing more you could have done. Vairë weaves all threads."

Something relaxed a little in the back of his head, and that let the pain wash over him again. It wasn't that which made his eyes fill and slowly drip tears, though.

"*Ú-belin cuina* . . . I may not live while the slayer of my kinsman walks beneath the stars," he whispered.

Lips touched his forehead. "Ritva is coming, but you should sleep now," she said. "You're going to need all your strength. We all will."

Ioreth was back. A sting in his arm. Soft black washed over the world, life falling very slowly.

CHAPTER TEN

"T"hese are very handsome horses," Reiko said, smoothing a hand down her mount's neck.

"Hard on the arse as any," Egawa said, obviously deep in thought. "Majesty," he added hastily.

Reiko smiled slightly; she found she could do that naturally now, though the pain remained.

"I've heard the word before, General-san," she said dryly, reproof and forgiveness in one.

Poor Egawa. Now he has to treat his lord's daughter as his lord, and sometimes he slips while juggling the cups.

The pain was like a wound indeed, scabbing over very gradually, the scars themselves pulling unexpectedly on the inside when you moved. But she had been raised to control pain. Pain hurt, but that was no reason to let it affect your doing what was proper. You let the hurt *happen*, without concerning yourself too much with it, and trying to block it was paying attention. That was more difficult with a hurt to the soul, but the principle was the same.

The Japanese party were all mounted on animals that had been waiting at the train stop; a wagon bore what baggage they had brought on the headlong trip northward. By their standards the horses were once again sleek muscular giants, all at the least a quarter again taller than the biggest she recalled ever having seen at home. She shuddered at what it must cost to feed them, having seen herself now that they ate grain that might have gone to humans, as well as grass and hay.

Japan had enough food now in years of good harvest, enough that nobody actually starved—not to death, at least—even in poor ones, but there was never much surplus and what there was had to be jealously guarded as a reserve against bad times or losses from enemy attack. Food was life and thrift was a necessity. Even at a feast for the wealthy and powerful there was more emphasis on quality and arrangement than lavish quantity.

The mounts—they were called *destriers*—ridden by their two-score armored escorts were larger still, though long-legged and deep-chested and surprisingly graceful for animals that weighed over a half-ton apiece, and wore armor themselves—articulated plates riveted to soft padded leather backing, protecting head and neck, shoulders and chest. Egawa had examined them with an attention that might as well have had a microscope involved, and she was interested herself; how far and how fast could even these great horses carry the weight of that protection and an armored rider?

But arrows are the weakness of cavalry, neh? Horses are such large targets. The armor will help.

Fast-moving horsemen were the standard response to a *jinnikukaburi* raid, but you had to be cautious lest you run into an ambush or a hail of archery. These looked like they could ride down any raider crew ever born. Though . . .

I doubt these are very agile, but with those long legs they might well work up a fair speed given a little while to run, and maintain it long enough for a charge. Certainly they came down on the jinnikukaburi *like a hammer on an egg in our last fight, though I only saw that at a distance.*

Her memories were blurred by the shock of her father's death, but she *did* remember afterwards seeing the bodies of men lying skewered like pieces of grilled octopus on a splinter of bamboo, the lances driven right through both sides of the tough Korean plate-and-mail shirts by the terrible impact. Or bodies trampled into half-recognizable bags of flesh inside their armor, or skulls crushed through the helmet by the serrated war-hammers the riders also carried.

There was a rattle and ring along with the massive hollow *clock* of their shod hooves on the smooth pounded crushed rock of the roadway as they paced along at a fast walk. This trip wouldn't take long at all, from the description. The men-at-arms in their black harness rode with their visors up and their shields across their backs, blazoned identically with a *kamon* in the form of a flame-wreathed lidless eye, crimson and yellow on black. Twelve-foot lances with bowl-shaped metal hand-guards just ahead of the grip were their primary weapons, colorful pennants fluttering below the bright blades.

There was a fair bit of traffic on the road with them, riders on horseback, carts and wagons and carriages, bicycles and pedestrians, now and then a Christian monk or priest or nun in their long robes pacing along or praying at the little roadside shrines with their crucifixes and images of saints or the blue-robed Virgin.

Reiko felt a little irritation at the naked stares she and her followers attracted.

Though I must admit, if as many Montivallans were riding through Sado-ga-shima, with our samurai escorting them, the peasants would stare and point as well. The shi would have better manners, I hope.

Their party didn't slow for any of it; a single scream from a trumpet and a harsh bark of *Make way! Way, in the Crown's name!* and everyone pulled to the side of the road, bowing to a degree that varied with their rank as the riders went by. That much was homelike in general outline, if not the details.

She could smell dust ground out of the pavement by steel-shod hooves and steel-rimmed wheels but little of it rose, because the season of rains was just tapering off. Low mountains rose in the west, forested and green-blue, just on the edge of vision though rising a little with every pace; higher ones stood even farther behind them to the east and fell away as gradually, including peaks with snow on them and one tiny white cone as perfect as Fuji, called Mt. Hood.

This is a beautiful country, even just the bones of it, she thought. *I wish I could see more of it, but I have no time to spare.*

Here in the valley the land was for the most part flat or only gently rolling; the road swerved several times to keep the gradient low and avoid hills or ridges covered in oaks, firs, maples and trees she did not recognize. But those were exceptions, as were the odd clumps of trees and bushes growing over the site of a pre-Change building whose foundations were too tough to be removed without excessive trouble. The occasional creek was always followed by a strip of forest on both banks, fenced against livestock with poles and rails, or quickset hedges of hawthorn starred with pink-and-white flowers in this season.

They hadn't seen any fields abandoned since the Change today, though those had been common enough farther south in the Willamette; now one cultivated stretch succeeded another as they did on Sado's central plain, but for far longer. Beech trees stood beside the highway beyond the verge-side ditches, planted in neatly spaced staggered rows on either side; the road was lavishly wide for one through arable land, thirty feet including the shoulders. The trees had leaves of a striking purplish-bronze color, sometimes meeting overhead and turning the long road into a tunnel of shade and flickering brightness. From the countryside to north and south of the roadway came a smell intensely green and fresh, a scent of vigorous growth and damp soil. It was stronger than the familiar odor of horse and leather, and occasionally livened with the pungent scents of manure or a deep flowery sweetness.

What she saw was wholly different from the rural parts of her own country beyond the most basic elements of forested hill and river and cleared cultivated soil in areas that were not too steep, but she recognized the slightly metallic green with hints of blue, wheat or barley rippling around knee-high, and some of the other crops—potatoes and turnips, flax and beets and more, though it was odd not to see any rice or millet or soybeans. Where the worked soil showed it was a very dark brown, deep and stoneless, moist but not wet, looking as rich as the sweet adzuki bean paste filling in the buns on a street-vendor's cart.

No terraces here, either, she thought.

Parts of Sado were staircases of green up the hillsides.

They don't need to use every inch, you can see they farm carefully but it's all so . . . lavish. Lucky! If we could just get free of the jinnikukaburi *long enough to really re-settle the main islands we might have more good land than we needed too.*

What caught her eye was the sheer size, fields that were regular squares that must cover hundreds of acres, each bordered by hedges and trees. That was bizarrely huge compared to the paddies of Japanese farms. By cocking her head and looking closely she could see that though each big field was planted to the same sort of crop they were subdivided by ankle-high ridges within into a patchwork of rectangular strips each of seven or so acres.

Which is still larger than the whole of a good-sized peasant's farm back home.

Peasants were at work among the crops, quite a few though never as densely as she was used to, cultivating with some very ingenious-looking horse-drawn machines as well as long-handled hoes or just stooping and pulling up weeds. They stopped to remove familiar-looking conical straw hats and bow deeply as the mounted party passed, with the hats held in their hands; Heuradys d'Ath waved back at them with her riding crop, and a few of them replied with waves of their hands and called her name.

The men among the landworkers wore a long belted tunic that came to their knees and loose trousers beneath, of a cloth that mixed linen and wool, with wood-and-leather shoes on their feet. Women wore the same tunic over another that reached to the ankles, and the older ones had kerchiefs around their heads beneath the hats. Some of the children were barefoot, and most wore only the short tunic. From what she could see all the peasants were as roughened by work and weather as any country-folk, but big and well-fed as well.

The strips that divided the fields showed very slight differences in the precise texture of what grew, like a larger blanket composed of pieces that didn't exactly match. About two of every five of the large fields held a mixture of grass and clover, thick with crimson blossom now in late spring that turned them into sheets of an almost lurid red.

Sometimes the bees working among them were numerous enough to make the horses shy a little as they crossed the road bearing pollen and nectar back to their hives. Cattle with hides of black or creamy yellow or red bodies and white faces grazed the fields, or sheep looking comically naked after their shearing in others, and now and then they saw sounders of pigs or herds of horses. Calves and lambs and colts born that spring played, kicking up their heels and butting at the udders of their dams, a sight that made her smile a little.

The sweet smell became overpowering when the field to their left was being mown for hay. Reiko looked closely; that wasn't much of a part of the farming she knew, since the limited number of oxen and horses her people kept were fed from verges and roadsides or with the by-products of crops meant for humans, while pigs ate scraps or foraged in the woods and chickens pecked for bugs and the odd spilled grain.

Here a staggered row of a half-dozen machines each pulled by two horses mowed broad swathes and left the cut grass behind to the accompaniment of a whirring, clacking sound. More horses pulled complex devices of wire and wood that raked the hay into swathes and left it to dry.

"This is wealth," she said quietly to Koyama. "They can afford to use nearly half of their land to grow food for animals! No wonder they use so many horse-powered machines."

He nodded agreement as he looked around at the countryside. "The more so as the Montivallans are not showing us this to impress us, I think. This estate is just the most convenient place to put us, nothing extraordinary."

"Wealth and *power*, Majesty," Egawa added. "I can see why they have much cavalry, too. Good country for it, difficult to find terrain features to anchor a flank, and lots of fodder."

Farther away in the same field workers with long-tined forks on six-foot handles were pitching the dried hay cut on earlier days onto carts with high latticework sides, these pulled by oxen.

Egawa grunted again. "And now we know how they can bind their bowels with all that meat they eat."

Koyama snorted, and Reiko ignored the byplay as she studied the scene. You could see the smaller strips were there too amid the hay once it was cut, and she thought she could see two groups—families, she supposed, they were each of men and women and children—arguing with each other as they pitched the fodder onto their respective carts. The dispute grew more heated, then stopped abruptly as the train of mounted warriors went by.

Heuradys d'Ath rode off the road and into the field, spoke briefly to the peasants, shaking the riding crop like an admonishing finger. There were more bows, but when she turned her horse back again one of the peasant men raised his hand to the other group with the fist clenched and middle finger extended, and got a clod of soil kicked back at him by a man who then spat on the dirt and ground his clog on it as if he wished it were an enemy's face.

Heuradys dropped back to ride beside the Japanese leaders when she returned to the road. Reiko was glad of it, though she missed Órlaith. Partly because of the simple ease of conversation, and partly because . . .

Because we share a loss and a burden no others do. We may become friends, I think, or as close as those in ruling families may be.

But Órlaith's retainer was able.

And someone to respect.

She also seemed to be someone very close to the Crown Princess; not a lover, Reiko judged, despite their sharing a tent and the obvious affection, but a confidant-friend-right-hand, truly a *hatamoto*, one who stood at the base of the lord's banner.

I have nobody that close, she thought a little sadly. *I have many loyal retainers, but few friends at all.*

"Your Majesty," Heuradys said politely, bowing in the saddle.

"Heuradys-*gozen*," she said. "Lady Heuradys . . . those strips in the big fields . . . they are what, please?"

The Montivallan noblewoman frowned for a moment as she bowed again, obviously thinking how to put the answer in straightforward terms to strangers. Reiko made an inaudible cluck of frustration to herself; she could handle spoken English much better now, enough to carry on most of the time without a sweat of concentration breaking out on her brow, but it was still *work*. Not like real conversation where the words did what you wanted without thought. And she was continually checked because she didn't know the common unspoken things everyone took for granted.

"These are the Five Great Fields of the manor," the noblewoman said.

She was making her speech slow and distinct without being too obvious about it; her manners were exquisite, though not exactly the same as those of a Japanese.

"The strips are each part of the peasant holdings; one strip of land in each of the Five Great Fields, as well as their toft in the village—"

"Toft?" Reiko said, frowning; she was *sure* she hadn't run across that word.

"Their home and garden and sheds. And with the holding go rights in the meadow, the common waste and the woodland—grazing for so many beasts, so many cords of firewood, the right to cut timber to repair houses and barns. They pay a part of their crops and of the yield on their animals . . . usually a quarter . . . to the lord, and provide a worker for the lord's demesne two or three days a week. Though the lord feeds the ones who work, on those days."

She pointed with her riding whip, using it as a conversational aid the way Reiko would have her fan.

"Those fields over there beyond that row of poplars are demesne land—you understand, Your Majesty, Montinore is where I was born, and my brothers and my younger sister; it is the home manor of the estate, right next to the castle. But all manors in the Association lands work in roughly the same way, that was established at the very beginning by the first Lord Protector, according to his plans. He was a scholar of the ancient ways, and in those terrible days it was a way that worked, so it was easy to spread far and fast. My lord my father's original estate, the Barony of Forest Grove, is just north of here."

"Demesne is lord's land . . . how different from peasant, tenant?"

"All that the demesne produces is the lord's; but a peasant's land and its product is his as long as he meets his dues, and he can pass the holding on to his descendants. On this particular manor a lot of the demesne is in vineyards; Montinore wine was famous even before the Change. And there are other dues, payments on inheritance and at marriage, milling and grape-press fees, cartage of firewood and building timber from the lord's forests, and service in the household."

Reiko glanced at her advisors. Ishikawa was looking at a tall slender windmill pumping water into troughs for the livestock in a field; it seemed to need no human attendance, and the water flowed when the animals pressed little flat levers with their noses. He was tracing the mechanism with his eyes, his lips moving silently as he analyzed; he was a good ship commander, but at least as much interested in things as people. Her folk used wind and water power a good deal too. That specific trick might be worth copying to save labor, especially in a fortress where many horses were stabled, though otherwise it was probably not worth the trouble and materials with the far smaller herds of her land.

Koyama and Egawa were both listening to Heuradys with close attention—land tenure was *important*, and just as important to a lord as to a peasant—and Koyama in particular seemed to be understanding a fair amount of the English, though neither spoke as fluently as she yet.

"Why sose . . . *those* . . . peasants we passed, they yell each other and shake fist?" Reiko asked.

Heuradys chuckled. "Your Majesty, one family accused the neighbors of taking a forkful of hay from *their* strip."

"That happens much?"

"Every once in a while, but those are the Johnsons and the Kowalskis. The bailiff should never have let them cart their hay on the same day but they probably leaned on him so they could watch each other."

"Families have quarrel? No, s . . . *those* families have *a* quarrel?"

"They've been at it as long as I can remember," she said, and rolled her eyes in exasperation. "And even they aren't sure how it started, though they'll talk about it for hours if you let them. They've been at it as long as my *mothers* can remember. A forkful of hay, a sheaf of wheat, a handful of potatoes thrown into the wrong basket—their kids steal apples from each other's trees and throw rocks at each other's dogs and the youngsters get into fights around the wine-barrel at festivals. We've tried fines, we've tried the stocks, by the Dog of Egypt, we had the heads of household flogged when they drew knives—that time was when they accused each other of plowing the boundary furrow wrong and shaving a sliver of land from each other's strips, which is serious business. And when we had the surveyor in to check it against the cadastral tenure map of the manor it turned out they'd *both* done it, so we fined them again and they howled louder than they had at the flogging. I think what made them really angry was that they'd each thought they'd put one over on the other!"

Reiko translated it; her councilors laughed, and she could see that several of her guardsmen were smiling behind their impassive faces. The details differed, but there wasn't a village where that sort of thing didn't happen now and then. Living at close quarters could mean, often meant, closeness. Unfortunately it also meant that if you quarreled with someone, you were stuck with the results for the rest of your life. That was what manners were for, in large part; to smooth over life's frictions among people who had to live closely with each other whether they liked it or not.

Heuradys shook her head. "But when we offered to move them to different manors, they wouldn't. I think they need the quarrel to give their lives savor, like salt on boiled potatoes."

"What does the lord owe, Heuradys-*gozen?*" Koyama asked, and only had to repeat it once before he was understood.

"To the tenants, protection and order, settlement of disputes—well, we try—fair judgment in court if things get that far, assistance in bad times or family emergencies, care for orphans and the sick, maintenance of things like drains and buildings and roads and bridges, the church and schools and clinic. And a sort of . . . mmm, general duty of help, what we call *good lordship*. Helping an able youngster get an apprenticeship, for instance, that would be good lordship."

Reiko had to translate that last, since *good lordship* wasn't a combination of words familiar from the pre-Change English they'd studied, but her retainers nodded. The *concept* was certainly one they knew, or something close to it.

Heuradys went on: "To one's overlord, or the Crown if you're a tenant-in-chief like us, the one who holds the fief owes the mesne tithes—a share of the revenue—and upkeep of the public works; we repair this road, for example. And of course service in war. Equipping and training your me-nie . . . your fighting tail, your armed retainers. Lancers, infantry spear-men, crossbowmen, to numbers specified in your indenture of vassalage. A baron or higher lord will have vassal knights in turn, either paid or enfeoffed with land of their own; we have three manors we keep in hand on this barony besides this one, and a dozen subinfeudated to our vassal knights. There's a peasant militia, but that's only called out in real emer-gencies. Associate vassals"—she touched the jeweled dagger on her belt—"can be called whenever there's need for as long as the Crown re-quires."

"Sank . . . *Th*ank you, Heuradys-*gozen*," Reiko said; the *th* sound was the hardest of all, and she reminded herself to press the tip of the tongue to the back of the front teeth to make it.

When the Montivallan noble had bowed again and legged her horse forward to talk to the commander of the escort, Koyama nodded thoughtfully.

"That sounds sensible, Majesty," he said, after making sure he'd caught the terms.

"Not precisely as we do things, but not totally different," Egawa said. "Perfectly workable way to organize their armies, if they take care about things . . . which it looks as if they do. At least here. This Montival is a very big place."

"And this Protectorate is only part of it, though itself quite large, and we have had only a glancing look at anything else. I was right that Mon-tival is a federation of sub-kingdoms with quite different customs," Koyama said.

"I wonder what they're guarding *against*?" Egawa said thoughtfully, looking at their escort; those included mounted crossbowmen as well, in lighter gear. "This looks like peaceful country. You can see nothing's been raided or fought over for quite a while. The peasants aren't carrying any weapons except knives on their belts, and those are tools. Most of the travelers we've passed have no more than knives and staffs, except for the *bushi*, and hardly any of them are riding in armor, they're just wearing their swords because they wear swords. If all this armor is precaution against us . . . should I be flattered?"

"They let us come near their Crown Princess armed, including armed with distance weapons like bows," Reiko said. "I think this escort is a gesture of respect."

Egawa was still having some trouble following English, much less speaking it, and was feeling a bit suspicious and resentful because of the sense that things were going on around him he could not understand. Of course, an Imperial Guard commander was *supposed* to be suspicious, and it must grate on him terribly that his charge was essentially helpless in the hands of foreigners, however polite.

"In this part of Montival, it is the mark of *shi*, *gentlefolk* is the English word, or Associate, those with the jeweled daggers, to ride horseback with their swords at their side," she went on.

She touched the hilt of her katana. Wearing the two swords was a mark of rank in the homeland as well, an old custom revived not long after the Change. She went on:

"And great lords ride with their warriors beneath their banner. The escort is to give us further consequence, I think."

Egawa's chuckle was harsh. "Not so very different from us, then, Majesty."

"And these are the Protector's Guard—the High Queen's own household men. Notice how all bow and give them passage."

"*Hai, Heika,*" he said with a pleased half-growl.

She nodded to herself at the sound of satisfaction in his voice. Most of it would be for her; a slight to his ruler would make him far angrier than one to himself. Likewise, a gesture of respect to her would impress him more. Unconsciously, that would also affect his analysis and advice.

And while I do not doubt their courtesy is genuine, I also think I have met several people here quite clever enough to see that themselves. Gestures are important—how else do we make ourselves known to each other, and what is speech itself but a set of complex gestures? On the other hand, when considering gestures . . . remember that even if you intend to kill a man, it costs nothing to be polite.

Koyama was more thoughtful.

"This is very different from anything that I expected," he said. "Here, especially. That Corvallis place, it was a dem-oc-ra-cy, more or less, from what I caught—some sort of representative assembly sent that delegation to Princess Órlaith. In the name of the *kokumin*—the People—and the Faculty Senate."

"She was much more polite to them than I would have been," Reiko said. "Those speeches!"

"*Hai*, Majesty, but her patience is itself significant. The McClintocks have their assembly to decide great issues under the Clan chief's direction, and they say the Mackenzies do as well. But this here . . . this is very strange."

"Why?" she asked. "We also have returned to many of the ancestral customs, Grand Steward. Or something fairly close to them. If I remember correctly, those ancestors of the Americans who came from Europe lived much like what we see here, once. My history tutors remarked on it, and said that the resemblance to Japan perhaps explained why we alone in Asia stood up to the Westerners successfully when they arrived. They beat the Chinese like dogs and burned their Emperor's palace, but they soon learned better than to try to bully *us* even though they had more deadly weapons."

"And soon ours were as good, or better," Egawa said.

"Yes, Majesty, Egawa-san, true as far as it goes. But our ancestral customs were much closer to us in time. After all, it was only two long life-spans from Meiji to the Change. So I would have thought them more . . . more accessible, as it were. More a part of the way our parents and grandparents thought even without knowing it, and so of what was natural for them to fall back on in the terrible times. *Americans* never lived so, not on this continent, whatever their more remote ancestors might have done many, many centuries ago. Something truly strange happened here—in this part of Montival in particular."

It wasn't very far from where the train had stopped to the *han* estate of the local *daimyo* . . .

No, manor of the baron, use their words, they are less likely to deceive with false assumptions, Reiko reminded herself.

"It is disturbing. But not the most disturbing of many disturbing things, Majesty," Koyama went on.

"I am disturbed myself," she admitted after a moment. "Principally by . . . There is such a great deal of this Montival place. We knew that old America was very large and populous, but I was not . . . prepared as well as I could have wished. Seeing a map and reading numbers is not altogether the same thing as traveling through real lands."

The trip up the Willamette valley had taken days, even traveling rapidly on the railroad—a wonder in itself of which Ishikawa Goru and Koyama and others of her party with engineering training had taken many notes. None of the islands of refuge were large enough to make it worthwhile, but when Honshu and the other great territories were reoccupied it would be time to consider it.

The valley began where the mountains ended, and there they had passed the ruins of Eugene. That was nothing strange in itself; she had seen the dead cities on the main islands of her own country, suburbs overgrown with renascent forest and the huge scorched, rusting, canted remains of the old world's buildings blanketing mile after mile at their centers.

But dangerous, and besides that haunted by the mad and savage offspring of those who survived the collapse by preying on their fellows.

They were few and lived on rabbits and birds and pine kernels now, but they were still ready to butcher and eat a salvager they caught alone. Her father's soldiers rescued their children where they could, those young enough to forget, but for the rest . . . the sword was the only true mercy.

We don't like to remember it, but they are just as Japanese as we in blood, Reiko thought; it was something her father had told her to keep in mind, if privately. *To become* jinnikukaburi, *one does not need to have Korean grandparents. Misfortune will do.*

No, what had been daunting about Eugene was the *scale* of the salvage work going on—long trains of railcars coming out, hundreds of tons stockpiled under unwalled sheds, from gearwork to be incorporated into modern machinery down to huge buckets of broken window fragments to serve the furnaces of glassblowers, and bundled rebar with lumps of concrete still clinging to it, stock for the anvils of blacksmiths. With officials to tax the process and the only soldiers needed a small bored garrison who enforced the officials' will and kept order between rival salvage groups. Eugene was dead, yes, but not the haunt of terror except in memory and dream. She did not think the workers there rested easy or would stay long by choice and they had to be careful where they put their feet or what might fall on their heads, but they were not in constant risk of attack.

"Do you notice that we haven't seen a single automobile or truck wreck on the roads for hundreds of miles?" Egawa said, echoing the direction of her thought. "Since we left the mountains, and there weren't many there. All hauled off to break up for useful parts long ago."

They nodded, thinking of the rusting hulks that still sprawled by the millions on the roads of most of Japan. Traveling up the valley of the Willamette and crossing it several times by bridge to let each important community say they had seen their High King's remains on their journey had been even stranger than Eugene. Corvallis was a *living* city, ten times larger within its wall than any of the castle-towns in modern Japan.

Fifty thousand people in one spot, in our world of today! And Portland and Boise are said to be even larger!

Corvallis was surrounded by manufacturing villages to take advantage of power from streams coming down from the mountains, as well as farms on the flats. A large part of the raw materials coming out of Eugene evidently went there, and the charcoal smoke of the forges and smelters and the ring of hammers and the hum of spinning machines had been noticeable.

And even with the vacant spots in this Willamette, gone back to swamp or forest, so much farmed land! she thought. *The first true wealth of any nation, tilled ground and the men and women who tend it, and their children. From that all else springs.*

The forms had varied—scattered farms of astounding individual size in the rural hinterland of Corvallis, each one with its house and barns in the center. Then clumped villages (called strategic hamlets, for some reason) in the area north of it inhabited by a group whose name seemed to be the Killers of Bears, and cottages and farms like strips strung along the sides of the roads in the area under the protection of an order of Christian warrior monks. Fortified villages behind great log palisades, surrounded by smaller hedged fields, among the kilted Mackenzies. Villages again here, huddled around castles and manors, a weird combination of the familiar and alien to her.

And all that only a fraction of Montival, she thought. *I hear of entire other domains, the United States of Boise and New Deseret and the Nakamtu and the San Luis and the Lakota Tunwan, weeks of travel away, and all part of the same kingdom. There is no inhabited area at home that cannot be crossed in a single day. Now the maps begin to seem real, and it is frightening.*

Koyama and Egawa both looked frustrated; they didn't have time to linger even if their hosts had allowed it, but they'd also wanted to spend time on their slightly different investigations.

"I was impressed by that regiment that lined the tracks in Corvallis," Egawa said. "Perhaps that is why she was patient with the speechmakers."

They had stood close by the passing train that held their High King's ashes and his heir, immobile as neatly ranked statues in a light rain, their weapons reversed and colors lowered. She had been close enough to see through the streaked window that many wept as they remained in their motionless brace. A group of middle-aged veterans, many with missing limbs or hideous scars, had grouped together under a unit banner that had obviously been sewn back together from tatters, bearing a slogan: *We Stood!*

Egawa had saluted, when he heard the story of how they'd earned it. His voice was musing as he went on:

"Those long pikes . . . the crossbow companies . . . and the field artillery. Not much use against small groups of *jinnikukaburi* raiding from single ships, but in a massed action . . . and the Bearkiller cavalry, also."

"And the production of food and goods that makes it possible, such as we see around us now," Koyama said. "I confess to bitter envy, Majesty. If we had such numbers, such power, we could crush the *jinnikukaburi* in a year or two at most, not fight all our lives to hold them off while trying to clear fields in the intervals between raids."

"And if it were not all six thousand miles away from Dai-Nippon, Lord Grand Steward," Egawa reminded them sardonically.

Reiko quoted an old saying: "*Fukoku kyōhei*. Rich country, strong army, neh? We are few and poor compared to these Montivallans now, but Japan has suffered disasters before, and by hard work and discipline has recovered. This part of old America has recovered so, from the Change and the wars that followed it, though much altered and diminished. That shows that they may be strong friends. We need such."

Then, firmly: "But someday we too will be a great and numerous and prosperous people again, strong and respected, a nation whose friendship is worth cultivating and whose anger is to be feared."

"Yes, Majesty," Egawa said. With a thin smile: "Good to have powerful friends. Even better to *be* a powerful friend, neh?"

"*Hai*, General Egawa, truly it is as you say. Until then, we will do as we must and as we can."

A thought formed, and she proceeded slowly: "And . . . even so we may be very fortunate right now. These people had a war against *jinnikukaburi* of their own. Not cannibals, but otherwise just as wicked, inspired by similar evil *akuma*. Princess Órlaith and I spoke a little of it."

"Yes, and they won," Egawa said rather sourly; he had spent his life in a perpetual holding action, like a farmer walking on the treadles of a pump against a rising flood, with decisive victory a wistful dream. "That's *very* fortunate, Majesty. For them."

Koyama looked at her with real respect. "No, I think I see what the Majesty means. What if they had *lost*, General Egawa? What if they had lost? What would that have meant for us—and for Japan—if we had come here and found a *jinnikukaburi* kingdom with the size and strength we have seen, ready to make alliance *against* us and *with* the *bakachon*?"

Egawa's face blanched slightly, though only one who knew him well would be aware of how much that meant.

"*Chikuso!*" he blurted. "Damn! That would have been a total disaster! Enemies on both sides of us, ready to grind us into paste like soybeans for miso!"

He fell silent as Heuradys d'Ath dropped back beside them.

"We should be at Montinore village and manor within a few minutes. Welcome to my family's fief, Your Majesty, you and your retainers. Our house is your house; enter and use all as you would your own."

Reiko inclined her head slightly. "Thank you, Heuradys-*gozen*. Lady Heuradys, I should say?"

"I thought *-sama* meant that?"

"*-sama* means that if . . ." Reiko frowned in thought. "If said from low person to high? It says also of the ranks of the one speaking and the one spoken of? *-gozen*, means *Lady* if from other person of high rank. *-dono*, also that, but it is . . . out of fashion. You do not have this difference?"

"Not really, or at least not formally. *Lady* is sort of ambiguous. *Sir* and the name is the title for a knight, but most Associate knights are men . . . a knight's wife or daughters would be called *Lady* or *my Lady*, or Lady and the first name, by almost anyone except close friends and family. And a noblewoman's daughters are called Lady unless you're using a specific title; since my mothers are a Countess and a Baroness I would be called *Lady Heuradys*. Or sometimes Lady Heuradys d'Ath, but that would only be in an official document or at court. That would be my title by birth, but in my own right I'm just a household knight and an Associate. It's a little complicated in my case because I was adopted by a woman, so I don't lose the honorifics due because my father is a Count."

"So this is your mother the Baroness' land?" Egawa asked, and Reiko translated it.

"Oh, we've been on her fief for an hour now. This estate stretches from the railroad to the crest of those mountains ahead, we call them the Coast Range," Heuradys answered cheerfully. "It was established early, long before the High Kingdom came to be, as Crown demesne . . . that is, land held directly by the Lord Protector of the Portland Protective Association. Then it was granted as a fief . . . *ban*, is that the word? . . . to my adoptive mother, Baroness Tiphaine d'Ath, about a decade after the Change, and added to afterwards, for services to the Crown."

Egawa blinked as he worked out the amount; an ability to make quick estimates of area and distance was an essential skill for a warrior. That was more land than any individual family in Japan possessed by a considerable margin, even counting lords with colonizing grants on the main islands that were still mostly empty. Whereas most of this seemed to be tilled land or carefully managed forest.

"A family of very wealthy and powerful *daimyo*, then, Majesty," he said calmly to Reiko. "Perhaps no insult is meant by not immediately lodging you in their equivalent of the Imperial Palace."

"They have their reasons," Reiko said. "If the circumstances were reversed, we would want time for ceremony and consultation among ourselves as well."

And besides, our Imperial Palace these days is just the old Shogunate provincial governor's house on Sado-ga-shima, which was a museum for a while, with a few modest extensions. We will be great again, my faithful bushi, but that time is not yet. You and I will not live to see it ourselves, but we will build the foundations and our descendants will raise the towers upon them.

She went on: "And we need a breathing space too, General Egawa. There is absolutely no point in worrying about home until we can do something about it. Focus, neh?"

They crossed a small river flanked by a strip of thick forest, on a bridge whose timbers boomed beneath the hooves. The road rose again; the mountains of the Coast Range were much closer now, and the ground grew a little hilly. They went past a mill with an overshot wheel twenty feet high and entered a largish village of several hundred people, with streets paved in patched and remelted asphalt bordered with trees. Cottages lined them behind fences, each at the head of a long strip of land ending in farm buildings, with a stretch of vegetable garden between; they were of different sizes and construction, with half-timbering and brick most common. There was a broad paved central square faced with a Christian church and what looked like other public buildings—she recognized the bathhouse and a tavern, and the workshops of blacksmiths and carpenters, potters and leatherworkers were obvious, just as they would have been in a castle-town at home.

People lined the streets, including many children; they waved little flags on sticks, the Crowned Mountain and Sword of Montival alternating with the Hinomaru of her Empire of *Dai Nippon*—the white flag with

the red sun-disk in its center symbolizing her ancestress the Sun Goddess. Reiko felt her eyes prickling a little at the sight.

"Sa . . . *Thank* you very much," she said to Lady Heuradys.

"Your Majesty, I'm as surprised as you. That would be my mother,
Lady Delia."

"She is . . . Countess, yes?"

"Well . . . ah, yes, as wife of my lord my father, Lord Rigobert, Count
Campscapell. But she, mmm, lives here as Châtelaine to my adoptive
mother Baroness d'Ath. And on Barony Harfang, our other estate, for part
of the year."

"Châtelaine is?"

"Sort of a manager—one who directs the estate officials, sees to the
household and to hospitality; usually a lord's wife, or a mother or other
female relative if he's a widower or single."

Reiko nodded; that was very much what a lord's wife did in Japan, an
okugatasama. Plus defending the home, when the lord was away.

"My lady my mother has been Baroness d'Ath's Châtelaine for a long
time. Thirty-six years. My eldest brother Lioncel and my younger sister
Yolande bear the name of de Stafford; I and my brother Diomede are
adoptive children of the Baroness as well."

"*Ah so desu ka*," Reiko said politely; that was all plain enough, without
being rudely blunt. "It is . . . very nice . . . gesture, you say? The flags."

"She has a . . . very nice sense of manners. And she's quick. The news
would only have gotten here a few days ago."

Reiko looked up as they emerged from a stretch of orchard. Off to their
right a castle stood on a hill. It was very unlike any in the homeland, but quite
similar to others she had seen here and to pictures of their European originals
she knew from books; tall crenellated walls, square machicolated towers and
a dojon-keep. Banners flew from the towers, and as they watched a heliograph began to snap bright flashes towards the east. The construction was
quite different from its ancient models, and much stronger. But it looked very
much like them, stark as a mailed fist raised against the sky.

"Castle Ath," Heuradys said. "My lord Egawa, we'll be quartering
most of your men there."

He began to stir a little restlessly, and Reiko made a sharp gesture with her fan. "Two men at a time will do for a ceremonial guard, in a quiet country place," she said to him. "All thirty-two could not protect me from treachery, if our hosts intended it. See to the rotations when we arrive, General."

"Majesty," he said to her, bowing; her tone had not been overly harsh, but it brooked no opposition.

Then to Heuradys: "Conclete, sis Castle?" he asked. "Wiss steel leinfolcement?"

"Yes," Lady Heuradys said. "Covered in buff stucco, as you see."

The rolling hills here were blanketed in green rows of grapevines, each with a flowering rosebush planted at its head, or with orchards. Reiko found the taste of wine rather odd compared to the beer and sake she was used to, though she could see it would grow pleasant with familiarity and she could already tell the difference between good and bad. The road wound again, and they caught glimpses of white buildings on a nearer hill through the trees. Then the road broadened, and there was a wall—not a fortification but a marker and barrier to stray beasts, stone posts joined by curling screens of black wrought iron. Two taller stone posts on either side of the road were each topped by a yard-high statue of an owl; between them stretched a metal arch, comprised of Latin letters that spelled out: *Montinore*.

The lancers and crossbowmen of their escort split and lined the road on either side with smooth precision, facing inward. Even the horses scarcely moved. Servants in tabards with the d'Ath arms—which Reiko found pleasingly austere, after the busy complexities of many of the Association blazons—pushed the iron gates open. Heuradys reined aside and bowed, moving an arm in a gesture of welcome.

As Reiko and her retainers rode forward a command barked out, and the long lances dipped as one until the points nearly touched the ground. They held as she passed, and then each came back upright—a long smooth undulating ripple like the spines on the back of a fish bristling. Trumpets sounded, a long brassy note; as soon as the last of the Japanese had passed the gate the commander raised his sword before his face in salute, another order was called, and the column of guardsmen reversed and trotted away in the same easy unison.

"As I said," Reiko said to her own guard officer. "To give us consequence."

"Yes, Majesty. Very prettily done, too."

The gardens beyond were a bit of a shock, totally unlike the spare, restrained Nihon style; there were sweeping green lawns like velvet, great trees of a dozen varieties scattered thinly or standing in clumps, brilliant flowerbanks beside winding pathways of white stone or frothing down terraced slopes, pergolas covered in an extravagance of purple wisteria, statues and benches and a tall fountain like an ascending series of shells where water leapt skyward. As the path rose towards the buildings they could glimpse a small lake beyond, and a hill westward covered in tall firs that seemed to mark the edge of the mountain forests.

"Gaudy," Koyama said behind her, with a bit of a wince as he looked about at the gardens. "And chaotic."

"Perhaps not altogether," Egawa said equally softly, surprising her a little. "It's not how I would do it, Koyama-san, but there is structure here, I think. I cannot see it yet—too unfamiliar. The flesh hides the bones too thoroughly."

"Like a message written in a different script. Hmmm. Perhaps. It will reward contemplation."

The buildings were in the Western style, familiar enough from surviving examples she'd seen in Japan, the central one with tall pillars, others looking as if they had been added from time to time in a different manner—windows topped with pointed arches rather than square lintels, for starters. They dismounted, and grooms came forward to take the horses. A small guard of spearmen and crossbowmen saluted and stood to attention; the servants knelt.

Reiko blinked. The tall slender woman of about sixty dressed in a darker version of Heuradys' costume was certainly the Baroness d'Ath. When their eyes met for an instant she saw with a shock that they were of an inhuman color stranger even than blue, a pale gray like ice on a winter's day. A slight chill ran through her, and she felt Egawa stiffen a little behind her, with an unconscious grunt of appraisal as his hand tightened on the hilt of his katana.

The middle-aged woman beside her would be Lady Delia, dark-haired and with those odd blue eyes by now half-familiar . . . and *she* was in a kimono. So was the barely-adult woman beside her who had a strong family resemblance; Lady Heuradys had mentioned a younger sister.

Delia's kimono was a formal *iro-tomesode* of a rather antique style, a deep crimson, with golden dragons below the obi and the full five *kamon*; her daughter's was pale sky-blue above with a pattern of a silver phoenix below. Baroness d'Ath used the flourishing gesture with the hat and a bow over an extended leg, respectful-looking even to one unfamiliar with the system of etiquette from which it sprang.

Lady Delia and her youngest managed a well-executed deep formal bow in the true Nihon style, only a little stiff and as old-fashioned as the kimono, but obviously something over which they had taken a good deal of care. So was the careful, and just-understandable pronunciation of:

"Heika! Youkoso irasshai mashita."

Reiko felt a melting of a tension she had not been fully conscious of until that moment.

CHAPTER ELEVEN

"The kimono was a nice touch, Mom," Heuradys said much later that night, stretching and leaning back in her chair.

"I was worried I'd do some sort of faux pas with it and ruin the effect, but it came off, I think. Of course, Yolande absolutely loved it. She's still slim enough that the padding isn't *too* bad. Kimonos can be absolutely lovely, but they really don't suit women who have breasts . . . or hips . . . *or* a waist. In fact, they're best for women built like the pillars holding up the porch."

The lamp left a puddle of light around the upper table in the Great Hall of the manor; they were the last ones in it, except for the tail-end of the clean-up squad waiting patiently by the doors.

"Reiko said it was perfect, in a very old-fashioned way," Heuradys reflected. "And that you carried it off in the same style. I get the impression that they've simplified things a bit there."

Montinore manor-house had started as a mansion, built in the later nineteenth century as a mining magnate's country place and becoming the center of a large-scale vineyard in the generation before the Change. Over the years Baroness d'Ath, or more accurately her Châtelaine once she had talked Tiphaine out of living in the castle, had added refinements.

The most essential was a true Hall, a necessity for a large household where everyone from highest to lowest usually ate their main meal in the same room and you had to do anything from holding the formal Court Baron to giving a masque with a big crowd after a tournament.

Other bits and pieces had been tacked on, including the royal guest suite necessary for a baron whose offices, first as Grand Constable and then High Marshal, drew monarchic visits. Reiko was now installed there, though they'd had to scare up some domestics for her since she hadn't arrived with a staff of ladies-in-waiting and maidservants.

Montinore didn't have quite the smoothly organized spaces of St. Athena manor-house on Barony Harfang out east, which had been purpose-built after the Prophet's War with modern methods for modern purposes, but Heuradys found the very irregularity charming. And of course rich with memories of her childhood, including the old bedroom she'd sleep in tonight. The windows were still open, letting in a breath of cool night air, and the scent of clipped grass and flowers. The dim light glimmered on the tile patterns of the floor and the bright hangings.

"It was all very mysterious," Delia said; she looked at a pastry filled with honeyed hazelnuts, unconsciously patted her waist and put her fork down with a sigh. "Getting your message, I mean, Heuradys darling."

From what people said and from the portraits she'd been a raving beauty, back when she first caught the eye of the newly ennobled and newly enfeoffed Tiphaine d'Ath and vice versa, though she'd been only a miller's daughter on this estate then and younger than Heuradys was now.

About Yolande's age, which is sort of strange when you think about it.

Class distinctions and relations had been more fluid in the Association lands in those days, though also often more brutal. The later promotion to Associate status and pro-forma marriage to Lord Rigobert de Stafford had been engineered by Sandra Arminger, Tiphaine's patron, as her protégé rose and wanted to share that with her girlfriend. Sandra had discovered that Delia's looks simply complemented a valuable talent for social skills, which she promptly had trained and put to work. And in any case she'd always been open-handed to her followers; and if you were loyal, she'd back you through thick and thin. Though if you *weren't* loyal . . .

Brrr. She died old, in bed, of natural causes, and without much pain. From what I've heard not one of those who crossed her that way managed any of those. She didn't kill people with her own hands and she didn't do it for kicks, but you ended up just as dead. Usually soon, though not as soon as you wanted by that point. That's why they called her the Spider.

Heuradys thought her lady mother was still quite beautiful in her fifties, in a comfortable . . .

. . . Matronly fashion, that's it, she thought fondly. *Matronly. And still the most brilliant facilitator and social manager I know. Go, Mom!*

Heuradys went on aloud: "I'm not absolutely sure—I don't have a magic sword that gives me special linguistic powers, and they're mostly the most stoic, low-affect people you've ever met, at least around outsiders. But I'm *pretty* sure they were feeling touchy as cats on the way here, even if Reiko is a sensible sort for a monarch. Very sensible for a girl who's just lost her father—and that hit her as hard as it did Orrey, I'd swear to that, too. But they're proud people, very, and they knew they were being stuck here like a document put in a file for future reference. The pride's more understated than your average Associate's bravado and less obviously bloody-minded, but it's there."

"You're right," Tiphaine said. *"Serious people."*

The three Associates nodded, knowing exactly what the term meant. Those who lived by their pride, and died by it.

"They appreciated you laying on a Japanese formal dinner, I could tell, the gesture as much as the meal. They know we've got the whip hand, they're feeling very isolated here, and showing respect really helps. How did you manage it, though?" Heuradys asked. "I like tempura as well as the next and sake is fine for a change, but I didn't know you could *get* some of that stuff out here in deepest rural-dom? I mean, edible seaweed? Wasabi?"

"Deepest?" Tiphaine said. "Nonsense. Ath is practically a suburb of Portland these days. Barony Harfang, now, *that's* rural. They'd have had to settle for roast mutton on the bone there."

"I have my methods, Watson," Delia said, smiling. "Actually I raided the best Japanese restaurant in the palace district in Portland; the grandfather used to work for Sandra and set up on his own after she died. She left him a bequest for it, in fact, money and the property. I just descended on them with a couple of fast carriages and lifted everything from the chef on down complete with materials and cookware, soothing objections with streams of gold."

The smile died. "Nobody's eating out much there right now anyway, what with Rudi dying and the Court in mourning. Goddess, it felt like the bottom fell out of the world. I could . . . *feel* something was wrong. Something terrible, something fearful. And then the news . . . I couldn't *breathe* for a while, I swear."

Heuradys nodded. Her mother wasn't just of the Old Faith; she was a High Priestess of its Wiccan branch, albeit a very discreet one; her mother had been one before her.

In the Lord Protector's day, if she hadn't been discreet, and had Sandra's protection to boot, that could have gotten her burned at the stake. We don't do that anymore, thank the Gods, but it was a real risk. I think that's one reason she still feels . . . obliged . . . to Sandra, despite everything.

Tiphaine nodded somberly and sipped at her brandy, glacial eyes hooded. Back in those days she'd been an actual atheist, though of course she'd learned better since. She spoke musingly:

"I have the spiritual sensitivity of mashed turnip, but I felt winded too when the dispatch came in. I never expected to outlive him. Completely aside from being older."

"He was so *alive*," Delia said, and Heuradys found herself nodding; she'd never met a man as . . .

Vivid, she thought.

"I know what you mean, sweetie, but three inches of edged metal in the wrong place does for the best of us," Tiphaine said. "It's . . . I expected to be the one who got it from a random arrow in some skirmish in the butt-end of nowhere, or—"

They all shared a look of agreement; if the High King hadn't appointed one Tiphaine d'Ath as Marshal of the High King's hosts when she retired as Grand Constable, and hence out of bounds for personal challenges under the Great Charter, she *wouldn't* have outlived him and they all knew it. Too many old feuds simmered from the days when she'd been Sandra Arminger's best and most feared enforcer-assassin-duelist, and she'd barely survived her last duel—in cold weather she still limped a little from the leg wound she'd taken in it.

More would have come as the sharks scented blood, or revenge, or just an opportunity for the fame of the one who killed Lady Death; after a certain point experience didn't compensate for a well-trained younger warrior's speed and endurance, especially in a dueling circle.

"Rudi . . . damn, it's like yesterday I brought him to Castle Ath during the Protector's War. Ten years old, alone among enemies and totally fearless . . ."

Tiphaine raised her glass, and they all sipped the brandy in tribute.

"Reiko *is* interesting, apart from being the only Empress I'm likely ever to have as a house-guest," Delia said. Impishly: "Cute, too. If I were her age and single . . ."

"Mom!"

"I'm middle-aged and monogamous, Herry, not dead or *blind*. That face . . . and that serious, tragic air . . . you want to pick her up and cuddle her like a kitten to see if she'll purr."

"*Mom!*"

Suddenly Tiphaine chuckled softly. Heuradys stared in mild astonishment; you could go for weeks without much more than a small smile from her adoptive mother. For a generation her title had been pronounced as *Lady Death* by some very hard men, and for good reasons. She swirled the brandy in her snifter and spoke.

"That scar-faced one built like a barrel is formidable," she said. "Egawa?"

"Egawa Noboru, the Imperial Guard commander, yes," Heuradys agreed. "I've seen him working out. One of those heavy quick men, like a solid block of catapult springs."

"Rare, dangerous," Tiphaine agreed. "Different gear and style, of course. Which brings back some very old memories."

Baffled, Heuradys raised a brow. You never got anything by pushing at Auntie Tiph, but sometimes just waiting receptively would work.

They sat comfortably in the half-light for a moment, and Tiphaine said meditatively, "Memories from before the Change . . . I'm showing my age . . . when I was this huge teenage nerd. Nerd or geek, I forget the distinction, but it was one or the other."

Heuradys blinked. Teenage was a term she understood though these days people said *youth* or *maiden*, but nerd was only vaguely familiar, something she couldn't quite pin down. And huge? It was *impossible* to imagine the woman who'd made her way to the top of the Association's warrior ranks despite the rampant plate-armored machismo, not to mention militant Catholicism—and that back when it was *even harder* than it was now—as being in anything but an absolute perfection of fitness and deadly skill. Even in her sixties she could make you sweat in a practice bout; some of the speed and flexibility was gone and the strength and endurance were less, but the form and ability to anticipate were utterly perfect.

Delia was gurgling her infectious laugh. "Oh, Goddess, darling, you *are* acting your age again. How many times must I tell you, it's not funny if you have to explain it? Humor was never your strong point."

"Applying stabby, slashy pointy things to people who needed it was my strong point, but I've outgrown that."

Heuradys asked plaintively: "OK, parents are supposed to bewilder children. Huge . . . geek? I thought you were an athlete . . . a gymnast? Headed for the Olympics in Greece?"

"Wherever they were held, actually, they weren't always in Greece," Tiphaine said. "Yes. Though I'd already gotten too tall to be an Olympic gymnast by the time I was thirteen, they were all pixies. I was starting to think of going for track and field instead, the pentathlon."

Heuradys nodded. She and Tiphaine had almost identical height and build, though they weren't related by blood at all. People who'd seen Lady Death at her peak said the young knight was as fast, too, which was enormously flattering. Though . . . there was also a reason there were fourteen little notches in the black bone of her adoptive mother's sword-hilt, each filled with a bit of silver wire hammered smooth once and then polished every day.

We don't do that sort of thing as often anymore, either . . .

"But I was *also* a huge nerd. Or geek. It's a term describing character and interests, not physique. You know people who can't shut up about . . . oh, their falcons? It's falcons morning, noon and night, jesses for breakfast and hoods at luncheon and gloves for dinner with fewmets for dessert? They're falconry geeks. Or nerds."

"You were a falconer?"

"Think general, not specific. Norman and Sandra were *giant* nerds . . . giant truly evil nerds, it turned out when they got a real country and real people to play with . . ."

"Darling!" Delia said reprovingly. "I won't say anything about Norman, but Sandra was very good to us. She was only . . . well, *sort* of evil."

"Oh, I was pretty evil back then too, sweetie. But nerds they were, being in the Society all their lives when other people grew up and moved on. I was much younger and just blossoming into full-blown nerd-hood when . . . well."

The young knight could see the older woman take pity on her. "All right, let's put it this way. There were questions that nerds discussed obsessively, far into the night. Sort of like this."

"Like arguing whether Harris Hawks are too easy to train to be real falconry? Oh, Lady of the Shield, I've heard *that* one! Futility incarnate, but Corbus here"—she named the estate's chief falconer—"can thrash it over all day if you let him."

"Exactly. Though I basically agree with him on that. But *this* night I've finally seen that it's actually possible to *answer* one of those questions. One that tormented Society people as they talked in circles."

Delia sighed; she'd been a small child at the Change, and didn't remember it at all beyond occasional nightmares. "What is it, darling, this unanswerable question which can be answered now?"

"Sweetie, it's this: *Knights versus Samurai.*"

She laughed aloud at their incomprehension, one dry quiet peal.

"Well, I'm very glad *you're* amused," Delia sniffed. "Now I've got to go and take this outfit off. No sense in waking Melisende, you don't need a tirewoman for a kimono the way you do for a cote-hardie."

"Oh, I'll help," Tiphaine said.

Then she turned her head towards Heuradys, and gave one considering nod of approval that spoke pride more plainly than the words:

"Good night, infant. You did well. And may you live in interesting times; we've had ours, thank you very much."

They left with their arms around each other's waists and Delia chuckling again as Tiphaine grumbled about the awkwardness of the big complex knot that held the *obi* sash at the rear. Heuradys sighed a little herself, and poured another brandy. It was good to be home with the family for a while, and she had interesting work ahead. . . .

But I'm worried about Orrey. How are things going at Todenangst?

CHAPTER TWELVE

The thirst was the worst part of it. Her head throbbed with pain, and the feel of her own tongue swelling was like continually being on the verge of choking. Dazzle hid the greenery ahead as heat shimmered off the baked off-white ground. She couldn't even taste the alkali on her lips anymore, but it still stung like fire in their cracks.

Ahead of her Reiko stumbled and caught herself on the hilt of her sheathed sword, bowing over the hilt as if it were a cane. Her breath came in sobbing rasps, though her face was lost in intensely black shadow beneath the straw bowl-hat.

Órlaith looked behind her, to make sure nobody had fallen out. When she turned again she had to blink and squint to make sure this wasn't another of the mirages. Those towers, and the greenery that surrounded them—

"Hnnnn!"

Órlaith came awake, gasping, and made her hand relax on the hilt of the dagger beneath her pillow—a sheathed one, of course, nobody in their right mind slept around razor-edged naked steel.

The fragments of the dream faded away as she grasped at them; exhaustion, a terror that caught the breath in your throat and squeezed like an armored gauntlet. And thirst, and a dry deadly heat not like anything she'd felt in the waking world. And beyond the shimmering sand, a dragon . . .

"Anwyn's hounds, that's the third night in a fookin' row!"

She scrabbled for the glass of cold herb tea by her bedside, half wishing it was a brandy-and-soda and still gulping it with huge relief. Sweat cooled on her flanks and she pressed the glass against her forehead for a moment. She'd had a full eight hours but she didn't feel fully *rested*. Mourning with your family was work as exhausting as a dawn-to-dusk day spent pitching sheaves onto a wagon—something she'd done more than once, on visits down in the Mackenzie dùthchas, where there was little rank and everyone did the needful in harvest-time.

"Bad enough without nightmares on top of it."

She poured more from the Bohemian glass decanter and looked at the clock next to the nightlight as she drank, suddenly conscious of a full bladder. It was five in the morning, before she'd planned to get up but not all that much, and not really worth going back to sleep since the sun would be rising soon and like most people she rose with the dawn unless something very unusual happened. Instead she touched the Sword of the Lady where it rested in a sandalwood rack beside the bed—whether magic or not, doing that always made her feel a little clearer-headed—then rose and threw off her night-robe. She preferred a short one anyway, pretty much like a tunic, since the longer variety always got tangled up. And some people were so obsessed by style they wore *lace* on theirs.

Heuradys had been known to do that, saying style was *worth* some sacrifices, particularly when she wasn't wearing it to bed alone and only had to keep it on until the gentleman in question got the full effect and reached for the laces. But then, she enjoyed wearing the full cote-hardie, too, which Órlaith merely put up with when she had to, and even danced well in one. Considering that you actually had to be sewn into some of the more elaborate Court versions, that was *dedication*.

Thinking of it and her friend cheered Órlaith, and the dream receded further.

A cat raised its head from the foot of her bed, a blue-eyed beast with silky white fur and a pushed-in face. It meowed with the petulance of someone whose sleep has been needlessly interrupted, but at least it hadn't decided to fight her for the pillow tonight or drape itself over her face while she slept. These had been her Nonni Sandra's rooms, high in the Silver Tower, and the Lady Regent and later Queen Mother always had a clutch of the creatures around. Her granddaughter had heard her say more than once with her infectious chuckle that you couldn't come up with a really satisfactory evil plot without a Persian cat in your arms.

And the cream of the jest, which I was too young then to appreciate, was that she actually did come up with more than one truly evil scheme in her day . . . while stroking the Persian cat she held in her arms. Also she genuinely doted on the beasties, and they her. Though I never saw one dare to claw the furniture.

The three surviving ones were getting old and creaky, since it had been more than seven years since Sandra Arminger died and they hadn't been kittens then, but Órlaith had never had the heart to exile them from what they probably thought of as their beloved home, or possibly their ancestral ranch. Even more than humans, cats rooted themselves in the familiar. If you looked at it from their perspective the mob of them had more right to this place than she did, having been there longer and much more consistently.

Several of them had gone looking for Sandra with moans of distress in the days after she'd been taken from her deathbed—this great oval bed she'd just woken in, though that had never given her nightmares before. At least they had according to the servant in charge of feeding them and cleaning their boxes. Órlaith wasn't sure whether or not that was simply the servant cunningly defending her adored charges. The woman in question was over seventy, had held the same post since the castle was built, and Órlaith was fairly sure she'd been quite mad since the Change, though reasonably functional.

And the irony of that is that I don't particularly like cats, except for kittens. I prefer dogs, and to be sure I miss Macmac sore, but Nonni's ghost would haunt me if I let a dog in here.

The cat landed on the ground with a thump and a slight feline grunt—

whoever started that story about the silence of cats hadn't been around them when they weren't *trying* to be quiet—yawned, stretched and padded off to have a drink of cool pure water, or cream, or nibble at the salmon and chicken waiting in their little porcelain bowls, or the small pots of rooted grass or fresh catnip, or track down a really satisfactory patch of sunlight to nap in without inconvenient princesses rudely thrashing about. Órlaith had thought more than once that few humans—save perhaps a Count's spoiled favorite daughter—had lives as easy.

The main rooms were a series of interconnected spaces linked by pointed-arch doorways in the Association's style—what the books called Venetian Gothic—walled and floored in pale marbles that mixed white and gray and very light green. The ceilings were mostly groin-vaulted carved plaster in motifs of vines and flowers or sometimes simple abstract tracery. The furniture was similarly pale, spindly and delicate, though the tapestries were colorful enough, and the rugs.

Órlaith hadn't had the décor altered much despite her own more robust tastes, except to send some of the artwork to the gallery in the City Palace in Portland that was opened to the public on the innumerable Catholic feast days. Even the slight scent of lavender and patchouli and wax was still as she remembered it from her grandmother's day. It wasn't as if she had to live here all the time, and for now and then it was a pleasure.

Almost as much as power, Sandra had loved beautiful things, and her searchers had scoured abandoned mansions and museums and galleries throughout the western half of the continent from before the end of the first Change Year to her final illness, fighting their way in and out where they had to. She'd patronized the Protectorate's own makers lavishly too. Some had been given away to nobles or institutions she favored, some simply stored where they were safe from weather and decay, and the very best went here.

Walls and niches and plinths still held many of the results; a tall Soong-dynasty Chinese goblet of green nephrite with handles carved in the shape of dragons, a many-armed goddess of ivory dancing creation and destruction on a lotus blossom, a Renaissance missal open to a page with a saint's face shining in gold and indigo, a painting by a Victorian Englishman named Leighton that might have been a portrait of Heuradys' mother with a peacock feather fan in her hand, but wasn't, a row of glittering Fabergé eggs . . .

The bronze statue of an athlete crowning himself with laurel had—probably—been done by Lysippus of Sicyon, Alexander the Great's court sculptor. It was basically intact save for the feet, but the carefully patched hole made by a crossbow bolt was much more recent, product of a murder attempt by the magus-assassins of the Church Universal and Triumphant in the year she was born.

And apparently they never stop trying, she thought grimly. *All you can do is delay things.*

Workshops in Portland had supplied the tapestries that showed lords and ladies mounted on unicorns and hippogryphs hawking in a forest carpeted in asphodels, miniature dragons on their wrists, and the lively woodcarving in golden bird's-eye maple of a plainsman on a galloping horse, his Stetson flying off as he turned to bend his short recurve bow and shoot backward over the animal's rump. The libraries occupied several large rooms all on their own, though of course there were far larger ones in other parts of the palace-fortress, and the immense archives.

Órlaith padded naked into the bathing suite, where Sandra had *really* let herself go; the most restrained element was the big tub of polished white granite carved into an abstract seashell. According to Todenangst legend, passed down from one servitor to another, the first time she'd used it she'd slipped below the hot scented foam and then cried when she emerged:

"At last I can start living like a human being! And screw you, Nero, you piker!"

Órlaith contented herself with a simple shower, or as simple as you could have in an enclosure of cast glass etched with designs of willows and wildfowl with hot water spurting from half a dozen nozzles, tied back her hair, threw on a fluffy white robe and walked out onto one of the fan-shaped balconies. Todenangst was fortress and palace both, and this high—the Silver Tower soared hundreds of feet into the air, and had the almost unthinkable luxury of a functioning elevator—defense could take second place. The balcony was several hundred square feet, with a balustrade of carved marble and the inner three-quarters roofed by a lattice of wrought-bronze rods grown with vines; foot-long cream clusters of Shiro Noda wisteria blossoms hung beneath it, against a background of bronze-green leaves and gold-pink rêve d'or roses in full musky-sweet splendor, dropping their scent through the cool air as dew pearled the flowers. A few petals lay on the tile. She sat and quelled her mind as they'd taught her in Chenrezi Monastery, focusing on a rose-petal and imagining it turning slowly in a pool of absolutely calm water.

Dawn was just breaking, painting the snowpeaks of the Cascades to the east pink and tinting the cone of Mt. Hood. She sat and watched it as the light spread over the great castle; drums and trumpets marked a change of watch, and an orca-shaped observation balloon rose with a smooth rush from the Onyx Tower on the other side of the keep, its tethering cable making a long pure threadlike curve. As the rim of the sun cleared the horizon she stood; on impulse she took the Sword of the Lady across her palms as she lifted her arms and chanted the Greeting softly. Alone and in a high place was always best for her when she made that rite; it made her feel as if a cool wind had blown right through her, a wind of light. The Sword felt *alive* as she did. Nothing dramatic, but . . . there.

Her brother John came with the servants bringing breakfast shortly afterwards. She sprang up and embraced him; he hugged back hard. He was nineteen and still an inch short of her five-eleven, so he probably never would overtake her, but well-built and getting very strong, and the unfortunate spots were gone. His coloring took more after their mother's side of the family, medium brown hair still worn in a squire's bowl cut and eyes on the greenish side of hazel, and square-chinned good looks which older people said favored Norman Arminger. Normally his face had a lazy good nature to it that she more than suspected was a mask he wore. Now it was stark enough. He hadn't been as close to their father as she had—there *had* been some head-butting with the two of them—but he'd been getting over that, and they were close enough.

"Thank you, Dame Emilota," Órlaith said. "And thank you too, Claremonde, Douceline."

Dame Emilota oversaw the two girls carrying the trays; she was a middle-aged woman in a white wimple and green day-kirtle and a black mourning armband, an Associate lady-in-waiting originally from the High Queen's household and transferred to Órlaith's here when she moved into the old Queen Mother's quarters. She was always extremely good at her job, in a way that managed to be irritating as well much of the time. Órlaith had never been quite sure if her mother just didn't notice that part or if it was a very subtle joke.

"Now you two just eat yourselves a good breakfast," she said, beaming blue-eyed benevolence.

Just as if we were both still ten, Órlaith thought with resignation, as Emilota went on:

"Don't your Highnesses go neglecting yourselves because you're stricken."

"We won't, Dame Emilota," John said dutifully.

"It looks delicious, Dame Emilota," Órlaith added.

"Grief or no, you have to keep your strength up," she said, blithely ignoring them both. "So you eat, now!"

John winked to one of the serving-girls as she bent to put down her tray, provoking a fit of shocked giggles stifled with an effort that nearly made her drop her burden.

"Riding dress today, please," Órlaith said. "Breeks, not a habit. Something plain and dark. Just lay it out."

Emilota sighed—she truly came alive when Órlaith dressed for festival and ceremony—curtsied and left, trailing the maids; after a considerable tussle, the Crown Princess had managed to convince her that she really preferred to dress herself unless it was something like a cote-hardie. *That* absolutely required skilled assistance, just as much as plate armor did.

"Mom's still in bed," John said as he poured coffee for them both.

It was expensive, but not impossibly so anymore. Her father had disapproved of *that* sort of ostentation. Órlaith added cream and honey to hers, frowning in worry; her mother had been very glad to have her here, and Órlaith had felt an overwhelming relief when she saw the familiar face, but they'd found little to say and you could only hug and cry so long.

I really am an adult, she thought sadly—she could remember when she'd been wildly eager for that to happen. *I know mother can't make it all better. And on the whole, I wish I didn't know it. I can see why housecats enjoy being sort of like kittens all their lives. Of course, they're not cursed with a sense of duty or knowledge of their own mortality . . .*

It wasn't like her mother to simply lie abed in sheer misery, either, no matter how great that misery was. Her last pregnancy had gone wrong, and she'd come back from that with grim fortitude, not least by refusing to miss a single day's work that she was physically capable of. High Queen and Lady Protector Mathilda Arminger Mackenzie was a woman of strong will and, usually, very disciplined habits.

"Give her time," John said. "Vuissance and Faolán are with her and that'll help, and she's been spending a lot of time with Chancellor . . . no, *Father* Ignatius. He's wearing his spiritual-counselor hat, and he's good at it—he's kind, but he doesn't cut you any slack to wallow either. I think the memorial Mass will help too, they've been making arrangements for that. Also . . . did you know she's expecting?"

"No, I didn't!" Órlaith blurted.

She was obscurely shocked both at the fact and that her mother hadn't informed her. Of course, she'd been away—her mother might not have been certain before the Westrian tour began. Her father would have been, the Sword let its bearer see things like that where the Royal kin were concerned, but he'd told her he didn't speak of what it told him to anyone else unless there was some strong need. And since then other things had preoccupied them both.

"Well, she's only forty-six and healthy," John observed. "And . . ."

She nodded. Their parents had been reasonably decorous—very much so, by the Clan Mackenzie standards her father had grown up with—but you could tell that side of their bond was still very much present along with the bone-deep comradeship and the sheer comfort that radiated when they were together.

All acts of love and pleasure were pleasing to the Goddess, but it was still obscurely embarrassing thinking about your parents in that context.

Mother-of-All, be gentle to her who wore Your seeming to me and walked in Your power, however she names You. It must be like having a foot and a hand amputated, only inside. Worse for her than for me. I lost my father, and it hurts, oh how it hurts, but people do outlive their parents and that's what parents wish. That is the way the Powers made us. She lost the companion of all her life—they were anamchara when they were ten years old, even though their families were at war then, long before there was any question of marriage. All their lives after that they were friends, and when the time came lovers, and comrades-in-arms and parents and working partners in all the wonderful things they did. I can't imagine what it must be like to have that cut off after so long, only that it's worse than anything I've ever felt.

Her brother's hand tightened on the edge of the table.

"She's kicking herself—beating herself bloody inside, I'm sure of it— because she didn't go along on that trip with you and Father, and of course that was the reason, she suspected it even a month ago and didn't want to risk another miscarriage by spending weeks in the saddle. Damn, if I'd only gotten off my useless butt and been there instead of that troubadours' convention—"

"Don't you start beating yourself up either. What would you have done that I couldn't?" Órlaith said bluntly. "I *was* there, Johnnie, and it was just . . . too quick. If *he* wasn't fast enough—"

He sighed. They'd both seen their father slash flies out of the air in practice sessions in the *salle d'armes.* Órlaith went on:

"You think I haven't played it over and over in my head, thinking what I *might* have done, or he *might* have done? That knife was headed for *me.* I think it would have gone right into my eye. I'm *certain* it would have, and I couldn't have stopped it, I didn't see it coming in time. He swung me back, that's why he didn't have enough time to shield himself, that and the old wound to his right arm. Herry snapped her shield up in front of me, but that's her duty and she was too far away to do it for him, anyway."

Her brother sighed again and nodded, turning up his hands. Like hers they had thick sword calluses, but he'd never been quite her match in the *salle d'armes;* he was stronger now, but just a hair slower.

"I'd rather be in my schoon than yours right now," he admitted gently. "But do you think he'd make *that* decision differently, even knowing what it meant and with a thousand times to reconsider? And father usually made the right decisions, especially when he had to do it fast and dirty like that."

She nodded. Her brother had always been good at seeing what people felt. He also looked a little more haggard than was right even now.

"Not sleeping?" she asked.

John shrugged. "Not sleeping *well*, no."

He was in full Court garb, though the tight hose weren't parti-colored and the fabrics were all plain and none brighter than the indigo blue of his houppelande and there were no little golden bells on the upturned toes of his schoon and there *was* a mourning band on his left arm. The turn-out was immaculate as always, but he didn't seem to be as . . . *smooth* as usual.

"Bad dreams," he said.

She felt a chill, a prickle up her spine and arms the way you did when the moaning, coughing grunt of a tiger came from a swamp and the reeds stirred against the wind. He went on:

"Well, *odd* dreams, really. Usually I just have the common sort, you know, I'm playing a lute and suddenly realize all the strings are out of tune, or I'm in the *salle* and realize my breeks have fallen down and the audience are all nuns? These have been . . . different."

"Oh?" she said, very carefully. "Different how?"

"Nonsense, really. I'm floating in seawater, only it's *warm*."

They knew that was theoretically possible, but you were well-advised not to go swimming in the Pacific anywhere on Montival's inhabited shores without a wetsuit—a cold current hugged the shore, bringing richly abundant life to the sea but making falling into it a real risk of death by core-chilling.

"And then there's this really old man with a white beard and weird clothes shouting something I can't understand, but in the dream it seems really important. And there's a boat with skulls all along the gunwales. And storms and shouting and . . . just nonsense, really, however real it feels at the time. I've been reading too much Howard and Fraser."

"Possibly," she said, feeling the chill settle deep in her stomach, as if she'd eaten snow in winter. "Been bothering you a lot?"

"Just the last three nights, like going to the same play three times in a row. But . . . louder each time. Though I may have had it earlier and not remembered."

A jolt went through her. *That wasn't anything like my dream. Still, the dreams of the Royal kin . . . are not those of ordinary folk. Sometimes they're not, at least.*

Then she took a long breath, returning to what could be dealt with in the light of common day.

"OK, Mom's out of it for a little while, though when the baby comes that'll help. I'm not sure seeing me did more good than harm."

"Hey, she loves you too, Orrey! You're her first."

"Yes, she does love me, very much—I never doubted that, even when we were fighting about religion."

He made a slight grimace, for which she didn't blame him. Back when she was thirteen—and he eleven, old enough to remember it—she'd suddenly decided that she was of the Old Faith after wavering for years between the different beliefs of her parents. That had been just before Nonni Sandra's funeral mass, on the very day of it in fact. In retrospect she admitted to herself suddenly refusing to take communion at her mother's own mother's funeral was a typical thirteen-year-old's act of offensively, grossly inconsiderate narcissism. Especially since the Old Faith allowed for its followers occasionally taking part in other rites. It didn't make the same sort of ferociously exclusive claims that the Religions of the Book did.

At that age you were still rebelling against the notion that you weren't the center of the universe, or at least had the star role in the great drama of life. Their mother hadn't reacted well. A coldly furious Arminger was not something to be taken lightly. Still, that was years ago now—most of a decade—and it helped that John had chosen their mother's Catholic faith, along with her sister Vuissance.

And that I made a deservedly humble apology after I came back from that trip to Stath Ingolf. Which was no fun, but I felt better afterwards about myself. When you do something that wrong, some groveling helps all around. You can't really say sorry unless you acknowledge that you're to blame.

Órlaith went on:

"But I was there when Da died, and she wasn't, and she just can't help envying me the extra time we had together, and then feeling bad that she does. She did always say that she got terrible mood swings when she was pregnant—when it doesn't make her sleepy all the time. I was . . . frightened when I noticed her crying in public yesterday, but maybe that's part of the reason. So we'd better settle some things ourselves. The kingdom comes first. First off, we're going to have to finally get off our rumps and publicly declare you heir to the Protectorate. The time for artful ambiguity is past."

He winced and occupied himself with the plates. There were four small omelets a few inches across, fluffy things with golden-brown crusts and a scent of strong melted cheese and ham, hot rolls under a cloth, butter, jam, and small bowls of stewed dried fruit and nuts with whipped cream. Órlaith nodded thanks, said the Blessing, and ate a forkful of her omelet. She stopped and made herself actually taste it by an act of will: one thing her parents had always agreed on was that taking food for granted was an insult both to the Divine in whatever form you followed it, and to the people who worked to produce it for you.

Nine-tenths of the human race had starved to death within living memory, after all. That wasn't as real to her down in the gut as it was to her parents' generation, who'd grown up children of the survivors; and vastly less so than it was to those last few survivors of the great dying themselves, many of whom were slightly mad on the subject, but she could see the point. And the overwhelming majority of living humans worked all their lives in the fields as they had since the age of polished stone; she'd done a little of that, enough to know first-hand how hard it was.

The smoky flavor of the ham and the sharp Tillamook cheese went well with the creamy lightness of the egg and the hint of garlic and chili from the crust. The tastes awoke her stomach, making the day seem more real.

Her brother crossed himself, kissed his crucifix, murmured: *"Bless us, O Lord, and these Thy gifts which we are about to receive through Thy bounty, through Christ our Lord. Amen,"* buttered a roll and went on plaintively, in a fair imitation of a sulky three-year-old:

"Do I *hafta* be Lord Protector?"

He could have been a fair actor, if he hadn't been born a prince, in one of the troupes that shuttled between Corvallis and Portland and Boise. He might even have made it into the Lord Protector's Men and had a permanent slot.

"Yes, you have to. Absolutely. Eventually."

"There are all sorts of things I'd rather do than be Lord Protector. Hunt. Make music. Make love. St. Michael witness, I'd even rather carry a spear in a foot-company with a mean sergeant."

"You *absolutely* have to," Órlaith said firmly. "Besides the legal part. The barons want it, and the Church wants it even more badly."

"I know," he said, and added impishly: "My confessor comes down on me like an avalanche of anvils every time I tell him how I wish I didn't have to do it. Tells me there are no princes in a confessional booth, so take up the cross God's handed me, drag it up to Heaven's gate, and stop whining in the meantime."

Órlaith nodded; Mom would have picked the man, and she always chose conscientious ones for the Royal family. "Da was never Lord Protector; our grandfather Norman was the last man to carry the title."

"And he was a mad tyrant by all accounts, so it's not a good precedent."

"Mad tyrant or not, he built the Protectorate and it's a big part of Montival."

She made a gesture around, as if to indicate what that demonic will had accomplished, the bulk of the Onyx Tower, rearing even higher than this; the great circuit of the inner keep, with its round machicolated towers, the outer bailey and the linear town along the inside of the wall, courtyard and cathedral, garden and workshop and barracks and armories. The realm governed from here and from the City Palace in Portland stretched from the lower Willamette to the Peace River in the north, and inland to the borders of Boise and the Dominion of Drumheller. It was the largest single unit in the inhabited part of the High Kingdom, had at least a quarter of its people and wealth, and everywhere within it the patterns of life followed the Lord Protector's dream . . . or much of it, however modified by his wife, daughter, and less directly, his son-in-law, who was the son of the man who'd killed him.

Probably the Protectorate was rather more than that proportion of Montival's military power, which would be crucial when the summons went out, and the barons were the core of that.

"Mom's always worn that hat," John said.

"Mom made the office something different, with the accent on the *Protector* instead of the *Lord*. The commons up here in the north-realm love her for it, too, the way Nonni Sandra and then Mom reined in the nobility without ripping the place up."

"And she'll be Lady Protector for the rest of her life," John said, a little more cheerfully, evidently trying to look on the bright side. "Since she holds it in her own right of birth and I won't inherit while she's here. Mary Mother willing, I'll be the age she is now before I have to take it on, or older."

"Sure, and you can just slide into it as her apprentice, so to speak. She'll have more than enough work, being High Queen without Da until I come of Throne age, and Lady Protector to boot, so you can take some of that off her and then run in harness with her when I take the throne."

"Oh, Christ," he said mournfully, wincing. "Years and years working under Mom's supervision . . . you know the way *she* works, as if wading through documents and listening to bureaucrats and negotiating with backwoods barons were just one long course of cherry pie and brandied apricot ice cream with cittern accompaniment. I'll be an old man in twelve months! Or endowed with an enormous case of Bureaucrat's Bottom."

"Don't look at me with puppy-eyes as if you've been condemned to the squirrel cage," she replied dryly. "And if the lard gets out of control, you can always go down and do a volunteer stint."

The elevators in Todenangst were run by convict-manned treadmills in the dungeons; for some reason *squirrel cage* was what they were called, though they actually looked like an endless set of steps on chain loops. When the elevator wasn't in use the same treadmills pumped water from the deep tube wells to the cisterns high above, supplementing the windmills on the points of the witches-hat roofs of the towers.

It wasn't a sentence of death, not like the bad old days when men had just vanished into the lower reaches and never come out again except as pallid emaciated corpses. But it wasn't a pleasant way to spend a sentence of, say ten years, either. Even compared to making big rocks into little ones for the roads or digging drainage ditches or cutting timber and picking oakum for the Navy.

"You've got years and years—hopefully decades and decades—before you actually have to assume it fully," she went on.

"Christ and His Mother grant it, but don't I get at least a few years of being a carefree young lord kicking up his heels?"

"No, you don't, Johnnie, except what you can fit into your spare time: we're the Royal kin."

He sighed and rolled his eyes, but without real anger and nodded as she continued:

"Just be glad you don't have to do the whole thing now. But we need to get you *declared*, officially the heir. With some sort of ceremony, in that nice orthodox Cathedral with the Cardinal-Archbishop or someone like that presiding. There was a point to keeping it ambiguous while . . . while Da was here . . . but now . . . Look, Johnnie, face it: you're male, you're Catholic—"

"Mom is Lady Protector and they've accepted that."

"She's *also* Catholic, *and* she has you, *and* you're the son of the legitimate daughter of Norman and Sandra Arminger. I'm female and I'm of the Old Faith and my father was a pagan Mackenzie."

"He was my father too!" her brother said, sounding genuinely offended this time.

She made a soothing gesture. "Of course he was, Johnnie. Sorry I am, and I shouldn't have put it like that—but it's more obvious to outsiders with me, you know what I'm after saying? When was the last time you put on a kilt?"

He shrugged, the easy smile coming back. "You look better in skirts, Sis."

"It's the legs . . ."

"All right, I admit it, I'm an Associate in my heart," he said.

"Which is the point. Seriously, the Associates were pretty good about putting up with Da, considering that he was the son of Juniper Mackenzie and Mike Havel, and considerin' how many of their grandfathers stopped the pointy end of Mackenzie arrows and Bearkiller lances during the wars against the Association . . . not to mention that Da's father killed Norman Arminger—"

"Who's our other grandfather, yours as much as mine. And considering that Father founded the High Kingdom *and* won the Prophet's War . . ."

She nodded. "True. But *I* didn't do either of those things, the great fame and amazement of the world, eh? There is absolutely no way half or better of the baronage will tolerate a pagan High Queen Regnant who's *also* Lady Protector. Not to mention, say, Count Stavarov, can you imagine it?"

"I can imagine his head over Traitor's Gate," John said a little grimly.

"If Nonni Sandra could never manage that safely, do you think *you* could? Or me, for that matter?"

"Point," he said; he hadn't known her as well as Órlaith, being younger, but her reputation was yet green. Probably that reputation was what made him continue thoughtfully:

"Or he could just . . . have an accident, like so many of the people who got in Nonni's way did. Because he would just *love* to be Lord Protector, and to hell with Montival."

"We don't do that sort of thing so very much anymore, to be sure we don't," she pointed out.

Though not so much *isn't at all the same as* absolutely never, *and if he ever tries to set me up with his repulsive son Yuri again . . . who he would just* love *to see as Consort to the High Queen, and his grandson's fundament on the Raven Throne.*

House Stavarov was one of her maternal grandfather's bigger mistakes, in her opinion. He'd used their manpower in the early days, and while from all the tales he hadn't trusted *anyone* very much except perhaps Nonni Sandra, he also thought he could keep them inconsequential by putting their estates in the Chehalis lowlands, where the climate was too damp for really first-rate farmland.

That meant the ruins of Seattle lay in House Stavarov's fief of County Chehalis, and Nonni Sandra had had to confirm it as a House Stavarov demesne as the price of their support in the chaos after the Protector's War. It was one of the rare but always painful occasions when Norman Arminger's area of historical scholarship had played him false; in the early-medieval Norman kingdoms where his heart and mind had dwelt since his youth, salvage wasn't a crucial economic factor. Here and now after the Change it most certainly *was*. Seattle was the largest of the dead cities within easy reach, and even with the Crown Third taken off the top it produced a huge and influential revenue stream each and every year, capable of buying everything from knights to newspaper editors.

Odd that a man born before the Change had that blind spot. He would have done better to let them have the Skagit Valley baronies and kept Seattle in Crown demesne instead. Water under the bridge, and it isn't the most important thing right now. Da was right, a ruler has to be a six-armed juggler and just ignore the odd itch.

Resolutely she went on: "We'll just give him and the others absolutely no grounds to complain in the House of Peers. And by the Protectorate law of succession you *should* get it, so they'd have right on their side if you didn't. The Great Charter doesn't mention anything about who gets the Lord Protector's office, and local law always has precedence where there's no specific provision in the Charter to the contrary. None of the Associate peerage is going to quarrel with an uncontestable hereditary succession by primogeniture in fee tail; they have too much invested in the principle. But if we put it aside . . . sure, and it would be in the nature of a *free-for-all tale.*"

He frowned, winced when the feudal pun struck, and took a sip of his coffee, which he preferred black. She'd always found that just a little odd; austerity wasn't generally his style, but even brothers had their complexities. After a moment he said thoughtfully:

"I could do you public homage for it—I mean, as heir to the Lord

Protector's office. Heir to heir, as it were, since you aren't going to take the throne for years anyway. That way, by the time Mom passes, God and the Virgin grant it be a long, long time"—he crossed himself again; he was devout, though no fanatic—"most people still around will have spent plenty of time accepting that the Lord Protector is the High King's, or High Queen's, hereditary vassal and always will be. That it's not just a personal union because of Mom's marriage to Dad. Nobody who's got vassals of their own is going to publicly disrespect that, either."

"Right."

Johnnie's plenty bright, just a little lazy about using it sometimes, she thought, and continued aloud:

"It would be totally awkward to have Mom swear homage to me— even after I succeed to the throne."

He winced. "Yes, it would, wouldn't it? I mean . . . I just can't imagine it."

She nodded. "But this will handle that neatly, you see? Separating the lines of the High Kingdom and the Protectorate."

"I can *absolutely* imagine doing homage to you," he agreed, smiling a little. "Or Mom, for that matter."

His face went stark as his thoughts turned elsewhere, and she remembered descriptions of men sweating in fear when their grandfather gave them a glance.

"And I can absolutely imagine leading Protectorate levies when we find out who killed our father. Find out in detail. Whoever they are, I want to see them *burn.* Not just their soldiers. Their lords. I want blood."

She nodded; he generally wasn't a violent man, but now . . .

"That plate won't be stinted, Johnnie, I promise you. But you know the old saying."

"It's a dish best served cold, yeah. We can't go off with the crossbows half-spanned, we need more intel."

"Speaking of which, I ought to introduce you to the *Jotei,* to Reiko. Obviously that's going to affect how we deal with this. Absolutely not her fault, the Three Spinners wove it in the deeps of time, but the quarrel did follow them across the ocean, so to say."

He grinned at her, chewing a mouthful of roll, swallowed, and put a purring smoothness in his tone—exaggerating for effect.

"You want me to charm her? Got a dynastic marriage in mind, Sis? I hear she's cute. Exotic foreign princess . . ."

"Sweet Mother-of-All, no!" Órlaith said, sitting bolt upright. "Look, Johnnie, seriously, none of your tricks the now! She's a *Queen*. Empress, actually. I know you think you're Lady Flidais' own sweet special gift to women, but we have to be *very careful* with these people! Promise? Otherwise I'll damned well forbid you her presence and get Mom to back me up."

He made a little abbreviated court bow in his seat. "Of course, Orrey, my solemn oath. I was just tying your boot-laces together to see you trip. You're a bit solemn at times. I'm not stupid, you know."

"No, but you're a male and you're nineteen."

"*That* makes me stupid?"

"No, it makes you an engorged penis. With feet, but no brain except the Little Head half the time," she said bluntly, and was glad to see him laugh. She went on:

"And we do need to find out the full story. This isn't just normal politics, Johnnie. Not even a normal war. Things like the House of Peers or some Count's ambitions or who does homage to who for what . . . we can't neglect them, but for that an ordinary sword forged out of an old leaf spring would do."

She had the Sword of the Lady across the back of the chair. He looked at it and nodded as she said:

"The Powers are at work here."

He touched his crucifix again; the conversation was tending into a region that prompted that. "You think these guests of ours are on the side of the Angels?"

Most Christians in Montival believed that the Beings who'd aided her father on the Quest were just that—Angels, or possibly Saints, which he'd regrettably misconstrued as pagan deities. And that the Lady who'd gifted him with the Sword was their blue-mantled Queen of Heaven and Mother of God. Father Ignatius *had* had a visitation from Her in the mountain snows on that great journey, in which she'd called the warrior Benedictine to be Her knight.

I don't disagree, she thought. *Only with the names the other way 'round, so to speak.*

She nodded. "Or at least the *Nihonjin* are on the side of humankind. I don't think they're stainless, but they're good and bad on a human level according to our natures as They made us, which is to say as apes with a touch of wolf. That evil our parents fought and beat here in Montival is of the Powers too, Johnnie. That isn't going away and it isn't limited to the High Kingdom, it just takes different forms in different places."

He nodded. His Church recognized the constant power of their Adversary. In some ways it was an easier concept for him than for someone of the Old Faith.

She frowned a little: "But . . . the Nihonjin weren't lying to me, understand . . .

"But?" he said.

"They *were* leaving bits out, starting with what they were doing here in the first place. They didn't arrive here by accident, or simply because they were chased, though they were. And they didn't come here to talk to us, either, though they are eager to get our help now; they didn't know we existed any more than we knew that they were there. I also get the feeling that there are internal tensions involved in their group."

"Never a Court without faction," John said confidently. "And by your report, that's their court in miniature your new friend has along with her."

"A couple of their high officers of State, at least. The heliograph messages from Herry say they're relaxing a bit the now."

"She'd know, even with the language problems," John said with a smile. "Probably she's part of the reason—our Herry's a hell of a lot more perceptive about people than your average knight. Her mother's a wonder at setting people at their ease, too . . . the mother that wasn't an assassin and former Grand Constable and Marshal of the High Kingdom and whatnot."

He liked Heuradys d'Ath, and it was mutual; they had a great deal in common. They'd been—very briefly—lovers a few years ago. That was how her brother had lost his virginity, in fact, in the stereotypical hayloft on Herry's own manor out east. He'd been making up for lost time since she gently made it plain she didn't have anything long-term in mind, and doing well enough to have a bit of a reputation. A Prince had advantages that way, even one who extremely conscientious about good lordship. She had to admit their parents had gotten that well and truly into his skull even when the Little Head was in operation, which apparently for males his age was no mean accomplishment. As well, he was wary about those looking for advantage in the bed of royalty.

Being a Prince was something; when you added in being handsome, a man-at-arms who did quite well in tournaments, a more than talented singer, dancer and lutenist, and the best sort of dandy—one who could carry it off casually—the results were quite a swath. Considered in the abstract she had to admit he was charming; for starters he really *liked* women, liked their company and liked talking to them, rather than just sniffing around them the way a drooling dog did with a pork-chop. Though it always looked faintly ridiculous to her when she saw him using his moves on some cooing, blushing, dewy-eyed female—or working a slightly different version on a barmaid with a forty-inch bust spilling out of her bodice, a full lower lip and freckles.

But as Herry had said back when, it would have been rather odd if his *sister* had been able to see that side of John.

He finished his omelet. "What's the Empress the Empress of?" he asked.

"Japan," she said severely.

"I mean in practice, as opposed to theory. There are plenty of Rovers out in the forests and deserts who've never *heard* of us. There's not much to being ruler of empty ruins and wilderness with no people, either. So is it two villages and a pet ox, or what?"

"They've got more people than there are either Mackenzies or Mc-Clintocks, but less than both together, I'm thinking, from what they've let drop," Órlaith said. "Somewhere between a twentieth of what Montival has altogether and a tenth."

"*Más o menos,*" John said thoughtfully, waggling a hand.

A number of the Houses of the Associate nobility had originally been Spanish-speaking, and that tongue had influenced the north-realm's version of English, though not as much as the archaic French of Norman Arminger's obsessions. John had picked up stray expressions like that, then truly learned the language because its music and stories intrigued him.

"More or less," Órlaith agreed, and then suddenly made a choking sound.

"What is it?" John asked with alarm.

Órlaith put her hands to her head, wincing at the feeling of *expansion*, like an itchy swelling in the center of her brain for an instant. It wasn't pain, but she wasn't sure that wouldn't be preferable.

"Spanish . . . I just got Spanish . . . there are drawbacks to possessing the Sword, that there are . . . wait a minute . . . There's that poem you like so much, I've heard you sing it a dozen times. . . ."

Suddenly she began to chant, a slow smile lighting her face as she did, and felt the rough rolling majesty of the words in her mouth:

"De los sos oios tan fuertemientre llorando,
Tornava la cabeça e estavalos catando;
Vio puertas abiertas e uços sin cañados,
alcandaras vazias, sin pielles e sin mantos,
e sin falcones e sin adtores mudados . . ."

John made a clapping motion. "Nice! You've even got the old-fashioned pronunciation down. Better than I do, after years of work. See, it's not all bad!"

"No, it isn't, that," she said. "I can . . . I can *feel* that poem now. How it should *taste*. *Arra*, from the little bits I can remember, I can't wait to get to a copy of Cervantes or de Vega!"

He shook his head. "Back to business. So the Japan she's Empress of isn't enormous, but three hundred thousand people more or less isn't so small, either."

She nodded. There were at least two dozen sovereign states in North

America, kingdoms and republics and bossmandoms and tribes and self-governing monasteries (at least one of them Buddhist) and whatever. That was counting only ones well above the level of the single backwoods village or a band of musk-ox hunters on Baffin Island. A quarter or third of a million would be about middle-rank in that league, say on a level with the Kingdom of Norrheim. Montival was the giant, and that was because it was a confederation. On this continent only the Bossmandom of Iowa had even half as many folk in total, being much smaller but very densely populated by modern standards and actually having more people than it had before the Change.

There *still* weren't anything like a tenth as many people in the whole area between Panama and the Arctic as there had been the day before the Change.

"Reiko's lot are the descendants of what survived on offshore islands and a few settlements they've planted since," Órlaith said. "It reminds me of what we've heard of Britain, only the Japanese ended up with a very nasty neighbor next door instead of an empty continent they could take over."

"They're well-organized, though, from your reports, and Edain's."

Órlaith nodded. "From what I've seen and what they've let drop without really meaning to—just the way they act and the assumptions they make—they're organized right down to the boot-laces they don't have. Much more tightly centralized than us, or most of Montival's member realms . . . except perhaps the Bearkillers or Boise. Out of necessity. Something really nasty happened in Korea, much worse than just a collapse, and they've been living next-door to it ever since. We need to get our decks cleared here at home, because bad things are heading our way."

"Let's go see Mom, then," John said.

Órlaith blotted her lips with the napkin. "If we can get her thinking and talking business, it'll help. Help all around. And then we'll duck out and have a bit of a chat with Reiko, you and I."

"Sounds good. I think I've done my immediate family duty here, and I'd appreciate something to *do* so I don't have to keep turning corners and thinking *where's Father?*"

She raised her voice slightly. "Sir Aleaume!"

There was a guard not too distant—close enough to hear a call, if not to overhear ordinary conversation; that was as much privacy as you could expect in a palace, particularly just after a King died by violence. The officer of the Protector's Guard appeared a discreet minute later, his steel sabaton-shoes ringing on the marble tiles, and then going muted when he stepped on a rug. His helm was under his left arm as he saluted with a thump, his handsome albeit jug-eared face fixed under its fringe of rust-colored hair and his slightly slanted eyes haunted—it hadn't been easy for him, returning as the commander who'd *failed* to keep the High King alive.

Probably he was most dreading his own father's return: Baron Maugis de Grimmond was Grand Constable of the Association and a man of notoriously high standards.

"Your Highness!" A nod to John. "Your Highness!"

"Sir Aleaume, Prince John and I will be visiting Barony Ath—Montinore Manor, to be exact. We'll be taking a detail from the Protector's Guard."

Because if they tried to get out of Todenangst *without* one, the uproar would swallow the day even if her mother or the Lord Chancellor didn't get involved . . . and both of them would. She continued briskly:

"Nothing extravagant, a dozen men at arms led by a reliable knight who can keep his eyes front and mouth shut, and spearmen and cross-bowmen in proportion likewise. The ones who were with us in the south would do nicely, and I'd like to show that they're not in any disfavor. Ah, yes, make sure Droyn Jones de Molalla is one of them too."

Since she'd borne the Sword she had no problem recalling names—anyone she'd seen even once, in fact. But she'd known the escort well anyway, since they'd traveled together for more than a month on that final trip. There was gratitude in the knight's eyes as he inclined his head; it was an indication that *he* wasn't in disfavor, or his men.

"And from the High King's Archers, Your Highness?"

"No, Captain Edain has enough to do."

Mother's known Old Wolf a long time, and he grew up with Da as foster-brother, pretty much. They went on the Quest together, all of them. She needs him around now and I'll let him focus on that.

"Have a hippomotive laid on, and horses waiting at the Forest Grove station."

That way they'd be there before lunchtime; hippomotives could *move* and it was barely a morning's journey all up that way.

"Inform Dame Emilota that she's to send only the minimal selection of baggage. *Strictly* minimal, this is a matter of State and there won't be much socializing."

And if the order comes through you, I don't have to spend another hour talking her out of making a Royal Progress out of it. And with the court in mourning, she may actually not grumble too much.

"Your Highness . . . may I command the detail personally?"

Surprised, she looked at him; that was very junior duty for someone of his rank.

"Of course, if you wish, Sir Aleaume," she said; then she blinked.

That might actually be a good idea.

"My thanks, Your Highness. All should be in readiness within two hours." He bowed, saluted again, wheeled and tramped off.

Órlaith sighed and rubbed her face. "Let's get to it, then, Johnnie."

CHAPTER THIRTEEN

"How are the men doing, General?" Reiko asked.

They were trotting down to the *salle d'armes* beside the little lake; it was a mild June day with a few fleecy clouds in a slightly hazy blue sky, perhaps a little warmer than it would have been on a June morning on Sado-ga-shima, perhaps a little less humid, though both were well within the range she was accustomed to.

The two of them were wearing *hakama* and the padded upper jacket used for serious drill, with boiled and varnished leather practice armor of an almost-familiar type over it, the wire-fronted helmets under their arms. Both were sweating freely from the stretching routines and forced-pace *kata* and a moderate three-mile run up and down hill with an occasional sprint, ready for some serious exercise.

"The men are well enough, Majesty. The barracks in the castle are . . . barracks. Certainly nothing any real samurai would complain of, far better than shipboard. The roof is solid, it's dry, and there are cots and clean bedding and a bathhouse."

The practice weapons to match the armor would be at the *salle*, as the Montivallans called their dojo. She carried a *naginata*, and their real swords were at their sides, of course; just as two of the Imperial Guard were following a dozen paces behind. She couldn't remember walking under the sky without a guard and a blade of some sort at her own side since she turned twelve and was presented with an adult kimono by her mother at her *mogi* ceremony . . . and with a *wakizashi* from her father's hands, an heirloom by the master-smith Kunihiro. The latter had caused some controversy, for giving a weapon at all and for a sword rather than a *naginata*.

You must prepare, my Reiko-chan, he'd said to her privately then, after they'd knelt in silence for a while with the blade between them. *So that for those yet unborn there may be the brush and the poem and the* chanoyu, *for us today there must be a sword in the hand. And in our souls, the steel.*

The only time she *hadn't* actually had live steel on her person since were occasions of State when protocol dictated that an attendant walk behind her with the weapon just ready to her hand.

Egawa seemed to read something of her thoughts. He inclined his head before he went on more lightly:

"There's even a field outside for *besuboru*."

"Ah, they play that here?" Reiko said.

It was the most popular non-martial sport back home; she enjoyed it occasionally herself.

"Yes, a few differences in the rules but the same game. And the local people are friendly—in fact some—"

He coughed. Reiko smiled without showing it in the slightest. If she had been a man he was reporting to, even so exalted a man as her father, he would have joked about *how* friendly some of the local peasant girls had been to the exotic and romantic visitors. Instead he went on with scarcely a stumble:

"In fact, the food is too good, if anything. Like festival food. I haven't eaten so much *gyoza* and *yakiniku* and *tonkatsu* on successive days in my whole life. Captain Nakamura is working them hard, he's fully recovered from his wounds and it was best to give two days complete rest anyway, but it might be good to suggest something plainer for everyday diet."

Reiko nodded gravely. The Montivallans had somehow found a couple of Japanese cooks—they didn't *look* very Japanese, and none of them

spoke the language beyond words relating to the kitchen and they mis-
pronounced those, but they could produce something quite like the fancier varieties of the homeland's style. Except that rice was regarded as a
luxury product here, which was a major distinction: her language used
the same word for *cooked rice* and *meal*, but noodles were a perfectly acceptable substitute. Nothing except the raw fish was of precisely the same
taste or texture as it would have been at home, but it was much easier for
her followers than dealing with a completely alien cuisine.

Which is important not for itself, but again as a gesture, she thought. *I am not
sure we would have been so thoughtful to strangers, in such a crisis. Of course, we have
less to spare and we are not in a position to choose peace or war as we please and as we
think honor dictates.*

She was stretching herself and trying the local dishes. Some of the
foods were just horrible—the pungent cheeses came in that category in
her opinion—and some were treacherous; ice cream tasted delicious but
gave her nasty stomachaches. Others were quite pleasant once you deliberately stopped looking for the familiar. The scrambled eggs with scal-
lions, for instance, or sweet rolls with raisins.

Egawa's thoughts had been running parallel to hers. "Majesty, as far
as *gaijin* know how, they are treating us like greatly honored guests."

He'd been particularly pleased when he learned the set of rooms she'd
been given was called the *Royal Suite* and used when the monarchs of this
land and their kin came calling on the barons of Ath.

He went on: "They are doing that though we have brought them terrible misfortune. Why? They revered their High King much as we did
Saisei Tennō, I can see that now. And they know we are weaker than they;
you can tell they're surprised anything civilized survived in Japan at all."

This path to the *salle* ran down a steep slope, terraced with stone re-
taining walls; the flat spaces created were planted in colorful flowers,
red-and-white *komakusa*, which they called bleeding heart here, blue-and-
white columbine, fuchsia, lupine, hollyhocks and more between neatly
trimmed lilac bushes. They trotted easily down the steep switchback
stairs, treating going downhill as a rest and timing their words to their
deep controlled breath. At first glance it was just the local love of masses

of very vivid colors, until you noticed the swarms of bees, colorful moths and butterflies, and—

"*Uso!*" Reiko exclaimed in delight. "I don't believe it!"

They both stopped, to stare at a swarm of astonishing little birds smaller than her thumb, *hovering* as they stuck their slender beaks into the flowers. Their wings blurred like those of bees or dragonflies as they did, but they were unquestionably birds, not insects. One of them came and did a slow circuit around her head only a few inches away, a brilliant tiny orange jewel making a humming sound like a giant bee. Then it zipped back towards the flowers. They seemed to be combative little things, buzzing about in furious challenge if another came near their chosen blossom, pursuing each other through the garden in aerial dances of angry grace.

"*Ijōna,*" she murmured, smiling a little; even the eyes of the grim Guard samurai swiveled a little.

"Extraordinary, Majesty," Egawa agreed. "I think these plantings are for these . . . little creatures."

She frowned slightly as they turned and resumed their trot, and the previous conversation: "I think . . . I think they *do* think of us as honored guests. It is extremely important to them that when we met we fought the same enemy."

"*Hai, Heika,*" Egawa said; he could understand that in his bones.

"And they . . . most of them, Crown Princess Órlaith in particular . . . do not blame us for her father's death. They blame the *jinnikukaburi*—it helps much that their Haida enemies were at the side of the ones who killed him. He had fought these pirates before, when he was a young man, and since. Everyone here knows they are enemies, so any allies of theirs would be the same. And I think the Princess sympathizes with us . . . with me particularly . . . since we have suffered the same loss at the same hands. I understand; I feel much the same. Her father seems to have been a man of . . . exemplary character, to judge from his accomplishments."

She felt half-admiring, half-resentful about that.

My father was a very great man, wise and strong, gentle when he could be and hard when he must, she thought. *Truly and justly his era is called* Rebirth. *He never ceased to work for our people, night and day. He died for them. But what he was able to accomplish was so . . . so cramped by comparison to what Órlaith's could do. Fate was less kind to him than he deserved.*

Railing against Fate was unbecoming futility, and resenting the Montivallans for their better fortune would be ungracious and foolish . . . but she had to fight the temptation.

"You can judge a man by the hole his going leaves in the world," Egawa agreed, and grunted thoughtfully again. "I wish we could make some definite alliance, Majesty."

"So do I. Grand Steward Koyama has been sounding out Marshal d'Ath."

"Good, though I wish my English was capable of handling subtleties so that I could join them."

He added dryly: "At first I thought he had simply vanished into the library here, Majesty."

"It *is* tempting."

There were thousands of volumes, including both works that had simply not survived the Change in Japan and a wide selection of new material. Montival was at least sporadically and indirectly in contact with much of the world, and the Grand Steward was in a position to satisfy a lifetime's curiosity in one mad gulp. His resistance and focus on the essential had been very creditable.

She went on: "But I must consider how to . . . to make them understand my father's . . . visions."

He looked uncomfortable, and more so when she added quietly: "Which I have now had myself. Three nights in succession, unmistakably this time. Very much as Saisei Tennō described them, but . . . very vivid. And while his was . . . general, I see *myself* in them."

She swallowed, feeling the sensation of terrible thirst again. That dread, and the shadow of towers. Eight heads in darkness, and a long hissing . . .

"Majesty . . . have you spoken of that with Grand Steward Koyama?"

"No," she said. "Not yet."

"He is an extremely intelligent man, and has much scholarly knowledge," Egawa said.

It would have been grossly impolite for him to directly urge her, but there was no harm in pointing out the *reasons* for doing something. The two men had a certain rivalry, but there was also a solid mutual respect.

She nodded. "Yes. But he has read so much of the world before the Change that sometimes he is not quite at home in this one, my *bushi*, even if he has lived in it most of his life. Not as you and I are at home. You see what I mean?"

His heavy scarred features knotted. "Yes, Majesty. Yes, I think I do."

"Do not forget why we came on this voyage in the first place, General Egawa. It was not to make alliance with Montival. We did not know that this place *existed*. Koyama was the most reluctant of you all. Finding Montival allows him to . . . repurpose the expedition in his mind, into something more . . . mundane."

She could see that he would have preferred to do exactly that himself—the prospect of a strong alliance against their enemies had given him hope, something in sparse supply for far too long. The desperation which had made her father's vision at least a little plausible was less in proportion.

"Majesty . . ." he began.

"No, General Egawa. Saisei Tennō's reasoning remains completely valid. And consider the . . . sacred weapon the Montivallan High Kings bear. The *shintai*."

He did, baring his teeth a little. Even just lying in its scabbard, it was a mental punch in the solar plexus, the worse the more closely you looked. She drove the point home as if it were the steel of her naginata:

"The possibility of an alliance is *related* to our original mission. I have asked, discreetly. The Sword they carry was found after a quest that seemed as mad as ours. It is their founding epic—a very recent one by our standards, as if Yamato Takeru were someone your parents knew, but I suppose every story has to start somewhere."

He nodded. "*Hai*, Majesty. So sorry; I worry."

"Saisei Tennō decreed when we left that both at home and on the expedition there should be no worry until one year had passed, and no despair for two."

There was a very slight trace of the affection she felt in her voice as she spoke, though what she said was literally true. An Emperor could order that. People would worry just the same, of course, but they would be much less likely to show it. If you did not act on an emotion or display it, for all practical purposes it might as well not be there. More, human beings being what they were, suppressing the appearance of an emotion reduced the thing itself. She could see Egawa following the argument through and accepting it.

They ran onto the flat and slowed to walk into the *salle*, pausing to slip out of their boots and into soft practice shoes. The two Guardsmen took stance at either side of the entrance; she could tell they and their commander would have preferred to keep both at her heels, but she had forbidden. The complex was entirely of post-Change construction, a set of cloisters with big barn-like rooms, and courtyards enclosing different terrain.

It was handsome in a severely plain fashion she liked, built of stone and the long, straight timbers so enviably abundant in this land of tall mountain forests. Evidently maintaining it for the gentry of the fief was one of the baron's duties. The ground outside provided woods, hill and bare grassland for the students' use and mounted work. There were certain necessary, fundamental likenesses to the dojos she had grown up with, just as *hakama* and breeks had a similarity based on their common function of enclosing human legs.

A bit more surprising had been real common elements. The unarmed combat techniques here were closely similar to what she'd learned, and even used bits of mangled Japanese terminology. And there were Nihon-style practice weapons, *bokken* and *naginatas*; they studied them a little here, though in the main their styles were based on European models she hadn't been aware existed. It was a little flattering, if you thought about it.

Men were fighting; and a few women, though those were mostly younger ones learning unarmed combat, shooting crossbows on the

range, knife-fighting or working with glaives—bladed polearms not unlike the *naginata*, though the blade was shorter and straight, heavier, and
had a hook at the rear. Here as in Japan all noblewomen learned self-
defense but few made a career of the sword, though there were exceptions. Reiko suppressed a smile as a giggle rose behind them but did let
her eyes narrow in amusement since her companion couldn't see it: except for servants sweeping and cleaning, the *women* present wore clothes
very closely resembling her kimono and *hakama* . . . or her Imperial Guard
commander's uniform.

Egawa had seethed for hours when he found that he was, by local
standards, wearing women's dress, suitable for an elegant noble lady out
to take the air. And while he found breeks ugly he thought actual tight
hose, which was what Associates wore as the alternative, actively obscene; fortunately they usually went with something loose and conceal-
ing worn over it, down to thigh-length or the knees.

The men practiced with shield and sword and shield and spear, and
men-at-arms with shields and swords or using a two-handed technique,
or with various polearms; classes of beginners as young as six hacked at
wooden pells or practiced *kata*. The combat in full armor had looked
unsophisticated at first, but there was skill to it as well as straightforward
battling, hard and quick and murderous. A couple of trials had shown that
the big teardrop-shaped shields were both an effective protection and a
menacing weapon that was irritatingly hard to deal with, though the
Montivallan knights were also surprised with what a real expert could do
with the katana. Shouts and clatter filled the air and then faded behind as
they passed. There was an odor of clean sweat, cloth and greased metal
and leather and weathered wood in sunlight, things half-familiar and half-
strange.

She and Egawa walked through the corridors, nodding to bows, until
they reached a large open-sided room whose floor was covered in straw
mats over boards. Hooks showed where board panels could be put up
between the thick wooden columns to make solid walls in winter. Racks
around the pillars held weapons and gear, and there were full-length mirrors on the one solid inner wall. A dais at one end had chairs for specta-

tors; right now four of them were occupied, by Baroness d'Ath, Lady Delia and her youngest daughter Yolande. This household had a rather . . .

Unusual and distinctive set of domestic arrangements, she thought; even more so for this part of Montival than they would be for Japan, she gathered. *But certain patterns seem to hold in all these* han, *these fiefs.*

The fourth was a young man, younger than she but full-grown, in dark rich clothes though not black except for the mourning band. D'Ath rose and bowed. Both of the ladies curtsied to Reiko, the colorful skirts of their garments spreading like flowers, and she nodded in return, before she and Egawa racked their swords and she the polearm.

The young man made a bow too, but not as deep. Reiko blinked thoughtfully at him, memorizing the face, then put it out of her mind for the present. When you fought Egawa Noboru, even for sport and training, you did well to focus completely.

They took the practice weapons they would use in hand—he an oak *bokken,* a wooden katana, and she a *naginata,* a two-foot curved wooden sword mounted on a six-foot shaft—and she could feel his attitude changing. Long ago he had first told her that there was no rank in a dojo except that of student and teacher, and on a battlefield that of victor and vanquished. Then he had proceeded to run her ragged and on occasion administer fine sets of bruises.

They sank to their knees and sat back. Two figures in hose and black padded canvas doublets and wire masks attached to leather helmets much like the ones she and Egawa carried were facing each other in the center of the floor, with straight long swords and twelve-inch poniards in their gauntleted hands; the blades were edgeless and had rounded points. An instructor who worked here—an older man with a patchy white beard, a limp, and a scar on his face that crossed an empty eye-socket and took the tip off his nose—raised a white baton above his head.

"Ready!"

The masked figures raised their swords hilt-high before their faces in salute, the movements swift and smooth and definite.

"Position!"

That was left foot slightly forward and dagger advanced, knees a bit crooked, long sword held with the hilt high and point down. The white rod whipped groundward.

"Fight!"

Egawa gave a happy sigh beside her, having found something which did indeed make him stop worrying for a while. She blinked; the movements had been very fast, a blurring flicker and a *ting-ting-ting* of metal on metal, feint-strike-parry-strike-strike-parry, a brief grapple and hard blows with knee and elbow and the pommels of the weapons, and then they were apart again. They began to circle, feet rutching with careful swiftness on the mats, balance transferred without ever being lost.

Ting-ting-ting-crash. One of the contestants was thrown, but rolled head-over-heels and came back to her feet in guard position even as the other advanced with a series of stamping lunges. *Ting-ting-ting!*

Very softly, and without taking her eyes from the contestants, she said: "Mostly with the point."

"And cuts from the wrist," Egawa said. "Straight cuts, not drawing ones such as we use. Intriguing."

"But still, this is not altogether unlike Musashi's two-sword style," she observed.

Equally low, Egawa murmured: "And for comparable reasons, Majesty. This is their duelist's style, designed for fighting a single unarmored opponent."

She nodded. The great author of the *Book of Five Rings* had fought in some of the last engagements of the Age of Battles, but he had spent most of his martial career in the opening years of the long peace, when the samurai were warriors without wars to fight. For the conflict of one man against another in a duel or a scrambling affray in some feud he was unsurpassed, but he dealt less succinctly with the more linear and massive form of combat when organized groups collided.

Another exchange, a parry not quite complete, and a blunt-tipped sword flashed up under one figure's ribs, producing an *ooof* of expelled breath.

"Kill!" the man with the baton said. "Match to Lady Heuradys. Set to Lady Heuradys, five-two."

They saluted again, and Heuradys spoke while her liege-lady caught her breath:

"Thank you, Sir Bohort."

"Skewered my liver again, Herry," Órlaith wheezed, taking off her mask to show a face flushed and braided hair darkened with sweat and bowing slightly to the knight of the *salle*. "If I wasn't wearing padding I'd be peeing red."

"That'll happen for real, Orrey, if you keep getting overextended on those lunges. Stay centered!"

"Next pair," the one-eyed man said. "Lady Heuradys and Crown Princess Órlaith yield the floor *d'escrime* to Lord General Egawa and Her Majesty of Nippon."

Reiko and her *bushi* knelt facing each other, donned their mask-helmets. Then . . . slowly . . . each came to one knee. She held her *naginata* grounded with the butt beside her right foot; the Imperial Guard commander's right hand crossed to rest on the hilt of the wooden sword. She watched Egawa—not his eyes or hands or even the way his feet moved ever so slightly as his toes curled ready to grip, but all of them at the same time. The general was her height almost to a hair, considerably heavier, and much, much stronger. He wasn't *quite* as fast, but he was still lethally quick.

Without thinking, the tiny signs flowed through her to produce action *without* thought, like a stone sinking into still water. Thought was far too slow to play with naked steel. Thought was death.

"Fight!"

Egawa came up off the mat as if invisible cords had jerked him forward, the *bokken* flashing out and up and then down in the overarm cut, the pear-splitter. Reiko blocked with the haft of the *naginata* held horizontally above her head and one leg back, and there was a hard *crack!* of impact as the tough wood flexed under the heavy blow. A battle weapon's shaft would have had steel wire or strips to protect it. She grunted slightly as the force of it made her bent arms sink down like springs, absorbing some of the force with her knees, and swept the polearm in a blurring circle. Egawa blocked, struck, came at her in an appalling combination of speed and precision and hard power; she kept the shaft whirling . . .

The first bout ended with her knocked skidding on her back for half a dozen yards. The second left her dazed and blinking for a few moments after the *bokken* glanced off her helmet; the scar-faced supervising knight insisted on looking into her eyes before nodding and stepping back and making a sharp horizontal gesture with the wand to show that there was no concussion.

The third went into a continuous flurry of block-strike-block that lasted for a very long time for a fight—fully fifteen seconds or a little more, with Reiko holding her own though the continuous whirlwind battering forced her back a half-step at a time. Sometimes on a battlefield there was no space for fancy footwork; you didn't want to train bad reflexes in. There were no focusing shouts, no *kiai*, after the first—every particle of breath was for use.

They both stepped back from that one, conceding a draw. Only an effort of will kept her limbs from shaking and she ignored the spots before her eyes as they drifted and then faded away. Similar discipline kept her from panting, instead deliberately stretching her lungs to take in as much air as they could, holding it for an instant and then exhaling from the bottom of her rib cage.

"This will be the last," Sir Bohort said in his rasping damaged voice.

They had both picked up enough of the local etiquette of the *salle d'armes* to know that the knight of the ring's decision was final and beyond dispute, accepted instantly regardless of rank. Reiko didn't regret it; she felt as if she'd been dropped into a barrel with a tiger and rolled down the side of a mountain. It was some consolation that Egawa wasn't moving with *quite* the same deadly fluidity that he had been at first. He treated every single bout as if it was a duel to the death, pacing himself to the task at hand alone.

Old man, this is my time, she thought.

"Fight!"

With the *naginata* you had the reach of a giant and the leverage multiplied impact almost as much. A few seconds later the ball at the end of the shaft—representing the sharp butt-spike of a real weapon—struck Egawa on the rear of his knee. She was whirling and driving the blade down even as he fell, and his block was only two-thirds complete when the curved edge lay along his neck.

"Kill!" the referee said. "Match to Her Majesty. Set to Lord Egawa, two-one-one."

Egawa was struggling to suppress a grin as he came—cautiously—to his feet again. The first time she had ever managed to beat him, a little over a year ago, her instructor had bowed expressionlessly before he limped away.

And then, she heard later, ended the night celebrating at his favorite *izakaya* with a few old cronies, drinking and singing and roaring for more sake and plates of pickles and *yakitori* until the town watch had to fetch his two eldest sons to carry him home. Where no doubt their mother had had something interesting to say about the matter in tones of exquisite restraint that cut like shards of broken glass. Possibly without even using words at all.

The next bout he had pushed her twice as hard. By now she was winning about one time in four or five. With the *naginata*, of course; with swords, it was still an uninterrupted series of defeats, her only consolation being that some of them were now fairly *narrow* defeats.

"Your knee?" she asked.

"It will be all right in a day," he said now. Then he bowed deeply: "Majesty!"

She inclined her head slightly. "General Egawa. Also, how is your hand?"

He flexed his left. "The wound was very narrow, and struck nothing important, no bones or severed tendons. It is healing well, though my grip has not yet recovered all its strength. Using it helps prevent adhesions within and loss of flexibility. It will serve, Majesty."

There would be pain, of course, though both of them ignored that.

She caught his eye for a moment in emphasis. "It has already served *me*," she said. "I had an excellent view of the narrow point after you put that hand between the knife and my face—it was exactly on course for my left eye."

He bowed again and limped away once more towards the baths. Órlaith and her *hatamoto* fell in with Reiko after she had racked her *naginata* and practice armor.

"In your average Protectorate *salle* our part of the baths are an afterthought tucked away behind something," Heuradys said with a smile. "Not here, though. Three guesses why?"

"Ah . . . I think I can guess, yes," Reiko said.

She was getting to the point where she could catch humor in English, but not with absolute certainty, and sometimes that spoiled it even when you *did* realize the meaning.

"You have separate for men and women, yes?" she said.

She *thought* that was what Heuradys had just said, but best to check. When Órlaith wasn't using her uncanny command of Nihongo everything was frustratingly difficult.

"Yes, we do," Heuradys said.

"What's this *we*, northerner?" Órlaith said lightly.

"*We* do, at least, we Associates. The Mackenzies don't, except for guests who prefer it that way, but then they're barbarians from the backwoods—unless you count McClintocks. You have separate facilities in Japan?"

She nodded: on their journey northward she'd always had a bathhouse to herself for a while, with guards outside, when it wasn't a private stretch of cold river, and of course the one in her suite here was hers exclusively.

"For peasants, no, everyone same time. Village is like . . . family, neh? But for *shi*, gentlefolk, and in towns, yes, that is the custom. Usually women and small children in the morning, men in the afternoon."

"Your English pronunciation has gotten a lot better," Órlaith observed.

Reiko returned her smile, feeling more pleased than she would have expected. The more so when Heuradys said:

"The *Heika* works at it hard enough to leave *me* feeling exhausted. You can hear the difference from one day to the next, and my attempts to pick up Japanese . . . leave a lot to be desired."

Like every substantial bathhouse she had yet seen in Montival, this reminded her strongly of its equivalents in the homeland, though this one was very comely in a subdued way involving broad planks and slightly rough stone pavers; the equivalent in the guest suite up in the manor was much smaller but more lavishly decorated. There was a changing room, faucets to provide hot water, and then large tubs sunken in a tiled floor; you scrubbed down thoroughly with soap first, rinsed off and then soaked, then got out and rinsed again and used a hemp-pad scrubber, and soaked once more. There was a steam room here too, which was rarer, though the Imperial Palace at home had one.

A gaggle of chattering teenage girls passed on their way to take advantage of the room with the heated rocks; they were what they called maids-in-waiting, from lesser Associate families serving in the manor as part of their education. They curtsied, which looked rather odd in the nude. She was beginning to see that there was a code of manners and hierarchy here as elaborate as the one she'd grown up with; it just used different symbols, like a similar message written in a different script.

A couple of the young girls stared rudely, but those slightly older administered admonishing taps—or flicks with a wet towel, which produced a yelp and more giggles. She had to keep reminding herself that people didn't mean to be aggressive here when they made eye contact for long periods; it was just a difference in custom.

When she remarked on the similarity of the bathhouse to the *sentō* she was used to, the Montivallans laughed.

"Sure, and that's because we copied them from you," Órlaith said. "After the Change, when getting hot water became so much more difficult and single families couldn't do it each for themselves. I think the Mackenzies started it, but it spread fast. Nearly everywhere people didn't stop washing, that is—and since the Prophet's War, they've mostly gotten the message of cleanliness even out on the Hi-Line. There's no wood there, but they started digging a little coal again instead, once we got rid of the Prophet and his crew, who despised human bodies too much to bother washing them."

"Ah," Reiko said. "I'd heard of sitting and washing *in* the tub."

She shuddered delicately as she untied her sash in the changing room.

As she was used to, the attendant was a middle-aged woman who accepted the clothes, folded them to be sent to the laundry, and handed robes and washcloths to the bathers. Strictly speaking she'd transferred the washcloths from an oven-like arrangement to a basket with wooden tongs, then handed them the covered basket: the cloths were hot and damp and smelled slightly and deliciously of lavender, which was a nice touch.

"Yes, I think that used to be the way it was done. Although they had showers, too, of course. Washing *in* a bathtub? Repulsive, that it is, and for the reasons you said," Órlaith said. "Much better this way. As my grandmother Juniper says, when you steal, steal the best!"

"I think we *Nihonjin* did not use the *sentō* so . . . so only?"

"Exclusively," Heuradys said helpfully, peeling herself out of her hose, which required some indelicate contortions to get the skintight knit fabric off.

"Excrusivery, no, *exclusively*. Yes!"

Her ear was finally starting to pick up the difference between the sounds represented by *r* and *l;* she'd decided that the nearest Nihongo equivalent was about halfway between them. It was even harder when the two were in the middle of a word, but she was getting closer. English was an odd language in other ways—speaking it made it very hard to generalize with any subtlety, for instance, or to discuss something without backing other people into corners.

The very structure of its grammar was faintly . . . rude. On the other hand, it was a good verbal hammer to hit things as if they were nails.

"So *exclusively* before the Change. But for us also there was trouble finding the water, and the fuel to heat it. Terrible trouble with everything at first, of course, but so necessary to be clean to avoid sickness. And to keep up spirits, morale."

Reiko did find herself glancing out of the corner of her eye as they scrubbed and then doused themselves down in the cleaning room with its slatted floor and stools.

"See something unusual?" Órlaith asked, catching the glance and widened eyes.

"Well . . . so sorry, but you're both so . . . so very, very *pink*," Reiko said.

Órlaith grinned. "And hairy, I suppose."

"Ah . . . not excessively," Reiko said, turning her eyes aside.

That was true, though it was also obvious they didn't depilate except under the arms. From what she'd seen, the *men* here were often like monkeys, or the fabled Ainu of legend. There were some Japanese as hirsute, but not many.

But the colors! she thought to herself. *The same as on their heads . . . I should have expected that, but I didn't!*

"Do your back?" Órlaith offered.

"Thank you."

The soaking tubs were like sections of great barrels set in the floor, which turned out to be exactly what they were, old wine-barrels rubbed smooth and fitted with round bench-like seats at different heights inside so that you could get neck-deep. There was a slight herbal fragrance to the steaming-hot water, and it worked its familiar magic on stressed muscles and the odd bruise. There were even wooden dippers to pour over your head. They sat in silence for a while, and she admired the interlocking beams of the ceiling. Then she asked.

"The young man with you, he is?"

"My brother John," Órlaith said. "Prince John, technically. John-*denka*. He'll be joining us for lunch."

Reiko frowned. "Please, you have a brother and are . . . the heir?"

Órlaith nodded. "I'm heir to the High King because I'm the first child born to him and the High Queen Mathilda. The Great Charter says the eldest child inherits *that* title, and I'll be crowned when I turn twenty-six."

"It's technically called cognatic primogeniture," Heuradys said, and Reiko moved her lips to memorize the term.

"My brother is—is going to be—heir to the Protectorate, because Mother holds that title in her own right as the only child of her mother and father. PPA law says that the eldest *son* inherits that, and daughters only if there's no male heir."

"Classic primogeniture," Heuradys said helpfully.

"So the order there after my mother passes would be John, my brother Faolán, then me, then my sister Vuissance. Silly in itself, if you ask me, but there it is. I *certainly* don't want to be Lady Protector, and it would be politically . . . difficult."

"No dispute on the dumbness," Heuradys said. "Mind you, I wouldn't be seigneur of Ath for a bet, poor Diomede has to handle that, and as for being Countess-regnant in Campscapell . . ." she shuddered. "How my lord my father manages it without starting to run around screeching *off with their heads* is beyond me. Lioncel would be more than welcome to it as far as I'm concerned, even if he weren't older."

"Ah," Reiko said. "We have not settled the law of succession in Japan, yet, whether to keep the old system or make a new as some wish, or even to return to the law as it was before Meiji. There was my grandmother, and she had only a single son, no daughters. And my brother Yoshihito . . . was lost, not yet married, still very young, six years ago. So there is now only myself and my four sisters. So the law does not matter very much yet, *neh?* The issue does not . . . go up?"

"Arise," Órlaith said. "Or *come* up."

"Al . . . Arise. There is much . . . debate over it."

"Sometimes I forget it's been only two generations since the Change," Órlaith said, and poured another dipper over her head.

The pale yellow of her hair turned much darker when it was wet, the color of old gold with the hint of red more pronounced. Then she twisted it into a rope and wrung it before she went on:

"As it turns out, it's extremely politically convenient that John stands to inherit the position of Lord Protector. He's a man, he's Catholic—you know that House Ath aren't exactly typical Associates."

Heuradys laughed and stretched. "Oh, by the Gray-Eyed, it would be impossible for us to be less typical! Although my brothers *are* Catholics, and they inherit, so the next generation won't get so many odd looks or whispers."

"What we need to know, *Heika*," Órlaith said, "is why your father . . . and his heir . . . came here. We know it wasn't to meet Montival; you didn't know we existed. What was it, precisely? This is a time for truth. There are decisions that must be made."

Reiko had heard that the Sword of the Lady could detect falsehood. She believed it. And the sacred weapon wasn't here right now, which was a gesture of trust. The two pairs of eyes looked at her through the steam, amber and blue, like cats on a ledge seen while the sea-fog rolled in.

She sighed. *You think, consider and ponder. Then you act or do not act; there is no point in dithering.*

"I can only say the truth, even if it is . . . extremely odd. I owe you my life. There is in Japan . . . or should be . . . three things which are the Sacred Regalia of the Imperial line. Great treasures, very sacred and very old. So old that even duplicates made long ago for safety are also sacred."

"The mirror, the jewel, and the sword," Órlaith said, surprising her. A shrug of the strong sloping shoulders. "I've been doing a little reading up."

"*Hai.* Yes. The jewel, *Yasakani no Magatama,* the mirror, *Yata no Kagami* . . . and the sword. *Kusanagi no Tsurugi.* For abundance, for wisdom . . . and the sword for strength, valor."

"Uh-oh," Órlaith said, obviously seeing the pattern. "The Yurok *mahrávaan* and her vision. One of these treasures is *here?*"

"For some general value of *here,*" Heuradys said. "On this side of the ocean at least."

Reiko licked her lips, tasting salt, uncertain whether it was sweat or tears. "*Kusanagi.* The Grass-Cutting Sword."

Órlaith frowned. "Wasn't it kept in a shrine . . ."

"The Atsuta Shrine, yes. Very old, very . . . very *holy.* Venerable. But badly damage . . . damaged in the great war of one hundred years ago."

They both looked thoughtful. "World War Two," Heuradys said after a moment. "Against the ruler of Deutschland, wasn't it? The mad one with the little mustache and the big spiked helmet and the withered arm he was always sticking out? Giant balloons and poison gas and steel war-chariots."

"*Hai,*" Reiko said. "We call our portion the Pacific War."

According to the version she had learned, Japan had been selflessly attempting to bring peace and prosperity to Asia when the Americans had suddenly and brutally rained fire on her cities. She suspected the details might be a little more complex. Being raised at court had made her skeptical of political innocence on anyone's part, even a court as small, austere and tightly disciplined as that of post-Change Japan.

"The Grass-Cutting Sword has been preserved there at Atsuta for a very long time, brought only . . . brought out only for ceremonies of new Emperor. Not *seen*, you understand, even then, even by him. Kept wrapped by Shinto priests. From a thousand and nine hundred years ago, when the Venerable Shrine was founded to keep it by Miyasuhime-no-Mikoto, widow of Prince Yamato Takeru. Until the Change everyone thought it was there . . . then things were very bad in Japan."

"As bad as anywhere in the world, I should imagine," Heuradys said thoughtfully. "So many people packed together."

"*Hai.* The Seventy Loyal Men set out to take my grandmother, only one of my family to survive the first fires, from Tokyo to Sado-ga-shima, Sado Island. Seventy men at the start, and one girl with burns, and ancient armor and swords they take from . . . exhibits? Displays? Twenty-six came to Sado with her, a month after the Change. Half those were dead within a year, broken by what they see . . . saw, and did."

"Brave men," Órlaith said soberly.

"Very. They win absolute *meiyo*—"

"Great honor," Órlaith supplied.

"Yes, great honor to preserve dynasty, all bow, all are . . . inspired. Very necessary in terrible time, to give people symbol of hope, of . . . things going on?"

"Continuity," Órlaith said.

"Of continuity. My father said to me once, to fight and work and struggle people need more than fear—they must have a hope, a goal beyond their own lives, their own bellies. A flag, a living being, can be the soul of a dream. Egawa Noboru, his father Egawa Katashi was one of the Seventy; and Koyama Iwao, my Grand Steward's elder brother—both were part of the Regency Council later. But they can . . . could only bring my grandmother, who was a small child. And the *Yasakani no*

Magatama, the jewel—there with them at the palace in Tokyo. Many years later, in the time of my father, we sent expedition . . . an expedition . . . to the Shrine to find the Sword. But it was gone."

She took a deep breath. "Then, half a year ago . . . my father saw it. Saw it in dreams."

She said it half-defiantly, ready for politely veiled disbelief. There had been enough of that at home. What she saw in those odd cat-like eyes was more disturbing in its way: acceptance. She went on.

"In a castle, in a desert, across the ocean. And . . . I have had these dreams too, since we came here to this fief. Three times. Heat, light, thirst, fear."

Órlaith made a gesture that involved thumping her fists on the sides of her head as she squeezed shut her eyes.

"*Arra*, that was what she meant! Past the dead City of Sky Spirits, to the Valley of Death! The thing that didn't belong there!"

Reiko looked from one to the other. Heuradys was puzzled too, if not as completely as she.

"City of Sky Spirits?" she said.

"*El Pueblo de Nuestra Señora la Reina de los Angeles del Río de Porciúncula*," Órlaith said. "City of Angels, it was called, and most thoroughly dead. And past it . . . Death Valley."

Heuradys snapped her fingers. It wasn't a gesture Reiko was familiar with, but the sharp wet pop caught her attention well enough.

"That report from the Dúnedain at Eryn Muir!" she said. "It wasn't just leftovers they tangled with."

"Leftovers who killed my cousin," Órlaith said grimly. "Once things get organized Mom's going to be doing something serious about that. Past time San Francisco and the Bay cities were dealt with. They just pushed themselves up the priority pole."

"Yes, but the Rangers said the Koreans and Haida and the Eaters with them disappeared *to the south*. Three guesses as to where they're going!" Heuradys said. "You can get to Death Valley *overland*."

Órlaith said something in the language she called Gaelic. Reiko had to read the tone, but that was swearing if she'd ever heard any.

"But a castle?" she said, in English again. "By Brigit the Bright who sends knowledge, we need to do some research!"

Reiko didn't know why she was smiling, for a moment. Then she realized it was because now she could feel something besides bleak determination. It was unfamiliar enough that it took a little while to truly know what the sensation was: hope.

The pavilion was a pleasant open-sided place of wood left to bleach to a natural silvery-gray, on a little tongue of land running into the lake not far from the *salle*. It was connected to firm ground by a plank walkway with carved railings on either side, and it had a view out over reeds and water to the wooded hill to the west; if you turned you could also see the walls of Castle Ath glowing umber in the afternoon sun. The air smelled of water, silt and greenery; a trout jumped in the still blue beyond, leaving a widening ring of ripples.

Two of her Imperial Guard stood by the entrance to the walkway, with their bows slung over their backs and their tall *su yari* spears in hand, foot-long blades glittering in the sunlight; a pair of knights in the black gear of the Protector's Guard were on the other side, with their shields on their arms and drawn swords resting on their armored shoulders. Both groups saluted in their various ways as the three young women passed.

Music sounded as they approached, a slow melancholy tune on a stringed instrument, she thought what they called a lute here, very much like a *biwa*. Reiko knew that Western music had strongly affected Japan in the century and a quarter between Meiji and the Change; and that at least the Change had not undone. This was only strange, not incomprehensible:

> "So, we'll go no more a-roving
> So late into the night;
> Though the heart be still as loving,
> And the moon be still as bright.
> For the sword outwears the sheath

And the soul wears out the breast
And the heart must pause to breathe
And love itself must rest—"

A man in the same colorful after-bath robe as they waited by the tables there, rising to bow and lay his lute aside. She studied him as they were introduced. Very tall by her standards, a few inches above average here. Damp brown hair, and eyes of normal brown but flecked with catlike green. A handsome face in the beaky fashion of his folk, and he carried himself like a warrior.

Reiko chided herself for the childish pleasure she felt when she saw that the table in the pavilion held several plates of sushi—chirashizushi style, the rice in a box with several types of sashimi topping, and futomaki rolls with chopped tuna filling, as well as cucumber and carrot. It really wasn't important . . . but after growing up eating rice nearly every single day you *craved* it when it was removed, and the smell of it pickled with vinegar in the rolls made her mouth water. It would be easier to ignore the pain of a stab wound, in the long term.

She'd been slightly surprised to find that people here actually knew of sushi, much less ate it. Albeit rarely, and as a treat for the wealthy. Prince John and the others could even use chopsticks with some facility, enough so that she felt even more horribly self-conscious about her progress with knife and fork.

You are distracting yourself because the serious matters frighten you, she thought, as she poured soy over a pat of wasabi in the center of a shallow dish. *Stop doing that, Reiko!*

"Dreams," Órlaith said to her brother. "It's just going around, that it is. Tell Her Majesty about yours."

His eyes went between Reiko and his sister as he did so, going wide.

"Her too?" he blurted when he'd finished and seen their reactions. "You too, Orrey? Why didn't you tell me this morning?"

"Once is coincidence, twice can be happenstance . . ."

"The third time is either enemy action, or someone sending you a message," Heuradys supplied. "You've had three dreams each on successive nights, and it's three people, two of whom are having the *same* dream. That's someone . . . no, Someone . . . talking. As plain as a sign in glowing letters written across the face of the moon."

Reiko didn't speak aloud, but her glance flashed to Órlaith.

"Just the last three nights," the Crown Princess said, then nodded to her brother. "Well, just the last three nights *definitely.*"

"As if it was far away, at first, and now is close enough to speak clearly. Or more clearly, or as clearly as may be," Reiko said.

Órlaith nodded approvingly to her and went on to her brother. "And her dream and mine are the same. Heat, thirst, desert, a strange building."

John looked at Heuradys with a question in his eyes.

"No," she replied to the glance, and shook her head with a broad gesture. "Just us faithful vassals here. You two . . . three . . . are the sacred monarchic types. You get the messages from the otherworld. And I don't envy you *one little bit.*"

John frowned. "You two got the heat-fear-castle one. I'm getting the warm-water-old-man-ships one. What does it mean? Couldn't they be a little more *precise*, by the Saints? Since they *are* Saints, or angelic visitations."

"Dreams don't work that way, Johnnie. Remember how Da . . . I don't know if he told you, but before the Quest, when he was our age, he had a dream of the Sword. He said that all it did was sort of alert him to the possibilities involved. No detailed instructions. The Powers who are friends to our kind don't tell us what to do; They speak in the terms we understand because they must, and They offer choices. We have to make the choices and succeed or fail. And by the sound of things, in Korea whoever They gave the choices to failed. Oh, how they failed. Probably not for want of trying, but they did."

John shook his head. "No, he didn't tell me that one. Well, you're the heir, you've got the Sword, it was more relevant to you."

"He didn't like talking about it unless he had to; said the bards were inventive enough on their own."

She grinned. "And you have the disadvantage of being a Christian, dreams aren't an important part of the apparatus for you Book people. The real question is, what are we going to *do* about them?"

Breath hissed between his teeth. "Basically you want to up and go after this . . . Grass-Cutting Sword, right?"

She shook her head. "No. Our friend from Japan here wants to go after it, for that it belongs to her and through her to her people and the Powers that watch over them."

"For the lord and the land and the folk are one," Heuradys said.

Evidently it was a proverb. Reiko blinked; that was something one of her own people might just as easily have said. Reiko shot her a glance, nodded crisply and looked down again.

Órlaith went on: "I want to *help* her. Then we set about dealing with the folk who killed our fathers, together."

Reiko nodded again, and busied herself with her chopsticks and a roll. She might still have a little difficulty with this language, but she could recognize something she agreed with down to the roots of her soul.

"Well, our lady mother the High Queen isn't going to be pleased," Prince John said. "Though . . . when Uncle Ingolf came into Sutterdown with the Prophet's killers on his tail, babbling a weird story about magic lost islands and glowing swords, she went along with it. Hell, she ran away without asking Nonni Sandra's permission to join our father when he went east to Nantucket."

"She didn't ask because she knew the answer would be no," Órlaith said dryly.

"And," he added thoughtfully after a moment, "that was *before* we had their example. Everyone in Montival's grown up on the story since."

"Aunt Fiorbhinn's 'Song of Bear and Raven,'" Órlaith said. To Reiko: "My father's youngest half-sister is a notable bard, and somewhat of a poet."

"There's hardly a ranch out in the backwoods where they don't sing 'Bear and Raven,'" John said. "In which much is made of her rebellious decision to run off to the east with Father. The Catholic princess and the pagan chief, the ones whose fathers killed each other in battle, coming together to create something greater than either."

"Not to mention creating you and me. Yes, and that was when she was our age. People change when they get older. They get more . . . cautious. They've been hit harder and more often. It doesn't mean they're stupid or timid—Mom is extremely good at calculating chances, I think, and she's certainly brave, and Ignatius is a man who just doesn't pay any attention to fear as such. But sometimes just . . . just jumping in *is* the better way to do it. The risk you avoid may be the worst risk of all."

"The *Heika* here seems to have her advisors under control, at least," Heuradys said.

Reiko shook her head emphatically. "So sorry, but I have noticed, here in Montival you are not very . . . no offense, but your feelings show."

"Funny, we Associates say that about Mackenzies. Yes, I've noticed your people don't show theirs much, even by north-realm standards," Heuradys said. "So your vassals are not as absolutely obedient as they look?"

"Some, one, two of the leaders. Others no; and these my father brings are most loyal of all."

"He left the ones he wasn't sure of?" Órlaith asked, interested. "Sure of their loyalty?"

"All loyal to Japan, to Emperor as . . . Emperor, the symbol of the nation. But my . . . Saisei Tennō had ruled from young man, younger than I am now when he take . . . took real power, when Council of Regents step aside to become advisors. Ruled strongly all those years, wisely, led in battle, made policies that work well. When *he* spoke, they listened— not just to the Emperor as a symbol on a flag, but to the man, you understand? I am . . . young, female, inexperienced. Very difficult to go against . . . what is the word, the thought everyone shares so much that they can hardly see it? Like a binding of roots below the soil?"

"*Nemawashi*," Órlaith said absently, using the Nihongo word Reiko was trying to convey.

"Consensus," Prince John said.

"Yes. They may override me if I try to lead them in ways they very much do not go to . . . want to go, against their consensus. Some, at least.

I cannot *make* them obey, not yet. Tennō in Japan always . . . *has* always been able to command like Great Kami come to earth, in . . . theory. Often, not in . . . reality world?"

"The real world," Órlaith said.

"*Hai*, thank you, the real world. People say they obey, they bow, very polite, but sometimes lock the Emperor up in a little court away from things, use him like stamping seal on documents, and courtiers have to sell calligraphy to buy rice for the household. If the Emperor disobeyed, they would remove him and exile him to a distant small island, and put another of the kin in his place. Saisei Tennō told me, often, never never give order you know will not be obey . . . obeyed. That is the first step on a bad road."

Órlaith smiled with a twist of pain in it. "And didn't Da say exactly the same thing at times?" Her brother nodded.

"Theory versus practice," Heuradys said, and Reiko nodded gratefully herself; she knew she was being understood, but it was still frustrating to be less than fully fluent. "Theory versus real world."

The *hatamoto* smiled. "We have a saying, Your Majesty: *It is easier to beg forgiveness than seek permission.* If what you do works, that is. In this case, we really won't have to worry about forgiveness if we fail, I suspect."

Reiko worked that out mentally, then laughed. Sometimes thinking about humor did *not* spoil it. Though the joke there was like umeboshi in a rice ball, rather sour.

Órlaith nodded, took one of the rolls in her chopsticks, dipped it in the wasabi-infused soy, and ate it. Then she spoke, looking out over the water.

"We'll have to prepare to do what my mother did when she went after Da. Abscond. That'll take a while, getting the details straight, and coordinating things over distances."

"We'll need a way to convey messages that doesn't go through normal channels," John said.

"And we're going to need some troops. Not many, not a huge force— the logistics wouldn't work—but some. People with appropriate skills, and personally loyal to you, Orrey," Heuradys added. "If those people the Dúnedain encountered down along the bay *are* heading for the same place, it'll take more than nine Questers. Even if the number is canonical."

"I have some ideas along those lines," Órlaith said.

Then, with a slow thoughtful smile: "And I'm probably going to need a nice Persian cat. Fortunately I know where to get one, and a messenger nobody will question when they're riding about."

CHAPTER FOURTEEN

ERYN MUIR
(FORMERLY MUIR WOODS NATIONAL MONUMENT)
ITHILIEN/MOON COUNTY, CROWN PROVINCE OF WESTRIA
(FORMERLY MARIN AND SONOMA COUNTIES, CALIFORNIA)
HIGH KINGDOM OF MONTIVAL
(FORMERLY WESTERN NORTH AMERICA)
JUNE 25TH (NÓRUI 25TH), CHANGE YEAR (FIFTH AGE) 46/2044 AD

Susan Clever Raccoon rode into the center of Eryn Muir on an afternoon in June, and drew rein after she'd looped around a farmer delivering what looked like sacked potatoes piled high in an oxcart. The man in the shapeless undyed linsey-woolsey tunic, floppy canvas hat and battered leather britches gave her an odd look, but she returned it with a smile and nod and his hand stopped unconsciously moving towards the cocked, loaded crossbow resting butt-down in a scabbard beside him. Getting stared at was a stranger's fate nearly everywhere except a few of the largest cities, and even there a Courier got the hairy eyeball sometimes.

Although just getting ignored was about as common in the really big places, as long as you stuck to the main streets and the places transients stayed. She found *that* sort of creepy and unnatural, far worse than curiosity and stares and suspicion. Most people seldom saw outsiders, after all. In a city like Portland *everyone* was a stranger outside their neighborhoods, which was downright unnatural.

Then she looked around to size up her destination, coming out of the fixed mile-eating focus of her trade and letting it sink in . . .

"Whoa!" she muttered, and the horse sidestepped under her at the conflicting signals. "Sorry, Shine. But . . . whoa!"

There wasn't much to see at ground level, just a few stone-and-redwood stables and haystacks and such flanking the old road, a pathway now mostly surfaced with natural stream gravel. One looked as if it might be an inn, from the sign carved with a prancing pony and the mix of people sitting at tables outside. It took a moment to realize that the buildings were in fact full-size, and that the people around them weren't midgets—were nearly all taller than she was, in fact.

The *scale* of the tree-trunks all around had thrown her off. Their bases were more like basalt pillars she'd seen in the Badlands once than trees, more like geology than vegetation. But their surfaces were infinitely more *alive*, a fibrous red-brown like the hide of some monstrous beast. Not a hostile one, but something that might crush you into insignificance if it decided to pick up and walk. Then her head went back and back as her gaze went up and up . . . and up, into a green haze like a dream of walking beneath the Pacific. The early-summer sun baked out scents like spices and sap as the long day drew to a close, warm and green and intensely fresh.

A grin split her high-cheeked bronze face, and she laughed with pure delight. There was awe in the sound as well, though she'd never considered herself more than conventionally reverent. But even she felt the *Wakȟáŋ Tȟáŋka* sometimes.

More in certain places and times than others; for her it had been strongest during summer lightning storms on the *makol*, watching the clouds build up into forever and come striding over the sky and land with flashes of lightning from horizon to horizon turning the thunderheads into huge caves, gates that reached through to another world. There was something of the same feeling here, though strange and subtle and different.

"Well, *girl*, you wanted to see the world," she said quietly to herself. "By *Wóȟpe*, this sure counts!"

She was tired and hungry, but that was normal working conditions for a Crown Courier. *This* was worth it and more. She'd seen forests all over Montival, ranging from the lodgepole pine of the Black Hills in her own folk's territory to the sunny oak groves of the Willamette to the tall dark Douglas-fir woods of the Cascades, but . . .

"But nothing like this before, eh?" a voice said down by the head of her horse.

She looked down and saw a middle-aged woman in Dúnedain garb, jerkin of dark gray doeskin with the white Tree and Stars and Crown embroidered on it, soft boots, and loose shirt and trousers of a green much like the flat needles of the giant trees high above. She was slim and slightly tired-looking, with short curling brown hair and a black-leather satchel held by a band over one shoulder. That had a silver rune on it like a capital X with vertical bars framing it on either side. When Susan leaned over to shake the offered hand the other's grip was dry and firm but didn't have a warrior's calluses. With a hand over her heart, she bowed and spoke:

"*Mae govannen;* well-met. I'm Ioreth Taconi, the *nesteleth* . . . healer, doctor, here." More formally: "Of Stath Ingolf and the Folk of the West."

"You're right, I've never seen nothing like *this* before!" the Lakota courier said. "I'm Rider Susan Mika."

Susan swung down, landing lightly; she was tired, but she'd known far worse. This didn't even come *close* to what you felt like after a long day up on the *makol* in February, coming back to a collection of *ger* in the dark, the cold seeping into your very bones until even the sight of warmth and light and the smell of food left you indifferent and numb. As if you were doomed to ride on forever, never quite reaching the corral, and didn't even *care* anymore.

"Yes, I was told to expect you. That would be . . . Rider Susan Clever Raccoon, wouldn't it, in the Common Tongue?"

"Yeah," Susan said, mildly pleased that the Dúnedain woman had taken the trouble to check. "Of the Lakota *tunwan* and the Oglála folk, ma'am, originally, now of the High King's Household and the Crown Courier Corps."

The Lakota had retaken a fair chunk of their old territory after the Change, and the Seven Council Fires in the person of her grandfather Red Leaf had been among the first to swear allegiance to the new High Kingdom of Montival during the war against the Prophet—the Church Universal and Triumphant's stamping-grounds had been just west of them, something nobody in their right mind thought tolerable. Under the Great Charter they were the Guardians of the Eastern Door, and while mostly nomads who followed their herds and hunted buffalo they tended to be homebodies when it came to leaving their own ranges. She thought she might be the first of her nation to be seen here since the Change, something that made her smile more broadly for a moment.

A teenage boy dressed like the woman came up and bowed slightly to Susan with his hand over his heart.

"*Mae govannen, rochon,*" the youngster said grinning broadly; he had reddish hair to his shoulders and freckles.

Susan knew enough to translate the greeting as: *well-met, rider.*

"*Haŋ kolá,*" she said.

Which was polite for a woman greeting a friendly male stranger, and she held up her right arm with the palm out. She'd have said *hi* and held it out for a shake if the boy had used English . . . what the Dúnedain called the Common Tongue, and which was English with pretensions in her opinion.

The doctor and the kid—

Well, younger teenager, she conceded. *Looks about thirteen.*

—spoke for a moment in the liquid elegance of Sindarin, which sounded odd with at least one involuntary pubescent squeak thrown in. Susan thought she caught the word for *horses,* and was sure the boy blushed when his voice betrayed him. A little reluctantly she handed over her reins and the leading string for her two remounts, then threw her bowcase over one shoulder, unhooked the shete scabbard from the front of her saddle and reached for her bags.

"I can send the saddlebags up with your roll and the pack, my lady," the boy said unexpectedly, bowing again. "No need to carry them."

I think he's shy and hiding it, she thought, which made her a little more sympathetic.

"OK . . ."

"Fingaerion's on stable duty," Ioreth said.

"It's no trouble at all," the boy went on. "These are really nice horses, my lady. They look like they could go forever."

He fed her mount an apple from a pocket, which Shine accepted with dignified eagerness; it had been a long day for her remuda too. Then he ran a gentle hand down the mare's neck, eased forward, felt her legs and got her left forehoof up and examined it. Even for a Lakota, Susan was fond of horses; that was part of what had gotten her in trouble at home in the first place. She recognized a kindred spirit, and an expert hand.

"Look like they could use a rest, though . . . say two days, and then light exercise? Re-shoe them then?" he said.

She gave him a look that plainly intimated she wasn't going to have her mounts reshod by someone whose voice hadn't finished breaking, and he went on:

"Don't worry, my lady, I'm not the farrier! I just help her out."

"Yeah, thanks," she said, reassured. "I'll come visit 'em later. Air the saddle and tack, though, please."

"Clean, soap, and air. And I'll go over the seams, too, my lady," he nodded and led the animals off. "I'll ring the bell for your kit."

Whatever the hell that means, she thought.

He tentatively stroked the buffalo-robe bedroll strapped to the back of the saddle as he went, as if he'd never seen one before. He might not have. The *Pty Oyate,* the Buffalo People, numbered in the millions once more out on the high plains after nearly half a century of careful management, but the Lakota *tunwan* limited the number of hides outsiders could buy. That kept them moderately expensive, especially since they were also in demand as high-quality power-belting for machinery.

And no foreigner hunted on Lakota land except the most honored guests. Her folk regarded horse theft as an amusing rough-and-tumble sport and didn't grudge anyone else who accepted the risks trying to turn the tables, but they took buffalo poaching *seriously.*

"Seems to know what he's doing, ma'am," Susan said with approval. "Polite, too."

"We're a bit shorthanded here right now, nearly all our warriors out patrolling, but I try to see that my son learns his lessons properly," the doctor said, and chuckled at her double-take. "You're exotic twice over to Fingaerion, you know. Lakota *and* a Crown Courier. He'll be peacocking in front of his friends for months because of this."

Dang, I suppose what exotic *means depends on where you're standing when you point and say it,* she thought.

Before she'd left the *makol* it had never occurred to her that anyone would regard her people as exotic and strange. They were just people who lived the way people lived.

And I thought Crown Couriers were exotic and romantic until I was one. Still do, come to that.

Susan's smile died. "I'm here to see Faramir Kovalevsky and Morfind Vogeler," she said.

And I want to do it without attracting too much official attention, so it's likely best they're all busy here.

"I've got dispatches," she went on aloud. "Ah . . . the Crown Princess wanted to know their condition, though, too. She was concerned about the injuries of her cousins, from the reports. And . . . she was upset about Malfind's death."

"So are we," Ioreth said grimly. "So I gathered from the message from *Hîr* Ingolf. Looks like we're finally going to get the backup we need."

Susan nodded. "But my messages to Faramir and Morfind . . . from what I understand, they're personal. And the Princess really wants to know how things are going with them."

Ioreth frowned, obviously marshaling her professional side. "Besides quite severe general battering, they both had concussions—his worse than hers."

Susan nodded; being knocked out was no joke. Sometimes you never did get completely better. One of her cousins back home had blinding headaches every week and forgot things all the time because he'd gotten kicked in the head by a mean stallion.

"And she had a nasty cut to the face from an axe, though it's healing well. Fortunately even Faramir's headaches have tapered off and I can't detect any long-term injury. They're both fit for full duty, if that's what you mean and if it's absolutely necessary," she said. "But they're both rather young—ah—"

Susan nodded. "So'm I, ma'am," she said. Dryly: "I'd noticed that myself, sorta."

It was the Dúnedain's turn to do a double-take, and she waggled a reproving finger and gave a snort before she went on.

"And I was frankly a bit worried about them, about possible long-term trauma. That was why I delayed putting them back on the active roster as long as I could."

She sighed and went on: "I'll take you to them. Activity is probably what they need, now. Can I give you a hand with your gear?"

"Thanks, but I can manage," Susan said, shouldering her bow, bowcase, quiver and shete.

She was a smallish young woman, but wiry and enduring, and she prided herself on handling everything she could personally. Often enough there was nobody else to depend on, when she was out in the parts of the High Kingdom that didn't have heliograph nets or railroads or even mail service. She'd slept in snowdrifts and lost remounts to tigers and been treed by grizzlies, exchanged long-distance arrows with bandits more than once, and it had come to at least a show of blades in rough places now and then. Knowing you'd be well avenged was comforting, but she preferred to keep it on a theoretical basis and make sure others respected the High King's badge herself. Mostly that was a matter of being visibly ready for trouble, though not someone who was looking to start it. A lot of Couriers were more pushy, but then a lot of Couriers were guys, little ones, with little-guy problems.

"Here's the lift then," Ioreth said. "I'll show you the ropes." An impish smile. "Literally, I'm afraid. Heights don't bother you, I hope?"

"No," Susan replied, and it was true.

Well, not much.

The lift rested on a low fieldstone base approached by a ramp. The vehicle itself was a circle made of two cross-lapping sets of planks with a pillar in the center, its rim surrounded by a chest-high wall of thin woven laths. It swayed a little as they opened the door and entered. Susan's eyes went up again. The supports for the breastwork were structural ribs as well, and they curved in to join the pillar well above their heads. A cable ran straight through the central column; she realized it was probably fixed in the stone base. A barrel-like arrangement stood out from the wood, with a crank-handle on either side.

Ioreth pulled out an anchoring pin. Susan put her burdens down and took her place at one of the cranks without needing to be directed; she'd never been shy about chores. The doctor nodded at an unasked question.

"This isn't the only way up," she said. "Just the easiest for people. One of the big trees is hollow, and we've rigged a spiral staircase in that one. And there are rope ladders and simple climbing ropes all over the place, and baggage hoists. This is the one that, ah, visitors usually use, though. The trees are strong, but you have to be careful about balancing the lateral strains above the base or you could pull one right over the way storms do. A redwood makes a very long lever."

They turned the cranks. It wasn't much effort, and the platform rose steadily though rather slowly. From that smoothness and the low whining sound, Susan guessed the cranks were linked to high-ratio worm gearing within. Mostly she watched as they rose, her lips shaping a silent whistle.

She'd heard they used treehouses a lot here. The *flets* were treehouses, she supposed. Just as the *makol* was *rather flat and quite wide*.

The lowest looked to be around fifty feet up, the highest twice that. In shape they were more like burls or pods, each supported by a circle of graceful curved wooden beams that started in a broad support collar built around the bark and fanned out to end in a ring-beam around the outer edge of the building. Most of the *flets* were one-story, surrounded by wide verandahs overhung by the mossy shingle roofs, though she saw a couple that were taller. Flowerboxes or similar constructions for small herb-gardens ringed the balconies, often dropping long tendrils of flowering vines.

Walkways joined them, light airy flexible things rigged like suspension bridges, looking shaggy and green for some reason. The trees often grew close together anyway, in tight clusters like sections of a circle where they'd sprouted from the roots of some ancient fallen ancestor. A few lanterns had already been lit as the sun dipped westward, and they glowed in cool complement to the warm yellow of the last sunbeams slanting down into the enormous stillness around them.

The wooden surfaces of the lift's structure had all been carved, in lacy patterns of interlocking tendrils. As she rose higher she saw that the structures of the houses and walkways had been decorated likewise, images of leaf and vine, bird and beast, warriors and spirits, all in a elongated style a little like what Mackenzies used but more delicate and intricate. Some of the larger ones showed scenes from tales, a giant wave overwhelming a mountain, two huge wolf-like beings fighting, a one-handed man with a star on his brow, a tall kingly figure kneeling before a shorter one.

The basic construction material was crimson-tinged gold-brown redwood, which she knew was light and strong and easy to work and very resistant to decay. It had been generously supplemented with other woods, and just touched here and there with decorative tile or glass. It was a substantial settlement . . . and it was lost in the immensity of the trees, ramming home the scale of what she was seeing again. Her mind kept stuttering that way at what she was seeing.

"It isn't as grand as *Tham en-Araf* over on the other side of the valley, but we at Eryn Muir like it," Ioreth said.

The words were modest, but pride rang underneath them. Susan found she didn't mind that in the least.

"I've seen a lot of big, pretty stone buildings," she said.

Though she had been rather impressed with *Hîr* Ingolf's dwelling at Wolf Hall, recently built on the ruins of a structure burned long before the Change in the Valley of the Moon. And more with its surroundings, mountain-backed grove and vineyard and woodland. Though the household had been understandably quiet and serious, with his eldest son so newly dead.

"I've never seen *anything* like *this* before," she added honestly.

There was a *click* as they came level with the middle of a walkway. The lift wasn't secured to it; instead cables stretched out to half a dozen trees from a big multilooped steel anchor-point just above, and those were in turn braced with more thigh-thick ropes to others to spread the strain. The arrangement wasn't rigid, and neither was the walkway. Everything was moving as the trees swayed, very slightly and slowly but continuously, to a murmur and sough and creak. Susan swallowed slightly—she wasn't afraid of heights, but she'd been raised on very solid, and mostly very *flat* ground where the highest place was your head when you were sitting on top of a horse.

The Dúnedain opened a door in the side of the lift, and another in the walkway. The walking surface was planks and it was about ten feet wide; the railings to either side were latticework with openings just large enough to pass a thumb. Every six feet or so the lattice arched over the walkway in a high curve; the side-walls and the roofed sections were both thickly overgrown with Morning Glory vines rooted in wicker tubs hanging a little below. Round pink-and-white flowers starred the glossy green, busy with bees and hummingbirds and big colorful moths of some sort.

"The last time *Hiril* Eilir visited, she said that *Hiril* Astrid would have loved it," Ioreth said; the note of pride was in her voice again, and Susan recognized the names of the Dúnedain founders.

When they were on the planks of the walkway Ioreth jerked a cord and the lift sank away with a mechanical whine. The cranks freewheeled, but the bottom struck the stone rest below with only a muffled thudding sound, cushioned by a matt of shredded redwood bark.

Half a dozen children a few years either side of six ran past playing some game, giving a little pause in mid-stride to bob their heads to the doctor. As they walked on another—about twelve this time, in practical mottled hunting gear with a light bow over her shoulder—nodded to Ioreth, gave Susan a curious glance, then tossed a coiled rope over the edge, swung herself over and slid away downward. Ioreth stopped to pull the rope up and coil it again and hang it from a wooden hook, apparently a chore everyone did if they passed one.

Susan could see some of the other walkways clearly from here. The passages were busy without being crowded, here a man carrying a wicker basket of white-feathered chickens, there a woman with a bundle of spearshafts over her shoulder and a serious expression, or a young girl with flowers in her hair, a frown and a hot pot held between two pads. Woodsmoke drifted from under the conical tops of the tile chimneys, and cooking-smells made her stomach rumble to remind her that it had been a long time since breakfast and that lunch had been hard-tack and jerky in the saddle. Families and groups were eating at tables on their verandahs, laughing and talking; it made her feel a little lonely.

The music of some stringed instrument sounded in the distance, and a song rang. More and more of the parties took it up, until the words were plain:

> *"So leave the fire and come with me*
> *To walk beside the dreaming sea—"*

They turned onto a shorter branch walkway that ended at the verandah gate of one of the *flets*, flanked by two structures that turned out to be nest-boxes for a colony of purple martins. A cat was sitting looking at the birdhouses with the tip of its tail twitching slowly and steadily, obviously trying to figure out how to get around the sloped wicker barriers, until it darted away as they walked up.

"This is *ohtar* housing," Ioreth said. "For young warriors who don't have a family dwelling here. North is twelve o'clock, right here. Jakes are at three o'clock, bathhouse at eight, the kitchen and common dining area at nine. You're assigned to seven, and Morfind is in ten. Faramir will be there soon if he isn't already—his mother and father have a *flet* here, but they're out with a patrol right now. I'll let them know you're coming if you want to wash up first."

"Thanks, ma'am," Susan said sincerely; a courier or a herder or hunter spent a lot of time being grimy and smelly, but she'd grown up washing when she could. "See you later, maybe."

"Certainly," Ioreth said, making the hand-to-heart gesture again before she left. "It's been a pleasure."

Round housing plans didn't confuse Susan either, the way they would have many people. These days Lakota used tipis for ceremony, and built permanent structures in rammed earth for their few small towns and to store bulky goods at selected spots along their seasonal migration paths. Most of the time they lived in *ger*, a type of circular lattice-work tent with double-layered felt walls and conical tops. An exchange student from Mongolia who'd been a friend of her grandfather's at SDU in 1998 had shown him how to make them, and they'd spread like wildfire afterwards since they were simple to make and maintain from available materials and suited the harsh climate perfectly. They were easy to move around either knocked down or on wheeled platforms, too. Even the biggest weren't as large as this *flet*, but the principle was the same, and at the summer hunt and festivals thousands might be parked near each other.

Number Seven had a number 7 carved into the plank doorway, and two glass windows to either side of it. Inside was a compact room shaped like a wedge of cheese with the point bitten off. There was a bed across the inner wall with brackets that showed it could be converted to multiple bunks, a cupboard, a table and chair and a lamp on a bracket, and a shelf with some books. She didn't even recognize the *alphabet* in the three fat leather-bound volumes, but from the illustrations it was from what the Dúnedain called *The Histories*, sort of like the way you'd find a copy of the *Book of Mormon* nearly anywhere you stopped in New Deseret. Graceful carvings ran around the edges of the furniture, and in bands under the ceiling. It looked comfortable, especially for summer, and even on a cold wet day it would beat hell out of a lot of barracks that she'd seen.

A bell sounded, but she couldn't see where for a moment. Then a bump under the floor accompanied it, and she realized that the inset bronze ring marked a trapdoor. When she opened it a pulley-and-basket arrangement with a rope loop running to the ground was revealed, loaded with her kit; when she'd heaved that out onto the floor she could see Ioreth's son waving from far beneath.

She waved back and spent a few moments arranging things. When she had two remounts she usually put a light saddle pack like this on one and switched things around when she transferred her gear to a fresh horse. Thirty pounds didn't burden a good animal of the sort the Courier

Corps used, and it made her life a lot easier. After she'd thought for a moment, she decided to wear her good clothes once she'd used the bath-house.

It was gear from home, a bleached deerskin tunic with fringes and beadwork, leggings likewise fringed and strap-up moccasins decorated with colored porcupine quills. Her work involved taking hospitality fairly often, and while she had to maintain the credit of the Royal Household you couldn't possibly carry sets of dinner-guest garb in all the dozens—possibly hundreds—of different local styles current in Montival.

Anyone who didn't like Lakota formal dress could do that other thing. For that matter, this was pretty much *men's* fancy dress back home, except for the blue-and-red yoke of beadwork and elk teeth over the shoulders, and so were the two feathers she pinned over one ear when she re-did her long braids. Anyone who objected to that could do the other thing too, and she wasn't going to drag a three-skin robe around. When she came out of the bathhouse wearing the garb—the facilities were much better than nothing but she suspected that something more elaborate was down on the ground at the nearby creek—she walked around the verandah to where Number Ten should be, holding the dispatch in her hand with the High Kingdom's seal—the Sword of the Lady and a crown—prominently displayed.

The *flet* was largely empty, which she'd expected from what Ioreth had said about everyone being out; if it hadn't been, she'd have suggested a stroll out on one of the walkways to get a little privacy.

The two she was after were sitting at their table on the verandah; or rather Faramir Kovalevsky was. His cousin was doing a handstand on the railing, with her legs extended and ankles crossed in the air, lowering herself slowly until her forehead touched the carved wood and then pushing up again until her arms were straight. When Susan came in sight she flipped up in the air and did a back-summersault with a nonchalance that made the young Lakota woman blink, given the seventy-foot drop at her back, and landed lightly on the balls of her feet. She was wearing soft loose trousers and elf-boots, but not the shirt-tunic, and the knit sports bra showed the long lean muscle rippling on her torso and arms. The face above it would have been striking except for the long red-purple mark of a fresh deep scar that wound from just beside her nose to her left ear.

It's a badge of honor, Susan reminded herself, as they made the introductions.

Faramir smiled. *Whoa, cutie!* the Courier thought, then made herself turn objective.

They're both actually sort of cute, in a wašicu *sort of way,* she thought.

Not that she had anything in particular against *wašicu;* it wasn't like the old days. Nobody pushed the Lakota around anymore; the last to try had been the Prophet's killers before she was born, and that hadn't ended well at all . . . for them.

Her father's *ger* had a ceremonial war-shirt in it with twelve scalps from that time.

And it didn't do to be prejudiced. For that matter, her own maternal grandmother had been a green-eyed redhead. People had moved around a lot right after the Change. There were sure-'nuff Lakota who looked pretty much like Faramir, though usually not among the most prominent families.

Though he's looking sort of grim underneath the smile and that cut makes it hard to read her expressions.

The table was actually more distracting right now, with an elegantly turned maple-wood tureen of steaming mushroom and ham soup, a cold raised venison pie, a salad of wild greens, fried potatoes, a round loaf of fresh white bread, butter and soft cheese and a pile of blackberry tarts with whipped cream and some things she didn't recognize.

When the meal was finished—it was the first time she'd eaten olives, and they were pretty good—the Dúnedain both looked through her message. They spoke together briefly in Sindarin, then Faramir squinted his blue-gray eyes at her.

"Basically, this"—his hand touched the stiff paper with the broken seal, where the message was written in the same odd-looking script as the books in her room—"says that you speak for the Crown Princess. So, speak, guest."

His English had a slight accent to her ear, fluid and a bit singsong, though it was obviously his other native language. He probably thought hers was a nasal drawl, and their word-choices were noticeably different.

And yeah, no question that's what it says. What the Crown Princess said to me was that I was supposed to evaluate you two. She knows you but wanted an outsider's appraisal. My appraisal is that . . .

"OK, there are two ways to interpret your report about the fight here last month," she said. "One . . ."

"Is that we're crazy," Morfind said flatly. "Or making excuses for screwing up with that Haida."

The scar turned redder when she flushed. Susan held up a hand.

"Yeah. The other is that you saw exactly what you said you saw. Princess Órlaith sorta inclines to that interpretation which frankly scares the shit out of me . . . and I don't scare all that easy."

"Us too," Faramir said, and Morfind unconsciously touched the long bone-hilted knife at her belt.

Susan continued: "So fill me in on what happened afterwards. That news hadn't all gotten north yet when I left."

The Ranger cousins looked at each other. Faramir went on neutrally:

"We found the enemy ship run into an inlet up north, around *Côf en-Amlug* . . . Drake's Bay."

"*We* meaning the Rangers of Stath Ingolf," Morfind put in; Susan got the impression she liked precision. "*We* as in Faramir and I were in the infirmary."

Faramir nodded. "As far as we can tell, what happened was that the ship just barely made shore. It's not a Haida orca, but it's the same as the ones the High King's party found in the Bay, except it wasn't on fire. This one didn't make it that far. Out of food, out of water, missing a mast, and it came ashore hard and broke its back. Stripped of pretty well all its gear."

"But with some bones split for the marrow on the beach," Morfind added grimly.

Susan signed agreement. Wendigo weren't part of her people's legends but she was familiar with the concept. Faramir continued:

"Then someone from the ship went south and made contact with the

Eaters . . . my guess is the *skaga*, because they didn't eat him before he could try to talk, and that would take supernatural intervention. They sent parties to sneak through Ithilien and bring back the crew."

"And we stumbled on the last bunch," Morfind said, a note of bitterness in her tone. "Faramir and my brother and me."

"But there the trail vanishes," Faramir said. "The *yrch* bands south of here are boiling like a pot left on the fire, though. It'd take a big force to find out exactly what happened."

"You may get that," Susan said. "I had dispatches from the Marshal's office and the Chancellor and the High Queen to *Hîr* Ingolf. I don't know what's in them, but your uncle . . . and your father . . ."

She nodded to Faramir and his cousin in turn.

". . . looked sort of satisfied. Looked downright scary, in fact. So I think it must have been news about reinforcements."

The cousins looked at each other again. Then Morfind leaned forward with her elbows on the table and her chin on her thumbs.

"But that's not why the Princess sent you to *us*," she said softly. "Not with personal dispatches and a personal message through you. Is it?"

Susan licked her lips. She'd loved the High King and she wanted revenge for him, but these two *burned*.

"No," she said. "The Princess . . . and her, um . . . guest. They think they know what this is all about. First thing you've got to do is swear not to speak a word of it, whatever you decide to do."

Another of those glances, and then they made their oaths. Susan was satisfied; Órlaith said their word was good, and she ought to know. Her own impression was likewise, for what it was worth. Faramir poured their glasses full again from the clay carafe of wine.

"You're not just talking to us about this, are you?"

"Oh, Hell, no," she said.

Susan was more used to beer and whiskey—they were what was available where she'd been born, though fermented mare's milk was more common still. The same friend of the family who'd shown people how to make *ger* had introduced airag, once her grandfather had talked him out of trying to ride a horse back to Ulan Bator and he'd settled down on the *makol* and married her great-aunt instead. Wine was nice, though. This one had an agreeable fruity aftertaste. She wasn't more than slightly elevated, since she never did that among even the most friendly strangers, but she was a little relaxed.

"I've made a bunch of stops. You're last. You want in?"

The young Dúnedain man said something softly in Sindarin, and his cousin nodded strongly. Susan raised a brow.

"In the Common tongue . . . *I may not live while the slayer of my kinsman walks beneath the stars.*"

Susan threw back her head, laughed, and said something in Lakota. The Rangers looked at her coldly, until she spoke again:

"That's one of *our* sayings. And in Common English, it means exactly the same fucking thing, you know?"

They relaxed, and she went on. "The High King was my uncle by adoption, and he was there for me when I really needed it. I figure I'm due a piece of this. The Princess invites you to the dinner. And I think you want a slice of the meat too, right?"

The two Dúnedain began to grin: this time it looked wholly sincere, though perhaps not very nice. She returned the expression as if in a mirror and tossed off the glass.

"Here's what's been happening," she said.

CHAPTER FIFTEEN

Órlaith sat and chewed on the end of her pen and blinked at the paper her hostess had dropped into the tangle of notes. On the High Kingdom's stationery, signed:

Baroness d'Ath, Lord Marshal of the High King's Hosts, and sealed with her Vee-and-Delta.

The text essentially read: *All requests by the bearer are authorized, and shall be carried out immediately without question or attempt to refer to the chain of command for confirmation.*

That would be very useful, when it was obeyed. She suspected that would be much less often than she'd prefer; bureaucracies double-checked things the way rabbits ran in zigzags when a hawk was after them, by reflex. Military bureaucracies were sometimes an exception . . . but on the other hand, sometimes they weren't. Heuradys' official mother rose from the table.

"And no, don't tell me what you hooligans plan to do with it," she said. "I don't want to know. When I got authorizations like that in the old days, people didn't want to know, either."

A formal bow of farewell. "Your Highness . . . Your Highness . . . Your Majesty . . . my appalling offspring . . ."

The Sword of the Lady rested on the table before the heir to the Kingdom, looking so normal against the burnished surface of the black walnut. Deep within her, there was a feeling like a bronze bell sounding a mellow note.

Truth.

"I'm going hawking," Tiphaine said. "You infants carry on. What I don't know, I can't be duty bound to tell."

Órlaith looked around the table at her . . .

Co-conspirators, she thought; herself, John, Heuradys, Reiko.

They were using an out-of-the-way conference room. Ruling at any level seemed to involve a lot of sitting around and talking, and this was just a pleasant chamber with a window overlooking gardens and a distant view of fields and, on the edge of vision on a fine summer's day, Mt. Hood. The normal sounds of everyday life came through it, along with the sweet smell of cut grass, birdsong, a horse snorting, the whirr of a push-operated lawnmower, the slow steady *tock . . . tock . . . tock . . .* of someone splitting wood with an axe. John fingered his lute—it was actually soothing when he did it like that, and it was good cover. People made music together all the time.

"All right, there's going to be a lot of people who'd say that we're crazy," she said. "Too young to think straight. Or too pagan and witchy, in my case."

John grinned and strummed and sang lightly:

"Guinnevere drew pentagrams
Like yours, mi'lady like yours
Late at night when she thought
That no one was watching at all . . ."

Órlaith scowled at him: "Or too foreign, in . . . dammit, we're going to have to use names, among ourselves. Is that all right?"

"Yes," Reiko said. A slight smile: "I grant official permission . . . Órlaith. We are in your land; in this we should follow your custom."

"Oh, Powers, you can say Orrey, Reiko. All my friends do."

Reiko lowered her eyes and swallowed, which was the equivalent of an emotional outburst from her. The Crown Princess of Montival had a feeling that Reiko hadn't *had* many friends, growing up.

"Ah . . . Órlaith . . . what does it mean? Does it mean anything?" she asked.

Órlaith grinned; Japanese names all had a meaning apart from being an arbitrary noise attached to a person. Reiko meant Courteous Lady, more or less, though *ko* had several alternative readings.

The which is appropriate indeed, for she is very much a lady and unfailingly courteous. Though to be sure when you're facing her in the salle *you might think differently!*

Egawa Noburu's first name meant *Arise* and Koyama Akira's meant *Bright Intellect.* Her grandmother Juniper had told her that English names had been that way once, compounds like *Friend of the Elves* or *Cunning in Battle* or claiming relationship with a particular Power. Between the Bible and the Norman conquerors they had gotten out of the habit, because after that their names came from foreign languages they didn't understand.

"Órlaith is *Golden Princess,* in the old tongue. And I can't even be called immodest, for it was my parents who picked it, and none of my own doing."

Reiko laughed, holding a hand before her mouth. "Most of us here are monarchs' children anyway, *neh?*"

"Right. Some will say *too foreign,* in Reiko's case. My mother and Chancellor Ignatius would listen to us, think seriously . . . and then possibly send an official expedition. In about six months, after the . . ."

An unexpected lance of pain hit her. *Doing something makes it feel better.* She sighed, waited an instant, and continued:

". . . after the High King's funeral in Dun Juniper, after things have settled down. An expedition which would not include us. Does *anyone* here think that's after being a good idea?"

"No," Reiko said decisively, snapping her fan from one side to the other. "It would be too late, if the *jinnikukaburi* . . . and our other enemies . . . are already on the track. And it would fail. And also . . . we Nihonjin did not come here to completely hand our mission to strangers . . .

even friendly strangers, or even close friends. The Grass-Cutting Sword is *ours*, as the Sword of the Lady is yours."

"I agree," John said. He ran a hand through his hair. "The problem is that if I hadn't had those dreams and someone else was telling me about it, I *wouldn't* agree. I'd be strongly inclined to think the one telling the story needed a long rest somewhere quiet with lots of chamomile tea."

"Right you are, Johnnie-me-boyo," Órlaith said. "I might believe such a one myself—but I might not, so, if I had no Sword. Or even if I did, for what someone *believes* to be true *feels* true, do you see?"

Reiko's eyes sharpened on her. "Your Sword . . . it does not reveal truth? This is what I understood?"

"When I'm listening to another, it tells me if they believe what they're saying, which is not quite the same thing as truth. I can sense the intent to deceive, you see?"

Reiko gave a quick nod.

No flies on that one, indeed. Though there are other things it can do, from what Da said. She went on:

"The second problem we're having here is that the . . . other side . . . obviously know something about this, too. That's clear from what went on down at Eryn Muir."

Reiko made a gathering gesture with her fan. "And from the fact that my father's ship was pursued almost as soon as it left Sado-ga-shima. Pursued relentlessly, regardless of cost."

Órlaith made a gesture of agreement. "And the Haida cooperated with them; Da always suspected that their shamans and chiefs were in contact with the . . . the Malevolence, and that it was building them up as a second arrow on the bow if the CUT failed. Our enemies are not going to be sitting about with their thumbs up the orifice and the mill-wheel of their minds disengaged from the grinding stones. The Powers are at work here, though They must mostly act through human beings. And our enemies are not necessarily stupid. A great pity, but there it is."

Heuradys nodded. "As it was before the gates of Troy," she said. "Let's just assume we're not the Trojans."

Órlaith looked down at the list she'd drawn up, thought for a moment, and scribbled a note. Then she went to a door, and rang a handbell for a varlet.

The door opened immediately. "Dicun, take this up to the heliograph station at Castle Ath," she said. "It's a summons for a Royal courier, a Lakota woman named Susan Mika. She'll be at Todenangst, so she ought to arrive in a few hours. When she does, send her straight up here."

"Courier?" John asked.

"Susan Mika's about our age. And she was very grateful to Da for taking her in and finding her work she loved, hard prideful work. I think she'll . . . cooperate. And that gives us a way to communicate that doesn't involve message logs that someone with the Royal codes . . . like our mother . . . can query any time they want to."

"Ah," Reiko said. "Clever! Yes, I remember her from Di-ar-muid's home."

"And that's one of the places I'll send her," Órlaith said. "Larsdalen first—"

"Luanne?" Heuradys asked. "Good choice, though she's a bit impulsive."

"Grimy arse, said the kettle to the pot. Then Dun Fairfax, for that Karl Aylward Mackenzie would never forgive me if I didn't, then Diarmuid's steading, then Eryn Muir for my cousins, and back with the answers . . . not that I much doubt any of them. Reiko, you need to get your guard commander on side. There's no chance of just walking off with that one not looking, is there?"

"No," Reiko said. "He is a dedicate . . . dedicated man. His father . . . remade . . . the Imperial Guard, and raised him very . . . sternly. And he knows me from very small. That is good and bad. And we need the men under his command. Some would follow me anyway, I think, but all would be . . . disturbed."

The folk around the table were all within a few years of twenty either way. They all nodded in unison; their worlds were full of authoritative people who were either their parents or who'd known them as infants or at least before they were toilet-trained.

Sure, and Da said one of the drawbacks of hereditary succession is that you spend your twenties with your parents and uncles and aunts being one and the same with your political superiors, Órlaith thought.

She had seen enough of the alternatives in stubbornly republican parts of Montival like Corvallis or the Free Cities of the Yakima League to know that she preferred the system she'd been born to, but still . . .

People who knew you when you were bubbling and dribbling have a hard time seeing you as an adult, and they can be downright irritating and give laughs like a braying donkey if you point out that you're not a wee puling babe the now.

Reiko apparently had that problem too, only worse. She wasn't going to let it stop her. Órlaith looked at the set of those almost-delicate features, and decided she liked that a good deal. Under that careful, gentle courtesy, there was a fair bit of tiger. She went on to her brother:

"Now, what you need to do, Johnnie-me-lad, is look up an old friend of the family in Newport; I met him not so long ago, and I've been in that city in the last few years."

John made a gesture of agreement; Órlaith had spent a few semesters studying at OSU in Corvallis, both because it was an excellent seat of learning and because it was politic for the future High Queen. Newport was a part of that city-state's territory and its principal outlet on the Pacific, a natural place to visit.

"But you haven't. Either one," Órlaith went on.

Her brother had been taking classes at the Protectorate University in Forest Grove instead, and at Mt. Angel. Both were heavily Catholic, which was perfectly appropriate since he was heir to the Lord Protector's position.

He looked puzzled, but only for an instant. "Oh. That's why. Nobody in Newport will know *me* from Adam if I'm careful."

"Exactly; or we can hope they won't, you see? We're going to need a ship, and we're going to need money."

Everyone nodded, even Reiko. Money—and the things it symbolized, like arms and armor and ships and fighting men and horses and food— greased the axles on which the wheels of kingdoms turned. Wise rulers kept an eye on how much of it was going where, and a very close eye on disruptions to the usual flows. The High Queen and her closest advisors would do that by ingrained reflex, especially if there was a sudden loan to the heirs. Wise bankers would automatically report any large irregular advance made to any highborn client, for related reasons. Certainly any operating in Portland or Astoria would, and there was no time to use financial houses in Walla Walla or Boise.

"We'll need a lot more than our allowances, or what we can borrow in the ordinary course of things without word getting back to Mother or the Chancellor. Here's what you'll be proposing—"

"Newport!" the conductor said in a voice that managed to be loud and a bit blurred and utterly bored all at once.

She blew a whistle and repeated it as brakes squealed and steel wheels rattled on rail.

"Newport!"

And not a moment too soon, Prince John of the House of Artos thought. *Mary Mother, I hate rail travel.*

He'd done a fair bit of it with his parents, as a child and youth, and it was annoying if you were naturally active. Carriages were worse, but you didn't normally stay inside one nearly as long. He'd rather bump his backside against saddle leather anytime, or walk for that matter.

All I've done is sit and watch trees and hills go by for hours and I feel tired out by it as if I'd been hacking at a pell or riding at the ring wearing a suit of plate. It's a mystery. And it seems unnatural to see a town without farms outside, just a few turn-out pastures and truck gardens. Here they plow the sea.

"End of the line! All off for Newport!"

But at least the weather's all I could want, he thought happily, yawning with his hand over his mouth and looking out the window.

There was a fine drizzle coming down. With a wind off the cold current that ran southward along the coast, it was also a bit chilly. Throughout Montival west of the Rockies summer was the dry season, but hereabouts on the ocean side of the Coast Range they got at least a few rainy days every month. Even a summer's day like this could suddenly dip into the fifties. The cold current running south down the shore from the Arctic made the weather undependable compared to the interior valleys.

Which is lucky. People will be keeping their heads down, not strolling along looking at strangers. Even in a fair-sized city like this, people usually notice outsiders.

The railway station was post-Change, a barn-like wooden structure with an overhang next to the tracks and a pavement of bricks salvaged here and there and brought in as ballast, which showed in the different shades of brown and red. His valet Evrouin slung his own smaller suitcase over his back and took his lord's canvas-and-leather bag and cased lute from the overhead rack and followed him as he hopped down. The servant would make him a lot more plausible.

The other passengers hurried off, some whistling for porters. There had been a score or so of travelers in each of the passenger cars but he'd simply put Evrouin in the aisle seat, pulled his hat down over his eyes and dozed or pretended to. That discouraged conversation and everyone would just put it down to Associate snootiness, which people in this part of the High Kingdom were always ready to believe in anyway.

The return passengers were waiting for the cars to be swept and looking at watches if they had them or the station clock if they didn't; stevedores were already slinging barrels and bundles and sacks and bales and boxes from the freight cars onto horse-drawn wagons and replacing them with *other* barrels and bundles and sacks and bales and boxes; clerks were ticking things off on clipboards; the chain team of twelve massive draught horses was being led away to the stables and paddocks and their replacements munched the feed in their nose-bags as they waited to be hitched to the other end of the train. This short workaday route that handled a lot of heavy freight usually didn't rate a hippomotive and made do with horses on their own four feet.

Everyone was moving just a little faster than he was accustomed to, not because they were in any tearing rush but simply because that was their customary pace. Corvallans had a reputation for bustling along, and apparently it was well-justified. Since he didn't have his head down and wasn't charging for the door a small group of touts also headed his way, holding up signs with the names of the inns they fronted for. *That* was perfectly familiar from train stops everywhere; a combination of golden spurs on your heels and no cordon of flunkies drew them. He flung up his hand and then pointed.

One of the touts bore a sign with the name *Seagull's Roost*. He had a stiff left arm and a rigid claw of shiny melted-seeming flesh at the end of it along with a few smaller spots of white-and-pink scar tissue on the left side of his face and scalp. That accounted for his occupation. Several of the others were also too disabled or young or too old for a full day's work; this was a thriving town where a strong back and willing hands could always at least pick up enough day-labor for a bellyful of bread and fish stew, a doss and the odd mug of beer. The leaping horse badge on his jacket was something Corvallans only granted to wounded veterans of the Battle of the Horse Heaven Hills, along with a small pension if the wounds were crippling, which accounted for the injuries *and* the occupation.

John had grown up around veterans of the Prophet's War, and the Horse Heaven Hills had been where it was won and lost, though the fighting had gone on for more than a year afterwards—years, if you counted chasing down the last bands of fanatics in the vast tumbled wilderness that made up much of Nakamtu Province. There had been a lot of catapults throwing glass balls full of napalm in the great battle, and footmen had had no option but to spit on their palms and brace the pike while they stood and took it. From the look of it one of the incendiary roundshot had split in midair, and he'd thrown up his hand at the last instant to protect his eyes from a spray of liquid fire.

He'd succeeded . . . mostly.

He also looked clean, neatly if cheaply dressed and not as if he escaped his fate daily at the bottom of a bottle or a pipe of maryjane as soon as he could scare up the price, though you couldn't have blamed him if he did. John wouldn't have picked that inn if he had, though.

"I've heard praise of your hostel, goodman," John said with charitable untruth, and gave a respectful inclination of the head. "Evrouin, please accompany him and get us rooms; we'll be staying for some time. I'll take *Azalaïs* with me."

That made the valet stir a little and shoot him a glance as he handed over the lute in its tooled-leather case. He was a dark hard-faced man in his late thirties, just barely old enough to have fought in the Prophet's

War, and an Associate himself. Though of the lowest class within that order—from the sort of family who got a double-sized peasant holding, what was technically a fief-minor in sergeantry, and supplied crossbowmen and spearmen to the manor lord instead of paying rent and labor-service. He'd been chosen by the High Queen when John turned sixteen, and over the three years since had displayed a number of talents beyond laying out a suit of clothes. They got on reasonably well and Evrouin was always impeccably polite, but he had an uneasy feeling that the man regarded him more in the light of an idiot younger nephew who had to be protected from himself than anything else.

"I think I'll be safe enough in Newport, Evrouin. I'll see you this evening."

"Yes, y . . . Sir Guilliame."

John was hiding *who* he was, but he had decided it was probably better not to try and hide *what* he was, which was essentially an Associate noble. Hopefully people would see that and not look further, and if he tried to be anything else his own clumsiness might attract unwelcome attention. You could put him in a kilt and he'd look like an Associate in a kilt, not a Mackenzie.

Hence his long hooded cloak, calf-boots, breeks, jerkin and light houppelande coat with long dagged sleeves and chaperon hat and liripipe, and the small golden spurs on his heels; also the long sword and poniard on his belt, crimped with the lead-wire peacebonding local law required. He had a mourning band on his arm, but then so did more than half the adults he saw—the tout for the *Seagull's Roost* had, for instance.

PPA gentry traveling outside the Protectorate on business or pleasure were plentiful enough in other parts of western Montival that seeing one didn't automatically make your mind run on royalty, and there were any number of reasons one might be here—selling the wool clip or brandy from his father's demesne to a shipper, for instance, or looking for a better deal on farm machinery or a hydraulic ram than he could get from Protectorate workshops. He'd picked solid sad colors of brown and gray, with just enough color—a little gold thread at the collar of his jerkin, a ring or two, and a jeweled buckle—to be credible. The arms of an uprooted tree, argent on gules, in the shield on his jerkin were mythical, but skill at heraldry was rare here in the south-country.

The rain gave a perfect excuse to swing on his cloak and pull up the full hood as well as he walked out of the front gate of the railway station and looked around the main street running down to the docks, leaving his face in deep shadow. The air above was loud with the harsh cries of seagulls even in bad weather, and more stood about looking cross and giving way reluctantly as people crowded them. Now and then someone would kick at one, and it would half-open its wings and give the avian equivalent of a curse.

The same misty drizzle that ran in little drops off the wool—woven undyed in the grease—made the wooded hills on three sides disappear into trailers of green and gray as the fog wound through them.

Newport wasn't particularly new, or very big, and it didn't have a town wall. It had been founded around a century and a half before the Change, and on that March day in 1998 the city on the shore of Yaquina Bay had been home to about ten thousand people. Half a century after the old world crashed in ruin it had at least that many once more, which made it a step down from the really big centers like Portland or Astoria or Boise or Corvallis, but still very substantial. And none of the others had anything like the numbers they'd had back then or ever would, which put it a step *up*, if you looked at it right. John strongly suspected that was precisely how the locals looked at it, from the brisk steps and the prideful looks he got, inviting the rube to admire the sights.

A scatter of new streets and rising frameworks of bright timber on the outskirts showed how it was growing, and the rhythmic *bang . . . bang . . .* of a pile-driver from the waterfront marked where new piers were being driven out into the bay. The works of human-kind still nearly disappeared against the great stretch of water and salt marsh and forest that made up the country around. The arches of the ancient steel bridge soaring high across the river mouth against the blue-gray Pacific were the only things of man that rivaled nature, they and the long breakwaters that extended the waterway out into the ocean. The city smells of woodsmoke and cur-

ing fish and sawdust and cooking and horses blended in the greater sym-
phony of salt water and brackish marsh.

Prince John looked around at the buildings with interest as he trod
the plank sidewalk; some were white-painted wood, more left to the natural silvery-gray of timber after a few years in the damp salt air, and a few
of brick or stone or half-timbering, though that wasn't as common here
as in the Association towns. Many of the roofs showed thick bright-green
moss on their shingles, and the number of workers up there hammering
on new straw-colored ones suggested patching was a continuous process.
He couldn't recall being here before, though he might have come with
his parents as a child—it would be in the back issues of the Court Diary,
but the important thing was that if he didn't remember it, there were
probably not many people who'd know him on sight, the way they would
have his father or his elder sister. Montival wasn't the sort of place that
slathered pictures of the ruler's family on every available space.

*They'd notice Orrey, though! She's a lot more conspicuous than I am—a five-foot-
eleven blond princess just stands out—and she spent half a year at the university in
Corvallis town.*

Buoy-bells added a distant ringing from beyond the harbor, and a pre-
Change lighthouse stood on a rise to the south. The wings and mewing
cries of seagulls were thick overhead; from the harbor a deep chant and
the rhythmic boom of a drum came as a tug pulled a three-masted ship
out beyond the breakwaters where it could spread its white-canvas wings
and fly. The twenty oars flashed into the gray water and came back up
dripping in perfect unison with the tune, like a dance. Someone jostled
him as he watched, and didn't bother to apologize either.

*I like visiting cities. They perk you up and put you on your toes. But by God and
His Mother, I wouldn't want to live in one, even one you could walk out of in ten
minutes. Wilderness I can handle for a while, too, but when you come right down to it
I'm a castle-and-manor lad.*

Before the Change this had been a very minor port, important only
for shipping out lumber and as a base for fishing boats. The harbor was
too shallow for most of the monster ships the ancient world had used,

ugly steel behemoths of thousands or even *tens* of thousands of tons, drawing scores of feet laden. You could still see their wrecks in some places along the coast, mostly sunken where they'd drifted ashore. Those ships had used ports like Astoria, or gone up the Columbia to Portland and Vancouver, or into Puget Sound to lost, dead Seattle.

Here remoteness had protected them from the witless hordes streaming out of the doomed cities and the plagues that had broken loose from the refugee camps to scour the Willamette clear of human kind save where luck or ruthlessness or both had enforced quarantine. Frantic adaption of the fishing fleet to oars and sails on boats not intended for them had kept famine at bay for the first year. A little later smoked and salted fish had provided something to trade for grain and potatoes.

Halfway through the first decade of the Change Year count Corvallis had extended its sway to the coast, sweetening the deal with the restoration of the railroad that wound through the lower passes of the Coast Range to the Willamette. That gave the ambitious city-state a shorter access to the Pacific . . . and just as important, one that was all their own without going through PPA-controlled ports on the Columbia and their jealous Guilds Merchant and the border tolls that had existed before the High Kingdom brought free trade throughout Montival.

Even the largest of today's ships were tiny by comparison to those of the ancients, sleek graceful dancers with wind and water, and Newport was quite deep enough for *them*. The place fairly bustled about him this working Friday in June, with traffic thick and hooves and wheels loud on patched asphalt and cobblestone streets; wagons and drays, bicycles and riders and pedestrians and steaming carts selling roast potatoes and fish sandwiches and sausages the contents of which John wouldn't have cared to guess.

Mother likes to say that sausage is a lot like politics that way.

There were scores of masts at the docks, from little fishing smacks and dories to the schooners that harvested the sea as far away as the Mendocino coast and Alaska, and the bigger ships that went far-foreign for cargo.

The ribs of more rose on half a dozen slipways, amid a continuous hammering and sawing, a clamor of smithy-work and a pungent smell of hot tar and oakum. Tall cranes hoisted thick curved shapes of wood and bundles of long planks from horse-drawn wagons. The mountains here-about were thick with magnificent timber for beam and spar and mast, and their rivers gave abundant power for sawmills.

New-built warehouses and ship's chandleries and dosshouses and stores full of the sort of things sailors bought lined the streets near the docks; as he watched a wagon was loaded with barrels of sharp-smelling pitch out of a shop that distilled it from scrap timber, laborers rolling them up two planks to the accompaniment of blasphemy and scatology before they were tied down and the team leaned into the traces. A huge sausage of sailcloth was handed from a second-story loft, down to fifteen waiting shoulders, and then went at a trot towards the yards.

The folk were mostly locals, and those mostly ruddy-faced and fair, often with the rolling walk of people who spent a lot of time on moving decks, dressed as often as not in oilskins and sou'westers over thick sweat-ers on this damp cool day. Men and women alike generally wore loose pants and boots and brimmed caps, often with a bell-guard cutlass hang-ing from a broad belt. But there were plenty from other parts of Monti-val, and outright foreigners were common.

He thought the rugged-looking couple in luridly colorful print tunics were probably Hawaiian, remembering what diplomats from that poly-glot kingdom had worn. And the man with the black goatee and curled mustachios with a rapier at his side was probably from one of the Spanish kingdoms of the far south, Arica or Puerto Montt or Esmereldas. But where did the dark man in the baggy pantaloons and long silk tunic em-broidered with crossed triple-bladed daggers and the enormous plumed, jeweled turban come from? Or the one shivering in a batik sarong and an incongruous-looking sweater, with an odd but extremely businesslike wave-bladed knife through his belt? Or the big blond woman with the broad-brimmed hat that had a tiger-skin band and a dozen corks on strings dangling from its edges?

Or that one? John asked himself.

That one was a tall, very black man of about John's own years in a splendid flowing robe of striped cotton under a rain cape, and a curved sword at his waist with a jeweled guard and hilt. His face was marked with chevrons of scars that were too regular to be anything but deliberate; he had a tuft of wiry chin-beard but a shaven head, covered by a broad beaded skull cap, and he strode along like a lord.

Which is probably what he is, at home, wherever that is.

Another black-skinned man in similar but plainer dress followed him, carrying various burdens on his back. He tugged at his master's sleeve and spoke in a throaty language.

The tall man stopped and glanced at his wrist; it bore the luxury of a watch. John had one too, right now stowed in the pouch at his belt to avoid the attention drawn by a display of wealth. The man in the robe nodded. He and his follower looked about, unrolled a pair of small carpets from the servant's backpack on the covered verandah of a shop that had a *closed for inventory* sign in the window, washed their hands and faces from a canteen and knelt facing westward, bowing their foreheads to the ground and murmuring prayers in a guttural tongue different from the one they'd spoken before. John didn't understand either one, but his musician's ear caught the rhythms of both.

Ah, John thought, with delighted surprise. *Now that I haven't seen before. They're Saracens! Moors, Muslims.*

There hadn't been many of that faith in Montival-to-be before the Change, and those mainly recent arrivals in the big cities where famine and plague struck first and hardest. His maternal grandfather Norman Arminger had given Protestants and outright unbelievers in the lands the Portland Protective Association seized a choice of exile—which meant almost certain death then—or conversion to his version of Catholicism; in the first ten years after the Change nobody here had known whether there even *was* a universal Church still functioning. He had grudgingly tolerated Jews provided they stayed discreet and paid his taxes, because even his chosen schismatic antipope Leo had argued that they had to endure until the end of the world and Christ's return.

Saracens the Lord Protector had simply and pitilessly put to the sword wherever he or his men found them, without regard to age or sex, to the old Crusader war-cry of *Deus lo Vult*, which meant *God wills it.*

John crossed himself. He didn't think God had willed *that*, and it was one of any number of reasons he prayed for his grandfather's soul quite regularly.

In that year of the great dying nobody had much marked a few more deaths amid so many. These days the Holy Father off in the Umbrian hill town where the Church now centered had sternly set his face against persecution of non-Catholics in any of the many lands where the children of Mother Church held power; for that matter, so had his two post-Change predecessors, though nobody here had heard from any Pope until about a decade after the old world fell. But that was rather late as far as this part of the world was concerned.

John knew Saracens mostly as figures in the romaunts and chansons like *The Song of Roland* or the *Song of the Lionheart* or his favorite, *El Cantar de Mío Cid.*

He suppressed his curiosity; the world was too wide and various to satisfy that itch anyway. Instead he watched the Moor walk away, and did not even ask the brown man in the gaudy turban why he glared hatred after him and put a hand longingly to the hilt of *his* peacebonded sword, muttering what were obviously curses in a liquid singsong language.

Instead he flipped a coin—a groat to his PPA sensibilities, known as a nickel here even though it was of silver—to a grinning tow-haired urchin who snatched it out of the air like a trout rising to a fly.

"What's the Sir Knight need?" the boy said.

John suspected he'd been gaping around like a hayseed from the Peace River baronies on his first trip to Portland. The urchin was about eight or nine, and the words were much more respectful than the tone and accompanied by a cheeky grin; Corvallis was one of those places that made a point of being elaborately unimpressed with noble blood. It also had free and compulsory schools of which its citizens were immensely proud, but those were out for the summer and most children did whatever they could to help the family budget or pay for minor treats.

"I need to find the merchant and shipmaster Moishe Feldman, lad," John said. "Can you direct me?"

The boy squinted at a church tower not far away with a clock set in its side. "Noon an' a bit. You'll find Cap'n Feldman at the Mermaid right now, Sir Knight, regular as clockwork when he's in port. It's halfway between his offices and the docks, and his fancy new house is out o' town a bit, too far to walk for lunch. Here, follow me."

He did, past a largish three-story building with *Feldman And Sons, Merchant Venturers est.* CY 11 painted above the main doors and the house sigil of a stylized ship heading upward into the sky. It was better if he met the man he sought outside it to start with. There might well be well-traveled people in there who *would* recognize him at a glance, and as yet they had no reason not to point and loudly exclaim something on the lines of:

My goodness, what's Prince John doing in Newport with false arms on his jerkin?

The Mermaid turned out to be a restaurant-cum-tavern, of a sort common in this town full of transients and sailors, with a large and gaudy carving of the mythical creature above the door. Despite her scaly tail, the lady was definitely a mammal. The boy ducked his head inside, nodded, turned and said as he jerked a thumb over his shoulder:

"That's him sitting beside the hearth—reading a newspaper."

John flipped him another groat, and got a brisk: "Thanks!"

The boy scampered off, dodging by a two-wheeled cart heaped high with dripping wicker baskets of weird-looking writhing crabs, things like armored spiders. John suppressed the thought that they were glaring at him through the walls of their woven prisons as if they foresaw the boiling water and drawn butter and blamed it all on him, and went in himself. A smell of roasting, frying and stewing met him, along with the smells of wine and beer, and of more tobacco than was common in most parts of Montival; exotic habits like that were more likely and easier to keep up in a port. From their looks this was a haunt for skippers and ship's officers and businessfolk and the like who could afford such indulgences.

The plank walls were decorated with souvenirs; from floats and nets to odd-looking weapons, the skull of a saltwater crocodile nearly as tall as a man, a cloak that seemed to be woven from colorful feathers, and masks made of painted coconut hulls and seashells. The weather was coolish under the gray sky outside, but body heat and what escaped from the kitchens kept the big rectangular room comfortable without a fire in the hearth, or in the tile heating stove set into the wall beside it. It didn't occur to him to wonder what his great-grandparents would have thought of a standard of *comfortable* that considered it perfectly normal to wear a sweater or coat indoors.

He made his way between the tables and through the fug of smoke and noise. Feldman was where the urchin had said; he was a lean, rather dark man of medium height, in his thirties and dressed in plain good clothes, with a close-cropped black beard that showed a white streak along one jaw that probably marked a scar, and bold boney features. There was nothing unusual in his outfit except for a kippah—a small round skull cap—on the back of his head. His back was to the wall beside the empty fireplace, and his cutlass rested on the bench beside him. It was peacebonded too, hilt and scabbard joined by thin lead wire crimped with a seal, as the law required for blades longer than six inches within the walls of Corvallis and inside the other towns of the city-state's territory.

You could jerk the wire loose quickly enough with a strong pull, but you had better have a very good reason to give the constables. At that, far more people carried blades here in Newport than in Corvallis town itself, a walled and tightly-policed city in the now-peaceful Willamette. Haida reavers had struck this far south within the last decade, and once you were out of sight of land, pirates were as real a threat as bad weather, if usually less common.

"Professor Feldman?" John said, extending a hand. "I'd like to speak with you, if you have the time."

The merchant snorted and folded his copy of the *Newport Commercial Bulletin*, with its subtitle of *Salve Lucrum*. He'd been doing the crossword puzzle.

"Save that Professor nonsense for Corvallis town," he said, giving a brief firm shake. "Mister will do, or Captain if you have to have something fancy, Sir Knight."

Feldman was a little wary in a hard, ready-to-respond way; some Catholics from the Protectorate had no use for Jews and didn't mind showing it. His hand was dry and very callused, from ropes as well as his cutlass-hilt. Technically a prosperous merchant in the territory owing allegiance to the People and Faculty Senate of Corvallis would be a tenured professor of the Economics Faculty of OSU; it was equivalent to being a member of the Guild Merchant in a chartered town up north or of the Chamber of Commerce in Boise or New Deseret. It didn't always involve giving formal classes, though they were expected to take on apprentices, for some reason called adjuncts.

Evidently Feldman didn't take it all as seriously as some.

"Sit, Sir Knight, if you've business to do—though this is my lunch hour," he added, as a hint not to waste time.

John bowed a polite acknowledgment and removed his cloak, doubling it and setting it on the seat of a spare chair before unbuckling his sword-belt. Then he removed his hat and set it and the slung lute case on the cloak. The older man's expression changed as John sat and his face was fully visible, turning fluid with astonishment for a brief flash and then setting into immobility again. He hadn't expected to fool Feldman, or wanted to.

"I'm called Sir Guilliame de Forreste," John said, and thought:

I'm glad I don't play poker with this one. He took a big shock with only a flicker. But then again, maybe I will, if this comes off.

"I'll bet you are," Feldman said, and John nodded confirmation. "Why, exactly, wasn't I told to expect you?"

"Pro . . . Mr. Feldman, this has to be strictly confidential. Confidential from *everyone*. If that's a problem, I can leave right now."

Feldman locked eyes with him for about twenty seconds, then slowly nodded. "I have obligations to your family. Your grandfather . . . on your father's side . . . helped *my* grandfather get out of Portland when the Lord Protector's men were after him."

A grin. "Granted the Lord Protector was *also* your grandfather, on your mother's side, but the principle holds."

John nodded. It wasn't everyone who could say that their paternal and

maternal grandfathers had killed each other in a spectacular single combat between their assembled armies. That fight on the Field of the Cloth
of Gold between Norman Arminger and Mike Havel was legend in the
Protectorate—and among the Bearkillers, his father's father's people, and
famous throughout Montival. He'd toyed with doing a chanson on the
subject himself, but it might be a bit tactless. Feldman went on:

"And there have been favors on both sides since. Discretion and an
ear I owe you. Anything else . . . we'll see."

A waitress came up. "The Tuna special, Cap'n Feldman?" she said. He
nodded.

"That'll do fine, Julie."

She turned to John with an expectant air. He smiled at her, and got
one in return. She was very nice-looking in a mature way, about thirty,
and he liked the alert expression in her blue eyes, not the glazed boredom
you saw so often with people in her line of work. He'd lately come to the
conclusion that attitude was more important than sheer looks.

Of course, this place was likely to be more *lively* than most; you could
probably pick up materials for epics just listening to the table conversations.

She also had no wedding band or mark where one had been taken off,
and he filed that away in the just-in-case section. Fornication was a sin for
which he'd tried to repent; however, even St. Augustine had prayed *Lord,
give me chastity . . . but not yet.* Adultery was *really* a sin and while he knew
he was a weak and fallible man, not to mention a *young, vigorous* man, he'd
never committed that one.

"The Tuna special is something special, mistress?" he asked.

"The best," she said. "Our meat and poultry dishes are fine, but the
fish here is even better, Sir Knight. My sister Kate uses her special mari-
nade. And the albacore, that's fresh as fresh—off my cousin's boat this
morning and caught last night. Only the people who catch it get it
fresher. Packed in ice or no, you won't get anything as good in an inland
town, not if you pay its weight in gold you won't. So unless you're from
Astoria or Victoria or Tillamook or someplace like that . . ."

"I'm not, so I'll have that too then, please. I can't resist so eloquent a
persuasion."

It came quickly; Feldman remained quiet until it did, and so did John—he wasn't one of the people who felt compelled to break silence. The merchant nodded slightly, and John flushed—he didn't particularly like being tested, but it was always good to pass one. Even if the substance of it was *not a jittery young idiot.*

The Tuna special turned out to be pound-weight steaks an inch thick, marinated in honey, mustard and vinegar and then grilled with a little oil, accompanied by the seasonal treat of a green salad and the usual loaves of bread and wedge of cheese. John crossed himself and kissed his crucifix and murmured:

"Bless us, O Lord, and these, Thy gifts, which we are about to receive through Thy bounty, through Christ our Lord. Amen."

Feldman broke off an end of his loaf, took a bite, and recited:

"Baruch atah Adonai Eloheinu Melech Haolam, hamotzi lechem min haaretz." He cocked an eye at John and translated. "Blessed are You, HaShem, our God, King of the Universe . . ."

". . . who brings forth bread from the earth," John said, cutting in as he completed it.

Ignatius and the other clerics who taught him had once tried to pound in a little Hebrew along with the Latin before they gave it up as a bad idea; not much had stuck, but that had. That had been about the time that he came to the realization that while he was a loyal son of Holy Mother Church, he had no slightest trace of a vocation for the life of a religious.

"Same ultimate overlord, different chain of vassalage, Mr. Feldman," he added.

"Well, that's a uniquely Associate way to look at it," the merchant said with a chuckle.

John shrugged. "The . . ."

Best not say Crown Princess *aloud.*

"My older sister is as much a Mackenzie clanswoman as anything; and she's of the Old Faith. I loved my father very much, but I'm an Associate and a Catholic like my mother." He sighed. "I'm going to be Lord Protector of the Association eventually, so I might as well do it whole-heartedly."

Feldman nodded. "Good attitude. Now, this whole affair has something to do with the . . . interesting Japanese-looking people who accompanied your sister north after the High King's death, doesn't it?"

He touched one corner of his jacket; John saw that it had been torn,
the ritual gesture of mourning in Feldman's faith. He looked aside and
blinked: keeping busy helped, but every now and then it struck him
again.

"I lost my father two years ago, and there is a hole in your life that
takes a long while to close," Feldman said gently. "But the Lord gives; the
Lord takes; blessed be the name of the Lord."

John nodded, took a deep breath, and went on: "What happened, and
what we want to do about it, is this. They really *are* from Japan, it turns
out there are survivors there, and they came here because—"

He continued, with an occasional sharp question to clarify some
point. Once Feldman said:

"You're sure they were being candid?"

"My sister is sure that they were telling the truth as they knew it," he
said. "And she carries—"

The man across the table nodded. "I've seen the Sword of the Lady.
It's . . . disturbing. And no offense, it's particularly disturbing for a Jew."

John smiled wryly. "None taken, Mr. Feldman. I've been around it all
my life. And *I* find it disturbing . . . as a Catholic, and for that matter a
human being. I'm deeply thankful I won't have to carry it. Unless something happened to . . . my sister. Which God prevent."

"*Alevai, omayn,*" Feldman sighed. "I hoped they were mistaken or lying.
That particular evil . . . I was hoping my father's generation dealt with it
for good and all."

"So did I!"

He paused when the waitress came and removed the plates, replacing
them with raisins and nuts and mugs of small beer—John recognized
Sophomore, a Corvallis brew, tasty if deliberately weak. He sipped while
the merchant sat back, his eyes hooded. He thought for perhaps ten
minutes before he spoke again:

"Let me sum this up. You want me . . . my family . . . to not only transport this expedition of yours, but to lend you the money for it, because this Japanese lady had some dreams. Oh, pardon me, you and your sister had dreams too. The only security you offer being your promise to pay us back later. Which would of course be worthless if you get killed, in which case the High Queen Mathilda, the Lord bless and sustain her, will want my head on a pike, if there's anything left after bankruptcy court gets through with me."

"Yes, Mr. Feldman, that's pretty much it. She wouldn't break the law to get it, and we're not asking you to do anything technically illegal, but she'd want it."

They both knew his mother never forgot a friend . . . or an enemy, come to that. Feldman's links had mostly been to his father's side of the family, not the Armingers. The merchant nodded and went on:

"And there's a distinct possibility that diabolists, of the sort who killed this Japanese woman's father and burned her ship and then killed the High King, may be involved. And may attack *my* ship. In other words, you're asking me to fight devil-worshipping sorcerous cannibal pirates."

"Quite correct."

"Possibly Haida too, who are all of the above minus the cannibalism— and what happens to your body after you're dead, is that really such a big deal? And assorted other low-lifes, possibly, including Eater bands in Los Angeles."

"That's pretty much the situation, Mr. Feldman. Actually according to our sources there may be Eater bands from the Bay area involved, too."

Feldman's face suddenly split with a grin, very white against his black beard. "I have to consult with my brothers and my mother, but I'm currently head of the family business and essentially I'm inclined to agree. Subject to negotiating the details, of course; though I insist on captaining the ship myself. Hmmm, the *Tarshish Queen* would do nicely."

John had been feeling a little discouraged. He blinked.

"You're saying yes?" he said, and managed not to let his voice break in a humiliating squeak for the first time in years. "Why?"

Feldman spread his hands in an eloquent gesture. "For a whole bunch of reasons. I have a debt to your family, but which part of it is most important? Which generation? I think you and your sister. She'll be High Queen, and you'll be Lord Protector of the Association. Good to have you both looking with favor on my family . . . and good for the High Kingdom for the Royal kin to have good relations with some of the prominent merchant families here. Of which I intend the Feldmans to be one, by the way. How can I expect loyalty and favor from House Artos, if I don't show loyalty now when you really need it, need it badly enough to ask, and when it takes real effort and real risk for me to help? Some of my more ambitious and less sensible colleagues here in Corvallis—"

Like most, he used the term to refer to the whole of the city-state's territory as well as the city proper.

"—think they are, or could be, the second coming of the Venetian Republic. Too much time with the history books."

"Third coming," John said absently. "Or the local version thereof."

News did travel around the world, if slowly; failing all else, the Papal couriers carried it on their rounds and clerics gossiped like other men. It turned out that Venice, or some part of it, *had* survived, and was a trading city once more. No doubt its defensible island location had helped, and local accident whose details were lost in the mists of time and distance.

Feldman nodded, taking the point that John kept himself informed.

"But unlike *La Serenissima*, we aren't an island," he said, putting his finger on the same factor. "We're part of Montival and we need the High Kingdom to be strong. Your father was a strong king, and just, but I think his heir will do as well. So would your mother, but she only holds the position for another five years in any case."

John frowned, thinking. "But why are you going to captain the ship yourself?" he asked. "I thought you'd manage things from here."

"And stay to face your mother?" Feldman chuckled.

"A definite point!"

"And I'm not going send one of our skippers into a place I won't go myself. And on a more personal level . . . you know what Feldman And Sons do . . . Sir Guilliame?"

John spread his hands in turn. "You ship cargo under charter, and trade on your own account, and in quite distant lands," he said.

"Right. My father helped open the Hawaii trade, back when that was risky. He was jumped by pirates off Maui once. Suluk corsairs out of Mindanao, and they chased him all the way to the Mendocino coast, down in California—excuse me, Westria, your grandmother Lady Sandra renamed it after those books . . . quite good books, incidentally. He found a little civilized community there, too, opened up that trade as well."

"The Barony of Mist Hills," John nodded; his father had confirmed the self-conferred title when contact was restored.

The merchant continued: "I took the first Montivallan ship into Darwin myself on my maiden voyage as skipper."

"That's the Kingdom of Capricornia, isn't it?" John frowned, calling up lessons and things he'd heard from the Lord Chancellor. "Northern Australia."

"Just so. Very lively place, big entrepôt, and I made some deals so sweet . . ." He kissed his bunched fingertips. "But right now I'm outfitting my *Tarshish Queen* to do a trip so far west it's far east, past Darwin—that Capricornian trade's getting crowded, and that means buying higher and selling lower."

"Where to?" John asked, distracted and intrigued.

He loved hearing of those faraway places with strange-sounding names. Not least for the contrast with the workaday, everyday modernity of Montival.

"Bali first—they've got some lovely stuff and they don't much like sailing themselves, though they've been settling some of the surrounding islands, they're densely populated, since they came through the Change better than any of their neighbors. Then New Singapore for rubber goods and lenses, they make some excellent lenses there . . . and then we're going all the way to Hinduraj on the Bay of Bengal as a speculation based on what I heard in Darwin. The Andaman islands on the way there are a pirate haven, but that's why the prices are so good, and there are people in Hinduraj interested in trade now the wars there have died down."

"They have?" John said, searching his memory; faraway places might

be enjoyable settings for romantic fantasies, but they didn't really impact . . .

*Wait a minute. Father was killed by people from the other side of the Pacific
Ocean who we'd never even heard of. Maybe we ought to be less casual about writing
a place off as unimportant because it's so far away.*

He coughed; from Feldman's ironic look he'd followed the thought.
John went on aloud:

"It's been thunder and blood from that part of the world as long as . . .
well, I can remember my parents talking about it when I was barely able
to understand."

"It's more peaceful lately, mainly because Maharaja Mahendra the
Purifier—"

"Ah, the mystery man," John said wisely; nobody knew much beside
the name and a reputation written in fire and blood.

"Not so mysterious now I've done some research, though a nasty piece
of work: his original name was Ravinder Kumar Pal, for example, and from
what I've been able to learn he reminds me of your maternal grandfather,
on a larger scale. He and his son finally finished killing nearly all the many,
many people they didn't like. The ones within reach, at least, which means
within a thousand miles or so of their palace in Sambalpur. So there's peace
of a sort there. His grandson took the throne two years ago and seems to
be much less of a maniac. A very hard young man, but . . . rational, which
is fortunate considering how very many people he rules."

"What's worth going there for?" John said dubiously.

"Hinduraj has indigo and saffron, spices, cotton and silk cloth, tea,
coffee, worked brass—artwork in general—semiprecious stones and
some really spectacular intaglio work, rare woods . . . they want raw salvage metals, tools and machinery. That route means a big crew and an
armed ship. The Royal Capricornian Navy patrol where they can, but
most of those seas are completely lawless, everyone with a dugout canoe
and a rusty kitchen-knife thinks he's a budding Pirate King. You know the
point of doing trade like that? Two points, really."

John had had excellent tutors. He hadn't enjoyed studying economics, but . . .

"Reward's a function of risk."

Feldman made clapping motions. "An Associate who doesn't think *wealth* is just another way to spell *wheat*, and vice versa! A miracle!" he said, grinning to take away the sting.

"You can do without silk and cinnamon a lot more easily than without bread, but I take your point."

"Right. I'm not interested in sitting in a countinghouse in Corvallis trying to squeeze another tenth of a point out of the miserable five percent return you make on milk routes like shipping grain and linen to Hawaii these days, or the downhill run to Tillamook with Bearkiller brandy to swap for cheese. I'd rather go to Degania Dalet and farm myself."

"And the other reason?"

"It's related. Milk runs are *boring*," he said, with a chuckle. "Understand, I don't take unnecessary risks, I don't fly gliders or hunt tigers for fun, I'm a family man."

John nodded; he *did* do both of those things for fun, of course. On the other hand, he'd never had a boatload of screaming corsairs come over the rail waving their parangs amid a hail of blowgun darts. Feldman went on:

"But I do enjoy *overcoming* risks, by planning and improvising. Pitting myself against necessary ones and coming out on top, and seeing places and people nobody else does while I do it. Have since I made my first run as assistant supercargo and general dogsbody on my father's ship. I don't pick fights, either . . . but anyone who sends a roundshot through the hull of a pirate *prau* is doing a *mitzvah* for the whole world as well as a favor to some poor, suffering, hungry, deserving sharks."

John nodded. When you thought about it, it wasn't altogether unlike a knight-errant's search for honorable accomplishment. In both cases, you were doing worthwhile deeds . . . but there was an element of doing the deeds for the wild deeds' own sake, too.

"So I'll see you again on Monday with some detailed estimates," Feldman said, tilting the mug back and wiping his mouth with the napkin. "Right now I want to get home a few hours before Sarah lights the candles. I miss that often enough as it is. If it wasn't Friday, I'd ask you home for dinner, but . . ."

John smiled. "I understand completely, Prof . . . Captain Feldman; a family matter. We'll have other opportunities soon and I'll find something to do."

It must be a little awkward, he thought. *Having Saturday as your day of rest.*

Some people got Saturday as a half-holiday. Plenty didn't, and almost nobody got the whole day off unless they set their own hours—and most of those who did couldn't afford to take two days off, not every week. Still, Feldman seemed to manage somehow; maybe he used Sunday for work that didn't involve others. There was something to be said for the extra concentration you got when you knew nobody would interrupt.

The merchant dropped a silver coin and left with a wave to Julie; the hour was later than John would have expected, and Feldman only stopped at a few tables to exchange a word or two with colleagues before he left. The place had emptied out while they talked. The waitress came back with another mug of Sophomore.

John smiled at her and unlatched his lute case. He'd done his part for now. His sister had other messengers out, and a good deal depended on them, but for now there was nothing he could do but relax.

"Do you mind if I take Azalaïs out?" he said. "She gets lonely."

"You have a name for your guitar?" she asked indulgently.

"Please, Azalaïs is a *lute*, of noble lineage and herself a lady. She's named for a great poetess and composer, Azalaïs de Porcairagues, who lived long ago in the land of the troubadours."

Playing the lute was an accomplishment so common among Associate knights as to be virtually a stereotype. Few people objected to hearing a good musician; it wasn't as if you could just summon up music at will, apart from what you made yourself. Wind-up phonographs just weren't the same, and anyway cost the earth.

"Well, as long as you don't drive the other customers out," she said.

Then she folded her arms with a skeptical expression, waiting to hear if his music was music only in his own mind; there were far more not-so-good players than really competent ones. He tuned the instrument quickly, then touched the strings with delicate precision. After a moment the sounds became an old tune, somber and rhythmic and somehow sparkling at the same time; perhaps the chance encounter that afternoon on the way from the train station had prompted something in the backrooms of his mind. He sang:

> "He turned and looked upon them, and he wept very sore
> As he saw the yawning gateway and the hasps wrenched off the door,
> And the pegs whereon no mantle nor coat of vair there hung.
> There perched no moulting goshawk, and there no falcon swung.
> My lord the Cid sighed deeply for such grief was in his heart
> And he spake well and wisely: 'O Thou, in Heaven that art
> Our Father and our Master, now I give thanks to Thee.
> Of their wickedness my foemen have done this thing to me.'"

Her arms unfolded. After a moment she pulled up a chair.

CHAPTER SIXTEEN

W*e're good here and the Professor is agreeable,* the message read. *Having a great time, see you soon with full details.*

Órlaith read the note from John again and smiled as she and Reiko walked to the north of the manor-house a few hours after sunrise. There was a pleasant allée of ancient oaks there along a graveled roadway that led down to the rose-grown buildings of the winery, big trees whose branches met overhead at eighty feet or better, with iron brackets to hold lanterns at twice head-height. Saplings ten or fifteen feet high stood midway between each, which was what they called *grandparent thinking*—you planted oak trees for your children's children to get the full benefit. The big ones here must have been old before the Change. Blue jays flitted between them, their voices loud.

There was a dense fresh smell in the air, slightly diluted with woodsmoke, and as they approached the winery the faint ghost of old must and spilled wine and fermentation tanks. A muted sound of mallets on wood carried through the brick walls—there was a big barrel-making shop there as well as the stemmer-crushers and vats and cellars. They stopped halfway and sat on a stone bench, leaning their swords against it close to each right hand; the rough limestone of the seat's edge was cool against the backs of Órlaith's knees. Two of Reiko's Imperial Guard samurai took stance on her side of the bench, just beyond the range that would let them overhear casual conversation; two crossbowmen in half-armor and unvisored sallets were on that of the Crown Princess.

"The game begins," Órlaith said, holding up the folded note in two fingers.

She got an odd glance from Reiko as the *Nihonjin* took the paper and read; she suspected that the *Heika* found her slightly frivolous at times, and her brother John most of the time.

"*Ichiban*," Reiko said when she'd read it: *excellent.*

Órlaith took it back and tucked it into her sporran and nodded. Without a ship and funds . . .

Well, just trying to walk there is definitely not a good idea. That would avoid the ruins of LA, but the distance . . . no way we could cover it without a recall order coming up. I'm not going to openly defy a direct order from Mom. I've got to avoid getting the order.

Behind them the terraces fell to the little lake and the *salle d'armes*, with the wooded hill behind it and Castle Ath on the next rise northward. Ahead, eastward, vine-clad hills rolled down towards a roadway. On the far side of it was the manor's village, with its roofs and the church steeple peeking from among the trees. Beyond that fields and orchards dreamed green and quiet, roads stretching white between their rows of beeches, with a twinkle off the polished brass fittings of a carriage as it curved around a plodding oxcart. Detail faded into blue distance. It teased vision and mind with castles and towns of the imagination, until the line of the High Cascades put a wall on the edge of sight, sweeping southward from Mt. Hood's white cone along a line that floated ghostly against the sky.

"The calm before the storm," Órlaith went on.

"Or that instant between the arrow leaving the string and hitting the target," Reiko said.

"I'll be glad to be out and doing, but until then I'll soak it up," Órlaith agreed.

"*Hai.* This is . . . soothing. Very pretty, the contrast of the fields and then the mountains in the distance."

"The view from here is even better a month from now. The wheat is just turning golden then. Then there's the harvest, and the celebrations—nearly everywhere has one, all different."

Reiko nodded. "We have a great festival at the rice harvest, some parts very old, others new since the Change. The Emperor harvests the first sheaf and offers it, nobody may eat of the rice of the new harvest until that is done, and then there is a great procession with dancing and drumming, Sado was always famous for its drummers—"

She described it, and Órlaith fought to keep her brow from rising; apparently part of the celebration involved Shinto priests pulling giant vividly-painted wooden phalluses and vulvas through the streets while sake flowed like water, among much else. Not totally unlike what the followers of the Old Faith did at that season, but not what she'd have expected from what she'd seen of Reiko's people here and now.

It wouldn't do to think all these folk are always as I've seen these with Reiko, she reminded herself; it was unwise to generalize from a small sample. *And anyway they're human; they can't be solemn and grim all the time.*

She went on aloud: "We have something similar. Christian rites here in the Protectorate, and different ones everywhere . . . down among Mackenzies, the Chief of the Clan takes the first sheaf and a special bread is made from it. Then at the end of the harvest they take in the Queen Sheaf, it's shaped into the form of a woman and set up above the table, and the Chief breaks the loaf at the feet of the Queen Sheaf in sacrifice before the feast."

They laughed as they compared details, and then Reiko sighed. "But always a little . . . sad at those festivals, neh? As at the Moon Viewing. A feeling of . . . how we come and go, but the earth remains. And the cycle of the seasons, that takes no account of the briefness of human lives. Spring always comes again, but for us, never the same twice and in the end there is a last."

Órlaith looked up at the arch of leaves overhead, frowning a little as she summoned the memory of verses by a poet her mother was fond of, and whose work had struck her as well. More so as she grew past childhood, and more still as she felt now in the wake of her father's death.

"There's a poet . . . he lived in England three generations before the Change . . ."

Then she recited:

"*On Wenlock Edge the wood's in trouble*
His forest fleece the Wrekin heaves;
The gale, it plies the saplings double,
And thick on Severn snow the leaves.

'Twould blow like this through holt and hanger
When Uricon the city stood:
'Tis the old wind in the old anger,
But then it threshed another wood.

Then, 'twas before my time, the Roman
At yonder heaving hill would stare:
The blood that warms an English yeoman,
The thoughts that hurt him, they were there.

There, like the wind through woods in riot,
Through him the gale of life blew high;
The tree of man was never quiet:
Then 'twas the Roman, now 'tis I.

The gale, it plies the saplings double,
It blows so hard, 'twill soon be gone:
To-day the Roman and his trouble
Are ashes under Uricon."

Reiko had listened with keenest attention. When Órlaith finished she sighed.

"Ah. That is very good, the sense of transience. The style is more . . . more *ample*, more spread out than ours, but that one is very good. I have *read* poetry in your language before, a little, but . . . for poetry, you must be able to hear it in your head even if you read silently, *neh?* The flow and the rhythm of the speech; the sounds are as much a part of it as the meaning, like music. Now I can hear it a little."

Órlaith's mouth quirked and she touched the hilt of the Sword. "I'd . . . so *much* rather that this hadn't come to me yet . . . but there's good in every happening. Now I can really appreciate *your* verse, which I suspect would have taken more time and labor than I can afford, otherwise."

Reiko nodded. "The records say foreigners found our language very difficult." Then: "Do you . . . do you think there will be something similar for me, when we recover the Grass-Cutting Sword?"

Órlaith shrugged ruefully and raised a hand palm-up. "I have absolutely no idea, Reiko," she said. "I'd be surprised if it did all the *same* things as the Sword of the Lady, sure and I would. The Powers don't work that way, I think. As They shape the lands and folk . . ."

"So They are shaped in turn," Reiko said. "At least, the faces They show to us are."

"Like a dance," Órlaith agreed.

"But there should be some similarities. Because the *kami* have made them both *swords,* neh?"

"Exactly," Órlaith said. "And . . . my father said that he thought that . . . the Change made some things that had been only . . . potentials . . . grow. So that myths now walk openly among us, the Change bringing them to the light of common day as water makes a seed sprout and burrow up through the soil, not all at once but gradually and . . . inexorably. There's a place there, beyond the mountain . . . I can't tell all I know, the details are a secret of the Royal kin, but it's where the King-making is done. I'll have to go there when it's . . . my time."

Reiko nodded. "Strange to think that Mt. Hood is so very far away from here," she said meditatively, shading her eyes with her fan. "It seems as if I could reach out and touch it. So tiny and perfect." She murmured in her own language:

"*The evening clears—*
   On the pale sky
   Row on row of autumn mountains . . .

". . . I would very much like to visit it someday. When the . . . other things have been attended to, if they ever are. *Giri, ninjo.*"

Órlaith nodded; *giri* meant duty, in the sense of fulfilling obligation to others—very much the way an Associate thought when he said *honor.* *Ninjo* she couldn't really translate into English at all, though *human feeling* and *heart's desire* were part of it.

"There's a hunting lodge on Mt. Hood we visit often—Timberline, it's called," she said instead. "That's a Crown possession, with a very great deal of forest attached. Lovely country for hunting, or just to enjoy. The fruit orchards in the Hood Valley are worth a trip by themselves in blossom time too, and they're on the way. So is the Columbia gorge, where the waterfalls come down the cliffs, when you come up to Hood River from Portland by riverboat to the Duchy of Odell."

"I would like that. And someday you may come to Sado-ga-shima in April, and see the cherries in blossom at the festival, and then the wild yellow licorice on the hills against the blue sea."

They both smiled at each other, then sat and watched the view and the patterns of shade moving over the landscape as the clouds drifted.

Órlaith was wearing kilt and plaid and loose shirt and Scots bonnet; one of the advantages of being half-Mackenzie was that you had a really comfortable set of walking-out clothes in your repertoire. The downside, of course, was that this was just about *all* Mackenzies wore, except for the robes of the Old Faith's rituals, and arisaids for women on very formal occasions. The only real difference was that you left the plaid off in very warm weather; otherwise the same or very similar garments did for work, war, the hunt, or a dance, with different accessories ranging from a burlap apron to armor to a Montrose jacket and lace. You just used your newest kilt for the fancier things.

Reiko was in a gray kimono with a design of black flowers and branches, one of Lady Delia's collection, hastily and heavily modified by the Châtelaine's tirewomen. A simple two-crest open black *haori* jacket went over it. Órlaith cocked an eye at the ensemble.

"That looks different," she said in Japanese.

"Oh, it's altered to a modern walking-out style now, what gentlewomen wear since we went back to *wakufu* for everyday," Reiko said, touching her fan to the sleeve.

Órlaith's Sword-trained ear rendered *wakufu* as *real clothes* or *our own style* as well as *Japanese clothing* in a more technical sense. It had overtones of warmth and belonging and coziness that she didn't quite follow.

Reiko went on with a graceful gesture of her fan: "Delia-*gozen* has some beautiful, beautiful work in her collection but nobody wears those really broad, very stiff obi with the cords anymore except on the most very, very formal court occasions, or the really big bow at the back either. We use these instead."

She touched the sash that held the robe together, which was soft black satin about eight inches broad, tied in a complex but not very large knot at the rear, and went on:

"I think because we just couldn't make them after the Change, not for a while, the ones we still have were all done before then. And we don't make quite such a big difference in the length of a man's and women's kimono anymore—of course, you wear a shorter one with *hakama* over it; men wear those more often, but it's not . . . not like hose. For men, very formal always has *hakama*, for women not, many things in between. The sleeves are still different, though. And a farm woman would wear a shorter robe and *mompe*, trousers, and perhaps an apron. Or tuck the ends of the kimono up under the obi for work."

Órlaith nodded. Reiko's face was more relaxed and animated, as they chatted of things harmless and interesting and beautiful.

Not grim at all, she thought. *Charming, in fact.*

One of the estate cats came stalking down the allée, a big orange tabby, and looked at them a little suspiciously. Órlaith bent over and extended a hand, avoiding a stare—cats and Nihonjin had the same ideas about that, which wasn't the only point of resemblance she'd noticed— and murmured:

"Mi-mi-mi-mi."

Her Nonni Sandra had told her that *meow* was a compound word in feline, made up of *mi* for *hello* and *eow* for *keep your distance*. She didn't know whether that was right, but a lot of cats seemed to like it when you went mi-mi at them, particularly if you weren't one of their familiar people. Cats that knew you preferred *mrrrrp*.

The beast came over, sniffed her hand and consented to a scritch on the head; its ears were rather tattered. Reiko chuckled; that died at the scrutch of feet.

A man was approaching, in the dress of a manor-house servant: neat brimless felt hat with the d'Ath livery badge, breeks and charcoal knee socks, with a laced hip-length jerkin. The varlet uncovered his short fair hair—with a slight twitch of the eyes towards the bodyguards, especially the samurai—made a leg, and spoke:

"Your Highness, there's a Royal courier," he said.

Órlaith raised an eyebrow. Generally a message for her here would simply be sent over the heliograph net to Castle Ath—with a skilled operator modern fixed models with four-foot triple mirrors could transmit fifteen words a minute, and over distances up to a hundred miles with favorable geography and weather and powerful telescopes at the receiving end. From here to Todenangst was a single stage, and as near instantaneous as no matter; John's had probably taken about twenty minutes from Corvallis, faster than the time required to write it down up at the castle and have someone trot over here.

"Not a message?" she said.

"No, Your Highness; a riding courier in the High King's . . . my apologies, the High Queen's livery, the Crown Courier Corps. And looking like it's been a long hard ride too."

The varlet bowed to Reiko as well as to her, she was glad to see; the d'Ath household servitors were well-trained, and just as important they really wanted to please. There were usually plenty of applicants for jobs like his in the Association territories; it was a lot easier than what a peasant did, and while you didn't get the same things served at the foot of the lord's table as they did above the salt, there was always plenty of it and you didn't have to grow it yourself. On the other hand, not all commoners liked being around nobles all day, without much time to call their own, especially if the lords in question were bad-tempered or hasty. That wasn't a problem here.

"Send him through, thank you, Dicun," Órlaith said with a smile.

He coughed discreetly into a hand. "The courier is a lady, Your Highness. A Sioux lady, I believe, the one who came here some time ago."

"Ah," Órlaith said, feeling a quick thrill, the sort you did when the bushes moved against the wind on a boar-hunt.

The game begins indeed.

Beside her Reiko stiffened, an infinitesimal motion that still made silk and linen rustle.

"Well, send her along, then. And have some refreshments sent up here as well, she's probably had a hard ride."

"We've already sent for that, Your Majesty," Dicun said, confirming her guess.

She didn't offer him a tip, which would be gross and insulting, though she did smile and nod. She reminded herself to leave a vail for the staff when she left, though; normally the senior Household servant along with her would handle it.

Susan *Mika*—Susan Clever Raccoon—came walking up with a slightly bowlegged stride, amid a powerful odor of horse. She made a knee, and gave a tired grin at the same time. Using relays of horses wasn't the fastest way to travel overland, not where hippomotives were available, or the fastest way to send a message when you had heliographs . . . but it was considerably less conspicuous than either and left far less of a paper trail. And if you pushed it you could cover well over a hundred miles a day, which was fast enough.

Fast enough for government work, Órlaith thought with a trace of whimsy.

"Your Highness, from Dun Fairfax—" Mika began.

"*Lakhotiya Woglaka Po!*" Órlaith replied.

And blessed the Sword; she'd had only a little of the language before, since all of that folk spoke English too, and a fair number had only ceremonial Lakota. Especially the ones with a lot of white-eye in their background; people had moved around a good bit in the years right after the Change, and settled and married where they could. Whatever their myths and stories, few could trace all their blood from any one tribe or folk.

She remembered that Mika was fully fluent, though, and the chances of anyone being able to understand them were only marginally greater than it would be with Japanese. The courier dropped into that sonorous swift-rising, slow-falling tongue:

"—from the Dun below the sacred hill in the Mackenzie dùthchas: *Let the old man say what he will, we'll skip the harvest and meet you where the fairies dance.* From Larsdalen: *You're on!* From the steading of your friend in the land of the McClintocks: *We'd have been at feud if you'd left me out.*"

The grin got a little wider, and she went on: "From the lady with the garland in that place: *Don't get him killed and forbye keep your princessly hands to yourself the while.*"

She tried and failed to put a McClintock burr to the last.

"And from the tall trees: *I may not live while the slayer of my kinsman walks beneath the stars.*"

Then with an oddly catlike expression, she added: "Those two are real enthusiastic types."

Dicun came back with a tray in his hands and a boy carrying a little folding table behind him. The lad set out the table and whipped a coarse brown linen napkin over it; the varlet set down the tray and removed the cover on a big bowl. That proved to be a dense chicken stew with peas and carrots and potatoes, accompanied by slices of thick-cut buttered brown maslin bread and a wedge of a strong-smelling yellow cheese and some dried apricots. A turned-maple mascar of beer stood beside it.

"Go ahead, you earned it," Órlaith said. "And I'm going to ask you some questions while you do. This is about as private a place to talk as I can imagine."

She gave Dicun a glance. He smiled, bowed, and as he left grabbed by one ear the lad who'd been helping him; the ears in question had been fairly quivering with curiosity. Mika sat on the end of the bench and plied a busy spoon.

"*Wopila!* Been eating jerky and trail mix in the saddle," she said around a mouthful. "I must've lost weight and I don't have any to spare."

The questions were few and to the point, mostly about the condition of the trails.

"And I'm coming too," Mika mumbled at the end of the conversation, after she'd mopped the bowl with the last heel of bread and swallowed the last apricot. "No way will I miss this."

Órlaith nodded and slapped her on the shoulder; the feel beneath the leather was boney, but the slender muscle was like iron wire.

"Of course not, cousin. I may need someone who can really ride."

"Instead of being a blacksmith's shop strapped into an easy chair mounted on a horse's back," Mika said, slandering Associate knights and Bearkiller cataphracts alike, and yawned enormously.

"Go get a bath and a bed," Órlaith said.

The courier nodded, lurched up and stumbled away. Dicun met her at a discreet distance and lent a helping hand. Reiko's hand was tight on her sword as Órlaith translated, the thumb pressing against the guard in that unconscious gesture.

"That's got us a dozen each of Mackenzies and McClintocks, and a couple of Rangers, who'll all be waiting at Stath Ingolf," Órlaith said. "And at least one A-lister. Now I have to get us some men-at-arms."

"And I some samurai," Reiko said.

Reiko and Egawa Noboru knelt on the grassy level patch beneath the great chinar tree and looked out over the little lake where mist curled, pink dying to a glowing white as the moon shone brighter. The sun was setting behind the forested hills to the west, silhouetting the tall firs as the rim of red dipped beneath the crest, and birdsong fell silent above them. The night was mild but underneath it was a faint chill, the earth breathing a scent of falling dew. Dim yellow light shone through the slit windows in the castle's tower and keep half a mile away, and the first stars spangled the purple above them. Mist curled over the water, and a frog leapt.

Egawa spoke:

"Furu ike ya . . ."

An ancient pond . . .

She took it up:

"Kawazu tobikomu . . ."

A frog jumps in . . .

The soldier completed it:

"*Mizu no oto.*"

The splash of water.

They both waited in silence as the sound of their voices faded into the dimness; the evening stillness was departing, and wind soughed gently in the branches. That poem was a work of the great master Bashō. Egawa sighed and repeated another, murmuring softly as if to himself:

"*Tabi ni yande* . . .

Falling sick on a journey . . .

Yume wa kareno wo . . .

My dream goes wandering . . .

Kake meguru . . ."

Over a field of dried grass.

"I long for home as well, my bushi," Reiko said, and spread her fan. "And wonder if I shall see it again, and bear my father's ashes to his resting place beside my grandmother. We stand on the edge of deeds and times great and terrible, beyond the fields we knew."

The sat in silence for a while longer, listening to the alien night—loud crickets, something that buzzed in the tree above them, then the familiar threefold yipping bark of a fox setting out on the work of the night.

My namesake, perhaps, Reiko thought. *The Ghost Fox.*

"Having thought, you must decide," she went on, gently implacable. "The Grand Steward would, I think—with the best, the most selfless of intentions, thinking it only temporary—bind me to what he considers wisdom. And he would use you to do so. Setting you up as a new tent government, with a puppet Empress."

Egawa pointed with his own fan. "Beyond this hill the sun paints the path homeward," he said. "But my Emperor died on foreign soil. Am I to come so far, and outlive him, only to betray his heir? Yet what is true allegiance here? You are . . . forgive me, Majesty . . . still very young."

"You must decide if I am a child, to be constrained, or truly what you call me, the Heavenly Sovereign One," Reiko said. "Because if I am sov-

ereign, General Egawa, then ultimately I—and none other—am responsible to my ancestress Amaterasu-ōmikami in this matter."

They waited. Reiko let the silence and the sounds fill her. *Having
thought, I have acted*, she thought. *Let the arrow fly.*

In the end, Egawa startled her by laughing. She turned her head to
look at him, and saw him gather up his sheathed sword and tuck it
through his sash.

"My only regret, Majesty," he said, "is that I won't be here to see
Koyama-san's face when he finds we're gone. When we leave, at least;
perhaps I shall see it, when we return with *Kusanagi*."

He made his bow. "Majesty. I will have considerable work to do, to
prepare all quietly."

His feet padded softly into the night, almost soundless on the springy
grass of the path. Reiko closed her fan with a snap, after an instant studying the razor edges of the metal segments. It quivered in her grip. There
were things that you must be *prepared* to do that still made your soul clench
with a relief so strong that it was also pain . . . if you found you need not.

When she had command of herself again she studied the moonlight
and the frosted arch of stars overhead until they washed through her
being, then said at last:

"*Araumi ya . . .*"
The rough sea
"*Sado ni yokotau . . .*"
Stretching out towards Sado
"*Amanogawa . . .*"
The Milky Way
"I will bring you home, Father. You and all our people."

Heuradys thought Sir Aleaume de Grimmond was handsome, especially
when he laughed, which he didn't do all that often. He was smart
enough, well-educated in the things considered important among his
class and nation, a first-rate fighter, and extremely conscientious. The
last was the problem here, though it would probably make him a good
baron someday.

And it may be an opportunity as well as a problem. I certainly hope so.

She'd invited him—and Órlaith, of course—and Droyn Jones de Molalla for a morning of hawking. Falconry was the all-purpose social lubricant, and one that even conventional females—which neither she nor her liege-lady were, of course—could share. They'd had a successful few hours, with half a dozen ring-necked pheasants and a wild turkey in the game basket.

Then they'd retired to the edge of the field for lunch in the shade of the hedge and row of Lombardy poplars that marked its limit; they were hunting one of the demesne fields of Montinore manor, currently planted in grass and clover for pasture rather than hay. Those attracted game birds, for feeding and nesting and as convenient refuges to stage quick trips to the grainfields.

The guards were having their own lunch a little way off, in relays so that there were always four on watch, and the falconer and his assistants and the grooms in another group yet, since they weren't even the lowliest of Associates. She and Órlaith were both in a noblewomen's riding garb, jacket and divided skirt—something very similar to what Reiko and her samurai wore, which all three of the young women had had a good laugh over.

Reiko's not bad company at all now that she's relaxed a bit, Heuradys thought. *Though the Gray-Eyed Lady knows she's got reasons for that grimness. Still, she's smart and well-read and she has a nice sense of humor if you like it extremely dry. She and Orrey are getting on very well.*

Sir Aleaume had lost some of his haunted look, and if falconry didn't relax a young Associate noble—Aleaume was the eldest here and he was still a young man—nothing would. Heuradys enjoyed it herself, even when done with an ulterior motive. It wasn't exactly the most fun you could have with your clothes on; for that, she was divided between . . .

. . . *well, music of course* . . .

. . . steeplechasing and hunting tiger, with single-handing a small boat right up there, and dancing close thereafter, but it was definitely a pleasant way to spend some outdoor time in good weather. Not to mention controlling the bird and small game population and providing food.

They'd chatted about the differences between the sport here in the close-grown Willamette country and the open eastern ranges; the de Grimmond family's barony of Tucannon was near the Blue Mountains, out in the County Palatine of Walla Walla. That was very similar to the Palouse just north of there where Barony Harfang was located, and House Ath had a hunting lodge in the Blue Mountains anyway—the Counts had given it to her adoptive mother after the Prophet's War, as a thanks-gift for dealing with a Cutter assassination attempt.

The black-and-white birds were resting on T-poles driven into the dirt by the varlets, with their yellow taloned feet clutching the perches to which their jesses were tied and their hooded heads hunched between their shoulders, doing the Prairie Falcon equivalent of a post-prandial nap-and-belch on a couch after a good meal.

Raptors like these falcons were solitary by nature; they didn't even like each other except in the mating season, much less humans. All you could teach them was that doing what humans wanted would get them more of what *they* wanted, which was to kill, eat, mate and sleep.

"Might as well be men-at-arms," Heuradys said with a chuckle, and explained her reasoning. "Though at least falcons don't drink booze."

Everyone else laughed as well. The hobbled horses grazed content-edly, since this was the equine version of being turned loose in a field of pies and pastries, with one of the younger grooms keeping an eye on them to make sure they didn't overeat and bloat. The nobles and the Crown Princess had a basket with sandwiches and pear tarts, and a flask of Montinore pinot noir wrapped in wet woven straw to keep it cool, with a striped alpaca-wool blanket to spread on the sweet-smelling clover and ryegrass. Birds were mostly absent—prey species had absolutely no doubt what a falcon's outline meant—but bees buzzed about, butterflies with white-rimmed blue or bright orange wings fluttered, and clouds drifted in the fleecy sky.

She took a bite of the sandwich, and smiled as she chewed. Old Goodwife Pernelle in the kitchens knew her tastes; thin slices of roast pork loin with a strong-tasting cheese, capers, onion chutney and mayonnaise on crusty rolls fresh that morning.

With lettuce just plucked from the manor gardens, for the crunchy.

Heuradys strongly suspected they were going to be on plain field rations again soon and lucky to get that, and was determined to enjoy this while she could. When she'd finished the pear tart she untucked the napkin from the collar of her jacket, adjusted her Montero hat with the peacock feather, and cleared her throat.

"The yield? With your permission, gentlemen."

"By all means, Lady Heuradys," Aleaume said, and Droyn murmured agreement.

It was pro-forma, considering that both were guests of Barony Ath, but manners counted and you had to consult your fellow-hawkers before disposing of the kill. She called to the falconer.

"Corbus!"

Corbus Cornelli was a lean brown-haired man in his thirties in huntsman's green suede leather, wearing a huntsman's falchion at his waist and the heavy gauntlet of his calling on his left hand.

"My lady?" he said, rising to approach the nobles and then doffing his hat and bowing.

"The turkey to you and your family, goodman. The pheasants to Father Abrahil."

She nodded to the westward, where the spire of the church just showed over tree and hedgerow to mark the location of the village of Montinore. The parish priest would distribute the birds—probably in the form of soup—to the needy, mostly the ill and the aged without close kin. If he also had a pleasant Saturday dinner of roast pheasant out of it, that was perfectly acceptable. A village priest was usually a peasant himself, some bright pious lad selected for a few years of higher education by his predecessor, who'd often been his uncle or second cousin. Most lived rather plainly and they had a close touch on the pulse of commons; a wise lord took care not to alienate them.

And it never hurts for us in particular to make a goodwill gesture to the Church. Pagan lords aren't so common we can afford to be needlessly brusque.

"Thank you, my lady!" Corbus said. "Shall we see the birds back to the mews?"

"By all means, we won't be flying them again today. They've been gorged rather heavily for that."

"So they have, my lady. It's worth the trouble to feed them from the hand after a kill. You can't make a falcon love you, but you *can* convince its little bird brain that sitting on your glove means a full croup."

"Unless it's a Harris Hawk."

He snorted slightly. "Well, if you're a beginner, they'll do, my lady. Though they tend to breed unrealistic expectations for *real* falcons."

Harris Hawks were the only raptors that hunted cooperatively in packs, up to a dozen birds at a time, like wolves with wings. Sometimes you'd see them standing on each other's backs in stacks four deep atop a rock or tree to get a better look-out. They liked each other, and were affectionate to their human handlers if well-raised from chicks.

"They're very agile, particularly with ground game," Heuradys observed.

"Yes, but a Harris keeps trying to lick your hands and cock a leg to pee, my lady," Corbus said with conviction.

"Ah, goodman, you're a purist like my lady mother! See to it, then."

Órlaith rose, an unconsciously supple motion of foot and knee without touching her hands to the ground.

"Come, walk with us, messires," she said to Aleaume and Droyn.

The four of them strolled along the hedgerow, theoretically admiring the last of the hawthorn blossoms.

"First, I must have your oaths that you will not repeat what I'm about to say," Órlaith said gravely, bending to smell a flower. "Please, think carefully, because you may be asked to violate any such oath by . . . highly placed people."

Because her mother takes oaths seriously; but she also takes her children very seriously indeed. And Orrey's not carrying the Sword right now . . . which as a gesture of trust is beyond tactful, it's so reckless it's cunning. Damn, but she is good at this!

Conflicts of fealty and oath—often tragic ones—were of course the staple of modern literature in the north-realm; they were how a troubadour put some dramatic tension in. Protectorate society *ran* on oaths, and they were important in many other parts of Montival too, if not quite so

overwhelmingly or accompanied with so much ritual. The young noble-
men looked at Órlaith, then at each other, then shared a single sharp nod.
Then they crossed themselves, kissed their crucifixes, and murmured the
form of the oath. After that they were quietly alert. Using falconry as a
cover for intrigue was *also* a staple of the troubadour's art, for the simple
reason that it was a good way to have a thoroughly private conversation
for unimpeachable reasons.

"Gentlemen, this has to do with why my father was killed—who was
responsible, and what has to be done to frustrate their plots and begin
avenging him. Also to assist our guest, Her Majesty of Nihon, who suffered the same loss as I, from the same foes, and who needs gallant swords
about her now. Are we to leave all the honor and burden of that to her
own vassals? I intend to help her on the search which brought her to us,
and which her enemies and ours are trying their best to frustrate. There
is no time for the ponderous official mechanisms of State. We must out
steel and strike."

Well, dang, I can feel *the chivalry boiling up inside 'em,* Heuradys thought as
Órlaith filled in the details, complete with prophetic dreams.

It was right out of a *chanson,* a princess in need of brave and faithful
knights, with *another* beautiful monarch, an exotic quasi-exiled foreign
one at that, and a holy relic to sweeten the appeal.

I can feel it in myself, for that matter.

Aleaume evidently had more control over his reflexes than Droyon,
who was bursting with eagerness to volunteer as knight-errant.

Or squire-errant, she thought. *Though if he goes on this quest and survives, the
accolade is a certainty. Though-the-second, he's the son of a Count, and he'd be
knighted in a year or two anyway. Plus he's six years younger than Aleaume, which
has to make a difference. Girls become women faster than men stop being boys.*

"Your Highness . . . am I to understand that your mother . . . Her Majesty . . . has forbidden this?" Aleaume said heavily.

"Not in the least," Órlaith said. "She hasn't been informed, yes, that's
true enough."

He winced. "Better to seek forgiveness than permission, then?"

Droyon cut in: "Her Majesty High Queen Mathilda herself did much the same thing when she was Her Highness' age, Sir Aleaume. Against the express wishes of *her* mother, the Lady Regent Sandra."

Aleaume acknowledged that with a gesture; it probably also acknowledged that the High Queen was much less likely to have him killed for disobedience than her terrible, smiling mother would have been. Though quite likely to give you a memorable tongue-lashing, or to inflict whatever penalty strict law allowed. Far less to arrange an untraceable tragic accident or have a challenge issued by someone like Tiphaine d'Ath in her dreadful deadly prime. The Lady Regent Sandra had been known in her lifetime as the Spider of the Silver Tower, and for good reason.

They paced along in silence for some distance, until the lancers and mounted crossbowmen of the knight's little detachment turned and kept pace with them at a suitable distance. His brow was knotted.

"This is very difficult, Your Highness," he said at last. "There is a conflict of loyalties here. I am of the Protector's Guard, and your mother is the Lady Protector. You are not; you are also not her heir to *that* position."

"Your honor is your own to judge, Sir Aleaume," Órlaith said gravely. "And a knight has no more important duty. I will inform you that my brother John—who *is* heir to the Lord Protector's chair—is with me in this, actively. He will accompany us. As a matter of fact, he's off seeing to our transportation and supplies this very day. Successfully, I might add. All will be in readiness in Newport; a fast ship with good captain and crew, money, supplies. Otherwise I would not seek to take this forward."

His eyebrows went up. He nodded and said approvingly:

"You are moving quickly, Your Highness."

"There is no other way, if it is to be done at all."

They walked on for a few paces, and then she continued:

"Tell me, do you remember my father and mother's visit to your home during the Prophet's War, when the County Palatine was being liberated? You would have been very young then . . . and I was conceived but unborn."

The red-haired knight grinned, looking far more relaxed. "Yes, Your Highness, I most certainly do! I was just six—I remember the siege of our castle at St. Grimmond-on-the-Wold. My mother and Captain Grifflet held it, while my father led our men in harassing the invaders."

"Sharp memory, for a six-year-old!"

Aleaume laughed. "What I mostly recall is being allowed to pull the lanyard on a catapult, and our soldiers grinning and cheering every time I did. And yes, that wonderful day! Seeing my father again after months, the foe in flight, the news of the great victory at the Horse Heaven Hills . . . and then the High King came, like a paladin of old, like Roland or Huon or *Ogier le Danois* or Arthur himself. He knelt and let me put my hand upon the Sword, and told me of how he'd gained it, and spoke to me . . . I didn't understand it all, but I swore then to be his knight and fight for him as my father had! I don't remember much from that long ago, but *that* memory has never left me."

Órlaith nodded. Heuradys knew the story; she'd heard Rudi Macken-zie telling it to his daughter at a campfire once. She'd been charmed at the time; it summed up all the romance of being an Associate.

"And what did my father say to that?" the Crown Princess asked.

"He said if I was as brave and true a knight as my father I would in-deed be welcome at his side. Or . . ."

He slowed, and then turned and looked at her. "Or at the side of his daughter who was to be born that year, who would need such knights."

She waited, and after a long moment he nodded and went to his knees, looking up at her and holding his hands out with the palms pressed together. She took them between hers, and Droyn and Heuradys moved instinctively to stand between them and any onlookers and to act as witnesses—an oath was a legal act, and required observers who could swear they had seen it done in due form.

"I, Aleaume son of Maugis, of the House of Grimmond, a knight of the Association and the High Kingdom, pledge myself as vassal-at-arms to Crown Princess Órlaith of the House of Artos. I shall be your man, of life and limb and all earthly worship. To you I pledge fealty and obedi-ence unto my death or the ending of the world. Your enemies shall be mine and your friends likewise, and all my aid and help be yours, with goods and sword and counsel. So I swear by God the Father, Son and

Holy Ghost; by the most holy Virgin Mother of God; and by the especial patron of my House, St. Joan of the Bow; and on my honor as a knight."

Heuradys swallowed, for she knew the man meant exactly what he said. The moment was intensely solemn; there were times when you didn't need something like the Sword of the Lady to tell when someone was binding themselves with chains of faithfulness like bands of adamant around the soul. Órlaith's voice was equally grave.

"I, Órlaith daughter of Artos, of the House of Artos and the Royal kin of Montival, accept your fealty, Aleaume de Grimmond of the House of Grimmond. I shall be your liege-lady; to you I pledge fair justice and good lordship and all the aids due a vassal-at-arms, and my protection to you and yours. I will hold your honor as precious as my own, and whoso does you wrong does also the same to me, and at their peril. This I swear by Sea and Earth and Sky; by the Sword of the Lady and She who entrusted it to the line of my blood; and by my own honor as a knight."

She pulled him to his feet and they exchanged the ritual kiss on the cheeks with their hands on each other's shoulders. Droyn knelt to make his own pledge as Aleaume stepped back; then they all turned and continued their walk.

"Welcome to the Crown Princess' menie," Heuradys said, and exchanged handshakes.

She didn't mind; a great lord would have many personal vassals, and she was the first and Orrey's friend as well. The company was pretty good, at that. These were both men to respect, swords to stand about a throne.

What's that Nihongo word Orrey mentioned? Hatamoto, *yes.*

"Now we plan," Órlaith said.

After the explanation Sir Aleaume's eyes went a little unfocused. He'd had a fair bit of military experience in the Protector's Guard, including the undramatic logistical parts that made the rest possible.

"There are two ways to do this, Your Highness," he said. "A full expedition, pushing ahead bases and supply dumps through the dead lands, digging wells and repairing roads. And a quick and dirty in-and-out, which I presume is what you have in mind."

"Exactly," Órlaith said. "And sure, the latter is the only practical one . . . considering the circumstances. A great whacking do with engineers and the like would take far too long, that it would, nor could we do it without the Crown being involved. It isn't an expedition for destriers and full harness, either, no matter if knights are along. We'll have to equip lightly and move fast."

"Bicycles, I suppose?"

He sighed; bicycles were distinctly lower class, or middle at best.

"To be sure; we're not going to cram forty coursers on a ship—a few horses for scouts, and that's it. Frankly, I wouldn't take any horse I cared for on this trip. Now, first we'll get a hippomotive and train ready here at Montinore—"

CHAPTER SEVENTEEN

Luanne Salander was an A-Lister of the Bearkiller Outfit. That status was new enough that the little blue burn-mark between her brows she'd gotten at her Initiation still itched as she waited in the dark behind the wooden sheds that made up the train station. A single light burned there, the watchkeeper waiting and yawning and occasionally getting up to do a walk-around.

The skin between her shoulderblades itched too as she huddled at the base of a hedge, breathing the strong scents of ancient horse-piss and hay and the nose-memory of manifold freights centered on Larsdalen's famed wine and brandy that hung around the station and its warehouses on a summer's night. And not just because she was sweating and the night had its share of mosquitos and other buggy things. The glare of disapproving parental eyes in her mind made it feel that way. The fact that the disapproval was strictly speaking hypothetical—she hadn't told anyone she was doing this—didn't make them any less real in her imagination.

Her parents—hopefully!—didn't know where she was, but you couldn't count on that, though she'd gone out the second-story window of her bedroom with all the stealth she could. Her mother had been a military glider pilot for the Outfit in the Prophet's War flying reconnaissance missions, a hideously dangerous specialty, and she'd worked in the Intelligence Service since. She was a shrimp; her barely-adult daughter towered eight inches above her five-one, which put her about midway between her parents, but height was not a job qualification for pilots or spies, and Alyssa Salander-née-Larsson had a well-deserved reputation for wits of ample size and vicious sharpness. She'd earned it after the war as well, spending a decade winkling out the remnants of the Cutters—the Church Universal and Triumphant—from the mountains and prairies of what had once been most of Montana and was now known as the Crown Province of Nakamtu.

Luanne's father Cole Salander had been in the United States of Boise's Special Forces and had captured Alyssa when her glider crashed during the Prophet's War—after he shot the grizzly bear that had been trying to pull her from the wreckage like the kernel out of a cracked walnut. Once he'd gone over to the Montivallan side along with most of his compatriots the two of them had entered a Boise occupied by the Prophet's men under false colors and pulled off the spectacular special operation that had opened the city's gates from the inside. The Outfit had voted him A-Lister status unanimously, a rare honor for an outsider. Afterwards he'd led dozens of patrols into the Bitterroots on leads Alyssa had sniffed out, outsmarting bandit-partisans on their own ground and running them to earth. And usually to death, by the blade or at the end of a rope, since the amnesty had long run out by then.

Which means I can't count on my parents being idiots. Middle-aged stick-in-the-muds, yes, stupid or unobservant or slow, no. Mary Mother be thanked I took the hint and talked to the courier where nobody could hear! Which was sort of cool in itself, I must say.

The whine of gearing and rumbling metallic clatter of wheels sounded northwards, and around a corner and a woodlot came the harsh yellow light cast by a hippomotive's headlamp. It flickered as the track curved and the trunks of the big Chinar trees along this stretch of the West Valley Railroad cut the beam one after another.

Right on time, she thought. *Less than an hour out from the Montinore siding, probably.*

The Outfit's chunk of the western Willamette was directly south of the Protectorate—if you didn't count the little autonomous Brigittine monastery and its clutch of allied freeholder villages—and stretched south to Corvallis. Eastward were the ruins of Salem where the new capital was being built, and beyond that the Queen of Angels Commonwealth and the Mackenzies and the odd enclave of Mithrilwood, where the Dúnedain had their headquarters. Westward the Outfit's domain went to the Pacific. Though few lived beyond the Coast Range, only a scattering of villages and the salt-works at Lincoln along the sea despite on-and-off talk of making a port.

Montinore and Forest Grove were right north of here, and Todenangst not far off to the northeast. The cryptic message from Órlaith had arrived just after dinnertime, and had said the train *wouldn't* be stopping for horses here at the Larsdalen station because their journey was *pressing and interesting*, and that it was *possibly very regretful* they wouldn't have a chance to visit and discuss it either here or in Corvallis.

The Crown Princess had left it to Luanne to tool on down to the station if she wanted to and could figure that much out, and find when a quick-passage train under a recent High Kingdom military override authorization was scheduled to pass through. That had turned out to be twenty-four hundred hours in the notation Bearkillers used, or midnight to most others. Which meant they'd left Montinore not much earlier, and at a time deliberately calculated to find most people asleep and to get into Newport with the largest possible share of the whole trip done in the dark. That was much the same thing since few but the wealthy stayed up long after sunset, especially in summer's short nights. Ordinary trains stopped for the night on sidings, too, which meant the route would be clear.

If I wasn't up to figuring out that this has to have something to do with the High King's killing and the mysterious strangers who were on the funeral train, I'd deserve to be left out and read about it afterwards in the Bearkiller Gazette, *she thought. Damned if I will be, though. Jumping on here is a safer bet than waiting for them in Corvallis, it's much busier there.*

Larsdalen had a couple of thousand people behind the cyclopean wall and famous Bear Gate; Bearkillers didn't build cities and had few towns of any size.

Whether she'd be able to get *on* the hippomotive-drawn train was another matter. An ordinary train traveled no faster than the team pulling it along hoof-on-gravel, which was usually at a brisk equine walk, equivalent to a slow jog for a human. Horses could pull a lot more on rails than they could on a road, about ten or fifteen times as much, but both ways they did it at a pace they could sustain all day. Like men, horses could walk a *lot* farther than they could run. A hippomotive's treadmills and gears and driving wheels translated some of that tractive power into speed, trading off cargo weight they could have pulled otherwise.

All that went through her mind automatically; logistics were part of the standard Bearkiller education, calculations of time and weight and speed and distance. They generally regarded Associates as play-actors and dilettantes who wasted time on galliards when they could be playing *kriegsspiel*.

Figuring out what was going on needed smarts, mostly. Actually getting on the train would require more in the way of speed, strength, agility and a willingness to risk going under the wheels and getting cut in half, which implied a lot of motivation.

So cousin Órlaith is testing me for brains, brawn, nerve and commitment all at the same time. Not to mention luck. Economical, Orrey! You deserve to be High Queen!

She thought she could manage it. In height and build she took more after her father, who was a tall sandy-blond man of mostly *Svenska* descent. There were big fair men on her mother's side too, like her grandfather Eric Larsson; but *his* wife had been born Luanne Hutton, and *her* mother and father had been what the ancient world called black and Tejano respectively. Luanne herself thought that she'd gotten the best of what her ancestors had to offer. She was tall for a woman, she could bench-press more than twice her hundred and fifty-five pounds, and even her weapons instructors agreed she was quick and precise and learned fast and had excellent situational awareness, which she thought she got from her glider-pilot mother. Pleasing a Bearkiller armsmaster wasn't at all easy. Her grandmother and namesake admitted she was first-rate with

horses; Luanne Larsson had been horse-mistress of the Outfit for a generation, and *her* parents had been breeders and wranglers with a ranch in
Texas before the Change stranded them in Idaho delivering stock to a
customer.

What she saw in the mirror every morning was perfectly satisfactory
in her opinion, and other people found it attractive as well, which was
nice or in some cases very nice. Dark gray eyes, olive skin that tanned
easily, slightly curly hair of a warm medium brown, and features with just
enough African and mestizo fullness to moderate the beaky Nordic
hatchet-face that prevailed on her great-aunt Signe's side of the family
and which only looked good for a short while. These days Signe's nose
and chin were making acquaintance, and her lips had practically disappeared. While grandmother Luanne had a weathered handsomeness at
sixty-two that showed you what a peach she'd been when Eric Larsson
fell for her with a dull thud just after the Change.

*Of course, Signe's lips might have gone away because her favorite expression is
thin-lipped disapproval,* Luanne thought with a grin. *Thank God Mike Jr. is Bear
Lord now, and that he's got a better disposition than his mom. Even if I get caught, he'll
probably commute it to . . . oh, a couple of months public-service call-up or going out
and working on one of the Outfit's ranches down south. Unless I get killed, of course;
he'll be really pissed off then.*

She'd always gotten along well with her first cousin once removed,
even if he was Asatruar, which faith Luanne regarded as one of Great-
Aunt Signe's less inspired decisions.

The train was getting closer. Luanne held up her index and little fingers, used the known distance to a familiar tree, and estimated speed.

Doing close on twenty miles an hour, she thought unhappily. *Hand-gallop
speed. A horse couldn't keep that up more than a couple of miles, but a hippomotive . . .
they could barrel right through the station without slowing down since they've got a
military priority order to clear the tracks.*

You *could* deal with objects moving that fast. One of the tricks her
grandmother had taught her mother, and her mother her in turn—the
lineage ran back to skills learned in rodeos before the Change—was to
grab the saddle-horn of a horse as it galloped by and swing up onto the

beast's back in one movement. Things like that were very impressive and even occasionally useful. The downside was that if you failed, even on turf or sand or sawdust you could easily dislocate your shoulder or break half your bones—or your spine, or your skull. Luanne had done that training with nothing worse than a lot of bruises, a broken collarbone and a mild concussion or two, but the equivalent with a moving vehicle, at night, on uneven ground with steel and rock and unyielding cross-ties all underfoot . . .

I sure hope cousin Órlaith has that thing slow down a bit! she thought.

She was carrying a lot more gear than she did at gymkhanas, too. Granted most of it was in a knapsack she could hopefully toss on board, she was still wearing a mail-lined leather tunic and a sword. She hurriedly took off the backsword, tied the guards of the sword and dagger to the scabbard-lip with a leather thong, and slipped it through a loop on the backpack and cinched it tight. That left her unarmed except for the hold-out daggers in her boot and collar, but needs must.

Closer now . . . was it slowing down or speeding up? She started taking rapid but deep and controlled breaths to build extra burst endurance. No lights except in the hippomotive itself, the cars were dark . . . well, it was midnight. Presumably most of the people aboard had been woken out of a sound sleep to be hustled onto the train; you didn't give information out before it was absolutely necessary on a clandestine movement. Now they were trying to make up the lost sack-time. All her instructors had said you slept whenever you could. She crossed herself and touched her crucifix, and murmured inaudibly:

"O God, You know me to be set in the midst of great peril. Grant me such strength of mind and body, that those evils which I suffer for my sins I may overcome through Thy assistance. Through Christ our Lord. Amen."

The open-sided power car came closer, with the moving shadows of the twin four-horse teams within, massive muscled shapes in the moonlight. Then four slab-sided wooden rectangles on wheeled bogies. The rear car would have a bit of open platform at its end behind a railing, and she could just make that out.

She was a little to the south of the main station building, where the salvaged solid metal rails gave way to the more modern steel-strapped wood; there was a clear straight stretch here. She turned and began running along the track before the hippomotive passed, working up to a full sprint just as the rear carriage swept by. Crushed rock ballast crunched under her boots, and the creosoted cross-ties tried to throw her off. It would be just perfectly glorious to trip, twist her ankle, bang her head on the rails and then get it cut off by the hippomotive as she lay unconscious.

The length of the train passed her. She estimated distances in the dark, and—

Thump-clung!

The backpack swung out of her hand and landed on the boards. She used the motion to help her leap and her hands in their fingerless kid-leather gloves clamped down on a rusty rear rail of salvaged pipe. She took one more bounding step. For an instant her arms felt as if they were being wrenched out of their sockets and then she had her feet snatched up and braced against the floor. One foot slipped a little, the hobnails skittering on smooth fir boards, and then she held it with a desperate pressure. If it *had* slipped it would have gone right into the bogie up to the knee and been cut about three-quarters of the way through. Of course, the motion of the wheel would have dragged her right down and underneath as well. Which would have killed her, but not as quickly as she'd have wanted by that point.

Phew! she thought, as she did a slow forward roll over the railing and came to her feet.

Then she froze. Contrary to what bards sometimes said, swords didn't ring when they were drawn unless you were stupid enough to use a metal scabbard and then ruin the edge against it. There was a faint, distinctive *whisk* of oiled steel on wood and leather, though.

Which is what I just heard. Uh-oh. Is this the foreigners' car, those Japanese we heard about? Will they speak English or just slash at anyone trying to board—

She opened her mouth to say she was friendly, but before she could arms grabbed her from behind; a man, mostly bare, shorter than she was and very strong. She started an automatic counter, and the man thumped her under the sort ribs with his left hand and dug the thumb of his right expertly into her neck as he forced her chin back, all the while evading the stamp against his bare instep. She could smell him, not dirty but distinctively different, a more vinegary scent than the usual body-odor.

"*Uff!*" she wheezed.

The immobilizing hold turned to an unpleasantly thorough grope as the man determined what he was holding in the dark, backing into the body of the rail-car while he did, where the dark was Stygian. He laughed and said something in an unfamiliar language and turned the investigative grope into something even less pleasant.

"Hey!" she tried to shout, though it came out more as a croak, and made a futile grab for her boot-knife.

There was a confused milling and series of collisions, and then a lantern came on and someone barked authoritative-sounding words in the same foreign language; she didn't recognize it, but the rhythms and sounds were distinctive. Luanne had no idea what the man was saying, but she could certainly recognize an exasperated officer snarling an order when she heard it.

Wow, a troll! she thought dazedly, whooping in breath and blinking against the light as the choke-hold was released, and reflexively rubbing at her throat and coughing.

The man standing before her was in something like a knee-length bathrobe, obviously just thrown on. The troll had his topknot tied, and was the oldest man present—in his forties or possibly fifties—with a squat heavy-muscled build and a truly impressive set of scars, including several that looked like the result of sword-cuts on the face.

Her mind chimed: *Experienced and extremely dangerous* when she looked at this one.

Luanne's immediate world had been at peace all her life, but she came of a warlike people and had been raised among the veterans of the long savage campaigns against the Prophet and the Church Universal and Triumphant. She knew the look.

Chimes it very loudly, she thought.

One man in the car was in what she recognized as something very like samurai armor, with a bare sword in his hand. The troll pointed, and he did a smart about-face and went back out onto the rear platform and closed the door behind him.

The other thirty or so men who crowded the car were in loincloths of an alien type, obviously a length of cloth twisted so that it was sort of a thong-rope except where it formed a pouch for the genitals. Under other circumstances she thought it might have been rather fetching, especially given the perfect condition of the bodies, but alarming right now. Especially given the odd haircuts; all but half a dozen of the men had a strip shaven up the middle of their heads and long behind. A few had the long part in a topknot, and the rest had probably undone it for sleep, which went with the bedding-rolls on the floor of the carriage and the bags of gear neatly piled up in one corner. Something nagged at her for an instant until she realized she was in a room full of men and taller than all but a few of them. Among a similar number of Bearkillers half would have had more inches than she.

A car full of nearly naked muscular shrimps with strange hair.

The troll's face was utterly impassive as he bowed to her and spoke: "Suh solly."

Wait a minute, is that so sorry? *I certainly hope so . . . Christ, that was really scary. More than getting on the train.*

She decided it *was* "so sorry," as he motioned her out of the way. She side-stepped, and the other men in loincloths scrambled to get out of *her* way, as if she was either contagious or red-hot. Then they stood in rigid, braced ranks.

The one who'd been holding her started to say something, and the troll barked at him again. Whatever he'd said, it produced a nice *attention,* as motionless as was possible in a moving railcar and looking a little strange in a loincloth. The troll stepped nearer and said something to the man who'd grabbed her, snarling it with their faces inches apart. There was an instant of silence, then—

Whamp!

The open-handed blow to the face sounded like two oak boards smacked on each other. The man who'd groped her was only about five-six, but he looked as strong as he'd felt, in a wiry fashion. He rocked and staggered and then came back to attention without the slightest attempt to dodge or block, his face blank despite the blood running from his nose and a cut lip.

The troll turned to her and bowed again. "I General Egawa Noboru. I sray . . . say . . . to he, bling disglace."

Bring disgrace, she thought. *I said he brought disgrace on us. Well, that's a positive attitude, good zero-tolerance for inappropriate behavior there.*

She had just about figured that out when the troll turned back to the groper and said something else in the same grating snarl; if broken salvage glass in a grinding machine spoke Japanese, it would sound like that.

Whamp!

He hit with the left hand this time, but it didn't seem any weaker than the other and even expecting it the motion was a blur in the dim light. The younger man staggered a little longer, and his face was already swelling, but it was still stolidly fixed.

"I s . . . say he blake—"

At her baffled look, he made a stick-snapping gesture with his hands.

"Break?" she supplied.

"*Hai,* brrreak. Break hos-pi-ta-ritry."

Breaks hospitality, she translated.

Another sentence to the younger man.

Whamp!

This time the man being beaten buckled at the knees and slumped to the floor; he wasn't unconscious, but his eyes had rolled up, and he was leaking blood from both of them, his nose, mouth and one ear.

"I say he . . . *bakayaro eta* . . ."

The troll squinted his narrow eyes, obviously working out equivalents in his head.

"*Bakayaro* . . . in Engerish . . . *flucking idiot. Eta* is . . . filthy shit-man."

He gave her a nod, and snapped his fingers; someone handed her backpack and sword to her with a bow, and she took them in a slight daze.

"Come, prease. *Heika* . . . Majesty . . . your Majesty . . . I bling you to."

Whoa, Luanne thought, looking down at the bleeding body of her assailant and then at the rigid lines of men around her staring fixedly ahead. *And I thought we Bearkillers had discipline!*

"You want klick . . . kick?" the troll asked politely, indicating the fallen man.

Want to kick him? she rendered it. She'd been genuinely frightened, but . . .

"No, thank you," she said, returned his bow and thought of the hasty reading she'd done since the rumors started going around. "Ah . . . good job. *Ichiban.*"

At that he smiled slightly and turned, motioning her politely ahead of him.

Well, this is going to be interesting. And I thought Mackenzies were strange.

CHAPTER EIGHTEEN

"Well, brother, we're ready," Karl said quietly.

Karl Aylward Mackenzie and his brother Mathun shared a room in their family's farmhouse in Dun Fairfax, one that had been half a bedroom before the Change. They'd shared it for a long time too, ever since they got too old for cribs in the nook adjoining their parents' room. That experience let them pack their gear for a secret pre-dawn departure without more than an occasional collision in the dim light of a single tallow candle, and no more quiet cursing than you'd expect.

Karl had been twenty for a few months and his brother was a year younger. That made them men grown by Mackenzie standards, though just barely. They were eligible to *take valor* and fight with the First Levy, if still a few years short of the age most were handfasted and so became full adults. They'd scuffled like pups in a litter most of their lives, but it had never gotten out of hand and they were as close as most brothers, which was fortunate since the room had just enough room for the two-tier bunk bed, two clothes-chests and a few things hung on the wall.

What was that kenning Lady Fiorbhinn used? Karl thought. *Literal and meta . . . phor? We're close enough, and then again in here we're close enough.*

They looked alike as well, enough to be taken for twins by those who didn't know them. They were both a little under six feet, with builds that would be more long-limbed and rangy than their stocky father even when they were his age. That was a legacy of their mother's side of the family, like straight barley-colored hair and eyes more blue than gray. Their square straight-nosed faces with the jutting cleft chin were his, though; like most clansfolk of their generation they wore that yellow hair in a single thick horse-tail down the back when it wasn't clubbed up and tied with an old bowstring as now, and like most Mackenzie men without the neck-torc of handfasting they shaved their admittedly still wispy beards.

Right now they could scarcely keep from grinning like loons at each other—at least, Karl thought Mathun looked like a loon when he did it, and he suspected that he wasn't much better. He felt about ready to burst with pride and eagerness too, and just a trace trickle of fear down in the roots of his soul.

The Princess sent for us, for us, to guard her back and help avenge her da! 'Twould be an offense against nature if none of the Clan Mackenzie were on this faring, there's scarcely a one that would have said her nay, but it's our very selves she picked for the message.

They tiptoed about in their sock-hose this hour before dawn, stifling the odd curse as they bumped into each other while stuffing their gear into two smallish sacks by the light of the candle in the wall-sconce; the window was firmly shuttered to keep the light from showing outside. Apart from a spare kilt and plaid each and oddments such as sock-hose and the linen drawers which Mackenzies did, contrary to rumor, wear beneath their kilts, it was mostly things you needed to live in the field. Some salt, hard-tack and trail mix, firestarters, a pot for Mathun and a frying pan for Karl, tools like hatchets, light sleeping bags folded small, their first-aid boxes, extra arrowheads and glue and bowstrings and wax, water purification tablets, a kit of wax-and-pigment color-sticks to apply warpaint. Nothing new to either of them; they'd gone on war-games with the Dun's fighters, and hunted in the mountains and wilderness for weeks at a time ever since they were big enough.

They were already wearing the brigantine torso-armor that any Mackenzie eligible for the levy kept—a jack of two layers of soft green leather with little steel plates riveted between, and short mail sleeves. The open-faced sallet helms they strapped to the sacks, the steel also painted green. Next to last they buckled on their belts, with the broad-bladed stabbing short swords and long dirks, the little soup-plate-sized buckler on its clip on the sword-scabbard and the special sporran with a brigantine-like backing that protected the Gift of the Lord, hopefully. He winced a little at the thought. No matter how brave you were, some injuries didn't bear thinking of.

Last of all were the baldrics with the quivers. For hunting you used a small one with five or six arrows. The war quiver was much larger—it held forty-eight arrows of various types in its tube of hard-boiled and varnished elk-hide—and had loops for carrying your longbow strung or unstrung, and pouches on the outside for various bits and pieces like an arrow-hone.

They each took two bows, not the hunting poppers but the great battle tools that took a hundred and twenty pounds of pull to bend past the jaw with a clothyard shaft on the string. Those could kill at three hundred paces, and at close range even the best armor wasn't proof against a square hit from a bodkin-head shaft. They'd made the war-bows themselves, from yew and walnut root-wood they'd cut and seasoned and bits of polished antler from their own kills for the nocks. The bowyer's bench and tools occupied part of a big room that had been some sort of vehicle storage before the Change, and where the household had its looms as well. Bowyering was a family tradition, passed down from the grandfather they scarcely remembered and that as an old man nodding by the fire.

The songs remembered him though, the first Aylward to bear the title *the Archer*, the one who'd taught the whole Clan the bow back in the beginning.

And they sing about Da's deeds too, on the Quest and in the Prophet's War and after. He's the Archer now, and seven times he took the Silver Arrow at the Lughnasadh Games, and there's all the things he did by the High King's side from here to the

Sunrise Lands and back. Well, now they'll sing about our deeds! Karl Aylward Mackenzie, the Archer . . .

"Ready when I find my rabbit's-foot . . . ah, here it is, with the blessing," Mathun said, touched it to his eyes and lips and rubbed it on his head before he tucked it into his sporran.

"And sure, now you know where it is, and your lice do too. Well, we're ready as we ever will be," Karl said, setting his flat Scots bonnet on his head.

He propped the note for their family on his neatly-made bunkbed. Like all Mackenzies he could read, write and cipher—it wasn't the most important part of what you learned in Moon School, but it was there. He even read for pleasure. He'd traded six deerskins and some Black Cohosh he'd gathered wild for the dog-eared secondhand copy of a modern *King Conan* printed in Corvallis that he'd stuffed into his sack; that was a lively historical novel set in ancient times. With it was a pre-Change edition of Donan Coyle's *The Free Companions* inherited from his father, about a more modern land rather like the Association territories. He'd been given it at his last birthday along with a gruff admonition that if he ever went on campaign he'd spend a lot of time being bored.

Writing beyond a list wasn't something he enjoyed, though, and he'd sweated over the message as he grasped the goose-quill in his callused fingers. He put the thought of his mother reading it, possibly even weeping, out of his mind.

And Mathun Aylward Mackenzie will be in the tales too, the faithful brother who does and says things that make everyone listening laugh, though brave and true in the end.

He didn't add that last thought aloud, not wanting a quarrel right now. Besides which, Mathun's knobby fists had developed a respectable wallop these last few years, as he had reason to know. Once their mother had separated them with a bucket of cold water.

The weight of all that gear was solid, about sixty pounds including the armor, but nothing very much to big young men who'd grown up farming and hunting and lumberjacking, digging and building and working at crafts.

And who'd drawn bows of ever-increasing weight at least dozens and usually hundreds of times just about every day since their sixth year. They said you could tell a longbowman's bones at a glance.

Both of them could wolf-trot all day under more than this, and had. Karl remembered a time just before last Samhain when he and his brother had packed out an incautious young bull elk, one that Cernunnos had guided into an upland meadow at dawn when they and their dogs had been waiting behind a thicket of blueberries. Fifteen miles over mountain trails to get it back before dark; even drained, gralloched and minus head and hoof that had been better than two hundred pounds of meat and hide all up. They'd been well and truly tired after that, but they'd done it, and he'd danced through the gate of the Dun with the antlers on his head and Mathun behind him giving the elk-call.

"We're as ready as we will be—and we'll remember something forgotten ten miles down the road," Mathun said, with another of those loonish grins. "And rend the air with curses, we will. Come along, Fenris, Ulf. And you too, Macmac."

Their dogs rose with doggy grins of their own, huge shaggy gray-brown beasts with mastiff and Dane and wolf in them. They might not know the details, but they could tell their masters were about something, and as usual were delighted to join in. Macmac was the Crown Princess' current dog and of the same breed, the descendant of her first, sent here for safekeeping by their father along with spare horses and gear left behind in the dash northward after the High King died. He'd been moping without his mistress and isolated among strange canines, and now looked eagerly hopeful that any break in routine meant he'd be reunited with her.

Karl sobered for a moment, thinking of the High King; Rudi Mackenzie had been a presence in their lives as long as they could remember, often as not at the table in their kitchen yarning with their da with a mug in his hand, and the brothers competing for the honor of drawing a new one for him from the special barrel of Old Thumper by the door. Not only was their father commander of the High King's Archers, and one of the Companions of the Quest, but Dun Juniper was just up the hill from

Dun Fairfax—you could do it in half an hour at a walk without pushing, if you took the direct footpath.

It's hard to believe he's just not there anymore, he thought, then brightened again. *And sure, we're to avenge him! Us, not Da!*

"The princess will be glad to see Macmac again," he said softly. "There's nothing like a dog you raised from a pup for consoling grief."

"Poor lass," Mathun said. A grin, lickerish this time. "And I'll be glad to see her for more reasons than him. What a woman! Perhaps she'll cast an eye on me, and *I* could console her."

"And then you awake from the dream needing a bath," Karl said dryly. "Hush now."

He took one last look around the room where he'd slept most of his life. There was a tiger-skull on the wall; the whole dun had turned out after that one took a cow, and the skin was in the covenstead for the use of the Tiger Sept, but he'd shot the first arrow. There was a dreamcatcher hanging from the ceiling over the bunks that their grandmother had made, trimmed with wolf fur—he and his brother were both of the Wolf Sept, that being the totem-dream they'd had. Most Aylwards got that one. And a few other knickknacks, among them a whimsical green pottery toad his first girl had made for him, she being from a family of potters—though she'd gone off to handfast with a beermaker in Sutterdown, the Clan's only real town.

Mathun caught his glance. "Can you blame her? The man had a brewery all his own, for Goibniu's sake!" He smacked his lips. "Not so fine as Brannigan's Special, but well worth drinking. I might have married him meself, with that in prospect, despite liking the lasses so."

Goibniu was a patron of smiths, and also had a sacred vat of never-failing mead. Maltsters called on Him as well as metalworkers.

"Hush, I said!"

Karl stuck his head out into the corridor. It was dark, for all that there were windows at either end. The Aylward house was the biggest in Dun Fairfax; in fact, it was the farmhouse that had stood here for nearly a century before the Change. It was honestly made of timber joists on a stone-walled cellar, unlike a lot of the gimcrack stick-built stuff put up in the last part of that hundred-year span, and looked good for another century at least, with care. It needed to be big, for the Aylwards had thriven mightily and bred lustily.

They padded down towards the stairs, holding their ankle-boots in their hands and taking care to step near the wall where the boards didn't creak. The dogs followed quietly save for the slight click of nails on the polished wood; they were well-trained beasts, who knew when their masters wanted silence. Down another set of stairs, and—

"And where are you two going?" their mother asked.

Karl didn't jump; he'd had *that* trained out of him long ago. His stomach still squeezed as he squinted into the light of the suddenly uncovered lantern. Asgerd Karlsdottir stood there like an image of the Norns, her graying blond braids over her shoulders and her arms crossed on her bosom. She was a tall woman, and not a Mackenzie by birth—their father had met and won her when he was on the Quest, in fabled far-off Norrheim on the shores of the Atlantic, what had once been northern Maine. She wore the garb of her folk, a hanging dress of embroidered blue wool and a full-length apron of white linen fastened at the shoulders with silver brooches.

"I asked where you were going, Karl, Mathun?" she asked again.

Her voice had never acquired the Mackenzie lilt; she had a sharp way of speaking and odd expressions—*ayuh* for yes and others—and a slow sonorous roll when she was moved or speaking formally. Karl's mouth opened as his mind hunted frantically for an excuse.

Her hand shot out, pointing a forefinger at his face. "And don't . . . don't . . . *don't* you tell me you're off for a day's hunting with armor on your backs, sword at your belt and your war-bows slung!"

He sighed and closed his mouth, and followed her pointing finger when it swung to indicate the door into the kitchen. Light flooded out as he opened it; the alcohol lanterns on the walls had been lit.

He heard Mathun muttering as he followed, and the dogs padded after them and thumped down heavily in their current favorite spots. Dogs had keen noses for rank and authority. The kitchen—which included what had been the living room or parlor of the original building—

was the core of the household. There was the hearth against one wall, with the altar and the images of the Lord and Lady over it, the cast-iron cookstoves, the icebox, the working counters. And sinks with faucets, since Dun Fairfax had running water.

Net bags of onions, strings of garlic and red dried chilies and burlap-wrapped hams and a flitch of bacon and coils of dried smoked sausage hung from the beams of the ceiling. Around the wall beneath it was a broad band of carved boards, wrought with running designs of vines and faces from myth and story. Below that were bright hangings woven by the household's own hands; other stretches of wall held tools of the sorts used indoors or that you might want frequently when you went out, and over by the door that led to the exterior vestibule were racks for weapons, conspicuously lacking the share he and Mathun were carrying.

Right now there was also a big mask woven of green fir-boughs hung over the long table where the whole household ate, a face with slanted eyes and a mysterious smile. It would be Litha at the end of the month, the Feast of Midsummer at the solstice, and Jack-in-the-Green presided over that. He sighed a little again, on a different note. The Green Man was master of summer's abundance, wildness and sweetness. In the berry-time before the shattering labor of getting in the grain, at least: then He became the dying-and-reborn Harvest Lord. Lithia was a fine holiday for a young man in a Dun of the Clan.

Well, maybe I won't be missing it anyway, he thought sourly.

His grandmother Melissa was also there, sitting in one of the chairs at the end of the table; she was in her white High Priestess' robe, with her rowan-wood staff with the silver Triple Moon on its finial leaned against the chair, and he winced slightly at that. She was old now, a bit bent and gnarled of hand from a life that had known its share of hardship and toil; she didn't stand long if she could help it, but the eyes beneath her white brows were still shrewd. She could simply pronounce what he wanted to do *geasa*, and it would be that-which-is-forbidden under sanctions even a reckless young man wouldn't dream of breaking.

His mother leaned back into the stairwell. "Down!" she called.

Mathun groaned behind him as the whole household filtered down the stairs. His aunt Tamar—his father's elder half-sister—and her man Eochu, a friendly sort and a fine leatherworker though quiet and unambitious, and their children. Except for the three eldest, one of whom was off with the High King's Archers, another who'd gone south to Dun Barstow, and the third who was a millwright up in Dun Juniper. His uncle Nigel, who was only a few years older than he himself. He and his twin sister Nola had been grandmother's last, after a long gap; Nola had moved out to a new dun with her man, as had Karl's aunt Fand and uncle Dick. Nigel's wife Caiomhe, and their first child, a babe in arms. And Karl's other siblings; his brother Cathal, who was gangly, sixteen and looking at him and Mathun with bitter envy, his sister Gunnvör, twelve and doing her usual quiet cat imitation, and little Aoife, looking a bit bewildered at it all with her great blue eyes troubled and her stuffed unicorn clutched close, for she was the baby and only six.

"If you grassed us up, Cathal, then by the Threefold Queen and the Lord of the Dance I'll smack that pimply—" Mathun began.

"Quiet!" his mother said. "Did you think to slink off without a word?"

"And *just* before the harvest," Nigel added.

Karl winced; that *had* bothered him. "I, um, wrote a note . . ."

Then his grandmother began to laugh. "Oh, stop tormenting the boys, you two, for sweet Brigit's sake," she said. "Look at them stammering and flushing the now!"

He exchanged a glance of sudden hope with his brother. His mother snorted.

"They deserved a bit of a scare, for deceiving us. Or trying to."

"Sit," she said shortly, and they did. "It was the Princess who called you to her aid, didn't she?"

Karl and Mathun looked at each other, and their mouths set: they couldn't speak, not when the first part of the message had been an oath of silence. Asgerd nodded approval.

"Good. You *can* keep your mouths shut."

"Though they couldn't *befool* a blind three-legged pig itching with mange," Aunt Tamar added. "Walking about looking at things and thinking 'will I see this again.'"

"I didn't say anything of the kind!" Karl said, and his brother nodded vigorously.

"No," his aunt said dryly. "But you thought it. You thought it *very loudly.*"

Their mother added: "After a Royal courier I know to be a friend of Órlaith comes, and then you tiptoe around like bears trying to dance, and sneak off into corners to whisper with a few of your friends . . ."

Suddenly she grinned, and for an instant you could see the wild girl of the stories beneath the grave matron who was known to be a bit dour and stern by Mackenzie standards.

"Did I ever tell you *why* I was ready to go off with your father, when he and the King and the others came to Eriksgarth to guest with King Bjarni? Why I was a shield-maid? Which is not so common a thing among my folk as it is here, though we all train to arms."

They looked at each other again. "No, Ma," Karl said.

"I'd been betrothed, and not to your father," she said, shocking them a little. "And my man was killed by the Bekwa when he went a-viking to the dead city of King's Mountain for goods to start our own garth. I pledged to the High One on the oath-ring of the Bjornings—"

They knew that the High One meant Odhinn, Lord of the Slain and Giver of Victories; she'd told them the tales of her people. The One-Eyed wasn't much worshipped in the dùthchas, though He was given due respect, and had followers elsewhere in Montival. Among the Bearkillers, particularly, and in Boise where the Thurstons, the ruling kin, were His. That was an unchancy One, from all the stories. You didn't use His proper name casually, lest the ravens called Thought and Memory fly too near. Even in Norrheim, red-bearded Thor who brought rain and warded the world of men from the giants was more popular with most.

"—that I would send him ten lives for the one taken, and that by my own hand. My kin were unhappy with it, though it was within our customs . . . just barely. But your father, ah, your father just nodded and took it as a thing needing no speech. That was the start of my love for him. He was just the age you are now, Karl, and you favor him in your spirits as well as your faces, you and your brother. You're men grown now, not to be taken by the ear and swatted on the backside when you're naughty. Only hiding what you meant to do angered me. Your grandmother is not in her dotage, and neither am I!"

At that all the adults were laughing, at him but with him as well. The two brothers shed their brigantines—they fastened under the right arm with clasps that could be undone quickly—racked their weapons, and hung the armor on the pegs by the door. They'd resigned themselves to missing breakfast, but that was quickly put right with bowls of porridge from the crock kept warming overnight at the back of the stove, with nuts and berries and thick yellow cream atop it, and a hasty dish of bacon and mushrooms and slabs of toasted bread and yellow summer butter.

Karl looked down as he chewed, thinking of the line he'd just heard from the Blessing: *And blessed be the mortals who toiled with You.*

"Going to be strange," he said. "Every day eating food I didn't help grow. About the harvest—"

Eochu shrugged, something he could do quietly, somehow; he was still strong and hale though he was older than Karl's father and his hands were marked and scarred with the wounds of his trade from knife and awl and waxed thread.

"We have enough for the Aylward croft, what with Breinan and Evora, and Cathal getting tall enough to do most of a grown man's work, and even if we didn't the Dun would help," he said.

That was the rule if a household was short labor due to public duty or sickness or unavoidable necessity, war or other emergency. Mackenzies didn't have lords; they looked out for each other. The tight bonds of a Dun could chafe, growing up next to someone didn't always mean your stomach wouldn't knot at the very sight of them, but it meant safety too, and protection in a world always hard and sometimes merciless.

"And sure, Edain may have stopped screaming and running through the treetops and heaving boulders by then, enough to come home and toss a sheaf or two himself," Eochu added with another chuckle.

Nigel nodded. "I wish I was going with you," he sighed, then looked at his daughter as she nursed. "But . . . no. Not until the First Levy's called out, if all this comes to war. Which it likely will, in the end, with our

High King dead. The wings of the Morrigú will be beating over this, Gwyn ap Nudd will lead the Wild Hunt riding, and many a Woman of the Mounds will keen from the rooftree at night."

And I'm just as glad you're not coming, Karl thought, without saying anything aloud.

His uncle was a first-rate fighting man, clever and hard; but if he'd been along, he would have been the first among them, for all that he was only four years older. When they'd finished they gave hugs and the kiss of farewell all around, then knelt before their mother; she put her hand on their heads, and murmured a blessing in the singsong tongue of her ancestors, the one her far-off Asatruar kindred used for worship. Then:

"Be brave, be cunning, shirk no duty, and hold to loyalty above all things," she said. Then with a catch in her voice: "And come home to me, my boys."

More matter-of-factly. "I'll talk to your father. He'll rage, but it won't last, for he'd have done the same thing in his time."

Their grandmother pushed herself erect. "When your father left on the Quest . . . we didn't know it would be that, then, of course . . . I blessed him. Shall I bless you?"

Karl and Mathun looked at each other, and nodded. She signed the air above them with the Invoking pentagram—point up first—and her voice rang out, cracked but strong:

"Through darkened wood and shadowed path
Hunter of the Forest, by your side
Lady of the Stars, fold you in Her wings;
So mote it be!"

Once outside the brothers lifted their bicycles down from the pegs on the wall, loaded their supplies into the panniers and pushed the machines along. Three others joined them, outfitted much as they were and around their age. Lean Ruan Chu Mackenzie had dark hair that developed red highlights in summer, and was son to the village healer. He and fair round-faced Feidlimid Benton Mackenzie, whose father was Dun

Fairfax' master-smith, were lovers who'd sworn the oath of Iolaus to-gether last year. Karl suspected that was the only reason Ruan had de-cided to come along, though his partner was wildly enthusiastic. Ruan had picked up a good deal of healing skill and herblore, and Feidlimid could do metalwork, and they were both good men of their hands. The rangy black-haired, black-eyed girl was named Boudicca Lopez Macken-zie, and was clever and could skulk quietly with the best; he'd seen her take deer by sneaking up to them and cutting their throats with a knife. The pair and the young woman both had a hound at their heels, of the same huge hairy breed; there was a moment of sniffing and tail-wagging, but the animals were used to each other too, and bouncing-glad to be off with their folk.

Boudicca looked back over her shoulder. Ruan and Feidlimid had a tuft of elk fur in the badge on their Scots bonnets to mark their sept, but Boudicca had a bit of fox tail that swayed as she tossed her head. People of her disposition often saw Sister Fox in their questing dream, and there was something of that One's sardonic grin in her voice.

"So much for stealing away unseen. Like reiver ghosts in the night, wasn't that how you put it, Karl?" she said with one strong eyebrow raised. "The stealth of tigers slipping through a thicket we have in-deed . . . except that we do not, so."

"Not so skilled at deceiving our own kindred, eh?" he said with a shrug. "Hopefully we'll do better with foemen."

She shot a respectable eighty-pound draw, but carried a glaive as well as sword and bow. The glaive was like a heavy pointed butcher-knife with a cruel hook on its rear, set on a six-foot shaft of strong ashwood with a butt-spike on the other end. The origin of the polearm was as a hedging tool; it could be wickedly effective in a fight and was surprisingly useful in other respects.

"Perhaps we should be tootling a pibroch upon the pipes instead, or beating a Lambeg?" she added. "Ah, well, at least I got a bag of supplies out of it—I thought me ma would load enough into it to rupture a pack-mule, weeping and carrying on the while and dashing back for one more thing I'd die without and that sure and certain."

"Ours had something to send along too," Mathun said, and the pair nodded that theirs had done likewise.

Which is convenient, I thought we'd have to stock up at Sutterdown, which would have cost good money and even more precious time.

Boudicca dug into the canvas sack lashed across the panniers on her bicycle and handed around some very nice apple-and-hazelnut-filled pastries, sweet with honey that tasted of fruit-blossoms. Karl had just had a good solid breakfast, but decided there was room, and anyway they wouldn't keep.

"And two cheeses wrapped in dock leaves," she said, jerking a thumb at the lumpy beige mass of the sack. "Those will travel a bit, at least."

Everyone perked up. Boudicca's mother Una, as all the world or at least all Dun Fairfax knew, was a dab hand as a baker and made a truly fine sweet sheep's-milk cheese with bits of dried fruit in it that traded five for one with the ordinary sort, and another with flecks of hot peppers that was almost as good. Her daughter went on:

"Nothing else she gave me will last out three days. There's loaves of risen bread, a crock of butter, tomatoes, eggplant, six pork-chops—"

The youngsters all nodded; the Lopez family's sharing-circle had just killed a pig. The households in a circle took turns furnishing a beast, which was the most economical way of doing it. There was at least a hundred and fifty pounds of butcher's meat best eaten fresh on a good fat summer hog, far more than even a big household could consume easily. Fall and winter were the seasons for preserving hams and bacon and salting down pigmeat in general.

"—and a head of *lettuce* from the back garden, by the Lady's eyes . . . the onions will keep, but nothing else. She tried to tuck in a dozen eggs, for all love, but I put me foot down there."

Mathun groaned in sympathy; the rest of them had things like dried smoked sausage and twice-baked crackerbread and hard cheese and sacks of nuts and dried fruit.

"How did your mother ken what we were up to?"

"*Your* mother told her, how else? Just last night, I will grant, which was shrewd. She'd have been a puddle by now, else."

"She packed you *lettuce?* Didn't she know we'll be gone months?" Mathun said. "Lettuce won't even last until we're past the last place we can buy garden truck."

At which Boudicca just snorted and rolled her eyes, and everyone shrugged agreement.

All the world or at least all Dun Fairfax also knew that despite her skills Una had trouble remembering to pin her plaid in the morning, or realizing that her children weren't kittens, and was in general a blithering flibbertigibbet. Her man had been even worse, until he tripped over his own feet one dark and muddy October afternoon while looking at a bird flying south. That wouldn't have been so bad, except that he fell right under the hooves and then the blades of a four-horse team dragging a disk harrow across a field due to be put in winter wheat. The pyre had been lit as soon afterwards as the wood could be got together, and the body on it had been tightly wrapped in old sheets from head to toe and then waxed canvas.

The next crop was very good in that field, which only stands to reason, Karl thought. *Earth must be fed.*

He'd sniggered with a fourteen-year-old's lack of mercy as the mourners tried to find something beside *not fit to be let out without a keeper* to say about the deceased.

Earth must be fed . . . still, a pity. Looking back he could say that Calbhach had been a fine shepherd at least, and a good-natured neighbor.

"We'll eat from yours the first couple of days and then you can share ours," Ruan said briskly.

Perhaps by way of reaction to her parents Boudicca was hard-headed and sensible, like the rest of her four younger sibs. She'd been applying the hatchet to feathered necks when her family needed a chicken since she was nine, for example, because whacking off a bird's head always made Una start to blubber. Even before she'd finished the prayer of thanks and apology, with the steel wavering dangerously in her hand before she struck. Legend in the dun said that sometimes she'd *closed her eyes* while she swung.

Folk were stirring and lamps lit behind windows as they passed; this wasn't the busiest season of the year—that was just ahead—but a farming Dun never lacked for work and rose with the early summer dawn. The air was taking on a tinge of woodsmoke and more than a tinge of the mouth-watering scent of baking bread—not every household had bread ovens, but the others swapped each morn with those who did. Other scents were present, livestock among them, but nothing very rank; Mackenzies were a cleanly folk, something enforced with Clan-wide *geasa*. And al-most as bad, songs from the bards at festivals if you fell below acceptable standards. Nobody wanted a mock-epic about *Dun Stinkard* sticking to you like dung to a boot.

Even the ducks and geese were stirring on the pond at the center of the green, and a cat gave them a blue-eyed stare from a fencepost, hissed half-heartedly at the dogs and leapt up to the turf of a roof to send pi-geons fluttering away.

Fairfax held a little less than four hundred souls all told, and was the oldest of all the Clan's farming settlements—Dun Juniper, up the hillside to the northward, was something else again; the portal to the Other-world, some said. That number was about as many as you could have and still keep all the fields within reach without wasting too much time going back and forth on foot. When a Clan settlement got too big for comfort it split and founded another, often in league with two or three more Duns with the same problem, and that newly established settlement took fresh Clan common-land under the plow. There was no lack of space at all, even here in the Willamette.

Dun Fairfax was named after the couple who'd owned the land here before the Change. They'd been very old, and besides that sick with some chronic illness which needed medicines that wouldn't keep. Mod-ern healers could identify it, though not help enough to mention. But their supplies and tools had aided that first band of Clansfolk to survive, and their graves were honored yet.

Most of the little settlement was houses along graveled streets bor-dered by nut or fruit trees; the newer ones were of deep-notched squared logs fitted together on stone foundations below, the older often frame like the Aylwards', salvaged from the abandoned dwellings that had been common two generations ago before fire and weather finished their work. All had flower-starred turf roofs, and all had carving and paint on shutter and rafter-end and around doors and windows, in the sinuous curling style Mackenzies liked; all had small gardens of flowers and herbs on their lots too. Highest reared the covenstead, with the beam-ends of its rafters wrought into the shape of the totem beasts, home to ceremony and ritual and used for the Moon School and in bad weather for meetings of the Dun's *óenach*, the assembly of all adults whose vote settled serious matters and selected those charged with office and delegates to the *Óenach Mór* of the whole Clan.

That side of the village also held smithy and leatherworker's workshop, the bathhouse, granary, communal barn and storehouses for the gear that was used in common, like the threshing machine and reapers and mowers and the separator. He could hear its droning whine picking up as someone worked the crank and poured their first milking through it; the cream would be splashing out into a bucket, ready to be poured into the buttermaking barrel-churn, and the skim milk into another to feed the pigs being fattened for slaughter.

And Aunt Tamar was right. I am looking at it all with new eyes. Who knows when—if—I'll be seeing it again?

The thought didn't oppress him; no more than to any healthy youngster did his own death seem real to him.

Around the whole dun was a clear graveled street edged with a rectangular wall of great upright logs, thirty feet high, thick as a man's body and cut to points at the top, the smooth wood lightly carved and varnished against rot. They were set in stone and concrete at their bases, and beyond was a dry moat grown in short-cropped grass. The huge treetrunks were bound together midway and just beneath the points with bands of stainless-steel cable set in grooves; wooden blockhouses rose at the corners and over the gate. A fighting platform ran around the inside, with wooden staircases stretching up so that each household's fighters could run straight to their posts if the drum and horn-call came.

Outside the gate was the little shrine to the Fairfaxes over their graves, and the god-posts, black-walnut logs carved and inlaid with the forms of

Brigit holding Her flame and sheaf, Lug with His long spear and hand raised in benediction. Unlike most Clan settlements, Dun Fairfax didn't have its own Sacred Wood; it used the same mountain *nemed* as Dun Juniper for the great ceremonies of the Wheel of the Year, which was a source of envy throughout the dùthchas.

"We're off, Henwas," Karl said shortly, as they came to the gate. "Merry meet, merry part, and merry meet again—after you open the gate, if you would."

"Off on your greatly secret quest!" the man taking his turn at gate-guard said, leaning on his long-headed spear and laughing in his gray-streaked brown beard. "It's invisible you lads and lasses . . . and lass . . . are!"

He mimed surprise, looking about with wide eyes and putting a hand to his ear before speaking awestruck tones:

"Aye, there's a bootless voice coming from the clear air asking me to open! Now, is that a good sprite or the Fair Folk about their tricks?"

Laughing and twitching like a pack of dogs with a tickle up the arse, him and his, Karl thought sourly but did not say, as the gate-crew composed of Henwas' household and neighbors winked and nudged behind the older man. *But the toe of me boot would do better.*

Boudicca had her glaive's lower three feet in a scabbard on the rear of her bicycle. That left her a hand to express her feelings, middle finger raised from a clenched fist. The guard laughed again.

"Any time you wish to serve the Goddess so, just proclaim the victory," he said, whipping off his Scots bonnet and bowing, and making a bad pun on the meaning of her name.

He might be fond of his own wit, but he and the others worked the crank to slide the bar out of its brackets and then pushed the gate open. Nobody here except Karl himself understood just how much High Queen Mathilda would be upset when her daughter decamped; and in any case, though the High Queen was well-liked—she'd been a captive/hostage up in Dun Juniper during the opening days of the Protector's War—in any dispute ninety-nine in a hundred Mackenzies would take Princess Órlaith's side by reflex.

They'd have been opening the gate about now anyway. The rim of the sun was just clearing the Low Cascades to the east, and the Lambeg drum roared from the platform above as the pipes skirled. Karl and his brother had already made the Greeting at home, but most folk waited for the signal.

"At least we don't have to sweet-talk Henwas, that laughing jackass, into opening without telling him where we're off to, or why," Karl said resignedly as they pushed their bicycles over the gate's threshold, pausing to make reverence to the god-posts.

In peacetime there was no rule against leaving the Dun whenever you wished, say for night-hunting or just a stroll. Generally through the small postern after the main gates had been shut, but it was a little irregular not to tell the gate-guards why. The conversation necessary might have given them away.

If everyone and his second cousin hadn't already kenned it without our knowing, Karl thought.

Then he laughed himself. When the others looked at him: "Well, to be sure it's not quite as we planned it, but we're away, are we not? Nothing hurt but our vanity, as me ma said. To tell the truth, I'm just as glad to have my kin sending me off with the blessing."

The others gave grudging nods as they mounted their bicycles and pedaled off with gravel crunching and popping beneath the solid rubber wheels. The dogs trotted after them in a clump, heads turning to watch the occasional bird or butterfly—but these were well-disciplined beasts, and they'd ignore even rabbits or deer.

"And it's a fair summer's day, and we're off for adventure!"

He put out of his mind some sour things his father had said on the subject of *adventure;* it was the way of nature for an old man to be a bit like a plaid on a wet day in the Black Months, soaked and flat and clinging and heavy. It *was* a fine day, and the valley of the little tree-fringed creek ran westward before them, opening out like a triangle with its broad base the edge of the wide Willamette.

The first little bit outside the walls was in strips of low-growing vegetable garden mulched with sawdust and walnut shavings. It was law to keep nothing above knee height within bowshot of the defenses. The days when folk feared the lurking, crawling terror of Eaters were gone and had been before his father's beard came in, and it would be a very bold and very stupid bandit chief indeed who led a band right into the innermost heart of the Mackenzie dùthchas. For that matter invading armies hadn't come this way in a long time either; the heartlands of the realm had been at peace since the end of the Prophet's War just before he was born, and that had mostly been fought in the eastern marches anyway. Though here south of the Columbia the foe had come as far as the passes through the High Cascades, and met the Mackenzie arrow-storm. But the rule about keeping the space before the walls clear remained, and was kept.

Beyond the garden strip the gently rolling land was in smallish square fields, edged about with close-trimmed hawthorn hedges or lines of trees or both, in pasture or grain, flax or row-crops like potatoes, with an orchard of apples or peaches or cherries or other fruit now and then, those mostly set with beehives as well. In a few hop-vines climbed tall arrangements of poles and ropes; Dun Fairfax didn't have a brewmaster, but Dun Juniper had a very fine one indeed, who swapped for hops and barrel-staves and such if they met her standards.

Karl recognized each plot with knowledge he'd acquired through skin and hands and feet, and knew who held it. The folk of a Dun did a fair bit in common and helped each other at need, but each family had its own croft. Even specialists like the smith or the potter had a field or so. Sheep and cattle grazed, the watchers who stayed out with them overnight waving to the party, and then they were out into the Willamette itself, with only the low distant blue line of the Coast Range to break the westward horizon as the last stars faded.

He turned and looked at the edge of the Cascades beneath the dawn, the Low Cascades blue-green, the snowpeaks of the High catching the morning sun that tinged their whiteness pink, and laughed for the sheer joy of youth and strength and a fair prospect stretching ahead.

A little after noon they were near Sutterdown, cycling past the water-powered mills along the canal from the Sutter River that sawed timber, ground grain and spun linen and wool into thread to sell to weavers and turned hemp into rope; they were mostly shut down in this season when water was low and folk busy getting ready for the grain harvest.

What with his father's profession Karl had seen the great cities, Corvallis and Portland and once even Boise. Despite that, he still felt an echo of the awe he'd known as a child of six seeing Sutterdown for the first time, there in its bend in the river. This was the largest town in the dùthchas, with fully six or seven thousand folk within its high thick rubble-and-concrete wall. That was stuccoed, and painted along its upper fringe below the crenellations with green vines and colorful flowers and lurking spirit-faces. The god-posts outside the gate showed the Lord and Lady as Apollo with his bow and Aphrodite rising from the foam; it was a famous work of the great wood-carver Denis Martins Mackenzie, and they all halted and pressed their palms together before their faces in a reverence.

There were still a few cast-steel roundshot embedded in the town wall, left as flaunting badges from the unsuccessful Portlander siege during the War of the Eye—what they called the Protector's War up in the PPA fiefs. That had been a decade before any of them had been born, but they all grinned proudly at the sight. The arrogant northern knights had retreated a good deal faster than they'd advanced, the ones who didn't stay forever with bodkins from Mackenzie longbows driven through their mail.

All Mackenzies were taught to sing, many did it well, and most played an instrument; hadn't Lady Juniper herself been a wandering bard before the Change? Karl whistled a bar from a familiar tune and they all sang a verse, a jaunty marching-song from the War of the Eye:

> *"Hey, hey, laddy-o*
> *Nock a shaft and string the bow:*
> *Jeweled belt and golden rowel*
> *Flinch at the sound of the Clan's wolf-howl!*
> *Fie what their lords bestow;*
> *They'll be gettin' their reward*
> *From sword and bow!"*

The kilted guards at the gate laughed as they leaned on spears and Lochaber axes and their unstrung bowstaves, being of course Sutterdown householders themselves taking a turn at this duty. A few of them might have been on the wall back then, or for more their parents or grandparents or for some of the youngest great-grandparents. The High Kingdom was united and at peace now, but that didn't mean the Clan had forgotten the wars against the Association.

Then back on the bicycles and over the slow-moving lily-grown green waters of the river-moat and through the gate. The guards gave them a cursory glance and waved them on, since they were obviously Mackenzies and several were known to them by sight. They pedaled past antique frame buildings and modern half-timbered ones with plastered brick nogging, dodging carts and wagons and carriages and wheelbarrows until it was easier to hop down and push instead.

"Heel!" Karl said sharply, and the dogs obeyed, even when their town counterparts barked challenge at the intruders.

They came to a rambling building with a sign hanging from an iron bracket, a wheat-sheaf and sickle carved and painted gold against the brown oak. The *Sheaf and Sickle* inn had songs about it too—Lady Juniper had made one before the Change, even, in honor of Brannigan's Special Ale. They stowed their cycles in the stands outside the big rambling building—it had grown by incorporating the structures to either side and adding second stories of half-timbering to some, and within it was a warren of steps up and down and odd dogleg corridors. Their dogs drank from the trough at the edge of the street, then flopped down by the bicycle rack at a command of:

"Stay! Guard!"

He didn't worry about their gear; Sutterdown was not quite as absolutely safe for loose property as a Dun where anonymity was impossible, but there was nearly a quarter of a ton of hound waiting, heads on paws but teeth ready and eyes peeled. He recognized some of the other cycles, at that, and he knew their guardians as well. A few doggy grins and flopping tails greeted him, but they stayed close to their charges and alert lest he treacherously try to make off with a cycle. His father had once told him he'd known a lot of soldiers worse at their trade than a well-trained Mackenzie greathound.

The main taproom was clear enough, though the floor was on two levels. All the windows were open on this warm summer's day and bees buzzed in the petunias and impatiens in the windowboxes outside, along with less welcome flies. They hung up their brigantines and bows and sword-belts on oak racks polished by long use, just inside the doors and under a fresh Jack-in-the-Green mask, and called greetings. From the number of bows and quivers custom was good, though there were fewer jacks—clansfolk carried bows and swords whenever they went far from home, but in these days of peace and prosperity armor was for war-practice or foreign travel.

The middle-aged granddaughter of the original owner who stood behind the brass-railed bar was named Bébhion Brannigan Mackenzie, and ran the place now with her kin. And the brewery and vineyard that were part of the property; the Brannigans were a family as prominent as any in Sutterdown, and usually contributed the senior High Priestess and High Priest of the town's clutch of covens as well.

"Merry meet, you bunch of young hooligans," she said, but smiled with it. "You're expected. The rest of your pack of redcaps and gossoons are over there, just got in."

She paused in polishing a glass mug to jerk a thumb towards the dimmer back part of the room.

"My thanks, fair lady Mayor," Karl said.

He touched the back of his right hand to his brow in the salute a polite male made to a hearthmistress, and got a snort; she *was* the mayor of Sutterdown, and *fair lady* was what her name meant in the old tongue.

Seven other young Mackenzies were waiting for them. There was a babble of greetings and hand-to-wrist handshakes and hugs and friendly-playful cuffs, but Karl spoke first to Gwri Beauregard Mackenzie, a woman of a few years more than his own age. Her name meant *golden hair* in the old tongue and was a bit of an odd choice, since hers was black and worn in a multitude of tight braids tipped with silver balls, which he thought went toothsomely well with smooth skin the color of pale cinnamon.

More to the point, she was daughter to the *fiosaiche*—seeress—Meadhbh Beauregard Mackenzie of Dun Tàirneanach, and had a reputation as a promising acolyte in that art. As long as she could handle herself well in other respects too, which Gwri could, he wanted someone with those talents on this faring.

Since it has more than a touch of the uncanny. Though to be sure, we'll have the Sword of the Lady along. Still, you put a dirk on the same belt as your long blade, and you tuck the sgian dubh *into your sock-hose too.*

When the noise had died down a little he caught her eye.

"No problems?" he said.

"None to speak of, we slipped away as planned," she replied; for a Mackenzie, she was short-spoken. "You?"

"None to speak of," he replied, and thought she caught the thought behind the words:

Or that I wish to speak of, to be sure.

One of the Brannigans came and took their orders; he chose a slice of the ground-mutton-and-onion pie and home-fries, and others called for cheeseburgers and souvlaki and catfish fritters and fried chicken and submarine sandwiches and the seasonal treat of a big bowl of salad to pass around. Once the beer came and while they were waiting for the food, he raised his stein:

"To the venture!"

Everyone lifted mugs to that; he sipped the cool hoppy bitterness of Brannigan's Special, and reflected that this was a brew to treat with respect, like the small barrel of Old Thumper his father kept for special occasions. No more than one pint with a long day's work ahead, any more would be weakness not strength for all that he'd be sweating it out again. With a bit of a push on a bicycle you could cover a hundred miles or better a day on reasonable roads, which they had . . . as far as Ashland, after which they'd have rutted dusty hill-tracks, if they were lucky, and deer-trails often enough, and they'd be using the bicycles as a handy way to carry gear more often than riding them, until they reached the point where their own feet would do all the work.

By then they'd have to be truly cautious about their surroundings, too. He wouldn't have felt easy about taking the whole trip down into Westria without at least a dozen good bows along, and more if possible. Those weren't lands under law, not yet, not even by McClintock standards. At best they were just thinly speckled with it, like the dust of a seeded and rolled field in the first light rain of autumn.

"Right, then," he said, when he'd set aside his empty plate and wiped his mouth with the brown linen napkin. "Now, we're off. First, one thing: a warband without a captain is meat for the wolves and ravens. Forbye my Sept totem is Wolf, yet I'm not anxious to feed His four-foot children just yet."

"And to willfully defy a bow-captain in the field is *geasa*," Gwri added. Pointedly: "Under a curse of death not long delayed, mind."

Karl slapped the table. "So I'm bow-captain of the Clan's archers on this faring, and Gwri is my second. Once we join up with the others, we're under Princess Órlaith's orders . . . which will come through *me*. Any questions?"

"You're to be bow-captain because your da is the Archer?" one of the crowd said, a hint of challenge in his voice. "There are more folk of Dun Tàirneanach here than of Dun Fairfax."

Gwri started to turn and scowl at the tall youth who'd spoken; his name was Tair Strum Mackenzie.

"Dun Tàirneanach, indeed?" a burly redhead said. "I and my sister here are from Dun Laurel, fairest of all Duns and most favored of the Lady, and I'll have you remember it, Tair Taylon's son!"

Karl put up a hand to stay him with a broad friendly smile; the last thing they needed was an inter-Dun pissing match. Nobody who'd decided to come with him was likely to be the shy or retiring sort. He spoke genially:

"No Tair, not because of that. Me da may well be after us hotfoot and in a rage, to try and drag us back by the ear like naughty toddlers. No, I'm to be bow-captain because the Princess asked *me* to form this party.

Also because I can and will whale the living snot from you if needful, Tair-me-lad, the which I can do now if you like. You'll have to keep up afterwards, mind, bruises and bloody nose or no."

There were four women in the dozen of them; without taking his eyes off Tair he decided that they all caught each other's gaze and rolled their eyes slightly. He thought that a bit unfair. From what he'd seen of life so far women were at least as concerned about status as men, and about as likely to make trouble over it. They were just . . .

A bit less straightforward about it when they have a choice. Usually.

Or as a woman would generally put it, they dealt with it more as humankind would, and less like a boar hog who'd been bitten on the scrotum by a horsefly.

He continued to the other young man: "Fair warning, but we'd best get it out of the way now if you insist, for there will be no time or place for such later."

He smiled while he said it and held out his hand. The other looked into his eyes for a moment, then laughed and shook; it turned into a bit of a squeezing contest, but both were reasonably satisfied.

"Any others?"

Heads shook. Gwri looked around. "*Geasa*, remember, and you consented to it if you stay. Last chance to walk away!"

Nobody moved, though faces sobered. Karl nodded and put his fist out above the table. One by one the others tapped theirs on it and murmured:

"So sworn. And so witness Badb, Nemain and Macha, who love a warrior's faithfulness; and by Lug of the Oaths."

"Well, we'll be off and on our way, then. We're to meet *feartaic* Diarmuid of the McClintocks in five days. Let's show the wild southern hillfolk who think they're so tough what Mackenzies can do, eh?"

CHAPTER NINETEEN

NEWPORT

TERRITORY OF THE FREE CITY OF CORVALLIS

(FORMERLY WESTERN OREGON)

HIGH KINGDOM OF MONTIVAL

(FORMERLY WESTERN NORTH AMERICA)

JULY/FUMIZUKI 6TH, CHANGE YEAR 46/2044 AD/SHŌHEI 1

"This way," Moishe Feldman said to Captain Ishikawa, on a bright brisk afternoon.

The Imperial Navy officer walked up the gangplank behind the merchant, dodging a string of stevedores running up it with bundles on their heads. The ship moved slightly at her moorings with all the coming and going, though the netful of cargo swinging by and down through an open deck-hatch probably had more to do with it, as the team on the rope chanted: *"She was makin' for the trades on the outside, And the downhill run to Papeete . . ."*

As he did the hull ground against the new hemp-rope bumpers of the dock, or the last tattered salvage tires doing that duty as well. He saw that the outside surface of the ship's side from the gunwales to at least the waterline had been covered in thin sheet metal secured to the planking with bronze nails. It wasn't armor, except possibly against shipworms; enough steel to stop a roundshot or bolt from a heavy naval catapult would make the vessel impossibly sluggish. But this would make it much harder to set the ship aflame with incendiary shot. Japanese shipwrights used the same trick, for vessels that expected to go in harm's way.

Ishikawa came up the narrow gangway with familiar ease, just lightly touching the manrope along the side. He didn't feel *too* conspicuous as he followed, even on this cloudless summer's day. Not in local dress for this Newport place, and with a knit cap pulled over his distinctive haircut with its topknot and shaved strip up the pate. The strange clothes didn't bother him very much; loose pants and *hakama* did roughly the same thing, as did a jacket and *haori*. He didn't feel more than half-naked without his swords either, as most samurai would, since you couldn't wear a katana all the time on shipboard anyway. Or just leave it thrust through a sash if you didn't want it lost overside. The *tantō* on his belt wasn't all that much different from the utility knife any seaman might wear, at least while it was in its sheath and you couldn't see the shape or the quality of the steel.

It's good to hear gulls and smell saltwater again, too, he thought. *And to feel the wind on my face and a deck beneath my feet.*

His mind skipped a little as he remembered the ice blowing into his eyes in the seas north of Hokkaido, the curling foam on the tops of the mountain-high waves ripped free and freezing as it came at him like catapult bolts until there was thick ice all over his oilskins.

Well, on a pleasant day like this, it is very good. Clear sky, a few clouds, a fresh offshore breeze . . . what more could a seaman ask of the kami of wind and tide?

His looks weren't impossibly unusual either. Most of the people native to this town were big, hairy, round-eyed and fair, but by no means all. He'd seen a couple who could have been Nihonjin in local clothes themselves . . . if they kept their mouths shut and didn't move, so that you couldn't see how their very stance and stride were different. Though if you looked closely . . . perhaps the language shaped the face as much as the blood did, or the genes to use the old-fashioned term.

And there were others from all over the world. *Which I envy.*

He loved the sea and ships, that feeling that *anything* might lie over the horizon, but all his sailing before the last voyage of the *Red Dragon* had been around home waters, keeping the scattered islands and new outposts together and intercepting *jinnikukaburi* raiders. Or once or twice striking back at *their* homeland, landing troops and burning coastal forts and shipyards. It was vital, necessary duty and ships simply could not be spared for anything else. . . .

But I have had my dreams. That is why I was so eager to volunteer for the Tennō's plan.

"I'll show you around," Feldman said slowly and distinctly.

Ishikawa followed that; he'd studied English for the professional literature in engineering and shipbuilding written in it, and since they got here he'd been trying hard to master the spoken form.

At least this man doesn't speak some eccentric dialect!

It hadn't occurred to him that English would have dialects like Japanese. He supposed it should have—the three written forms of his own language were much more uniform than what actually came out of people's mouths on different islands, and he'd visited every single one of *those* that still had more than a family or two. By now he could follow some of what he heard here, though he wasn't nearly as fluent as the *Heika* yet; he admired the way she'd mastered the spoken language by sheer applied willpower. Understanding was easier than speaking, and he could follow speech, if it was slow. Mostly.

She could even talk *poetry* with the locals by now.

What a woman the Majesty is, even so young! he thought. *What a ruler she will make! Fearless but not reckless, tireless, both intelligent and clever, and so good at getting people moving as one. With a will like the steel of a Masamune sword, supple and strong and hard at the same time. And now to work. General Egawa was most particular about my thoroughly surveying any foreign ship which will carry the* jotei. *Not to mention the rest of us.*

He found himself fascinated by both the similarities and the differences between this *Tarshish Queen* and his lost, beloved *Red Dragon*. The size was roughly similar, he thought twenty-five or perhaps fifty tons more than the four hundred he'd commanded, depending on the depth to keel.

He wrote *displacement? four hundred ton, more a bit?* on his slate and held it up.

"Four hundred and sixty tons displacement," Feldman said, confirming his estimate.

Dimension? he wrote.

"Two hundred twenty feet from bowsprit to rudder, thirty-five-foot beam, twelve-foot depth of hold."

The Japanese sailor easily converted feet to metric measurements, or to the more natural *shaku*, which were replacing them again in general use. A shaku was almost exactly the same as a foot anyway, smaller by well under a single percentage point.

"She's shallow draught, for inshore work, and for dog-hole ports," Feldman went on.

"Dog-hole?" Ishikawa asked.

"Places so narrow a dog couldn't turn around in them."

"*Hai*, understand," Ishikawa said, suppressing a chuckle; he'd gotten ships in and out of places like that often enough. "Back, forward, around, anchor and rine . . . line . . . and pull, much swear and yell."

"I've been there," Feldman said, and this time Ishikawa grinned at the idiom once he'd examined it in his head.

They had dedicated warships here, he knew from his dips into the library at Montinore, built for nothing but fighting other ships, though not many. A publication called the *Illustrated Naval Gazette* had been fascinating. Japan couldn't afford anything like that right now; her navy was of vessels designed for roughly the same purposes as this fast armed merchantman, carting cargo and people quickly into dangerous places, dealing with reefs and sandbanks and shoals, and fighting at sea or carrying troops onto hostile shores when necessary. The hull was moderately shallow, and he wondered how much leeway she'd make tacking. A deeper hull lost less distance that way, but of course it needed more water under the keel. . . .

There were three masts, each of them a single varnished trunk up to the topmast—he regarded them with soul-deep envy as he traced the standing rigging with his eyes. There would be trees like that somewhere in Japan's mountainous interior, but nowhere close enough in practice to today's shipyards, and his people used composite masts bound with shrunk-on steel hoops. These were better; and more beautiful.

They went below, dodging the net-loads of provisions and supplies swung down through the hatches and into the hold by the dockside cranes, and the laborers stowing it under the supervision of deck officers loudly concerned with the ship's trim. From the smell, only faintly stale, the bilges had been deliberately flooded with clean seawater and thoroughly pumped out recently or the ship was fairly new, or both. He approved; it was most literally a pain in the back, but worth it.

"Ballast?" he said, then spelled it out on his slate when the other man looked baffled at *barrus*.

"Bundles of copper pipe right now," Feldman replied. "Sometimes ingots or bars of various metals. Usually I sell it at the other end of the voyage and replace it with worked rock or salvage brick for the run home. Metal stock is cheaper in Montival than anywhere my firm trades, and you can always sell brick or ashlar here for a little something. The metal kills some things that try to grow in the bilgewater, too."

Ishikawa grunted thoughtfully and bent to look at the scantlings as they came back up into the main cargo hold, prodding occasionally with his *tantō* to check the soundness of the wood. The framing was again a mixture of the familiar and the strange; and they used a thick and apparently waterproof plywood extensively, which intrigued him—it gave much larger sections than ordinary planks and presumably was stronger, though he would worry slightly about the laminations in conditions at sea, depending on what they were using for glue.

Still, it looked as if it was holding up well, and the structural planking that strengthened the decks was magnificent—straight dense-grained baulks eighty feet long and eight inches through with scarcely a knot, beveled together at the edges and bolted securely to the beams and stringers. That turned the decks into elements in a hollow box girder of enormous natural strength. The construction and fastenings were to a very high standard too, as good as the Imperial Navy's shipyard on Sado-ga-shima. Much better than the wrecked or captured *jinnikukaburi* vessels he'd examined, which were fragile when they weren't over-heavy. The storage lockers held abundant spare sailcloth and rope, along with pitch and other naval stores.

He worked his way methodically back to the main deck, which was flush for about two-thirds of its length from the bowsprit, a lovely clean curve like a sword. Then it rose to a low poop-deck that held the binnacle and wheels.

The captain's cabin—which would be for the *Heika* and the other women of rank—was at the stern, with officer's cubicles on either side of a corridor running beneath the poop. He checked what would be the *Heika*'s quarters—quite adequate and already being modified for more bunks—and the navigation gear, which was good and almost exactly the same as the equipment he'd trained on. There weren't many different ways to make a sextant and chronometer and binnacle-mounted compass, and as far as he could tell the charts were good, based on pre-Change surveys but updated recently. This Feldman probably had a lot more experience with deep-sea navigation by sun and stars than he did, though he was sure his inshore skills were at least equal given that his experience was mostly of that sort.

"You design ship?" he said, as they climbed back to the deck; he thought so, from some of the other man's replies to his questions. "You build?"

"I designed some of the details and oversaw construction in the yard we have a share in, but this is similar to most of our . . . my family's . . . ships. My grandfather got the wreck of a big schooner that came here right after the Change, from San Francisco—bunch of refugees brought her in, an old vessel built about a century before the Change and used as a museum ship, called the *Thayer*. The town council let them settle because they figured anyone who could do that was worth their keep. My grandfather got the hulk for next to nothing because nobody thought she was good for anything but burning for the nails."

"Wooden ship still froat so rong, one hundred year?" Ishikawa asked skeptically.

"She'd been heavily restored about halfway through that, but even so . . . not seaworthy anymore, not really, not even at the beginning of the trip; it was a miracle she made it this far. She'd hogged badly, and there was dry-rot above the waterline, right in the ribs and hanging knees. It would have come apart like wet paper if they'd hit really bad weather. Sweet hull lines, though, a design originally meant for this very coast. We took her draught inch by inch, recorded everything as we dismantled her for the metal and fittings, and we've never found anything better for our line of work. There are ships three times as large and much deeper in the keel on regular runs now, but we go where the risk and the profit are."

Ishikawa nodded. *Risk* meant *battle*, among other things. "Catapults?" he said.

One merit of speaking the language badly was that nobody would expect him to know how to be really polite in it, which he'd realized was another language all on its own when he grasped that people weren't *trying* to be rude to him. In a way it was like being drunk; everyone automatically made allowances for things that wouldn't normally be tolerated.

"Right, here's the armament."

Eight complex machines crouched on the deck on either side, their snouts pointing at flaps that could be opened in the bulwark.

"We mount 'em topside because they'd take too much cargo space if a clear fighting-deck was left below."

"Why sixteen?"

"That's as much weight as we dare put so high above the keel, you see."

"*Hai*, unbarance if more."

Feldman peeled back the tarpaulin that covered the one he indicated, and Ishikawa bent over to peer at the mechanisms. A heady, familiar smell of well-lubricated steel and brass and a stranger one of something slightly like peanut oil greeted him.

The differences of detail were greater here—unlike wind and water or time and stars, there were more workable solutions to this class of problem—but the basics were similar. Springs of salvaged steel from railroad car suspensions were compressed when carefully curved throwing arms were drawn back, and snapped forward to pull the cross-cable that launched the projectile resting in a trough. The main frame was secured to a plate in turn bolted to the beams and carlins of the deck, with elevation and traversing screws moved by handwheels.

He rough-measured the components with outstretched thumb and little finger, since his were a convenient half-shaku long more or less, and decided they were near optimum in their proportions. Those had to be carefully calculated to transmit the maximum possible amount of the energy stored in the springs.

These weapons could be quickly rerigged to throw either eight-pound steel balls or four-foot javelin-arrows. Some of those had sickle heads to cut rigging or bisect anyone unlucky, and some of the roundshot were of glass filled with incendiary compounds and wrapped in cord that could be soaked in the stuff and set alight just before they were shot.

He traced tubing with his eyes, and grunted with delight—the recoil force was transmitted through cylinders of its own and used to partially recock the loading system, salvaging energy and speeding up the process.

Really very clever.

The Imperial Navy had something similar, but that was much easier with the purely mechanical cocking system his service used. In the bows and right aft at the curved stern of the poop deck were the chasers, single rather larger catapults running on steel tracks set into the decks, so that they could be rapidly traversed to cover a cone before or after the ship. Those had sloping steel shields built on either side of the throwing-trough to protect the crew while they reloaded and aimed.

"Cocking mechanism is . . . pump liquid . . . hydrauric?" he said.

"So desu," Feldman said, surprising him a little. "Long-stroke hydraulic bottle jacks from Donaldson Foundry & Machine in Corvallis, twenty-five-ton rating on the broadside pieces and thirty-five for the chasers in bow and stern. Those rocking-pump levers unfold and are clamped behind the piece for action. Forty-five seconds to reload with two hands on the pump, twenty-eight with four. Range is about fifteen hundred yards at maximum elevation with bolt ammunition, a bit more if you shoot on the uproll. More effective and accurate the closer you get, of course."

Ishikawa grunted again—that was a slightly better rate of fire than the ones he'd used; on the other hand, his threw heavier shot farther and he would bet that they took less maintenance and were more reliable than these.

Then he looked up. The long booms on the masts looked as if it was mainly a fore-and-aft gaff rig, but there were spars for square sails on the main and foremast.

"Sail plan?"

"There we did make changes. It's a topsail schooner rig now; gaff mainsails on all three masts, square topsails on the main and fore, jib topsail on the mizzen. That's a compromise, but everything's tradeoffs, right?"

"*Hai*," Ishikawa said, when they'd gone back and forth to make sure that *tradeoff* meant *torēdoofu*. "*Honto ni*," he added for emphasis. "Definitely truth. Anything better one way, not so good the other. Nothing *ichiban* all way."

This rig would sacrifice a little speed with the wind abaft the beam for more when you were working into the wind plus ability to point closer, and a very little less on a reach for considerably more with a following wind. For a ship that might have to either chase or run in any conceivable wind conditions, not just get from Point A to Point B regularly at least cost and time, it was a very sensible compromise.

Hoses were rigged to the dock. Rumbles came from below as the liquid gushed through them, filling the coated steel tanks below with fresh water.

"Crew?" he said.

With the work of loading going on so fast it was impossible to tell exactly who were part of the ship's complement and which were dockside workers helping out or shore-based carpenters making last-minute alterations. Neither type wore uniforms, just rough shapeless patched working clothes differing only in detail from their Japanese equivalents.

"You *can* handle her with as few as ten if you're not in a hurry— schooners are economical that way."

Ishikawa shrugged agreement. Gaff-rigged fore-and-aft sails like those on the lower parts of the *Tarshish Queen's* three masts could be raised, lowered and reefed from on deck, with most of the muscle-work done by winches, and they had them. For maximum speed the square topsails on the main and fore would need hands to go up the ratlines and out the spars. Plus there was little point in having catapults without crews.

"For foreign work . . . forty-five at least. That allows eight-hour watches with one on and two off in good weather, plenty of reserve for storms, and enough to help with loading and unloading if there aren't good harbors. And to fight, of course."

"Prentry vorunteers?" he asked.

The ones who definitely were sailors looked capable and they didn't have to be driven to work. They also looked as if they knew what they were doing. At first glance half seemed to be women, but when he counted it was more like one in three or four. He would have thought mixed crews could cause disciplinary problems, especially on long voyages, but presumably the locals knew their business.

I will have to tell General Egawa to caution his men about making assumptions; we want no problems there.

Women in Japan also did things now that hadn't been customary in the old days—the really old days, not the otherworldly-strange period between Meiji and the Change—because there simply wasn't any alternative. They helped crew family fishing boats, for instance, if usually not on bigger craft. And ladies of the upper classes did much of the Empire's routine administrative work.

Feldman nodded. "There are plenty who'll ship out to do one watch on and two off with a strong chance of a fight, rather than one on and one off, and there's no run without *some* chance of pirates anyway, even along the coast. And my crew works for a share in the voyage as well as a wage. That can double or triple straight pay rates, if we're lucky. I get my pick; no first-voyage runaways fresh from the farm for the *Tarshish Queen*. First-rate hands prefer to work with their own kind, too, not spend half their time cuffing and shoving and cursing at plowboys. I could ship half again the number I do without taking anyone I wouldn't want."

"Why not more hands?" Ishikawa asked.

"I'm not a government—I can't pay wages out of taxes."

"Tradeoff again."

"Yes. Speaking of which, just exactly how many . . . soldiers . . . am I supposed to pick up? The . . . Sir Guilliame said that wasn't certain yet, just that there would be a fair number."

Ishikawa's face remained impassive. His heart suddenly ached for the crew *he'd* lost. And which he'd recruited, trained, led and fought beside—fisherman's sons, mostly. He'd known every one of them, their names and natures and families. He took a deep breath and went on stolidly:

"I have eight sailor and self. Besides that, *Heika* . . . Her Majesty . . .

blings . . . brings thirty-two samurai Imperial Guard, herself, General Egawa, and party of Crown Princess—same number. Pick up twenty-eight more place you know. And six horses."

He thought Feldman winced slightly, and he sympathized; carrying large animals on a ship was nothing but trouble, and the farther you had to go the worse it was. He'd done it himself, mainly bringing breeding stock to new settlements or remounts to garrisons, and the memory was not a fond one. Pigs were bad enough, but oxen and horses . . . The man nodded stolidly and replied:

"For a voyage of this length, quite doable. The winds are from the northwest consistently this time of year, and the longshore current runs south most of the way."

"That herp . . . that will *help, hai,*" Ishikawa said. "If not storm."

Feldman laughed. "Oh, storms, of course. It's summer, but . . ."

Ishikawa had been grave, as was fitting. For a moment they shared a sailor's smile at the vagaries of the weather *kami.*

The merchant slapped the mizzenmast they stood beside. "We've weathered some storms together, this old girl and I."

Old? he thought, and remembered the smell of the bilges. He asked: "When built?"

"She's six years old this spring."

Ishikawa thought for a moment, then bowed. "This is a fine ship, Feldman-san. Must see sailing, but still . . . fine ship. I will inform the *Jotei.*"

And Egawa, he thought.

Trusting the Empress to a foreign ship, and a foreign merchantman with a civilian crew at that, had understandably put the general on edge. The voyage here had been bad enough, and that was with an Imperial Navy vessel and picked professional crew. Under an impassive face, the commander of the Imperial Guard was as jumpy as a cat on a salvage-metal roof in summertime.

Feldman returned the gesture, rather clumsily. Ishikawa didn't think the Montivallans were any better shipwrights than his people, but they had access to some materials that would give them an advantage. Some other things they did differently, though that mostly seemed simply different, not substantially better or worse, like the catapults. They definitely had *more* in the way of ships even though they were mostly concerned with the land and the interior of this huge continent. Newport alone had as many slip-ways as the Imperial Navy base at Ryotsu on Sado-ga-shima, and from what he understood there were bigger ports and shipbuilding yards.

"We're building another to the same draught and plan right now; she's just about ready to have her sticks mounted and standing rigging put up."

Feldman pointed to a hull in the fitting-out basin a mile away, under the big A-frame cranes that would slide the masts in.

"From what I'm given to understand, if she's ready when we get back, a certain sovereign-to-be plans to buy her and transfer her to another sovereign we both know so she can get home when she wants to go. By then you should be familiar with her elder sister here, Ishikawa-san, and ready to take command and sail her."

Ishikawa came to keenest attention, and felt a cold chill run through his belly. To have a ship again!

"*Ichiban,*" he said softly. "Sank . . . thank you very much, Feldman-san."

"*I'm* not the one giving you the ship, Captain Ishikawa," Feldman said, chuckling. "My family will be getting her full price, enough to replace her and make up the loss of a season's trade. But I would like to think she's in good hands."

Ishikawa didn't say aloud that he felt like a cripple without a deck of his own to command, but he thought that the merchant understood it.

"We load tonight," Ishikawa said instead. "Leave morning tide."

Droyn and Sir Aleaume settled their contingent in to the ship, more than a score of men-at-arms and spearmen and crossbowmen, all in plain civil garb now. Their equipment was bundled or bagged, the weapons in long canvas sacks, the half-armor for each man wrapped in padding and stuffed into big duffels, even the unmistakable four-foot teardrop shapes of the shields disguised by stacking them pointing in alternate directions and tying them up in sailcloth. The troops were visibly unhappy without their weapons to hand; it would be as bad as walking down the street in your drawers for them.

Órlaith stood at the gangplank and greeted each one by name, a brief word and a nod. When they were all by their gear and sleeping bags below, she stood and caught their eyes. The long low space of the hold was like a shadowed cave, only the glimmer of lights off the water coming through the open portholes. The lashed-down, tarpaulin-covered supplies rose like hillocks behind them, and the light stalls of canvas-covered wicker for the horses they'd pick up later. The air had the inevitable smells of troops in transit, slightly rancid canola oil on leather and metal, old sweat soaked into armor-padding so that it never quite came out, as well as the brackish water and tar and spoiled fish of a working port.

"You were with me when my father the High King fell," she said, not abruptly but without prologue.

Silence. That had been when he fell . . . and these men hadn't saved him. They'd won the brief savage battle handily and he'd actually been murdered by a prisoner, but many would still be smarting from the greater failure, and savagely determined to redeem their names.

Even if it wasn't their fault. Hearts have reasons that heads know not. I feel the same way and I know there's nothing I could have done.

"Now we have a chance to begin to avenge him," she said. "And as well to deal a heavy blow to the whole realm that sent the men who killed him."

A low grim mutter ran through them. She nodded. "Yes, comrades, I know exactly how you feel. We're going through the greatest and least known of the dead cities, and then into the wild lands. Those who fall will win honor, and I will not forget them or their kin. Those who return with me . . ."

A smile: "I'm assuming that I *will* return, of course; maybe that's unreasonable optimism."

That was a joke between warriors. The tension broke a little in a chuckle, and she went on:

"Those who return with me will stand with pride before the whole of the north-realm. And the whole of the High Kingdom of Montival. This enterprise is of high importance, and of great peril. I will share its hardships and dangers with you, for you are men I trust with my life."

Another growl, and then a barking cheer: "Órlaith! Órlaith! *Órlaith and Montival!*"

She raised her hand in salute, but swallowed and blinked as she turned away, thanking the darkness. The shout had always been *Artos and Montival . . .* until now.

The Japanese came aboard in the predawn hush, their weapons and gear in shapeless bundles on their backs. Órlaith had spaced out the movements from the Feldman and Sons warehouse; she wasn't exactly trying to be completely secret. . . .

But then, I'm not trying not to be, either, she thought, standing on the poop deck and watching them come up the gangplank. *I would really prefer that some curious, officious twit not burn up the signal net with reports heading for Mom until we're safely on our way. Better to seek forgiveness . . .*

The Japanese sailors and samurai—she knew enough to tell them apart at a glance now—stowed their gear under the direction of the ship's crew and found where they'd sling their hammocks. When they came on deck again they lined up neatly facing the poop-deck, knelt and bowed their foreheads to the planks of the deck as Reiko stood above them. She was wearing her torso-armor of lacquered steel and silk cord, and the broad flared helmet with the chrysanthemum *mon* on its brow, looming above them like some *kami* of war.

The night was nearly over, with the cool slightly stale smell you got just before the eastern sky started to go pale, and the tide would be making soon. The stern lanterns cast unquiet yellow light on their faces, turning them into things of bronze in the night. Reiko stepped up to the rail and looked down at them, with her left hand on the hilt of her katana.

After a moment she spoke.

"We have come a very long way together, my warriors," she said; it was a conversational tone, but it carried. "Come through storms and ice and battle, through suffering and thirst and hunger, wounds and death. We have lost dear comrades and friends. We lost . . . *Saisei Tennō.* But we have never turned back, and we have also found much. We have found strong allies against the enemy we have fought all our lives. Now they will help us find the thing that the *Saisei Tennō* sought, the great lost treasure of our people. That the enemy has put forth all their strength to prevent us shows how right *Saisei Tennō* was to seek it, how important it is that it be in our hands."

The bronze masks were immobile, but Órlaith could see a few eyes flicker in her direction. The wry smile was entirely in her mind, but it was definitely there behind her grave face.

Sure, and the words magic sword *become more than a story once you've seen one!*

Reiko went on, after she'd given them an instant to think of that:

"Please listen carefully. I know that every one of you is ready to die, for the Chrysanthemum Throne and for our homeland. I know that you of the Imperial Guard and the Imperial Navy feel a burning shame that my father fell and you survived him. Many of us already have died, half of those who began this journey with him. Their names will live forever just as those of the Seventy Loyal Men do, they who preserved the dynasty and the hope of our people . . . *provided we win.*"

A long silence; evidently that last phrase turned a platitude into something with impact. She continued.

"If we do not, *no* names will live. There will be no Obun festival at which to recite them or people who speak our tongue and follow our customs to burn incense and make offerings. It will be as if our ancestors died again, died without issue. All that we of Nihon have ever been, all that we might ever be, depend upon us now."

The silence stretched again, echoing. "So remember this: the reason we fight is not to show our courage or to win honor. Nor may you seek an honorable death because you feel shame that you survived. Worthy as those things may be in ordinary times, even to think of them now is selfishness. We on this expedition fight for our people; we fight that there may be uncounted generations to come. That they may plant their rice and raise their children and sing their songs without dreading that a sail on the horizon may bring death and horror. To protect them against the terror from the sea, to give them a future, we must *win.*"

She let silence fall for a moment before she went on: *"This is our inescapable duty.* I will need more than your deaths; I need your swords and the living hands that wield them; Japan will need them. They belong to me and through me to the nation, not to you, and you may not sacrifice them without dire need."

A whipcrack: *"Is that clear!"*

"Hai! Hai, Heika!" came the chorus, in unison from the samurai and ragged but sincere from the sailors.

"Show the same loyalty and discipline now that you have in the past, and no hardship, no enemy, no desert, no fortress can stand against us!"

"Tennōheika banzai!" crashed out from all of them as they flung their arms upward. *"Tennōheika banzai! Banzai! Banzai!"*

The Sword let Órlaith feel the wave of belief behind it, the bronze ring of truth.

"To the Heavenly Sovereign One, ten thousand years! *Banzai!*"

Captain Ishikawa came up to Reiko afterwards, along with Egawa, as the rank and file went below to the crowded hold.

"Majesty?" he said. "You summoned?"

"Captain, the Imperial Guard were helping a good deal with the *Red Dragon*, towards the end, weren't they?"

"*Hai*, Majesty. Mostly hauling on ropes and similar basic tasks."

"Our voyage south should take between one and two weeks. During that time, I want you to have both your sailors and the Guard helping with the work—familiarizing themselves with this ship and drilling on her armament as much as they possibly can without interfering badly. This is to be your primary task until we make landfall. General Egawa, see that your men cooperate fully. Captain Ishikawa, arrange the details with Captain Feldman on my authority."

Egawa ducked his head. "My men were already cross-trained on catapults, Majesty, but these are an unfamiliar model. They will learn them quickly, I will see to that."

She nodded. "Captain, you will have heard that we may be getting another ship, one very much like this?"

"*Hai*, Majesty!" the seaman said enthusiastically. "I would rather have the *Red Dragon* back in good condition, but if I cannot, that would be a very acceptable substitute. And once we get her back to the yards on Sado, there are a number of features we can study to see if they are suitable and practical for adoption, given our available materials."

Egawa looked less happy, but resigned. "A foreign ship is better than no ship, Majesty, and if Captain Ishikawa says it is suitable, I accept his judgment."

"Then training the Guardsmen to help sail *this* ship will be essential if we are to use *that* one."

Then Ishikawa cleared his throat: "So sorry, Majesty, but while General Egawa's men are strong and I am sure willing enough—"

"They had better be," Egawa said flatly.

"Ah so, gozaimasu-ka," Ishikawa said politely, obviously pitying any Guardsman who *didn't* show willing. "But that is a very short time to learn anything useful."

"They can learn routine tasks," Reiko said. Dryly, flexing her hands: "Besides pumping."

They had all pumped, the last two weeks before they made landfall; pumped day and night until they staggered away numb with fatigue and hunger to shiver themselves to sleep in bedding that was never dry or warm.

"And so free really skilled men," she went on. "There are not enough of your sailors left to manage a ship of this size on their own on the journey home, are there?"

"Not with any safety and not on such a long voyage, no, Majesty. With the assistance of the Guardsmen, we should be able to sail home, and even fight the ship, after a fashion, and of course they will improve with experience. I will split my sailors so that each watch would be commanded by a fully trained man . . . the Guardsmen will have to be ready to obey common sailors, of course."

"Then see to it," she said; Egawa's slight grim nod said there would be no discipline problems.

For a moment the Crown Princess and the *Jotei* were alone on the poop-deck, standing somber and silent; Órlaith thought they both felt the weight of the expectations on their shoulders.

Then the ship's captain came out on the pier; he shook hands with some sort of municipal port official, handed over a sheaf of papers, and came up the gangplank. Feldman was in a brass-buttoned jacket of dark blue and a nautical cap, with his cutlass on his belt; he gave the streaming colors at the jack a salute, and then another to Órlaith and Reiko as he came up to the poop-deck. They both nodded to him without speaking, knowing better than to interrupt a professional in the middle of a task.

The port official on the pier spoke sharply, and his workers went to the two bollards that held the *Tarshish Queen's* hawsers. Several sailors came padding up to take their place at the wheel, standing on the benches to either side of it and undoing the rope loops that held it. There was a quiet bustle on the deck—a few brisk orders, but everyone seemed to know where to go.

Glancing shoreward you could see Newport's streetlights going out one by one as the lamp-man made his rounds, and the yellow of flame coming on in windows as folk rose for the early tasks. Dark shapes moved in the streets, with here and there a bullseye lantern's spark as groups walked to work. The sky to the eastward had been paling for a while; now the stars vanished one by one, and the clouds there were tinged with red. Darkness faded, and suddenly you could see pale shadows, and wisps of fog out on the harbor that turned a glowing milk-white as the first low rays struck them. They weren't quite the first to put out; fishing boats were already out on the water, and flat-bottomed barges set their stubby sails as they worked across the broad bay.

"Mr. Mate! How does she trim?" Feldman called briskly, and followed it with a volley of nautical technicalities.

"Aye, Cap'n, well enough," the weathered dark man standing by the mainmast replied, and added details in the same jargon. He finished with: "Water's on the ebb, skipper, down half a foot."

"Then make her ready, Mr. Mate. Prepare to loose all."

The harbor tug came alongside the bows, there was a flurry of movement as the tow-rope was passed across and made fast, and Feldman took a speaking trumpet from its rack near the wheel.

"*Cast off, bows!*" he thundered through it. "*Cast off, astern!*"

The harbormaster's men thumped their mallets on the cross-rods of the bollards, then lifted the heavy loops of the hawsers free. Deckhands pulled in the thick cables and coiled them. The ship's motion changed a very little as she was no longer tied to the land and rubbing against the wharf's bumpers. Then the tug's oars all came out at once, like a centipede stiffening, poised, stroked the water, and the deck surged beneath their feet. The towing cable broke the surface in a smooth taut curve, jets squirting out of the hemp as the tension of the ship's hundreds of tons of deadweight came on it. The water of the harbor was quite still for a few moments as the tug took them down the channel; Órlaith could hear the call of *stroke . . . stroke . . . stroke . . .* in time to the hollow boom of the hortator's drum. Then a ripple flickered across the green water as the breeze freshened.

Feldman nodded and looked up at the pennants at the mastheads as they passed underneath the great arches of the steel bridge across the river's mouth; there was a sudden scent of hot tar from the maintenance crews up there, heating the preservative for another day in their ceaseless work. Waves surged white on the breakwaters to either side, and then the ship began a long porpoise-like heave and roll as they passed out into the waters of the larger ocean. The waves shaded from blue-green to deepest blue beneath them, streaked with lines of foam.

"Prepare to cast off the tow . . . *cast off!*"

The cable slithered forward through the hawseholes and splashed into water turning a lighter blue as the dawn broke. Little whitecaps marched towards them from a horizon still dark and lost in haze; the tugboat turned sharply northward and circled, returning to the harbor.

Always starting a journey and never completing it, Órlaith thought in a moment's whimsy. *Must be frustrating!*

"Hard a'port the wheel!"

The hands standing to either side spun it, and the nose of the ship turned southward as it coasted on the last of the momentum from the tug, the long slender reach of the bowsprit bisecting the view.

"Hands to winches, hands to heads'l sheets!"

The winches whined as the crew whirled their handles round, and the upper booms of the gaff sails rose like blinds being drawn. Canvas thuttered and cracked, and the ship heeled sharply as the wind snapped them out into smooth curves and the booms paid out to the limit of the sheet-ropes and travelers. There was a surge as way came on the ship, and the tossing turned to a purposeful lunge. Droplets of spray came sparkling down the deck like a handful of diamonds as the bow dug into a curve and broke free, like a spirited horse lunging as a journey began.

"Hands aloft to loose tops'ls!"

The rigging thrummed like plucked strings under the rush of feet, and the sailors edged out along the manropes of the yards that held the square topsails. Another billow and crack as they fell down and filled, and the ship bent further before the wind; on deck crews hauled to set them at just the right angle. Captain Feldman looked at the binnacle and gave a quiet command to the helmsmen, ending with:

"Thus, thus: very well, thus. Mr. Radavindraban, you have the deck. Keep this heading."

"Aye aye, skipper," the first mate said. "Steady as she goes."

Then the merchant-captain surprised her; he'd seemed almost alarmingly businesslike so far, even single-minded. Now he grinned, took a deep breath, looked about at sea and ship and sky, at the crimson and gold over the mountains in the east.

Then he recited softly, beneath the thrum of wind in the rigging, the gathering hiss of water along the sides, and the creaking groan of a wooden ship working:

> "Thy dawn, O Master of the World, thy dawn!
> The hour the lilies open on the lawn;
> The hour the gray wings pass beyond the mountains,
> The hour of silence, when we hear the fountains,
> The hour that dreams are brighter, and winds colder,
> The hour that young love wakes on a white shoulder,
> That hour, O Master, shall be bright for thee;
> Thy merchants chase the morning down the sea!"

Feldman turned to them again. "Your Highness, Your Majesty . . . we're under way."

CHAPTER TWENTY

The McClintocks were singing as they trotted along:

"I met a man in tartan trews
I spiered him wha' was the news—"

It was their turn, so Karl didn't try to start up a Mackenzie tune. He was feeling a little tired, too, but . . .

But I will bear the teeth of Anwyn's Hounds before I admit it, he thought. *And forbye, this Diarmuid is probably walking in the same schoon just now. Also it would be the whipped cream on the pie if me da were to catch us and beat me about the head and shoulders with my own bonnet before them all, and I've an uneasy feeling that's who'll come after us. Old as he is, set him on a trail and he does . . . not . . . stop.*

So he would *not* be the first one to suggest they stop for the night, though there was a good stretch of not-too-steep meadow just ahead and the sun was touching the peaks to the westward. There were a dozen men in the *feartaic's* party . . . eight men and four women, rather, the same balance as in his, typical for a faring like this in either Clan.

They'd left the bicycles at Diarmuid's steading, heading south on foot with six pack-mules to carry the essentials. That didn't include tents; it was high summer, after all. Pressing hard, ten hours a day or so at wolf-pace, alternately jogging slow and walking fast with a break every hour, you could cover a lot of ground even in the mountains. It might kill the mules eventually, tough though the beasts were. No other creature could rival humankind for work of this sort, not when you kept it up for many days.

Gwri of Dun Tàirneanach dropped back beside him. Her dark eyes scanned the woods around.

"I've an ill feeling," she said quietly. "But these are not our home ranges. It's . . . uncertain. Perhaps it's just the strangeness, feeling out of my proper place, but . . ."

"But it'd be a foolish thing to ask you along for your counsel and then scorn it," Karl said.

Also, second sight aside you're one who sees well and thinks hard, and no mistake.

As they'd come south the land had changed, gradually and day-by-day, until they were in country utterly unlike the mosaic of river, swamp, groves of fir and oak amid prairie meadows, overgrown ruins and patches of farmland that made up the Willamette, and more subtly different from the wet rugged forests of the Cascades where they'd all hunted and trapped. And more varied than their own mountains as well, according to aspect and history; these woods burned more often than the rainforests farther north, and you went from dense shade to open land to dappled savannas of grass and oak within a few miles. Just here on a north-facing slope the land was in tall widely-spaced sugar pines, old-growth trees mostly a hundred fifty feet or better with cones as long as a man's fore-arm. Sharp-leafed tan oak and silvery-barked madrone were thick in the understory and the edges of places too rocky to support the great coni-fers.

The scent sap was heavy in the warm dusty-dry afternoon air, and tough-looking plants with a few white-and-yellow flowers still marked the yellow grass. This far south, even in the mountains summer rain was rare.

That strangeness made it harder for Karl to judge risks. The distinc-tive pit-tit-tit of a white-headed woodpecker sounded, and the angry churring of a redbelly, but neither was a type that paid much attention to humankind. There weren't any bigger animals within sight, but most of them *did* pay attention to his breed, as they would any other predator, and would move off at sight or scent of the warband. Game was still thick enough that with Cernunnos' favor they'd never gone short of fresh meat, and with a score and six of them along they could finish off a big beast before it spoiled. Even in warm weather.

I think the Princess thought of it when she said how many to take, we're just as big a band as could live off the land without scattering and slowing down, provided we know what we're about, Karl thought admiringly. *Which means we don't have to carry a weight of supplies that would slow us down. She's a clever lass, and no mistake, our golden princess!*

Then he concentrated on the matter at hand. They were also just few enough that a really desperate or deeply stupid band of outlaws might tackle them, at least for a quick nip-and-tuck raid or ambush where the ground favored them, or if they split up for any purpose. No matter how badly the bandits were beaten in the fight that followed, the delay might be fatal.

If only because caring for the wounded would slow us so.

Besides deer and elk, mountain sheep and boar and feral cattle, they'd glimpsed bears of both types, and seen scat of cougar, tiger—or possibly lion, in these warm lands with much open space—lynx, and gray wolf. Bears weren't any more dangerous than the big cats, but they often had an attitude of surly indifference to humans rather than the sensible caution other predators displayed.

And we've seen sign of men, sometimes, though this is days beyond the edge of the McClintock settlements or even their regular hunting-grounds. Tracks, blazing, old campfires, cut-marks. Not many, but some.

"Better to take care when there's no need, than need to take care and have none," he said quietly.

"Should we string bows?" Gwri asked. "Casual-like?"

That was risky if they were being watched; you just didn't leave a yew stave strung unless you thought you were going to use it, because eventually that weakened it. When more than a score of Mackenzies strung their longbows and just walked along ready, no stealthy watcher with ill intent was going to think it was anything but readiness for an attack. If he was being dogged, he wanted the trackers to think their targets were entirely ignorant.

He snapped his fingers and called: "Mathun!"

"Aye, bow-captain?" his brother said.

Possibly with a little irony in the title of respect, but you couldn't complain about the words or even the tone.

"We're all going to play a game of rovers," he said.

Mathun nodded, then checked and looked at him . . . and winked. No, he wasn't stupid *all* the time. He might be clever too one day, if he lived.

"You and Gwri make up the teams," Karl said. "I'll call the marks."

Nobody observing them was going to be surprised if a group of his clansfolk did *that*. After shooting at the mark—a man- or beast-shaped target—rovers was the commonest way to practice archery. You walked forward, shooting fast at targets the overseer of the contest called at the last moment—an ant-heap, a bush, the stump of a tree, a stump *behind* a tree so you had to loft the shaft over its top and drop it onto the mark; it had the advantage of requiring instant judgments of range and elevation and windage, which shooting at a known target did not. Strangers had been known to claim that a Mackenzie lass might well take a bow to bed along with her lover, to practice shooting into the ceiling in the midst of baby-making, and it was a pardonable exaggeration. Any group of clansfolk on a journey would be as likely as not to while away the time by a rovers' match.

Bards like Lady Fiorbhinn called it a cliché or a trope to say that Mackenzies were a people of the bow. Like most such, there was a solid kernel of fact.

"And it's something we can do while we're moving forward," he said. "No shots under a hundred fifty paces, mind."

He dropped behind as Gwri and Mathun spread the news; there were a few happy whoops. Boudicca gave him a slow nod as she stepped through between bowstave and string, then strung the weapon with a twist of hip and shoulder and thrust of thigh.

When he came to the middle of the column he found Diarmuid Tennart McClintock standing on a little rise by the side of the trail, looking southward as the song came to an end:

"*—Upon the haughs of Cromdale!*"

The ground over the ridge sloped away more gently, down towards a little creek that was a series of slow-moving pools in this season. He had a short sleeveless mail shirt on, and a crossbow cradled in his arms; several of his party carried them, though he was the only one with steel armor. Normally Karl had a fine Mackenzie scorn for the mechanical shooting contraptions, but he did admit that you could carry one spanned and loaded for a long time without being conspicuous about it. And they were handy in any sort of close quarters, which a longbow taller than a tall man was *not*.

"You were in a great hurry," the McClintock said. "Now you're taking time to play at shooting games?"

"Gwri has a bit of a tickle," Karl said quietly.

"The dark lass with her hair in tight braids?"

"Aye. Not easy in her mind. Neither's Boudicca. It's a way to string bows without giving aught away, so. If I'm to be attacked, I'd rather it were at a time of my choosing."

"They have the foresecht?"

"Gwri, yes, a wee bit. Boudicca, no, but she can feel the wind with her skin, so to say. Might just be nerves. But then again, maybe not, eh?"

The smaller man hissed slightly between his teeth, keeping his eyes moving. "Forbye they might be right. This is bandit country, for a' that it's paarrt o' oor dùthchas by strict law. I dinna like the look o' that last claig-tail heidbanger we passed. Fear-*cùirn* he might be, outlaw or in league with sich."

Karl snorted agreement. They'd passed that last steading some time ago. It was a lone cabin built by a settler whose surly grunts indicated he'd come that way to live precisely because nobody else did but his harassed-looking wife and swarm of naked towheaded children. There had been nothing around it but a bad smell from the hides tacked to the wall, an empty corral and a small scruffy garden. He'd worn the Mc-

Clintock kilt, but his voice had held an odd twanging accent rather than their burr.

"I admit there are full plenty of deer hereabouts, but little else to steal," Karl said musingly; bandits went where the prey was, like any predator.

Diarmuid shrugged. They'd gotten on reasonably well, but he knew that the McClintock considered himself older—well, he was, by about six years—and more experienced.

The last is a matter subject to dispute.

Neither of them had marched to a real war, for the realm had been long at peace. Since before Karl was born, and while Diarmuid was still running about the place bare-breeched. Granted McClintocks had a wilder life, but Karl *was* the son of two of the Questers, and his father had been captain of the High King's Archers since their founding. He'd absorbed a good deal of the trade through ears, eyes and skin as his parents raised him, and then traveling often with his father.

"So what would bandits here steal?" Karl went on.

He took a swig from his canteen, which was salvaged galvanized metal encased in molded boiled leather to preserve it from bangs and knocks. The water had the slight metallic taste of the powder that purified it; even a spring bubbling out of rock was a risk in strange country. In your own you knew which water was safe, and were hardened to the local little beasties anyway, but you lost that protection the minute you moved into a new watershed.

If you weren't careful, travel could turn into one long session of looking for a place to squat with a twist of grass in one hand. The bards tended to leave that out of the tales of adventure, except the comic ones.

He handed the canteen to the McClintock, who swigged in turn and replied:

"More to reave hereaboots than ye maun think. We've been pushing south as oor numbers grow. McClintocks go this way in small parties o' late to salvage on their own from the dead cities in the great valley to the south, or to sell livestock and sich to the settlers there. And broken men

flee hereaboots—those outlawed for killin's or just hated out if they've
bad-angered all their neighbors."

Karl nodded to show that he knew of the custom. Mackenzies had a
way set down in law for getting rid of people just impossible to live with,
involving a meeting of the dun's *óenach* and a show of hands, though it
was a very grave matter and rarely evoked. McClintocks were less formal
about that, as with most things.

"Not just McClintocks, but other folk as weel. They can hide out and
strike north and flee back with their plunder, an' it's gae hard to track 'em
if they've learned the lay o' the hills."

Karl nodded slowly. This was a huge land, and it had been thinly
peopled even before the Change. Most survivors of the first years had
long since drifted off to better-favored areas, ones where enough folk
could dwell close enough together for something besides hand-to-mouth
savagery. Hiding would be a lot easier than finding, hereabouts.

"Would any be bold enough to attack a band like ours?" he said.

Diarmuid shrugged again, capped the canteen and handed it back to
him. "Hard tae say. Oor goods, beasts an' weapons and gear would be
wealth to such."

The Mackenzie nodded again; if you were on your own and couldn't
trade honestly, something as simple as a good splitting axe to cut the time
you needed to spend on firewood rather than gathering in food, or a mule
to carry burdens a man couldn't, would mean the difference between
surviving a winter or starving and freezing. Armor like the brigantine he
was wearing would be beyond price . . . Though to be sure you wanted
armor for the same reason it was hard to steal, the advantage it gave in a
fight.

"Also . . ." Diarmuid's voice dropped. "Few women go for outlaws.
That sort of man can be driven blood-mad by the lack."

Karl spat. "Aye."

He thought for a moment, remembering a conversation when he'd sat
on the lip of the stone flags before the family hearth, mulling cider. He'd
been ten at the time, and very proud of being trusted with the task. There
was a knack to it, heating pokers red-white in the embers, then tapping

them off and plunging them into the wooden mascars without getting ash in the liquid or damaging the mugs, in a hissing and smell like a mixture of juniper berries and meadowsweet and honey and roasted apples. It had been a winter afternoon, weeks after Yule, and sleet had been falling outside—the next morning everything had been shining silver for an hour after dawn, until the world turned back to the ordinary mud and gloom of the Black Months as it melted.

The High King and his own father had been sitting at the kitchen table after the midday meal, shelling walnuts by tapping them open with the pommels of their dirks and tossing the meats into their mouths while they waited for the drinks, playing a desultory game of fidchell and discussing a man they'd known during the Prophet's War . . . what had they said?

Aye. They said he'd have been a fine captain, save that he used anger at an enemy to avoid thinking instead of fuel to make thought flow hot. Yes, and the High King said:

"What most angers you about your enemy is the key to defeating them, and it's that which it's most needful to consider carefully."

Well, Karl-me-lad, let's see if you can use the lesson.

After a minute he spoke: "Now, if you were a bad man, one with fell and ill intent, hence denied the Lady's gifts . . . what would bring you running, heedless, tongue out and eyes bulging and ignoring all else?"

"Ah," Diarmuid said, glancing at one of the women.

Who had just loosed at a knot in the trunk of a dead pine a hundred and ninety paces distant. The hard thock of a shaft hitting wood cured hard by sun and wind overstepped the smacking thrum of the bowstring, and she took off towards it with a whoop, hurdling a chest-high bush without breaking stride.

"But how would we do that?" the McClintock said.

"Let's be trying this, if the lasses agree—it'll cost us nothing if we're *not* being followed save a very little time. For if outlaws *are* following us, they're being careful, which means they'll not close in until they're sure it's safe. The which they will not do until we make camp, the more so as we're playing at rovers now and hence have shafts on the string. We need them to attack, and soon, and on ground of our choosing, I'm thinking, if we're not to fight them later on their terms."

He listed the details of his plan. When he'd finished, Diarmuid looked at him with something between respect and alarm. He offered a flask, and Karl took a swig; it was pear brandy, distilled from perry, strong and sweet. He managed to do it with a calm face, though his heart was throbbing fast and he could feel sweat breaking out on his brow. Not at the danger ahead; he'd never been timid about that. What struck him with unexpected fear was the fact that if he failed others would pay for it. His mind winced at the thought of having to explain to his friends' parents . . . though he could take some comfort in the thought that he'd be unlikely to survive disaster himself.

"Ye'll go far," the McClintock said, taking a sip himself and screwing the cap back on before he stored the flat silver vessel in his sporran. "If ye're nae hung."

The first bandit stepped out of a thicket of bearberry, only a few of the small leathery-green leaves catching on his ragged clothes; part of that raggedness was bits and pieces deliberately sewn on as camouflage. A dozen more followed him, the setting sun throwing long shadows before them. The women below were splashing about in the water of the pool, eight of them, it had been so *long*. Their clothes and weapons were on the dry ground, or hung from branch-stubs on the trees.

It took them a moment to notice him; he was thankful that the Mackenzie dogs had all gone off to hunt with the men. His eyes took in the little clearing; the four mules hobbled, their pack-saddles lifted off but still bundled—just right for throwing back on and leading away. Then they could set up an ambush to deal with the frenzied pursuit . . .

He walked confidently forward. There was just time to wonder what the naked women were picking up from the bottom of the stream.

Karl looked down from the tree, only a few branches below him—this was the first big enough to hold a man securely. The war-cloak was excellent concealment up here once you'd filled the fabric loops with twigs and foliage; besides that, they were easy to make from mesh netting and easy to roll up into something compact and light. All the Mackenzies had a couple with them. He had a braided leather cord looped around the tree and his waist so that he could lean forward; the sugar pine wasn't as thick through as he was, not up here where the branches began. There were those who liked to hunt from blinds this way, though he'd always preferred a ground stalk. . . .

But deer don't carry weapons, so. Also they deserve more honorable treatment than these.

The *other* good thing about crossbows and their strings of stainless-steel wire, besides the fact that you could carry them cocked and loaded, was that they were more or less impervious to wet. Oh, the stocks might swell eventually, but that wouldn't be a problem for *hours*. Four of the young women who'd been dabbling and splashing came up with them in their hands . . . loaded and cocked. The range was about a dozen paces to the foremost grinning outlaws, who barely had time to let the smiles slide off their faces.

Tung-thwack!

The first bandit bent over with an *ooof!* like a man who'd been punched in the gut; unlike that man, he wouldn't be getting up again. It hadn't been a fist, it had been four hundred and fifty grains of ashwood, vanes and triple-edged steel hunting head, traveling fast enough to be a blur. He couldn't be sure from this vantage, but he thought it had lodged in bone somewhere—if it hadn't, it would have made a double blood-splash going in and coming out and might have killed one of his friends behind him. Three other women shot within half a second of her; only one missed, which with the juices of rage and fear hopping through the system was better than good.

They'd only had four crossbows. Gwri came up out of the water with a yard-length of leather cord in her right hand, widening into a pocket in the middle. The sling blurred around her head just once and she released the end of the strap; the smooth stream-washed pebble was a near-invisible blur as it left the sling until it cracked into a face in a spurt of red and cut-off bellow of shock. The women with crossbows dropped them and came up with the larger rocks they'd selected beforehand and piled beneath the water at their feet, just right for throwing—and every one of them had been knocking over small game with rocks since they were old enough to hit a rabbit raiding the family's carrots and lettuce.

Those of the bandits who had bucklers raised them and came forward crouched, calling out remarks of their choice. The rest milled about for a moment, shouts of raw rage replacing whoops of lust, except for a couple of wounded men screaming their hurt to the world. Attracted by the noise, the ones they'd left as rearguard came running up too, laughing at their comrades as they did—which said something of their sense of humor, since apart from the ones down with crossbow bolts through them the rocks had left several helpless with broken jaws and others spitting out teeth and howling and holding cracked ribs. There were a bit over two dozen of the reavers, as many as the warband to begin with.

One began whirling a lariat in the style of an eastern plainsman, protected by two fellows with larger shields made of raw planks and hide. The rest clumped together, cursing and dodging and pushing each other forward with cries of encouragement that amounted to *after you with the rocks.*

Now, Karl decided. *They're about to make a rush.*

It was the same instinct that let you judge when a group of beasts was going to stampede.

Quickly, now, boyo, he told himself. *The lasses are the safest people on this field . . . until those spalpeens understand the danger they're in. Then they'll strike to kill.*

He undid the catch of the war-cloak and let it fall back from his shoulders as he moved one foot out on the branch and drew, making a loud, vaguely squirrel-like chittering sound between his teeth as he did, the agreed-on signal.

It was awkward, with a heavy war-bow six inches taller than he was, and shooting down past his own knee, but he managed. The head wavered slightly, as something deep within him realized *you're shooting at a man, not a deer.*

Then he called on Father Wolf in his mind, and felt a ruthless calm fill him: possibly there was a whisper of *Oi, mind yer work, there.* For some reason, his totem always spoke to him in the accent of the grandfather he barely remembered.

He let out a breath and drew inside the bow, waiting until the flight-feathers tickled the skin behind the angle of his jaw. Possibly one of the ten bows in the trees about creaked enough to be heard over the shouts and screams and bellows and the women's hawk-shrieks of anger, for the bandit he aimed at looked up at the last instant. The face was a tangle of brown beard and hair more shaggy than a sheep's arse and not as clean, but the eyes in it went wide and the mouth gaped to show teeth about the same color as the hair.

The outlaw had just long enough to scream himself, at the sight of the broadhead pointing at him from only thirty feet away. Karl's hand was steady as he let the bow-cord roll off his three string fingers, but something deep inside winced a little. It helped that so much of his practice had been snap-shots at targets shaped like men. If you just got out of the way and let reflex do the job—

Snap!

An arrow from a longbow traveled hundreds of feet in a second. Thirty feet was a tiny *fraction* of a second, barely a flicker of motion, literally less than an eyeblink. The flat wet smack of the broadhead's impact was tooth-gratingly familiar, the same sound any hunter heard from a close shot. The point struck just over the bandit's collarbone and smashed downward through his lungs to lodge in his pelvis. Along the way it slashed through the knot of big veins over the heart. The outlaw dropped backward instantly and utterly limp, as if someone had hit him on the head with a sledgehammer, twitched once or twice and lay still with a diminishing stream of blood coming out of his nose and mouth. It was precisely the sort of merciful quick-killing shot—right through the body-cavity lengthwise, slanted across—that you tried for when hunting, to show your skill and please the Horned Lord and Lady Flidais. With a man walking upright the only way to achieve it would be like this.

Nine other bows snapped by the time he had the next shaft on the string. Every one hit, though not all were swiftly fatal: it was close range, the comrades he'd picked for this were all first-rate shots even by Mackenzie standards, and they had had time to be very careful about selecting their first targets among the close-bunched outlaws. Karl had put a dozen arrows ready to hand, lightly tapped into the bark beside him and angled so that he barely had to move his string-hand to grasp one. That made up for the odd position, and he shot them off in a ripple of snarling grunting effort in the time it might have taken a man to count to six ten times, nock-draw-loose, not consciously aiming at all—if you were a real master-bowman you just thought about where you wanted the point to go and there it went. The last one took a little longer to strike, since it was aimed at the back of a running man seventy-five yards away. He flopped forward onto his face, twitched and lay still, with the arrow standing from his spine like the mast of a ship sailing into eternity.

The bandits didn't have time to shoot back, though many carried bows; it took crucial seconds to realize where the arrows were coming from, more to spot the archers through branches and needles and war-cloaks, and anyway shooting right up was nearly as clumsy as straight down. Plus the band had aimed at the enemy archers first: a man with an axe or a spear thirty feet down might as well be unarmed. One outlaw with more presence of mind than most tried to run into the water with the women, which would be one place nobody in their band *could* shoot. Boudicca's hands came up from below the water again, this time with her glaive.

The bandit tried to stop his headlong dash as the polearm rose dripping with the point angled towards his gut, and succeeded at the cost of teetering for a moment with his arms windmilling. One hand held a foot-long knife and the other a small hide buckler, both completely useless now. Except that the panic-stricken violence of his movements might well have sliced his own skin or bashed himself in the head.

The slope down to the water gave a perfect angle for what Boudicca did next; she snapped the razor-edged inner curve of the hook on the back of the blade around the bandit's bare ankle and heaved. The outlaw went over backward with a shriek as the foot was pulled out from under him and the Achilles' tendon sliced across at the same time. That grew almost unbelievably loud as the Mackenzie woman snarled, drew the shaft of the heavy weapon back, and rammed eight inches of the point into his crotch with a convulsive two-handed thrust that must have cracked bone.

Karl winced at *that*, even as he slung his bow, kicked the coiled rope off the branch, jumped, caught and slid downward. Not that you could blame her, all things considered . . .

Where followers of his faith held sway, they punished rapists by burying them at a crossroads with a spear through them, to avert the anger of the Earth Powers at the profanation of the most sacred rite, the one that symbolized the creation of all that was. If the circumstances were aggravated, they might bury the culprit quick with the spear in the earth as a warning, for it was blasphemy and a profanation of holy things, not merely a serious crime.

He whistled sharply as he slid; the rest of the Mackenzies rose from their hiding places and shot as well. Fenris and Ulf and Macmac exploded out of their nests of leaves in the hollow of a fallen tree, silence broken in a baying roar, and the rest of the warband's beasts followed—the dogs had long since settled their own hierarchy of rank in their own fashion. Few bandits were still on their feet after hundreds of arrows landed on better than twenty-four men, and none of them were unwounded; three of them ran straight into the great dogs, and the whole went over in a snarling tumble of limbs and fur and fangs and blood and screams. Mackenzie hounds were gentle . . . with those they thought of as their own folk. Then the McClintocks hiding under their own war-cloaks behind rocks and under fallen trees where they'd crept back after loudly going out to "hunt" erupted to their feet.

"*McClintock Abú!*"

The ripping scream of the McClintock *sluagh-ghairm* cut through the brabble of bewilderment and pain, which was what a war-cry was supposed to do. Diarmuid led his folk, claymore in his right fist, target on his left forearm and dirk gripped in that hand. Behind him came two men carrying *claidheamh mòr*, the four-foot blades aloft above screaming tattooed faces, and the others fanned out in a wedge. There was a brief clash of steel.

Karl whipped out his short sword and took his buckler in his left hand as he landed, crouching and shouting:

"*Hectate's Wolves!*"

That was to rally the Mackenzies. Instead of the desperate fight he'd expected . . .

A man crawled away from him, the arrow through his lower back jerking and trembling as he crawled, blood and snot and tears running down his face. Boudicca walked over, glistening save for the dirt and blood on her feet, poised her glaive and thrust to the back of the neck, went on to the next. There weren't many.

He and Mathun both whistled sharply, the commands overriding each other, and their dogs stopped their worrying at the bodies of their kills, licking their chops. They sat back and looked around with satisfaction as the rest of the great shaggy hounds joined them, thumping the ground with their tails and grooming and doing a little good-natured sniffing and jostling—their pack had done very well. The blood-and-shit stink was heavy, especially by contrast with the purity of the mountain air, rawer and heavier than slaughtering-time back on the croft or on a hunt, and with a peculiar muskiness. Flies buzzed in the sudden silence.

Many of the young warriors of both Clans were pale-faced; Ruan sat down abruptly and hid his face in his hands, with his partner's arm about his shoulders, and their dog nuzzling and whining uncomprehending sympathy. Tair made a dash for a bush before he doubled over retching. Most doggedly went about retrieving their arrows . . . save for some so deeply embedded it would have meant cutting to a degree unpleasantly reminiscent of butchering a pig.

"Who's hurt?" Karl called sharply; it might be his first real fight, but he was bow-captain and found that made it easier to keep steady. "Sound off your names the now!"

All his party did. The women were giving him black scowls as they dressed, and then a couple of grudging nods as it became clear nobody had worse than superficial cuts or bruises. None of them had appreciated being, essentially, bait in the trap . . . though it had been bait with sharp teeth. One of Diarmuid's McClintocks had his sword-side forearm slashed deeply, enough that he'd have to be left at the next secure place. The tacksman's healer was working on that almost at once, evoking a loud yelp as she swabbed and then sewed and bandaged. Even just walking with that would be no joke, though there was no alternative either.

We can leave him at White Mountain; we're close, Karl thought doggedly, swallowing and then spitting to clear his mouth.

Diarmuid was a bit pale himself, plunging the point of his claymore into the soft earth of the stream-bank and then wiping it carefully on his sock-hose before he sheathed it and came over.

"Well, that worked as ye said it would, Archer," he said quietly.

Karl could hear the slight difference in the way he used the word, an emphasis that turned it into a title. Even then, there was a prickle of pride in it.

Diarmuid jerked his chin at a body wearing a kilt:

"There's that woodsrunner we met, the loon I thought might be in league with the outlaws. So he was, and little good it did him. Mind, against real warriors we might not have done so well. They fell for your little trap like trout rising to a fly, and didn't even sniff for a hook."

Karl shrugged agreement, not feeling chatty at the moment. It was a fair point; men well-supplied with foresight and discipline and self-control didn't usually end up in a raggedy-arse bandit gang.

"We might have paid a heavier bill even with these gormless shags if we'd given them a chance to come to handstrokes, or ambush *us*," he said. "Me da always did say that surprise was like having ten times your numbers, and that against men struck blind."

"A wise man, from what I saw of him," Diarmuid said, then jerked a thumb northwards. "D'ye think he's on our track?"

"That I can't say, but I wouldn't be surprised, at all, at all."

"I'll not fight him," Diarmuid said, warning in his voice; it was the manner of a man repeating something obvious that needed to be absolutely clear.

"Neither will I!" said Karl indignantly. Then: "Mind, I'll *run* from him with all my heart."

"The same, master-bowman, the same. So let's be about that, nae?"

The whole group was unwontedly subdued as they broke camp— mainly a matter of picking up packs and resaddling the mules.

Forbye it's a reminder of how easily you might die yourself, he thought.

He knew from listening to real veterans that everyone *tried* to make every fight a one-sided massacre. A fair share of them actually turned out that way. That was why everyone loved an ambush when they weren't on the receiving end . . . except that you couldn't count on that.

And . . . not that these outlaws didn't deserve it, but that man's wife and children . . . how will they cope, come winter? Maybe Diarmuid can have them sent for. It's not the wee lads' and lasses' fault, after all.

Someone would be willing to take them in. Pleasing the Powers aside, it was a rare household that couldn't use another set of hands, and even a small child could do things like baby-minding or bird-scaring to free stronger backs for more important work.

I'll mention it, casual-like, so as not to seem to think it wouldn't occur to him on his own. Now let's begone as soon as we may.

Gwri Beauregard Mackenzie did stop to use her lighter to kindle a small fire. Everyone fell in behind her as she stood before it and held up her arms in the gesture of prayer.

"You powerful God, you Goddess gentle and strong," she said, tactfully naming no specific names. "To You we pray, and to the *aes dana* of this place by whatever names they most wish to hear. By Your ancient law, if a man takes up a spear against another of his own will, he consents to the shedding of his blood as an offering to You, in Your forms as the Dark Mother and the Warrior Lord. We have killed from need, not wantonness, knowing that for us also the Hour of the Hunter must come."

"For Earth must be fed," they all murmured in response. "And we but borrow our bodies from Her for a little while."

She went on: "Yet these too were Your children, Mother-of-All; we ask that you make us clean of their deaths, that they may speak no ill of us to the Guardians of the Western Gate. Let them make accounting, and be healed of all ills of soul in the Land of Summer, where no evil comes and all hurts are made good. There we will greet them, each forgiving the other. So mote it be!"

"So mote it be," they all chorused.

Then each pricked a finger and let a drop fall on the fire, and passed their weapons through the smoke, bending and touching a pinch of dirt to their lips and then foreheads to symbolize their acceptance of their own mortality. Earth and air and fire and the water of life in your veins . . .

"For to kill is to know your own death," Karl murmured, an old saying of his folk, as he threw a helmetful of water across the little fire and stamped carefully, kicking dirt over any lingering ember.

"That's true when you kill a beast," Mathun nodded beside him as they took up the march; not one counseled that they camp here among the tumbled dead. "More so here, I suppose. If it must be done, best done quickly and well."

Karl nodded in turn. And something inside that felt like his father's voice noted that if the band had to be blooded . . .

Best it were an easy victory. Next time they'll be more confident and less likely to freeze or come down with the shakes.

The raven had been watching for some time when the living humans left. It was a young male, part of a flock of not-yet-mated birds that roosted together, though it was foraging on its own today. In the manner of its intelligent kind it had long known that groups of humans meant food, in one way or another. Either they left you food, or they became food, sometimes both.

Cocking its head and looking down at the scattered bodies it considered heading back to the roost and alerting its companions. Sunset was approaching, and owls made the dark risky if you were alone, though two or three ravens were a match for anything short of a golden eagle. On second thoughts it was hungry, and it could always fill its croup now *and* bring the others for the riper feast tomorrow.

A careful flit around showed no other predator-scavengers yet, though some would arrive soon, drawn by the intoxicating scents of fresh blood and slashed bodies—coyotes in particular could be dangerous to a lone raven, they were more agile than wolves. By tomorrow they'd have ripped the bodies open; or a bear might come along, or wolves, or one of the big cats. The scattered pieces would make better pickings for the whole flock then and they could defend each other and run off any buzzards.

Decision firmed. It glided down, pecked at the glitter of a broken-off arrowhead out of curiosity, then approached a body with cautious hops. The eyes were juicy treats, and relatively easy to get out with a little trouble. Humans almost never took them from their kills.

The eyes opened. They were black from edge to edge, like pools of tar. The corpse's head lifted slightly from the ground, and the limbs twitched.

The raven hopped backward, feathers bristling open, wings spread and making a startled high-pitched *keck-keck-keck* of alarm. This was *not* how dead animals were supposed to behave! There was an electric feeling of *wrongness* as well, like the taste of rusty metal.

The body slumped into motionlessness. The eyes became the lawful, tasty glassy white-and-brown. The tension faded from the air, and the raven's feathers sleeked against its body; it nervously groomed again to put everything in place.

The eyes looked very tempting. Still, it hopped a few feet away to another body before it began to feed.

CHAPTER TWENTY-ONE

The length of copper pipe flashed towards the back of her head, thrown with a hard snap and pinwheeling towards her, casting a shadow ahead of it. A shadow, a flicker of disturbed air, a sound, a *knowing*.

Órlaith spun leftward into it with the shield tucked up under her eyes—you learned that by practicing putting your left fist just under your chin. The sword in her right hand—the Sword—swung in a blurring cut across the narrow field of view the long vision slit in her visor left.

Clung!

The foot-long length of three-inch pipe clattered to the deck . . . cut smoothly top-left to bottom-right into two matching curved troughs. Metal formed by machines of inconceivable power in the ancient world, cut by something that was not quite matter as humans understood the term; if the engineers who'd made those machines could have seen the result, they'd have thought of lasers, or diamond saws. The blow had run up her wrist and arm, all right, but she'd had to overcome a lifetime's conditioning to use the blade that way. A dozen more of the bisected pipes littered the deck; one of the ship's apprentices gathered them up into a basket, looking at Órlaith with hero-worshipping puppy-eyes.

Heuradys snorted and sat down. "Well, there's always a place for you in the scrap-metal trade if monarchy palls," she said. "Although I'd miss the happy times throwing chunks of pipe at you, Orrey."

Órlaith snorted back and pushed the visor up with the edge of the shield, breathing deep and letting the wind cool the hot sweat running down her face. The visor was a smooth curve of top-pivoted brushed steel across her face, but the lower edge was drawn down into a point that suggested an eagle's beak and reached to the level of her chin, and the whole helm above it was scored with thin lines inlaid with gold in the shape of feathers. The decoration suggested her totem bird without in the least detracting from function, nor did the sprays of real eagle feathers at either temple.

And there's no harm in a little style. Plus your retainers need to be able to tell who you are at a glance, the which is not easy in full plate.

She grinned at the lad as she ducked out of the guige strap and dropped the point of the shield to the planks. He took it and proudly bore the four-foot teardrop shape over to the bench around the poop deck. Doubtless he was imagining himself a page.

The cool wind also felt good as it found the gaps in the flexible back-and-breast of overlapping steel lames she was wearing, along with sallet helm and vambraces on her forearms and armored gauntlets. Out here on the Pacific it was always cool, which made it perfect for the hard physical labor of working in armor; at that, half-armor like this was vastly better than a full suit of plate.

It isn't the weight that's the problem, it's the way it holds what your body exudes against your skin, and it's not just the sweat.

If it weren't for crossbows and longbows and catapults and pikes and glaives and war-hammers and Lochaber axes, and most of all if it weren't for heat exhaustion, men-at-arms armored cap-a-pie would be invincible.

And where we're heading, a suit of plate complete would be a sentence of death, not long delayed. Mind you, in winter armor also manages to be miserably cold. Da always said that was a miracle . . .

She and Heuradys and Reiko and Luanne Salander were taking the privileges of rank and using the part of the poop-deck between the wheel and the stern rail for practice; Sir Aleaume and Droyn were down below, working with the men-at-arms until the space was clear.

Nobody would object anyway, she thought. *But I'm using the Sword. They're not even* wishing *they could object.*

It was never really possible to believe the Sword was just a sword. A lot depended on what the circumstances were—why the wielder had drawn it—but there was . . .

. . . sort of a shock *feeling, so, when you do draw it, even for practice.*

As if it was too solid for the world, too *real.* She'd grown up around it, and she was the offspring of the pair who'd mingled their blood on the blade before they thrust it into the rock of Montival's bones at Lost Lake, during the Kingmaking. In her hand it felt right, but still rather . . . alarming. Heuradys treated it like something very dangerous that she knew well; Luanne was a little more alarmed, but hid it well. Everyone else sort of avoided it, deliberately or otherwise, except for Reiko's intent glances.

Even the way it looked as a physical . . . or sort-of physical . . . object could disturb. Right now in the bright sunlight it sparkled. Not the way polished steel did, though it was similar at first glance. There was something of the way a diamond glittered as well, and something altogether other. It was beautiful, but nothing like a creation of human hands. Reiko was looking at it with a brooding expression in her narrow eyes.

Nobody in Nihon today knew what Kusanagi-no-Tsurugi looked like. Nobody had actually seen it in well over a thousand years, except for the Shinto priests at the Atsuta Shrine charged with its care, and they had all died with the Change. Even while it rested there, Emperors were merely presented with a wrapped bundle *said* to contain it. The weapon *might* have been lost and recovered several times, depending on which epic poems or legends you believed.

And they've no earthly idea how it ended up here, though I have my suspicions, Órlaith thought. *Right now, my Sword helps keep the deck clear for our work.*

You *had* to keep it up if you were a warrior by trade, which she was among other things; if you didn't spend sheer sweating effort nearly every day you lost speed and, just as crucially, endurance. That was quite literally a matter of life and death, and not only for yourself. If you were a liability you endangered your friends as well. Even a general leading armies had to be ready to fight with their own hands, in the modern world—her father certainly had, even in the great battles of the Prophet's War, much less on the Quest before that—and right now she commanded the equivalent of about one understrength company.

And while I don't think hitting people will be the whole of this, certainly some bashing will be involved. So, work.

People in their trade usually found the whole process interesting as well, and treated it as something of a sport and tried out variations. She mentioned that, and Heuradys laughed aloud.

"Might as well be sex," she said.

Órlaith chuckled too, but . . .

At that, the itchy discontented way you feel after going without pushing yourself physically for a few days does *feel a bit like that particular need. Worse for men, I think, poor creatures.*

Luanne picked up the basket of sliced copper, touched a finger in wonder to the liquid-smooth surface of one of the cuts, then swore mildly when the edge of the metal sliced into her skin a little. Fortunately that was on a callus, but she dropped the bisected tube back among the others hastily.

She was a friend and a relative-by-courtesy; she was the granddaughter of Eric Larsson, the man who'd been brother to the woman who married Mike Havel *after* he fathered Rudi Mackenzie in a very brief if fruitful encounter with Juniper Mackenzie while on a scouting trip to the Willamette a few months after the Change. Signe Havel-née-Larsson had never entirely gotten over that. Mainly because none of *her* children with Mike Havel, the first Bear Lord, ended up as High King of Montival. Most of the rest of her family were happy enough with it, including Mike Jr., the current wearer of the Bear Helm, who'd never made a secret of the fact that he was perfectly satisfied with what he had. The High King and Queen and their family had guested with Eric Larsson and his descendants often, and vice versa, and she'd always gotten on well with them.

With Uncle Mike too, for that matter; he is my father's half-brother, after all, and kin is kin.

Still, Luanne hadn't been around the Sword as much as Heuradys. She affected an elaborate nonchalance.

"I knew that thing was sharp, but it's really *sharp*, isn't it?" she said. "I mean, it's *absurdly* sharp with a deeply absurd sharpness."

Órlaith nodded. "It's a *magic sword*, Luey," she said dryly. "It's . . ."

She pulled out a yellow hair that had wisped free of the coif under her helm, tossed it up and let the following breeze flick it against the upraised edge of the Sword. It parted cleanly, drifting on down past the wheel. No battle blade was ever honed to anything remotely approaching that. Even if you *could* get it that sharp it would make the edge impossibly fragile for something made to slam full-force into meat and bone, much less hard leather, wood and occasionally metal.

"Like an obsidian razor. But nothing harms it. Nothing. Nothing dulls it, nothing chips it, nothing *sticks* to it. You could pound it against a boulder all day long and you'd have the Sword and a heap of diced gravel. And if you dip it in oil it doesn't get greasy. My . . . father . . ."

She took a deep breath, remembering his endless patience from her first faltering grip on the hilt of a miniature wooden practice-blade.

". . . said that it took him most of the trip back from Nantucket to begin to grasp what it could do just *as a sword*, just as a battle-tool. You need some different reflexes to get the most out of it. And it may give you the gift of tongues and of telling falsehood from truth, but it *doesn't* suddenly give you extra swordsmanship points. Or invulnerability."

They all nodded soberly. Not wrecking your own weapon was one of essential points of learning the sword, and even work-of-fine-art swords from master-smiths were surprisingly delicate. Fighting with a sword that *couldn't* be damaged, even if you weren't at all invulnerable yourself, would be profoundly different.

"This is quite heavy," Reiko said, hefting the shield by the grip below the middle of the upper curve.

"About fifteen pounds," Órlaith agreed. "Larch plywood covered in bison-hide boiled in wax and then thin sheet steel. Concave so you can tuck your shoulder into it."

Fifteen pounds was around seven times what a sword weighed; the Sword of the Lady was slightly but definitely lighter than a normal weapon of the same dimensions, a bit under two pounds. Just heavy enough to give a blow conviction, but allowing a little extra speed and longer before you tired.

And sure, it's lighter for me than it was for Da. When I hefted it then, it was a bit over two, maybe two and a half. Plus I'd swear it's become just a little smaller overall the now, sized for me and not him.

Heuradys took the shield and began checking it over, tugging at the enarme, the loop you put your forearm through and the grip higher up and the section of rubber padding between where the forearm rested. The whole arrangement left your arm nearly but not quite parallel to the long axis of the shield. The inverted-teardrop form was about four feet long, as broad as your shoulders at the top and tapering to a blunt point below; on horseback it covered you from shoulder to shoe. In the olden days its predecessors had shrunk and then gone out of use when plate armor came in, but in modern times there were a lot more, and worse, missile weapons around than there had been in the age of Louis the Spider and the Wars of the Roses.

"You can tell a knight because he's slightly lopsided," Heuradys said, working her left arm to emphasize the point.

Her left deltoid and trapezius *were* very slightly larger, despite the fact that she used several routines designed to balance you.

"We Bearkillers use a smaller round shield," Luanne said. "Not nearly as clumsy."

She rolled hers over so that Reiko could compare them; it was a concave disk about a yard across, with the snarling face-on bear's head of the Outfit on its sheet-metal face.

"Same construction, pretty much, but you have to remember to move it now and then. It's perfectly adequate if you're quick."

Heuradys shrugged. "Girl, *you* can use that little soup-plate when someone's coming galloping at you with the weight of a man-at-arms and barded destrier all concentrated behind a lance-point. I'll take the kite shield anytime!"

Órlaith took the hilt of the Sword in both hands as they bickered amiably and began a set with flourish-cuts. It was a hand-and-a-half weapon, what some called a bastard longsword, with a double-lobed hilt of black staghorn and silver that let it be used comfortably either one- or two-handed. She did the forms as much to loosen up as anything; when you carried a kite-shield the style was very tight and contained, the shield battering or levering a path clear for the blade, working over the top as often as to the side.

She ran through the guards that made up the starting-positions and the strikes and blocks that flowed from them: the Ox, the Plow, the Fool, the Roof, and the Tail. Then she finished by short-gripping the Sword and using it for a savage flurry of stepping thrusts to her imaginary opponent's face/throat/belly/groin, blade punching in and out like the needle in a treadle-worked sewing machine. That sort of close-in finishing blow could actually penetrate armor even with a normal weapon. Reiko came half-erect with a gasp of alarm, probably expecting to see her fingers patter down on the deck when she clamped her left hand in its gauntlet on the midpoint of the blade.

"It's all right," Órlaith said when she'd finished.

She took off that gauntlet and bounced the blade on the skin of her palm. The impact felt like that of a metal ruler.

"It's a *magical* magic sword, Reiko. It won't cut or harm me—or anyone of the Royal kin."

Reiko's eyes turned narrow. "What happens if someone . . . else touch it? Not of your blood?"

Órlaith winced a little.

"Nothing good. Though how bad depends on their intentions. If it's just someone heedless or stupid, or a child, say, they get an overwhelming impulse to drop it. Otherwise . . ."

Heuradys spoke: "I'd been at Court three years and thought I was the toughest new-minted junior squire on the block when I saw . . . someone try to steal the Sword. It . . . well, let's put it this way: I heaved my cookies all over a very valuable pre-Change Persian rug."

"Cookies?" Reiko said. "Heave?"

"Puked. Vomited. Queen Mother Sandra was quite annoyed. About the rug, that is. Up until then I'd wondered why there was such a light guard on the Sword when the High King or Queen weren't bearing it. After that . . . I didn't."

Órlaith sheathed the weapon and sat down beside her knight; a weight was gone from the world.

"All yours, Reiko."

The three Montivallans watched Reiko practicing with her katana, the edge of the blade flickering as she danced with the steel, sure-footed on the moving deck in her *kegutsu*, leather slipper-like shoes.

That's right, Órlaith thought. *She has lots of practice at sea. Da loved sailing, but Ma gets seasick something fierce the first few days.*

The crowded waters about Newport were well behind them now and there were no other sails in sight, only the faint dim line of the Montivallan coast off to the left, dreaming under the morning sun. South of here was nothing but the odd fishing village, and even those faded out as you went down towards Westria province until you reached the mouth of the Klamath.

Port, she reminded herself. *Left is port when you're facing towards the bows.*

The sky was blue and cloudless, a summer's sky. The wind came from the northwest, cool and strong and steady and smelling very different from the brackish longshore scent. There was nothing in it but a quarter of a planet worth of ocean, down from the northern ice, and every breath felt as if your lungs were being laundered and delivered back fresh and clean.

"I thought Reiko might be a little light for serious work," Órlaith said. "But—"

"Says the big blond horse of a woman," Luanne jeered pleasantly; she was the shortest of the three at five-eight and a bit.

Then she leaned her elbows back on the bulwark and looked overside at the long shallow trough where the water curled away from the side of the ship.

"Damn, but sailing's fun. Like being on a galloping horse but less work."

The long spars of the gaff sails were swung out to the . . .

Port, Órlaith reminded herself again. *Not left, port. And the wind's from . . . the wind is broad on the starboard quarter, not just hitting us from behind and to the right.*

. . . to the portside, out over the rails. The canvas was in taut smooth curves, and the square topsails were set on the main and foremast as well at slightly different angles, a geometry of off-white-against-blue above crossed with the almost-black tarred hemp of the rigging. You could feel the wind's great hand pushing the ship over, pushing it along, and if you put your own palm to the standing rigging it hummed with a subliminal note of power as it transferred the thrust to the hull.

Ships . . . ships felt *alive*.

"I don't think Reiko's too fragile for hard work," Heuradys said.

"Certainly when she hits you with a practice blade in the *salle* you feel it!" Órlaith said . . . with feeling.

"The Japanese are none of them what you'd call big, but they all seem to manage," Heuradys agreed. "And Reiko's taller than half of them, so relatively speaking she's less of a runt than you, Luey."

Luanne gave a small shudder. "That one who grabbed me on the train was a shortie, but he felt like he was made out of cables attached to high-geared winches," she said. "I'm sort of glad Egawa came along! I would have had to hurt him to make him let go . . . not that he didn't deserve it, acting like an asshole that way, but it would have been undiplomatic. Mind you, Egawa *did* hurt him, which of course was OK because it was their own chain of command. Hurt him about as bad as you can without doing lasting damage."

Heuradys chuckled. "*He's* built like a horse. Granted he's built like a *short* horse, but I still wouldn't want him to hit me. Even less so with something sharp or pointy or both."

They all nodded. Other things being equal reach and weight, thickness of bone and sheer mass of muscle were advantages; that was one important reason women fighters were a minority even among folk like Mackenzies who didn't make much of a distinction between the sexes, pregnancy and infants being the other main cause. Fortunately other things often *weren't* equal, which was why they weren't all that *un*common either. Except where custom strongly disapproved, and there were usually a few even there. Those who made a success of it tended to be bigger than average for their gender and very, very good.

"She's certainly got first-rate situational awareness," Órlaith said. "And the way the deck's moving doesn't affect her blade placement at all, does it now? Like a surgeon, she is."

The waves came from the same direction as the wind, long smooth swells a blue deep enough to be almost purple, each with a crest of white foam. The bow of the *Tarshish Queen* rose to each of them as it overtook, then sank again as the whitecap hissed by along the big schooner's flanks, adding to its own wake and sending spindrift flying down the deck to put the taste of salt on her lips. Then the ship seemed to be scudding down-hill, her own foam breaking back from the bows. There was a long slow fore-and-aft pitch to the motion, but not much roll, and there were only a few human forms draped over the leeward rail.

Captain Feldman stood by the wheel in his brass-buttoned blue coat and, appropriately, sailor's cap, his arms crossed. Ishikawa Goru and one of his men were spelling the usual watch on the wheel, his eyes darting occasionally to the sails, the waves and the compass card in the binnacle before the helm.

The regular pair who'd have taken the wheel this watch otherwise—one hand stood on either side of the big spoked wooden circle—were watching *them*, and so was the captain-owner. Feldman caught her eye and gave a slight nod, but Órlaith wasn't surprised. The Japanese naval officer wasn't moving much, but he and his countryman still gave the impression of men dancing . . . or doing any complex physical task once it was so intimately familiar that it was graven into nerve and muscle.

And Goru looks happy, too, she thought. *There are few pleasures greater than practicing a useful skill you love and do well. And he doesn't have the sort of stone face that Egawa has, or even Reiko a lot of the time.*

Flags streamed from each mast, blowing off to . . . port; the ship was going faster than the waves but more slowly than the wind that propelled it. The house flag of Feldman And Sons streamed from the mainmast, a stylized ship rendered in a few black strokes on pale blue, headed up into the sky; the blue-white-green Crowned Mountain and Sword national en-sign of Montival flew from the place of honor at the mizzen; the orange-on-brown anthropomorphic beaver's head of Corvallis from the foremast.

Luanne Salander grinned at it. "My granddad Eric always said ol' Benny the Beaver looks *dorky beyond words*. Apparently before the Change it was a bit of a joke."

Heuradys spoke softly: "Right now it's a bit of a joke too, but tact, girl, tact. People have died for that flag. And *my* parents were among those who killed a fair number of them, something I'd rather not bring to the minds of the crew of this ship while I'm on it. Your people never fought Corvallis, but please remember mine *did*."

Bearkillers and Corvallans had been allies for a long time—since the wars against the Association began, not long after the Change, in fact. In all that time the Bearkillers hadn't stopped saying that the Corvallans were prone to showing up a day late and a rose noble short in anything serious and being greedy, conceited and sneaky to boot. The Corvallans hadn't stopped thinking, and sometimes speaking, of Bearkillers as arrogant, brutish killer rubes, either.

Both sides had a distinct point. It hadn't helped that the Outfit's territories had been between the city-state's anvil and the hammer of the Protectorate in the old days, either. All that passed for ancient history now, but it was living history as well.

And making cracks about how stupid someone's flag looks is not tact, Herry's right about that. Especially when you're on their ship. Benny the Beaver goes a lot of rough places these days. Am I only three years older than Luanne? Or . . . well, I remember thinking that I don't have a heimat *back when we were at Diarmuid's. There are advantages as well as drawbacks. You get more perspective, that you do.*

"That quick-draw thing is interesting," Luanne went on . . . more tactfully . . . nodding towards Reiko. "I'm not absolutely sure how useful it'd be most of the time unless you were planning on suddenly topping someone's head at a dinner party, but it sure is pretty."

Reiko was in the ready position again, kneeling with her left hand on the scabbard of her katana where it was thrust through her sash edge-up.

She drew with that hand this time, and thrust straight backward in the same motion. Then the blade flicked back as she rose with a smoothness that looked as if invisible cords were pulling her erect, up into the two-hand overhead position, down with a stamp and an *isa!* of controlled effort . . .

"Not too academic," Órlaith said critically. "I'd always thought of *iai-jutsu* as something in a book, but that's the real thing. You can tell, under all the differences of detail."

"Right," Heuradys said. "Sort of like the difference between Society training before the Change and the way we do it now."

Luanne snorted. "The way my grandfather tells it, the Outfit picked up their basic style from the ARMA—the Association for Renaissance Martial Arts, my great-aunt Pam was a member, the first Bear Lord found her up in Idaho of all places and she established the sword training program. And they were *way* more realistic to start with than the Society. Less dancing and prancing, more slashing and stabbing."

"Maybe to start with, but that's ancient history," Heuradys said. "I don't think there's *anyone* anywhere on *earth* more . . . realistic . . . about fighting than Auntie Tiph."

"Well, yeah. Point. I've only met her a couple of times and she's *scary.*"

Most people who'd spent a lot of time in a *salle* had tried their hand a little at the *nihon* style. As the texts described it, at least, but it wasn't a living tradition here except in a few out-of-the-way places. Seeing it used by people who actually knew it well was fascinating.

Heuradys nodded at Reiko. "Yes, you can see she's used it for real. More battle experience than us, I'd say."

"That wouldn't be difficult, Herry," Órlaith said dryly. "We've had one real fight between us, and that lasted about ten minutes."

I can mention it now without wanting to fall into a puddle and greep, she thought somberly. *Though it's there, back in my head. If I keep running fast enough, I'll stay ahead of it.*

Luanne Salander was the youngest of the four of them. "And I'm a combat virgin," she sighed.

"It's a lot less fun to lose than the other kind," Heuradys said soberly.

"Speak for yourself, you never slept with Edgar I'm-in-a-hurry Cumbreson," the Bearkiller said dryly, and they all chuckled. "Or at least I hope you haven't, for your sake."

"I thought you Catholic girls didn't?" Heuradys said.

"Oh, we do, we're just supposed to feel guilty about it afterwards. And let's put it this way: the penance my confessor set me was *more fun* than sex with Eddie. Saints, but my repentance was sincere!"

"Ouch, ouch," Heuradys said.

"That too."

"*Ouch.* Well, you'll have Prince John along on this trip."

"Dreamy, I will admit."

Órlaith shuddered. "Oh, euw."

The others jeered at her. Heuradys went on: "Unless he'd deteriorated since he was sixteen, no complaints there."

Luanne laughed. "You *didn't.*"

"Oh, yes, I did. No penance was more fun than him, I assure you. Poor boy, I was the only eligible female he knew who wanted to jump his bones and who he was *sure* didn't have ulterior motives."

"A sixteen-year-old virgin *boy* and he *cared* about that? I may have to take another look."

"He's sensitive, yes. Sings well, too."

Órlaith made a retching sound. "Might you be after switching the subject from the largely imaginary charms of my little brother?"

"In hose you can see he's got a really nice tight pair of . . . oh, all right, Orrey," Heuradys said, chuckling.

Then she sobered and watched narrow-eyed as Reiko went through a turn-cut-cut-block-turn-strike flurry.

"She's quick. I couldn't say if she's as quick as you or I, Herry," Órlaith said, "since she's not pushing it, but she's very definitely fast and smooth."

She'd been taught by those who knew from experience that a real expert—someone with first-class gear and lifelong first-class training— could drive down most battlefields killing at every second step, because most of what they'd be meeting was levied farmers blundering through half-remembered drills.

Until you run into another expert, of course. Or just run out of luck with the cross-bow bolts and arrows. Or some prisoner has a holdout knife . . . oh, Da!

A long breath and a resolute focus kept the sudden wave of emotion at bay.

Luanne was going over her backsword. Órlaith thought she'd been surprised at how fast things rusted in salt air; few Bearkillers went to sea. She finished wiping the slightly oily cloth down the blade, checked the edge—you didn't want to hone it unless it was necessary, oversharpening was always a temptation—and slid it home. A-listers used a more complex blade than the Associate longsword, basket-hilted and with an edge along one side and about a third of the reverse as well.

Thoughtfully, Órlaith said: "Are either of you surprised we're all so light-hearted?"

Luanne looked stricken as she wiped her hands. Heuradys put a hand on Órlaith's shoulder. The Crown Princess shook her head and gave it a reassuring pat.

"No, not Da. He'd be the last to say that we should mope for a year and a day; don't give grief less than its natural due, but no more either, was how he put it when my Nonni Sandra died. No, I was thinking . . . we're heading towards *Los Angeles*—"

It was a name to wake terror, even among the few salvagers who'd made lightning raids for treasures whose location was precisely known. And before that . . . the year of the Change had been bad absolutely everywhere, but the stories out of southern California had been bad even by comparison to the tales her father and Uncle Ingolf and the other veterans of the Quest had told of the death zones of the far east coast. At least there most hadn't lost their drinking water on the first day.

"—and we're going right through it. Plus something like the CUT is involved. But I'd say we're all . . . feeling more sunny about things than before we got away?"

Luanne shrugged. "I had to listen to stories about the Quest of the Sword all my life, since my aunts Mary and Ritva were *on* the Quest . . ."

Mary and Ritva had also met their men on the Quest, and eventually settled far south, not far from where the Montivallans had met the Japanese and their pursuers. Though they were Dúnedain, not Bearkillers.

". . . well, you would have even more, Orrey . . . and then the Prophet's War and my parents and *grandparents*, by the sword of St. Michael, doing the larger-than-life thing. And I've been thinking since I made the A-List, what was it all *for*? Thinking about an *entire life* spent on call-up drills and getting everyone in the Strategic Hamlet to keep their pikes in proper dressing when they're crossing an obstacle and deep conversations about whether the new mare is really sound breeding stock and whether the vineyards need Bordeaux mixture this year and the most exciting thing I do being hunt boar and breed and maybe visit Corvallis for the theater season. Not that I've got anything against hunting and sure, I want babies and a man of my own, but not *yet*, you know? When my mother was my age she was flying gliders against the Prophet and hanging upside down over grizzlies."

"I was worried about you, Orrey, until we got started organizing this," Heuradys said. "And, well . . . I mean, everything Luey just said, squared. By the Gray-Eyed, *cubed*! But I think something like this is what you need. Provided we don't get killed and have our hearts cut out and eaten, but *you're* not going to live a quiet, safe life anyway. It's not in your blood. And . . . your father was my King, too. I'm a knight of the High Kingdom and the Household, I want to avenge him. I *need* to do it. Maybe not as much as you do, but . . . a lot."

Órlaith sighed and nodded. "Thank you both. If I'm being stupid, at least it's in good company. And to be sure, the Powers seem to be pointing in this direction. It's never wise to ignore Them."

Reiko finished her drill; for her that involved a looping gesture like flicking blood off the sword and wiping it as it was sheathed with a piece of paper carried tucked into her sash. Then she joined them, breathing deep and with sweat running down her face despite the sea-breeze.

"Day . . . the day does not feel light . . . right! Right, without doing *kata*," she said.

"Me next!" Luanne said.

Her eagerness proved the point, and she bounced up into the space Reiko had vacated, bringing up her shield with the backsword reserved.

"I'd like to look at that sword," Órlaith said to Reiko, in her language. "It's lovely. May I?"

In Japanese, it was words that turned back into English would have been more on the order of:

Please excuse me, but may I ask that you do me the great favor of letting me look at your (prefix: beautiful/gracious/honorable) sword?

The Sword of the Lady gave her an instinctive command of any language she needed—she was being exactly as polite as she would have been in English—but she still *thought* about it occasionally as she spoke. When she did, it was a little like seeing a stereoscope image not quite properly aligned. A literal translation of the phrase that popped into her mind in English would have been *rude*, the sort of way you'd address a naughty child or possibly a prisoner. And if you translated the Japanese directly into English, it sounded silly. Yet the meanings were identical, native-speaker to native-speaker.

I don't think it's that the Sword gives me social skills, it's that some such skills are built into the way a language is structured and just absorbed as you grow up, she thought. *And I get that for free.*

She could tell by imagining it that she'd have used slightly different phrasing to a man, or if *she* were a man, or if they hadn't been of virtually identical rank. Reiko had told her a couple of days ago that she had beautiful conversational manners *in the modern style,* which probably meant the way things had gone in her generation.

The Japanese woman hesitated only an instant before saying: *"Hai,"* and touching the sheathed weapon. "It should be cared for soon anyway, in this damp salt air. But better we look below. There's too much spray here."

They went down the hatchway and down what sailors insisted on calling a ladder, though *very steep staircase* would have been more accurate, stowed their weapons and gear and took turns with the tiny cold-salt-water shower where you pumped with one hand and tried to wash with the other at the same time—even on a shore-hugging voyage, fresh water was limited to a little for wiping down with a cloth afterwards to get the salt off. As they went down the passage she heard John playing his lute in the little cabin he was sharing with Aleaume, Droyn and Feldman's first mate; this was probably the only time in the day when he had it to himself, and he was playing short fragments, stopping, playing again. Reiko looked a question at her.

"Composing," Órlaith said. "Trying out bits and writing them down." Reiko nodded. *"Rippa na kōdō,"* she said.

Which meant *worthy* or *commendable*, more or less—Órlaith had no-ticed the respect the Japanese party always seemed to pay to the arts, not to mention to disciplined effort in any field.

Then she gave a sudden shy grin: "But . . . drive you crazy, if you have to listen all the time in that little cabin."

She mimed screaming and tearing out her hair, throttling someone and then whipping a dagger out of her sleeve and stabbing herself in the throat. Órlaith laughed aloud; for someone usually so solemn, Reiko could be extremely funny when she let go a little.

"Tell me!" she said. "When we were younger and he'd just started do-ing music seriously, a lot of the time we were on trains—my parents took us around with them as they toured the Realm, that they did; to see and be seen, they said. Otherwise we'd have been separated too much. And we'd be cooped up with John as he practiced, and eventually I'd start throwing things and he'd dodge and *go right on*, and if Herry was along she'd stick her thumbs in her ears and go *LALALALALALAL!* Until Da came back and roared at us all to shut up and let a man think, petitions and children's choirs were bad enough . . ."

Reiko laughed herself, shedding years and layers of responsibility. "My father also traveled much by sea, to the other islands and the new outposts, and I with him after my brother . . . after I became the heir. Your brother is not . . . he is not that bad! Even composing."

"No, but he *was*," Órlaith said. "*De*-composing, I called it then. He's quite good the now, but when he was twelve and always trying things just a bit beyond his level it grated, that it did, and I don't have near as fine an ear as Herry does. . . ."

They went into the cabin. The roof overhead was the poop-deck, and the semicircle of inward-slanting windows at the rear was the stern of the ship. For shipboard it was spacious, although by any other standards it was the size of a modest bedroom, perhaps a hundred square feet, count-ing what was now taken by double bunks on either side, and the roof was just high enough that Órlaith didn't have much problem suppressing the urge to duck. Most of the center was taken up by a table; when the *Tarsh-ish Queen* wasn't under charter like this the ship's officers and the supercargo would dine there and perhaps a paying passenger or two, and fold-up benches ran up either side of it. The light that poured in through the windows was reflected upwards from the sea below, and it made shifting patterns on the overhead beams.

Reiko fetched a small lacquered box colored a deep red-brown with the chrysanthemum *kamon* of her House on it and laid the sword down carefully on the table beside it. Then she spread a clean white cloth.

"This is a very . . ." Reiko paused and obviously thought for a moment. "Revered sword? Old, very old."

Órlaith nodded with interest; some time ago she'd come to the conclusion that when Japanese said *very old* they meant either *very, very* old or *even older than that.*

"Before the Change, it was in a museum. But still a good sword for fighting. The leader of the Seventy Loyal Men, General Egawa's father, brought it from Tokyo, and used it many times to preserve the life of my grandmother along the way. He presented it to my father when he came of age to need a sword."

Órlaith had noticed that Reiko had two katana with her, but the other was securely wrapped in its gray linen bag in her chest, and in a special scabbard and hilt made for storage at that.

Reiko opened the lacquered box and brought out the contents, laying them out with an almost ritual neatness; there were a tiny bronze mallet, a ball of silk that she took out of a further cloth bag, a folder of wrinkled-looking rice paper, and a small vial of oil. The Japanese woman smiled, dropping back into her own birth-tongue:

"So sorry, I really need to speak Nihongo now. In the very old days, women weren't even allowed to touch swords like this. Not with their bare hands, at least; they had to wrap the sleeves of their kimono around their fingers first."

"Times have changed!" Órlaith said. "And I'm glad to see it."

"And changed and changed again," Reiko agreed. "Originally this was an *ôdachi.*"

The word meant great-sword, and in her mind it felt very much the same as the equivalent in her native dialect of English. Something on the order of *unusually big*.

"The blade was three shaku two *sun* long . . . about—"

"Thirty-eight inches," Órlaith said.

That was roughly as long as what a Montivallan would call a greatsword or *claidheamh mòr*, though curved and less massive.

Reiko nodded. "*Hai*, very close. It was shortened in . . . well, I will show you."

Órlaith watched with interest, propping her chin on her fists, but to one side and not leaning too close—this was a very sharp edge by any standards other than the Sword of the Lady, and unlike that it would cut anyone without exception. She didn't want to crowd.

Reiko drew the sword, set the *saya*-scabbard aside and laid the blade down with the cutting edge away from her. It gleamed in the subdued light of the cabin, flawless and beautiful, with the subtle waving line of the *hamon* running down behind the edge to show where it had been differentially tempered to an almost glasslike hardness at the cutting surface while staying soft and springy within. Órlaith had never seen a better creation of the bladesmith's craft, though these days that was becoming a high art in Montival, no longer just a matter of filing and grinding old leaf springs.

For something made to kill, this was . . .

Almost indecently pretty, she thought. *Nonni Sandra would have loved to have it in a glass case in her chambers.*

"This is a *soshu kitae*, a sword made with seven laminations, which are harder or softer in different parts of the blade," Reiko said absently as she worked. "That is done after the initial folding, which itself produces many layers . . . thirty thousand or so. It is what we call *jewel steel*."

Next she took up the little mallet, unscrewed a small bronze pin from its handle, and used both to tap out the two *mekugi*-pegs in the hilt. She set those aside with the same neatness. Then she took the sword in her right hand, blade-up, and tapped on her wrist with the fist of her left hand, two light but sharp blows. The *tsuka*, the hilt of wood and sharkskin and cord, came loose and she lifted it away, and then the *tsuba*, the round guard and spacers. Then she laid the naked blade carefully on the cloth without touching her fingers to the steel, putting the mountings to one side.

There was an inscription on the tang, above the two holes for the fastening pegs and on the same side as the edge:

朝倉篭手切太刀也・天正三年十二月・右幕下御摺上・大津伝十郎拝領.

Reiko pointed it out. "In our script, this is—"

Órlaith held up her hand, surprised and delighted: "Well, and Da didn't mention that! I can *read* the language too, whether or not it's in the Latin alphabet! *Asakura Kotegiri-tachi nari-Tenshô sannen jûnigatsu-Ubakka su-riage-Ôtsu Denjûrô hairyô.*"

Reiko's brows went up, and she smiled slightly. "This is a very old-fashioned version of our writing, and I think you even caught the original pronunciation!" she said. "Let me try and render it in English . . ."

Slowly and carefully she spoke: "This Kotegiri-tachi from the Asakura was shortened by . . . it says *Ubakka*, but that is a title not a name, a title of Oda Nobunaga, who was a great warlord of the Age of Battles . . . in the twelfth month of Tenshô 3, and presented to Ôtsu Denjûrô."

At Órlaith's enquiring look, she amplified: "Tenshô 3 . . . that would be in your calendar, 1575."

"Four hundred and twenty-three years before the Change; four hundred and sixty-nine years ago," Órlaith said, and whistled softly in respect.

She would have expected something that old to be a fragile mass of corrosion, especially as that was long before the art of making rustproof alloys. This looked . . .

Not new, no, but absolutely sound. It looks like a well-used but well-kept blade handed down from parent to child for a couple of generations. What a beautiful curve, shallow and clean! And . . . the internal structure must be as complex as a snowflake. Perfect form, perfect function.

"Four hundred and sixty-nine years!" she said again in amazement.

"Half a millennium, and it *is* still battle-worthy. Now that is a wonder and the wonder of the world, sure and it is."

Reiko chuckled and shook her head. "No, much older than that. Ten-shô 3 was when it was *shortened*, very long swords were going out of style then, I think because methods of fighting had changed, that was towards the end of the *Sengoku Jidai*, the Age of Battles. Just before the triumph of the Tokugawa and the long peace that ended with Meiji. It's right for me now as a katana since I'm so tall . . . well, tall back in Nihon, not here in the Land of Storks."

Her finger traced a line in the air over the curve of the blade.

"Two shaku two *sun*, six *bu*, five *ri*. Twenty-seven inches. It was already a famous sword when it was shortened, though. In Bunna 4 . . . 1355 AD . . . Asakura Ujikage fought with it in a battle in Kyoto, and cut through the steel archer's guard on an enemy's wrist. *Steel-cutter*, the sword was called after that. It was made earlier still, perhaps one generation or two, either by the great master-swordsmith Masamune, or by his student Sadamune."

Sure, and I'd feel paralyzed carrying anything that old into a fight! Órlaith thought.

Then she looked at the Sword of the Lady where it lay on her bunk, the belt wrapped around the scabbard and the whole tucked beneath the tight-made sheets and blanket.

Though to be sure, give that seven hundred years . . . but the Sword of the Lady came from the hand of the Goddess Herself, forged in the world beyond the world, while this is a weapon made of earthly steel by a human smith. I am impressed, so!

She sat in silence and watched as Reiko cared for the weapon; gently wiping it with the rubbed paper, tapping it with the ball of silk up one side and down the other—it held a mixture of a special clay and pow-dered deer horn—wiping it again, then applying a very little of the choji oil on still another paper before reassembling the hilt and resheathing it.

"Our master-smiths make good swords now, better every year," she said. "But . . . not like this."

Suddenly there was a tenseness in her silence. Órlaith looked up and realized with a shock that Reiko was weeping, slow tears dropping down an immobile face.

Uh-oh. I have absolutely *no idea what's appropriate here, that I do not,* she thought; dismay was like a cold knot in her stomach. *The Sword can tell me how to say things, but I don't even know whether I should* say anything.

Órlaith settled for gently touching the back of Reiko's hand for an instant. After a few minutes the Japanese woman spoke, her voice slightly choked:

"This was my father's personal sword since he was old enough. He often said he wanted me to bear it after him. My mother and my sisters will be waiting for the sails of his ship, hoping as we all hoped after my brother was lost, not knowing he is dead too. And I am here, all alone with his ashes and his sword."

"You're not alone, Reiko," Órlaith said. "I will be your friend, if you want."

"I have no friends."

"Well, you do now. *Shin'yuu.* Best friends."

EPILOGUE/PROLOGUE

TARSHISH QUEEN, PACIFIC OCEAN
TERRITORIAL WATERS, HIGH KINGDOM OF MONTIVAL
JULY 8/FUMIZUKI 8TH, CHANGE YEAR 46/2044 AD/SHŌHEI 1

R eiko knew she was dreaming. It was nothing like the previous dreams, with their terror and burning heat, yet there was some of the same enormous clarity, pressing on her like a falling mountain. Here she was an observer, not the center of the vision.

Though an observer fully present, as if the warm sun beat down on her own shoulders and she smelled earth and dust and growth and, somewhere, smoke amid the homelike humid silkiness of the air. Emotion was muffled, mainly a cool curiosity. What she beheld was extremely clear but distant, as if seen through lenses of inconceivable fineness that brought close that which was infinitely removed. Yet she was *there*, as if she walked through an unfamiliar landscape.

Time, she realized. *I am seeing through a vast reach of years, eons; the remote past or the distant future.*

A man was struggling through rank grass taller than he was, sweat sheening on a face twisted with effort and marked by a bar of tattoo below the lower lip and wedges on the sparsely bearded cheeks; behind him lay a horse bristling with arrows, flies already landing on the bloody wounds. It had been ridden with ruthless determination until it dropped dead in its tracks. Insects buzzed and glittered through the air.

He was Japanese, she thought—certainly of the same race as she— though oddly dressed, in a crude belted poncho of woven hemp and trousers of the same material. And straw sandals of a type she'd seen peasants wear. Long hair was in plaits held in bone rings on either side of his face, and escaped strands stuck to his cheeks and neck. A sword was in his hand, a straight single-edged blade with a ring pommel—it looked nothing like a *nihonto*, more Chinese if anything. The blood that ran like liquid red enamel along it was entirely familiar, and the coppery-metallic smell of it.

Voices rang in the distance, shouting back and forth, and the man started and darted a glance behind him. Reiko could hear the words, and they *sounded* a little as if they were in her language, but there was only a haunting pseudo-intelligibility, traces of the familiar in a harsh multi-syllabic strangeness.

The tone was clear and one she knew well, though; there was a deadly baying eagerness in it. That was men primed to kill. The savage call of a pack that had winded the prey as it ran along the blood-trail.

The solitary man ran faster, his dirt-stained hand clenched on the odd-looking sword. Then he slashed at the grass in two places as if forcing a passage, stopped, ran backward a dozen paces and jinked abruptly to his left, twisting and turning to avoid disturbing the grass more than he had to, and leaving little track on ground that looked as if it were hard dried mud. After a few dozen yards he went down on one knee, the knuckles of his left hand resting on the dirt, the sword held out to one side in a position she knew kept it ready to strike upward—he must expect horsemen to come after him.

This one is a warrior, she knew. *And a good one.*

That was plain from the cat-like ease of his stance, blinding speed held in check with trained reflex, ready to explode off the ground in an instant. His breath came deeply but controlled, no wild shallow panting but a disciplined drawing in of every possible atom of air and a slight pause to let the lungs suck what they could from it. On the run and alone, horse lost, comrades lost, enemies hunting him through this wilderness of grass, still there was no panic in his fine-drawn tension or the snarling grin on his lips. He was older than she but not by many years, and in his prime, slender but broad-shouldered and very strong; the muscle on his bare forearms was corded in ways that said he used a sword every day, and bore the dusty-white lines of scars against the pale golden-ivory skin. The man knew how to hide, too; keep low, keep motionless, wait out the pursuers. A fly crawled over his face and he ignored it.

I would not like to be the enemy who found *this man,* she thought. *He may die, but he will not go alone. That is what he hopes for now, not for life but for a chance to strike back.*

The voices didn't come any closer, but he looked up and she did too. Arrows whispered by overhead, dozens, long black-fletched shafts of bamboo. They trailed smoke as they flew, from tufts of burning fiber bound round them near the head. The rustling forest of grass was nearly tinder-dry. It caught with a roar, plumes of dirty-white smoke rising with flames licking a dozen feet into the air. They spread faster than a man running, left and right and ahead, closing in towards him with a blast of heat that dried the sweat on his face. The only clear direction was back towards the pursuers.

For a moment there *was* fear on the man's features. Then rage overcame it. He leapt to his feet and took the sword in both hands, slashing at the grass around him in a frenzy. Then he stopped. Fear and anger both left his face, astonishment filling it.

For the grass bowed *away* from him, rippling before the sweep of the steel.

The first time might have been illusion, a swaying in the fierce gusts of the building fire heading inward towards him. Then he swung the sword about his head again, and the air was a blast that bent the tall tough grass down as if it bowed in homage in a circle about him. Instantly he ran forward, the sword flashing back and forth, glittering where the dried blood did not hide the metal. The fire roared higher as the blast struck it, but now it was running before the man.

He laughed as he ran. In instants he was on charred stubble, coughing as he held a fold of the coarse fabric of his garment over his mouth. Smoke hid him; above the cloth she could see his narrow, intensely black eyes intent with thought.

He could escape now, she thought. *He could follow the fire—drive it before him and be concealed by the smoke.*

When he moved it was not away from his foemen, though. He looped out in front of a patch of flames and swung the sword again. Wind blasted, fanning the blaze. . . .

Driving them before him, she thought. *Using it like a whip of fire!*

Wordless before, now he shouted, his voice exultant over the roar of the flames:

"Swora yu to ki-nu yo!"

That had no meaning either, until suddenly she remembered leafing through an old history of Nihongo one of her elderly tutors had kept, intrigued at the way it claimed to be able to trace a language back through time. Even through the distant calm that possessed her, a prickle went down her spine as she recognized:

"I come, as if from the sky!"

In word-forms that had faded away centuries before the *Genji Monogatari* was written.

And in that instant the feeling of distance thinned, attenuating for a moment until it was less than the most translucent oiled rice-paper. The man turned and locked eyes with her, and she saw his expand in astonishment. He gasped and threw up a hand as if against an enormous light, the brilliance of the Sun Herself. That light shone from behind her, and *through* her, and for one eternal instant *was* her.

I am become kamigakari! Reiko knew.

She flung out an arm towards the man's enemies, and his awe turned to a redoubled fury . . .

. . . and she woke with a cry she stifled even as it passed her lips.

The cabin of the *Tarshish Queen* was dark, with only the swaying night-lantern casting dim blue shadow, less bright than reflected moonlight off the wake coming through the curved stern windows. The long slow rise and fall of the ship rocked her, and the hiss of water past its flanks. A tousled fair head rose from the pillow on the bunk above hers and peered down over the edge.

"Reiko?" the sleepy voice said.

"I have seen . . ." she said softly.

Then realization firmed in her mind: that had been the Grass-Cutting Sword, in the hands of Yamato Takeru himself, or at least he to whom that name had been given in legend.

"I have seen a myth being born," she said.